A SKY BEYOND THE STORM

ALSO BY SABAA TAHIR

An Ember in the Ashes
A Torch Against the Night
A Reaper at the Gates

A SKY
BEYOND THE
STORM

SABAA TAHIR

HARPER
Voyager

Harper*Voyager*
An imprint of HarperCollins*Publishers* Ltd
1 London Bridge Street
London SE1 9GF

www.harpercollins.co.uk

First published by HarperCollins*Publishers* Ltd 2020
1

Published by arrangement with Razorbill, an imprint of
Penguin Young Readers Group, a division of Penguin Random House LLC.

Map by Jonathan Roberts

Sabaa Tahir asserts the moral right to
be identified as the author of this work

A catalogue record for this book is available from the British Library

ISBN: 978-0-00-841165-7 (HB)
ISBN: 978-0-00-841166-4 (TPB)

Set in Electra LT Std

Printed and bound in the UK by CPI Group (UK) Ltd, Croydon CR0 4YY

MIX
Paper from
responsible sources
FSC
www.fsc.org
FSC™ C007454

A dedication

in two parts

i.

For every child of war
Whose story will never be told.

ii.

For my own children
My falcon and my sword
Of all the worlds wherein I dwell
Yours is the most beautiful.

Nevennes Range
Borderlands
Antium
River Taius
The Empire
Estium
Tiborum
Silas
Estium Garrison
River Rei
(Blackcliff)
Serra
Serran Range
Raider's Roost
Nur
Lake Vitan
Jaduna Lands
The Great Wastes
Borderlands
Navium
Karkaus

THE EASTERN SEA

Kauf
Prison

NERUAL LAKE

River Nerual

FARI BAY

FOREST OF DUSK

River Dusk

Delphinium

AFTAB BAY

Adisa

The Soul Catcher's
Cabin

MARINN

Sher Jinnaat

Ayo

DUSKAN
SEA

BHUTH BADLANDS

MALIKH ESCARPMENT

Taib

Aish

TRIBAL DESERT

Sadh

Lacertium

ISLE SOUTH

PART ONE

WAKING

CHAPTER ONE

The Nightbringer

I awoke in the glow of a young world, when man knew of hunting but not tilling, of stone but not steel. It smelled of rain and earth and life. It smelled of hope.

Arise, beloved.

The voice that spoke was laden with millennia beyond my ken. The voice of a father, a mother. A creator and a destroyer. The voice of Mauth, who is Death himself.

Arise, child of flame. Arise, for thy home awaits thee.

Would that I had not learned to cherish it, my home. Would that I had unearthed no magic, loved no wife, sparked no children, gentled no ghosts. Would that Mauth had never named me.

"Meherya."

My name drags me out of the past to a rain-swept hilltop in the Mariner countryside. My old home is the Waiting Place—known to humans as the Forest of Dusk. I will make my new home upon the bones of my foes.

"Meherya." Umber's sun-bright eyes are the vermillion of ancient anger. "We await your orders." She grips a glaive in her left hand, its blade white with heat.

"Have the ghuls reported in yet?"

Umber's lip curls. "They scoured Delphinium. Antium. Even the Waiting Place," she says. "They could not find the girl. Neither she nor the Blood Shrike has been seen for weeks."

"Have the ghuls seek out Darin of Serra in Marinn," I say. "He forges weapons in the port city of Adisa. Eventually, they will reunite."

Umber inclines her head and we regard the village below us, a hodgepodge of stone homes that can withstand fire, adorned with wooden shingles that cannot. Though it is mostly identical to other hamlets we've destroyed, it has one distinction. It is the last settlement in our campaign. Our parting volley in Marinn before I send the Martials south to join the rest of Keris Veturia's army.

"The humans are ready to attack, Meherya." Umber's glow reddens, her disgust of our Martial allies palpable.

"Give the order," I tell her. Behind me, one by one, my kin transform from shadow to flame, lighting the cold sky.

A warning bell tolls in the village. The watchman has seen us, and bellows in panic. The front gates—hastily erected after attacks on neighboring communities—swing closed as lamps flare and shouts tinge the night air with terror.

"Seal the exits," I tell Umber. "Leave the children to carry the tale. Maro." I turn to a wisp of a jinn, his narrow shoulders belying the power within. "Are you strong enough for what you must do?"

Maro nods. He and the others pour past me, five rivers of fire, like those that spew from young mountains in the south. The jinn blast through the gates, leaving them smoking.

A half legion of Martials follow, and when the village is well aflame and my kin withdraw, the soldiers begin their butchery. The screams of the living fade quickly. Those of the dead echo for longer.

After the village is naught but ashes, Umber finds me. Like the other jinn, she now glows with only the barest flicker.

"The winds are fair," I tell her. "You will reach home swiftly."

"We wish to remain with you, Meherya," she says. "We are strong."

For a millennium, I believed that vengeance and wrath were my lot. Never would I witness the beauty of my kind moving through the world. Never would I feel the warmth of their flame.

But time and tenacity allowed me to reconstitute the Star—the weapon the Augurs used to imprison my people. The same weapon I used to set them free. Now the strongest of my kin gather near. And though it has been months since I destroyed the trees imprisoning them, my skin still trills at their presence.

"Go," I order them gently. "For I will need you in the coming days."

After they leave, I walk the cobbled streets of the village, sniffing for signs of life. Umber lost her children, her parents, and her lover in our long-ago war with the humans. Her rage has made her thorough.

A gust of wind carries me to the south wall of the village. The air tells of the violence wrought here. But there is another scent too.

A hiss escapes me. The smell is human, but layered with a fey sheen. The girl's face rises in my mind. Laia of Serra. Her essence feels like this.

But why would she lurk in a Mariner village?

I consider donning my human skin, but decide against it. It is an arduous task, not undertaken without good reason. Instead I draw my cloak close against the rain and trace the scent to a hut tucked beside a tottering wall.

The ghuls trailing my ankles yip in excitement. They feed off pain, and the village is rife with it. I nudge them away and enter the hut alone.

The inside is lit by a tribal lamp and a merry fire, over which a pan of charred skillet bread smokes. Pink winter roses sit atop the dresser and a cup of well water sweats on the table.

Whoever was here left only moments ago.

Or rather, she wants it to look that way.

I steel myself, for a jinn's love is no fickle thing. Laia of Serra has hooks in my heart yet. The pile of blankets at the foot of the bed disintegrates to ashes at my touch. Hidden beneath and shaking with terror is a child who is very obviously *not* Laia of Serra.

And yet he feels like her.

Not in his mien, for where Laia of Serra has sorrow coiled about her heart, this boy is gripped by fear. Where Laia's soul is hardened by suffering, this boy is soft, his joy untrammeled until now. He's a Mariner child, no more than twelve.

But it is what's deep within that harkens to Laia. An unknowable darkness in his mind. His black eyes meet mine, and he holds up his hands.

"B-begone!" Perhaps he meant for it to be a shout. But his voice rasps, nails digging into wood. When I go to snap his neck, he holds his hands out again, and an unseen force nudges me back a few inches.

His power is wild and unsettlingly familiar. I wonder if it is jinn magic, but while jinn-human pairings occurred, no children can come of them.

"Begone, foul creature!" Emboldened by my retreat, the boy throws something at me. It has all the sting of rose petals. Salt.

My curiosity fades. Whatever lives within the child feels fey, so I reach for the scythe slung across my back. Before he understands what is happening, I draw the weapon across his throat and turn away, my mind already moving on.

The boy speaks, stopping me dead. His voice booms with the finality of a jinn spewing prophecy. But the words are garbled, a story told through water and rock.

"The seed that slumbered wakes, the fruit of its flowering consecrated within the body of man. And thus is thy doom begotten, Beloved, and with it the breaking—the—breaking—"

A jinn would have completed the prophecy, but the boy is only human, his body a frail vessel. Blood pours from the wound in his neck and he collapses, dead.

"What in the skies are you?" I speak to the darkness within the child, but it has fled, and taken the answer to my question with it.

CHAPTER TWO

Laia

The storyteller in the Ucaya Inn holds the packed common room in her thrall. The winter wind moans through Adisa's streets, rattling the eaves outside, and the Tribal *Kehanni* trembles with equal intensity. She sings of a woman fighting to save her true love from a vengeful jinn. Even the most ale-soaked denizens are rapt.

As I watch the *Kehanni* from a table in the corner of the room, I wonder what it is like to be her. To offer the gift of story to those you meet, instead of suspecting that they might be enemies out to kill you.

At the thought, I scan the room again and feel for my dagger.

"You pull that hood any lower," Musa of Adisa whispers from beside me, "and people will think you're a jinn." The Scholar man sprawls in a chair to my right. My brother, Darin, sits on his other side. We are tucked by one of the inn's foggy windows, where the warmth of the fire does not penetrate.

I do not release my weapon. My skin prickles, instinct telling me that unfriendly eyes are upon me. But everyone watches the *Kehanni*.

"Stop waving around your blade, *aapan*." Musa uses the Mariner honorific that means "little sister" and speaks with the same exasperation I sometimes hear from Darin. The Beekeeper, as Musa is known, is twenty-eight— older than Darin and I. Perhaps that is why he delights in bossing us around.

"The innkeeper is a friend," he says. "No enemies here. Relax. We can't do anything until the Blood Shrike returns anyway."

We are surrounded by Mariners, Scholars, and only a few Tribespeople. Still, when the *Kehanni* ends her tale, the room explodes into applause. It is so sudden that I half draw my blade.

Musa eases my hand off the hilt. "You break Elias Veturius out of Blackcliff, burn down Kauf Prison, deliver the Martial Emperor in the middle of a war, face down the Nightbringer more times than I can count," he says, "and you jump at a loud noise? I thought you were fearless, *aapan*."

"Leave off, Musa," Darin says. "Better to be jumpy than dead. The Blood Shrike would agree."

"She's a Mask," Musa says. "They're born paranoid." The Scholar watches the door, his mirth fading. "She should be back by now."

It is strange to worry about the Shrike. Until a few months ago, I thought I would go to my grave hating her. But then Grímarr and his horde of Karkaun barbarians besieged Antium, and Keris Veturia betrayed the city. Thousands of Martials and Scholars, including me, the Shrike, and her newly born nephew, the Emperor, fled to Delphinium. The Shrike's sister, Empress Regent Livia, freed those Scholars still bound in slavery.

And somehow, between then and now, we became allies.

The innkeeper, a young Scholar woman around Musa's age, emerges from the kitchen with a tray of food. She sweeps toward us, the tantalizing scents of pumpkin stew and garlic flatbread preceding her.

"Musa, love." The innkeeper sets down the food and I am suddenly starving. "You won't stay another night?"

"Sorry, Haina." He flips a gold mark at her and she catches it deftly. "That should cover the rooms."

"And then some." Haina pockets the coin. "Nikla's raised Scholar taxes again. Nyla's bakery was shuttered last week when she couldn't pay."

"We've lost our greatest ally." Musa speaks of old King Irmand, who's been ill for weeks. "It's only going to get worse."

"You were married to the princess," Haina says. "Couldn't you talk to her?"

9

The Scholar offers her a wry smile. "Not unless you want your taxes even higher."

Haina departs and Musa claims the stew. Darin swipes a platter of fried okra still popping with oil.

"You ate four ears of street corn an hour ago," I hiss at him, grappling for a basket of bread.

As I wrest it free, the door blows open. Snow drifts into the room, along with a tall, slender woman. Her silvery-blonde crown braid is mostly hidden beneath a hood. The screaming bird on her breastplate flashes for an instant before she draws her cloak over it and strides to our table.

"That smells incredible." The Blood Shrike of the Martial Empire drops into the seat across from Musa and takes his food.

At his petulant expression, she shrugs. "Ladies first. That goes for you too, smith." She slides Darin's groaning plate toward me and I dig in.

"Well?" Musa says to the Shrike. "Did that shiny bird on your armor get you in to see the king?"

The Blood Shrike's pale eyes flash. "Your wife," she says, "is a pain in the a—"

"Estranged wife." Musa says. A reminder that once, they adored each other. No longer. A bitter ending to what they hoped was a lifelong love.

It is a feeling I know well.

Elias Veturius saunters into my mind, though I have tried to lock him out. He appears as I last saw him, sharp-eyed and aloof outside the Waiting Place. *We are, all of us, just visitors in each other's lives*, he'd said. *You will forget my visit soon enough.*

"What did the princess say?" Darin asks the Shrike, and I push Elias from my head.

"She didn't speak to me. Her steward said the princess would hear my appeal when King Irmand's health improved."

The Martial glares at Musa, as if he is the one who has refused an audience. "Keris *bleeding* Veturia is sitting in Serra, beheading every ambassador Nikla has sent. The Mariners have no other allies in the Empire. Why is she refusing to see me?"

"I'd love to know," Musa says, and an iridescent flicker near his face tells me that his wights, tiny winged creatures who serve as his spies, are near. "But while I have eyes in many places, Blood Shrike, the inside of Nikla's mind isn't one of them."

"I should be back in Delphinium." The Shrike stares out at the howling snowstorm. "My family needs me."

Worry furrows her brow, uncharacteristic on a face so studied. In the five months since we escaped Antium, the Blood Shrike has thwarted a dozen attempts to assassinate young Emperor Zacharias. The child has enemies among the Karkauns as well as Keris's allies in the south. And they are relentless.

"We expected this," Darin says. "Are we decided, then?"

The Blood Shrike and I nod, but Musa clears his throat.

"I know the Shrike needs to speak to the princess," he says. "But I'd like to publicly state that I find this plan far too risky."

Darin chuckles. "That's how we know it's a Laia plan—utterly insane and likely to end in death."

"What of your shadow, Martial?" Musa glances around for Avitas Harper, as if the Mask might appear out of thin air. "What wretched task have you subjected that poor man to now?"

"Harper is occupied." The Shrike's body stiffens for a moment before she continues inhaling her food. "Don't worry about him."

"I have to take one last delivery at the forge." Darin gets to his feet. "I'll meet you at the gate in a bit, Laia. Luck to you all."

Watching him walk out of the inn sends anxiety spiking through me. While I was in the Empire, my brother remained here in Marinn at my request. We reunited a week ago, when the Shrike, Avitas, and I arrived in Adisa. Now we're splitting up again. *Just for a few hours, Laia. He'll be fine.*

Musa nudges my plate toward me. "Eat, *aapan*," he says, not unkindly. "Everything is better when you're not hungry. I'll have the wights keep an eye on Darin, and I'll see you all at the northeast gate. Seventh bell." He pauses, frowning. "Be careful."

As he heads out, the Blood Shrike harrumphs. "Mariner guards have nothing on a Mask."

I do not disagree. I watched the Shrike single-handedly hold off an army of Karkauns so that thousands of Martials and Scholars could escape Antium. Few Mariners could take on a Mask. None is a match for the Blood Shrike.

The Shrike disappears to her room to change, and for the first time in ages, I am alone. Out in the city, a bell tolls the fifth hour. Winter brings night early and the roof groans with the force of the gale. I ponder Musa's words as I watch the inn's boisterous guests and try to shake off that sense of being watched. *I thought you were fearless.*

I almost laughed when he said it. *Fear is only your enemy if you allow it to be.* The blacksmith Spiro Teluman told me that long ago. Some days, I live those words so easily. On others, they are a weight in my bones I cannot bear.

Certainly, I did the things Musa said. But I also abandoned Darin to a Mask. My friend Izzi died because of me. I escaped the Nightbringer, but unwittingly helped him free his kindred. I delivered the Emperor, but let my mother sacrifice herself so that the Blood Shrike and I could live.

Even now, months later, I see Mother in my dreams. White-haired and scarred, her eyes blazing as she wields her bow against a wave of Karkaun attackers. She was not afraid.

But I am not my mother. And I am not alone in my fear. Darin does not speak of the terror he faced in Kauf Prison. Nor does the Shrike speak of the day Emperor Marcus slaughtered her parents and sister. Or how it felt to flee Antium, knowing what the Karkauns would do to her people.

Fearless. No, none of us is fearless. "Ill-fated" is a better description.

I rise as the Blood Shrike descends the stairs. She wears the slate, cinch-waisted dress of a palace maid and a matching cloak. I almost don't recognize her.

"Stop staring." The Shrike tucks a lock of hair beneath the drab kerchief hiding her crown braid and nudges me toward the door. "Someone will notice the uniform. Come on. We're late."

"How many blades hidden in that skirt?"

"Five—no, wait—" She shifts from foot to foot. "Seven."

We push out of the Ucaya and into streets thick with snow and people. The wind knifes into us, and I scramble for my gloves, fingertips numb.

"Seven blades." I smile at her. "And you did not think to bring gloves?"

"It's colder in Antium." The Shrike's gaze drops to the dagger at my waist. "And I don't use poisoned blades."

"Maybe if you did, you would not need so many."

She grins at me. "Luck to you, Laia."

"Do not kill anyone, Shrike."

She melts into the evening crowds like a wraith, fourteen years of training making her almost as undetectable as I am about to be. I drop down, as if adjusting my bootlaces, and draw my invisibility over me between one moment and the next.

With its terraced levels and brightly painted homes, Adisa is charming during the day. But at night, it dazzles. Tribal lanterns hang from nearly every house, their multicolored glass sparkling even in the storm. Lamplight leaks through the ornamental lattices that cover the windows, casting gold fractals upon the snow.

The Ucaya Inn sits on a higher terrace, with a view of both Fari Bay, on the northwest end of Adisa, and Aftab Bay, on the northeast. There, among mountains of floating ice, whales breach and descend. In the city's center, the charred spire of the Great Library lances the sky, still standing despite a fire that nearly destroyed it when I was last here.

But it is the people who make me stare. Even with a tempest roaring out of the north, the Mariners dress in their finest. Red and blue and purple wools embroidered with freshwater pearls and mirrors. Sweeping cloaks lined in fur and heavy with gold thread.

Perhaps I can make a home here one day. Most Mariners do not share Nikla's prejudices. Maybe I, too, could wear beautiful clothes and live in a periwinkle house with a green-shingled roof. Laugh with friends, become a healer. Meet a handsome Mariner and swat at Darin and Musa when they tease me mercilessly about him.

I try to hold that image in my mind. But I do not want Marinn. I want sand and stories and a clear night sky. I want to stare up into pale gray eyes filled with love and that edge of wickedness I ache for. I want to know what he said to me in Sadhese, a year and a half ago, when we danced at the Moon Festival in Serra.

14

I want Elias Veturius back.

Stop, Laia. The Scholars and Martials in Delphinium are counting on me. Musa suspected Nikla wouldn't hear the Shrike's plea—so we plotted a way to *make* the crown princess listen. But it will not work unless I get through these streets and into the palace.

As I make my way toward the center of Adisa, snatches of conversation float by. The Adisans speak of attacks in far-flung villages. Monsters prowling the countryside.

"Hundreds dead, I heard."

"My nephew's regiment left weeks ago and we haven't had any word."

"Just a rumor—"

Only it is not a rumor. Musa's wights reported back this morning. My stomach twists when I think of the border villages that were burned to the ground, their residents slaughtered.

The lanes I traverse grow narrower, and streetlamps more scarce. Behind me, a tinkle of coins echoes and I whirl, but no one is there. I walk more quickly when I catch a glimpse of the palace gate. It is inlaid with onyx and mother of pearl, selenic beneath the snowy pink sky. *Stay away from that bleeding gate*, Musa warned me. *It's guarded by Jaduna and they'll see right through your invisibility.*

The magic-wielding Jaduna hail from the unknown lands beyond the Great Wastes, thousands of miles to the west. A few serve the Mariner royal family. Running into one would mean jail—or death.

Thankfully, the palace has side entrances for the maids and messengers and groundskeepers who keep the place running. Those guards are not Jaduna, so slipping past them is simple enough.

But once inside, I hear that sound again—one coin sliding against another.

The palace is a massive complex arranged in a U around acres of manicured gardens. The halls are wide as boulevards and so tall that the frescoes painted upon the pale stone above are hardly visible.

There are also mirrors everywhere. As I turn a corner, I glance into one and catch a flash of gold coins and vivid blue clothing. My heartbeat quickens. A Jaduna? The figure is gone too fast to tell.

I backtrack, heading to where the person vanished. But all I find is a hallway patrolled by a pair of guards. I will have to deal with whomever—or whatever—is following me when they reveal themselves. Right now, I need to get to the throne room.

At sixth bell, Musa said, *the princess departs the throne room for the dining hall. Go in through the southern antechamber. Place your blade on the throne and get out. The moment her guards see it, Nikla will be evacuated to her chambers.*

No one gets hurt and we have Nikla where we want her. The Blood Shrike will be waiting and will make her plea.

The antechamber is small and musty, the faint scent of sweat and perfume mingling, but it is, as Musa predicted, empty. I slip silently through and into the shadows of the throne room.

Where I hear voices.

The first is a woman's, resonant and angry. I've not heard Princess Nikla speak in months and it takes me a moment to recognize her intonations.

The second voice stops me cold, for it is laced with violence and chillingly soft. It is a voice that has no business being in Adisa. A voice I would know anywhere. She calls herself Imperator Invictus—Supreme Commander—of the Empire.

But to me, she will always be the Commandant.

16

CHAPTER THREE

The Soul Catcher

The stew tastes like memories. I don't trust it.

The carrots and potatoes are tender, the grouse falling from the bone.
But the moment I take a bite, I want to spit it out. Steam undulates in the
cool air of my cabin, conjuring faces. A blonde-crowned warrior standing
in a jungle with me, asking if I'm all right. A small, tattooed woman with a
whip dripping blood and a gaze cruel enough to match.

A gold-eyed girl, her hands on my face, imploring me not to lie to her.

I blink and the bowl is across the room, smashed into the stone mantel
above the fireplace. Dust drifts down from the masterfully crafted scims I
hung up months ago.

The faces are gone. I'm on my feet, the splinters of the rough-hewn table
I just built digging into my palms.

I don't recall throwing the bowl or standing. I don't remember grabbing
the table so hard my hands bleed.

Those people—who are they? They are in the scent of winter fruit and the
feel of a soft blanket. In the heft of a blade and the slap of a northern wind.

And they are in my nightly visions of war and death. The dreams always
begin with a great army hurtling itself against a wave of fire. A roar breaks
across the sky, and a maelstrom spins, sentient and hungry, devouring all
in its path. The warrior is consumed. The cold woman and the gold-eyed
girl disappear. In the distance, the soft pink blooms of Tala fruit trees drift
to the earth.

The dreams make me uneasy. Not for myself but for those people.

They matter not, Banu al-Mauth. The voice reverberating in my head is

17

low and ancient. It is Mauth, the magic at the heart of the Waiting Place. Mauth's power shields me from threats and gives me insight into the emotions of the living and the dead. The magic lets me extend life or end it. All in service of protecting the Waiting Place, and offering solace to the ghosts that linger here.

Much of the past has faded, but Mauth left me some memories. One is what happened when I first became Soul Catcher. My emotions kept me from accessing Mauth's magic. I could not pass the ghosts quickly enough. They gathered strength and escaped the Waiting Place. Once out in the world, they killed thousands.

Emotion is the enemy, I remind myself. Love, hate, joy, fear. All are forbidden.

What was your vow to me? Mauth speaks.

"I would help the ghosts pass to the other side," I say. "I would light the way for the weak, the weary, the fallen, and forgotten in the darkness that follows death."

Yes. For you are my Soul Catcher. Banu al-Mauth. The Chosen of Death.

But once, I was someone else. Who? I wish I knew. I wish—

Outside the cabin walls, the wind wails. Or perhaps it is the ghosts. When Mauth speaks again, his words are followed by a wave of magic that takes the edge off my curiosity.

Wishes only cause pain, Soul Catcher. Your old life is over. Attend to the new. Intruders are afoot.

I breathe through my mouth while I clean up the stew. As I don my cloak, I consider the fire. Last spring, efrits burned down the cabin that was here. It belonged to Shaeva, the jinn who was Soul Catcher until the Nightbringer murdered her.

Rebuilding the cabin took me months. The pale wood floor, my bed, the shelves for plates and spices—they're all so new they still ooze sap. The house and clearing around it provide protection from the ghosts and the fey, just as they did when they belonged to Shaeva.

This place is my sanctuary. I do not want to see it burn down again.

But the cold outside is fierce. I bank the fire, leaving a few embers burning deep within the ashes. Then I tug on my boots and grab the carved wooden armlet I always find myself working on—though I don't recall where it came from. At the door, I glance back at my blades. It has been difficult to give them up. They were a gift from someone. Someone I once cared for.

Which is why they don't matter anymore. I leave them and step into the storm, hoping that with a realm to protect and ghosts to tend to, the faces that haunt me will finally fade away.

«««

The intruders are so far south that when I drop out of my windwalk, the gale that raged around my cottage is little more than a rumor. The Duskan Sea mists my skin with salt, and through the crashing surf, I hear the interlopers. Two men and a woman holding a child, drenched and clambering up the glistening coastal rocks toward the Waiting Place.

They all have the same gold-brown skin and loose curls—a family, perhaps. The remnants of a ship float in the shallows beyond them and they stumble as they run, desperate to escape a band of sea efrits hurling detritus at them.

Though I remain hidden, the efrits look to the forest when they sense me, carping in disappointment. As they retreat, the humans continue toward the trees.

Shaeva broke bones and bodies and left them at the borders for others to find. I could not bring myself to do as she did—and this is what I get. To humans, the Waiting Place is simply the Forest of Dusk. They have forgotten what lives here.

The few ghosts I have not yet passed gather behind me, crying out at the presence of the living, which pains them. The men exchange glances. But the woman carrying the child grits her teeth and continues toward the shelter of the tree line.

When she steps beneath the canopy, the ghosts surround her. She cannot see them. But her face goes pale at their moans of displeasure. The child in her arms stirs fitfully.

"You are not welcome here, travelers." I emerge from the trees and the men halt.

"I need to feed her." The woman's anger swirls around her, tinged with despair. "I need a fire to keep her warm."

The ghosts hiss as the forest ripples. The trees reflect Mauth's moods, and he doesn't like the intruders any more than the spirits do.

The last time I took a life with Mauth's magic was months ago. I killed a group of Karkaun warlords with barely a thought. I use that power again now, finding the thread of the woman's life and pulling. At first, she grips her child more tightly. Then she gasps, reaching for her throat.

"Fozya!" one of the men cries out. "Get back—"

"I won't!" Fozya spits, even as I squeeze the air from her lungs. "His people are murderers. How many has he killed, lurking here like a spider? How—"

Fozya's words stick in my head. *How many has he killed—*

How many—

Screams erupt in my mind: the cries of thousands of men, women, and children who died after I let the walls of the Waiting Place fall last summer. The people I killed as a soldier, friends who died at my hand—they all march through my brain, judging me with dead eyes. It is too much. I cannot bear it—

As suddenly as the feeling is upon me, it fades. Magic floods me: Mauth, soothing my mind, offering me peace. Distance.

Fozya and her kin must go. I drain the woman's life away again. She nearly drops the child. With each step I take toward her, she stumbles back, finally collapsing on the beach.

"All right, we'll go," she gasps. "I'm sorry—"

I release her and she flees north, her companions hurrying behind her. They keep to the coastline, casting frightened glances at the trees until they are out of sight.

"Hail, Soul Catcher." The scent of salt overwhelms me as the waves foam at my feet and coalesce into a vaguely man-like form. "Your power has grown."

"Why so far inland, efrit?" I ask the creature. "Does tormenting humans hold such allure?"

"The Nightbringer requested destruction," the efrit says. "We are . . . eager to please him."

"You mean you fear displeasing him."

"He has killed many of my kind," the efrit says. "I would not see any more suffer."

"Leave them in peace." I nod in the direction of the departing humans.

"They are in your domain no longer, and they have done nothing to you."

"Why do you care what happens to them? You are no longer one of them."

"The fewer the ghosts I deal with," I say, "the better."

The efrit surges toward me, wrapping itself around my legs and yanking as if to drag me underwater. But Mauth's power shields me. When the efrit lets go, I get the distinct feeling that it was testing me.

"A time will come," the efrit says, "when you will wish you hadn't spoken those words. When Mauth can no longer magic away the screams in your head. On that day, seek out Siladh, lord of the sea efrits."

"Is that you?"

The creature doesn't answer, instead collapsing to the sand, leaving me soaked to the knees.

Once back in the forest, I pass on a dozen ghosts. Doing so means understanding and unraveling their hurt and wrath so they can release it and move on from this dimension. Mauth's magic suffuses me, allowing me swift, deep insight into the spirits' suffering.

Most take only a few moments to pass. After I finish, I check for weakness in the border wall, which is invisible to human eyes. The trees open for me as I walk, the path beneath my feet smooth as an Empire road.

It has been like this since I surrendered myself to Mauth. When I built the cabin, wood appeared at regular intervals, hewn and sanded as if by a craftsman. I've never been bitten nor suffered illness, nor struggled to find game. This forest is a physical manifestation of Mauth. Though to an outsider, it appears as any other forest would, he alters it to fit my needs.

Only so long as you're useful to him.

Screams and faces rise in my head again, and this time they do not fade.

I windwalk back into the storm to the heart of the Waiting Place: the jinn grove, or what is left of it.

Before I joined with Mauth, I avoided the grove assiduously. But now it is a place where I can forget my troubles. It is a vast plain on a bluff high above the City of the Jinn. Beyond the dark sprawl of that eerily silent place, the River Dusk winds, a serpentine glimmer.

I survey the blackened husks of the grove's few remaining trees, which stand like sentinels, lonely between drenching sheets of rain. In the five months since the Nightbringer freed the jinn, I have not seen signs of a single one. Not even here, in the place that was once their prison.

" . . . *guide me to Kauf Prison . . . help me break my brother out of there.*"

The words trigger a memory of the gold-eyed girl. I grit my teeth and head to the largest of the trees, a dead yew whose branches are blackened by fire. Its trunk is deeply scored on either side. Beside it sits an iron chain with links half the size of my hand, burgled from a Martial village.

I heft the chain and bring it down on one side of the tree trunk, and then the other, deepening the score marks. After only a few minutes, my arms begin to ache.

When your mind does not hear you, train your body. Your mind will follow. Skies know who said those words to me, but I have clung to them these past few months, returning to the jinn grove again and again when my thoughts grow unruly.

After half an hour, I am soaked in sweat. I peel off my shirt, my body screaming, but I have just begun. For as I heave stones and whip the tree and run the escarpment that leads down to the jinn city, the faces and sounds that haunt me fade away.

My body is the only part of me that is still human. It is solid and real and suffers hunger and exhaustion just as it always did. Flogging it means I must breathe a certain way, balance a certain way. Doing so takes all of my focus, leaving nothing for my demons.

Once I've exhausted the possibilities of the jinn grove, I trudge to its eastern edge, which slopes down to the River Dusk, swift and treacherous from the storm. I dive in, gasping at the frigid water, and swim the quarter mile across, emptying my mind of everything but the cold and the current.

I return to shore soaked and exhausted, but clearheaded. I am ready to face the ghosts that will be waiting in the trees. For even as I swam, I felt a great sundering of life far to the north. I will be busy this night.

I make for the old yew to collect my clothes. But someone stands beside it.

Mauth put an awareness of the Waiting Place into my mind that is much like a map. I reach for that awareness now, seeking the pulsing glow that indicates the presence of an outsider.

The map is empty.

I squint through the rain—a jinn, perhaps? But no—even the fey creatures leave a mark, their magic trailing them like a comet's tail.

"You have entered the Waiting Place," I call out. "These lands are forbidden to the living."

I hear nothing but the rain and wind. The figure is still, but the air crackles. *Magic.*

That face flashes in my mind. Black hair. Gold eyes. Sorcery in her bones. *But what was her name? Who was she?*

"I won't hurt you." I speak as I would to the ghosts—with care.

"Won't you, Elias Veturius?" the figure says. "Even now? Even after everything?"

Elias Veturius. The name conjures many images. A school of stark gray rock and thundering drums. The tiny woman with glacial eyes. Within me, a voice cries out, *Yes. Elias Veturius. That is who you are.*

"That is not my name," I say to the figure.

"It is, and you must remember it." The figure's voice is pitched so low, I cannot tell if it is a man or woman. Adult or child.

It's her! My heart beats too swiftly. Thoughts I shouldn't have crowd my head. Will she tell me her name? Will she forgive me for forgetting it?

Then two withered hands appear in the darkness and shove back the hood. The man's skin is pale as bleached linen and the whites of his eyes are livid and bloody. Though I have forgotten much of who I was, this face is burned into my mind.

"You," I whisper.

"Indeed, Elias Veturius," Cain, the Augur, says. "Here to torment you, one last time."

CHAPTER FOUR

Laia

Keris Veturia is in Marinn and she is just yards from me. *How?* I want to scream. Only days ago, Musa's wights reported that she was in Serra.

But what does that matter when Keris can call on the Nightbringer? He must have ridden the winds and brought her to Adisa.

My pulse pounds in my ears, but I force myself to breathe. The Commandant's presence complicates matters. But I must still get Nikla out of the throne room and to her apartments. The Scholars and Martials in Delphinium have few weapons, little food, and no allies. If Nikla does not hear what the Blood Shrike has to say, any hope of aid is lost.

Silently, I weave across the floor until Nikla and Keris come into view. The Mariner princess is poker-straight upon her father's massive driftwood throne, her face in shadow. Her burgundy dress is cinched tight about her waist and pools on the floor like blood. Two guards keep watch behind the throne, with four more on either side.

The Commandant stands before Nikla in her ceremonial armor. She carries no weapons, wears no crown. But she does not need them. Keris's power has always lain in her cunning and her violence.

Her skin gleams silver at her nape, for she wears the living metal shirt she stole from the Blood Shrike. I marvel at her size—she is a half foot shorter than me. Even after all the misery she's caused, one could see her from afar and think that she's a young, harmless girl.

As I inch closer, the shadows on Nikla's face shift and seethe. Ghuls, feasting on the crown princess's pain, swirling around her in an unholy halo that she cannot see.

26

"—cannot make a decision," Keris says. "Perhaps I should speak with your father."

"I will not trouble my father while he is ill," Nikla says.

"Then give in, Princess." The Commandant holds open her hands, as if someone else is speaking such abhorrent words. "The attacks on your people will stop. The jinn will retreat. The Scholars are a drain on your resources. You know this."

"Which is why I have encouraged their departure from Adisa," Nikla says. "However, what you ask is—" The princess shakes her head.

"I am offering to take a troubled populace off your hands."

"To enslave them."

Keris smiles. "To offer them a new purpose in life."

Rage makes my hands shake. My mother, Mirra of Serra, could scale walls with hardly a thought. Would that I had that same mysterious skill. I would use it now to leap upon Keris when she least expected it.

My dagger is in my hand—not the one I was to lay on Nikla's throne, but an older weapon. Elias gave it to me long ago. It is wicked sharp and coated with poison from cross-guard to tip. I run my gloved finger along the blade and inch closer to the throne.

"What of the thousands of Scholars you killed?" Nikla wags her head, unknowingly shaking off the ghuls, who chitter in vexation. "Did they have no purpose? You perpetrated a genocide, Empress. How do I know you will not do so again?"

"The number of Scholar dead was greatly exaggerated," Keris says. "Those I did execute were criminals. Rebels and political dissidents. You've disavowed your own husband for speaking against the monarchy. My methods were simply more permanent."

A steward steps out from behind the throne, face solemn as she bends to whisper in Nikla's ear.

"Forgive me, Empress," the crown princess says after listening. "I am late for my next engagement. We will speak in the morning. My guards can show you to your quarters."

"If you wouldn't mind," the Commandant says, "I'd like a moment to appreciate your throne room. Its beauty is renowned—even in the Empire."

Nikla goes very still, her fists tightening on the throne's intricately carved armrests.

"Certainly," she finally says. "The guards will wait in the hall."

The princess sweeps out, her soldiers trailing. I know I should follow her. Find some other way to carry out a threat so that she is taken to her quarters.

But I find myself staring at the Commandant. She is a killer. But no— nothing so simple as that. She is a monster in killer's clothing. A scrap of the hells masquerading as human.

She stares at the stained-glass dome above, where bright-sailed ships ply Marinn's turquoise seas. I take a slow step toward her. How much suffering would have been avoided if I'd had the courage to kill her months ago, out-side Serra, when she lay unconscious at my feet?

Now I could end her with one strike. She cannot see me. I fix my gaze on her neck, on the vivid blue tattoo crawling up her nape.

Her chest rises and falls gently, a reminder that no matter what she has done, she is human. And she can die just like the rest of us.

"It's the throat or nothing, Laia of Serra." The Commandant's voice is soft. "Unless you cut through my fatigues to the artery in my leg. But I'm faster than you, so you'll likely fail."

I lunge, but she's turned toward the faint *whoosh* of my cloak as I fly

28

at her. The impact of our bodies jolts my invisibility loose. Before I draw another breath, the Commandant has me flat on the floor, knees clamped around my thighs, one hand pinning my arms while the other holds Elias's blade to my throat. I did not even feel her take it from me.

I cringe but the high neck of my shirt protects me from the poison on the blade. The silver skin of her chest flashes. She tilts her head, reptilian gaze boring into me.

"How will you die?" she asks. "In battle, like your mother? Or in terror, like mine?" Her hand is grasped tight around the hilt of the dagger. *Talk. Keep her talking.*

"Don't you—" I gasp as she presses the weapon against my windpipe. "Don't you dare talk about my mother like that—you—hag—"

"I don't know why you bothered, girl," she says. "I always kn-know—"

The knife slackens against my throat. Keris's eyes dilate and she coughs. I squirm out from under her, rolling away. She leaps for me, and when she misses, stumbling instead, I allow myself a smile. She's losing the feeling in her hands. In her legs. I know, because I tested the poison on myself.

Too late, Keris notices my gloves. Too late, she drops Elias's blade, staring at the hilt, realizing how I got the poison onto her. If she'd ingested it, it would have killed her. But against her skin, it is more of an inconvenience. One just bad enough to give me the edge. The Commandant scrambles back as I yank a dirk from my boot.

But Keris Veturia has been at war nearly her whole life. Her instinct takes control and as I slash at her throat, she doubles me over with a quick hit below my sternum. My weapon falls, and I reach for my last knife. With a blow to my wrist, Keris sends it clattering across the floor.

Voices sound outside. The guards.

I lurch into her while she's distracted and she throws me off with such force that I smack into the throne, head muzzy as I ooze to the floor. She opens her mouth to shout for the guards—likely the only time she's called for help in her life. But the poison has stolen her voice and after struggling to stand, she finally collapses, limbs gracelessly akimbo.

Now or never, Laia. Where the skies are my blades? I'd choke the life out of her, but she might wake up in the middle of it. She'll be out for a minute, at most. I need a weapon.

The hilt of Elias's dagger pokes out from beneath the throne. Just as I get my hands on it, still gasping for breath, I am flung back like a rag doll.

My body slams into a quartz pillar. The throne room blurs, and then sharpens as a figure who is not the Commandant, but who certainly was not here a moment ago, makes its way toward me.

Pale skin. A dark cloak. Warm brown eyes. Freckles dancing across a wrenchingly handsome face. And a shock of red hair that's nothing compared to the fire within him.

I know what he is. I know. But when I see him, I do not think *Nightbringer! Jinn! Enemy!*

I think *Keenan. Friend. Lover.*

Traitor.

Run, Laia! My body refuses to cooperate. Blood pours from a gash on the side of my head, salty and hot. My muscles scream, legs aching like they used to after a whipping. The pain is a rope wrapped around me, pulling tighter and tighter.

"Y-you," I manage. Why would he take this form? Why, when he has avoided it until now?

Because he wants you panicked and off your guard, idiot!

His smell, lemon and woodsmoke, fills my senses, so familiar though I've tried to forget.

"Laia of Serra. It is good to see you, my love." Keenan's voice is low and warm. But he is not Keenan, I remind myself. He is the Nightbringer. After I fell in love with him, after I gave him my mother's armlet as a token of that love, he revealed his true form. The armlet was a long-lost piece of the Star—a talisman he needed to free his imprisoned brethren. Once I gave it to him, he had no more use for me.

He puts a hand on my arm to help me stand but I throw him off and drag myself to my feet.

It has been more than a year since I've seen the Nightbringer in his human form. I did not realize what a gift that was until now. Such concern in those dark eyes. Such caring. All to mask a vile creature that wants nothing more than to obliterate me.

The Commandant will be conscious soon. And while the Nightbringer cannot kill me—he cannot kill any who touched the Star—Keris Veturia can.

"Damn you." I look past the Nightbringer to Keris. If I could just get to her—

"I cannot let you harm her, Laia." The Nightbringer sounds almost sorry. "She serves a purpose."

"Curse your purpose to the hells!"

The Nightbringer glances at the doors.

"No point in shouting. The guards have found pressing duties elsewhere." He crouches beside Keris, feeling her pulse with a gentleness that bewilders me.

"You wish to murder her, Laia of Serra." He stands and approaches. "For Keris is the font of all your woes. She destroyed your family and turned your mother into a murderess and kinslayer. She annihilated your people and torments them still. You would do anything to stop her, yes? So what makes you so different from me?"

"I am *nothing* like you—"

"My family was killed too. My wife slaughtered on a battlefield. My children murdered with salt and steel and summer rain. My kin butchered and imprisoned."

"By people a thousand years gone!" I shout. But why speak with him? He's buying time until the Commandant wakes up. He believes I am too foolish to notice.

Fury floods my veins, numbing my pain, making me forget the Commandant. It colors everything red, and a darkness roars inside me. The same feral thing that rose within me months ago, when I gave him my armlet. The beast that lashed out in the Forest of Dusk, when I thought he was going to kill Elias.

The Nightbringer glares, mouth curling into an inhuman grimace. *"What are you?"* he says, and it is an echo of a question he asked before.

"You will not win." My voice is an unrecognizable snarl that rises from some ancient, visceral part of my soul. "You have harmed too many with your vengeance." I'm inches from him now, staring into those familiar eyes, hate pouring from my own. "I do not care what it takes, nor how long. I will defeat you, Nightbringer."

Silence stretches between us. The moment is impossibly long, hushed as death.

Then I hear an ear-blistering, eldritch scream. It goes on and on. The stained glass above cracks, the throne splinters. I clap my hands over my ears. Where is it coming from?

Me, I realize. *I am screaming. Only it is not me, is it? It is something inside me.* The moment I comprehend that fact, it feels as if my chest has split open. The dark light pouring from my body roars, as if freed after a long imprisonment. I try to stop it, to keep it leashed within.

But it is too powerful. I hear a rush of footsteps, see a flash of kohl-lined eyes. Coins tinkle—a sound I remember now. The headdresses of the Jaduna.

I have to run—I have to escape them.

Instead I collapse to my knees, and all the world goes white.

CHAPTER FIVE

The Soul Catcher

The emotion that explodes in me at the sight of the Augur's face feels unnatural. Like an animal, claws out, shredding my insides.

"I do not need your anger, Soul Catcher." The Augur grabs my shoulder and yanks me toward him. I nearly slip in the driving rain. "I need you to listen."

The ghosts sense Cain's presence and shriek so loudly it sounds as if there are hundreds of them instead of just a few dozen. Mauth's magic washes over me, dulling the screams and the cold, muting my anger. I force Cain's hand away.

"You disturb the spirits, Augur," I say. "The living are anathema to them."

"Living! Is that what you call this?" His laugh rattles around his rib cage like a loose stone. "If only the Nightbringer had killed me when he obliterated the rest of my kin. But I escaped his prison and he did not see that coming, did he—"

"Escaped?" The jinn and I have avoided each other for five months. I have no wish to tangle with them now. "What do you mean *escaped*?"

"They will be here any moment. Listen well, for I have little time."

"And I've none. You *cannot* be here." My ire surges, almost incandescent, and I wait for it to fade, for Mauth to take it away.

But a few seconds tick past and I feel no rush of peace. *Mauth?* I call in my mind.

"Your master is otherwise occupied," Cain says. "Battling a monster of his own creation." The Augur's mouth twists, and he glances over his shoulder, through the trees toward the mist-shrouded City of the Jinn. "The ghosts of our misdeeds seek vengeance. So I said to you long ago. And so it is. Our wrongs return to haunt us, Elias. Even Mauth cannot escape them."

"Mauth is not good, nor evil," I say. "There is no right or wrong with Death. Death is death."

"And death has chained you. Do you not see?" Cain's skeletal fingers crook toward me, and the jinn grove fills with a strange light, gold but with a shadow at its heart.

At first, it's too bright to see the source. But when it fades, I blink and catch the impression of thousands of ropes snaking around my body, binding me to the earth.

"You must escape this place. Tell me, *Soul Catcher*, what do you see when you dream?"

The warrior, the cold woman, and the gold-eyed girl flash through my mind. My hands curl into fists.

"I see . . . I . . ."

An eerie howl rises from the City of the Jinn. A wolf, I'd have thought, if not for the undercurrent of primeval rage. Others join it to create a hair-raising chorus and Cain stumbles toward me.

"The jinn have my scent," he whispers. "They'll be here soon. Listen well. You see a war, yes? An army breaking against a wave of flame. Beyond, fair blossoms blanket the ground. Above it all, a hungering maw. A maelstrom that can never be sated."

"You've been tampering with my mind."

"You think Mauth would let me into your mind, boy? He has you caged and chained, locked away. I did *not* give you the dreams. You see them because they are truth. Because some small part of your old self lives within you yet. It screams to be free."

"The Soul Catcher does not care for freedom—"

"But Elias Veturius does," Cain insists, and I find I cannot move, hypnotized by his use of that name. *My name. My old name.* "Elias Veturius yet lives. And it is imperative that he live, for the Great War approaches, and it is not the Soul Catcher who will win it, it is Elias Veturius. It is not the Soul Catcher who is an ember in the ashes, it is Elias Veturius. It is not the Soul Catcher who will spark and burn, ravage and destroy. *It is Elias Veturius.*"

"Elias Veturius is dead," I say. "And you are trespassing. The walls of the Waiting Place exist for a reason—"

"Forget the walls." Cain's face is feral. "For the ghosts, there is a greater threat. There are forces more powerful than death—"

The howls sound again, clear even through the downpour. Mauth's magic will protect me—already it rises around my body, a shield against the jinn.

But the jinn do not concern me. My duty is to the ghosts, and if something threatens them, I must know what it is. Questions flood my mind. Questions I need answers to.

"What do you mean 'forget the walls'?" I yank the old man toward me. "What threat do you speak of?"

But he looks over my shoulder to the figures emerging from the dark, their eyes burning like small suns through the curtain of rain.

"He belongs to us, Soul Catcher." The voice that speaks is sibilant and heavy with rancor. One of the jinn steps forward, a glaive in her hand. "Return him," she says. "Or suffer our wrath."

CHAPTER SIX

The Blood Shrike

Princess Nikla has not fled to her quarters. No alarm bells sound.

Instead, she strides down a long hallway toward where I lurk. The massive, carved doors of the state dining room—where she is not supposed to be—are across the hall from me and the ebony staircase I'm waxing.

There are a dozen Martials working in the palace, the Beekeeper told me. *You won't be an anomaly, but keep your head down. I'll send the wights when Laia has done her part and Nikla's in her quarters. They'll take you to her.*

When Laia says she'll do something, she does it. I hope to the skies she's not dead. The Delphinium Scholars will have my head if anything happens to her.

Besides which, she's grown on me.

My pocket rustles—the wights bringing me a scroll. I crouch, as if I've seen a scratch on the banister, and read the hastily scrawled message.

Keris Veturia in palace.

I hardly have time to comprehend how the Commandant got here—and how Musa's wights missed it—when the Princess approaches. She halts before the dining room, not ten feet away. Chatter leaks from the closed doors. Once she's inside with all those courtiers, she won't emerge for hours.

Do something, Shrike. But what? Kidnap her? Kill her guards? I'm supposed to secure a treaty, not start a war.

Bleeding, burning hells. I told Livia to send a diplomat. Avitas Harper would have been perfect. She could have dispatched him to Marinn and let me stay in Delphinium. I'd have been able to focus on Grímarr and the Karkauns. And I'd have been free of Harper and the maddening desire that muddles my mind and tangles my words whenever he's near.

But no. *The Mariner royal family needs to speak with someone who fought in Antium*, Livia said. *Someone who knows what Grímarr is doing there.*

Just thinking of it makes my blood boil. Four weeks ago, Grímarr ambushed a supply caravan headed for Delphinium. He replaced the food with Martial and Scholar limbs—those hacked off during his violent blood rites. One of his men hid in the caravan and tried to ambush me, shouting, "*Ik tachk mort fid iniqant fi!*" I gutted him before I got a translation.

When the Paters of Delphinium learned of the incident, they were horrified. Their support wanes, even as the Karkauns wreak havoc on my capital. We *need* this alliance.

So here I am, standing three yards from the crown princess of Marinn, bold as a Navium dock whore. I have no battle armor. No mask. Just a stolen uniform and my scarred face.

The princess doesn't enter the room. Instead she stares at the fish and shells and ferns carved in the door as if she's never seen them before. For an instant, she looks panicked.

The idea of lording over the Martials as an empress—and being subject to the politics and expectations of such a position—makes me ill. Perhaps Nikla feels the same.

One of Nikla's guards clears her throat. Half of the sentries I've seen here are women—something the Empire could use a bit more of. This guard is also female, tall and hawk-faced, with dark skin and a firm voice.

"Your Highness. It has been a long day. Perhaps your steward can make your excuses."

"You overstep, Lieutenant Eleiba." Nikla's shoulders stiffen. "I reinstated you into the guard at my father's request. Do not—"

Nikla turns as she speaks—and spots me. "You," she says. "I don't recognize—"

Don't kill the bleeding guards, Shrike. Treaty, not war. I rush the princess and she stumbles back, her feet caught in the hem of her dress. Before her defenders can call out, my dagger is in my hand. I ram it, hilt first, into the temple of the first guard, dropping him.

As he falls, I snatch his spear away and spin the butt of it into the face of the guard behind me. A satisfying thump tells me I've hit my mark. I jam the spear between the dining room door handles so that the guards and courtiers within cannot get out.

One of the soldiers, Eleiba, rushes away with the princess, screaming for aid. The third guard is on me now, but I disarm her and bash her with the flat of her scim. Before she hits the floor, I have flung a knife at the fleeing Eleiba.

It sinks into her shoulder and she jerks, nearly falling.

"Run, Princess!" she shouts. But I am too fast for them both. I spot a door. According to the map Musa had me memorize, it leads to a small meeting chamber. I herd Nikla and Eleiba toward it.

"In." I nod to the door. Eleiba growls at me, but I fix my gaze on the princess.

"Do you know who I am?"

She narrows her eyes and nods.

"Then you know that if I'd wanted to kill you, I could have. I'm not here to hurt you. I just want to talk. Tell your guard to stand down."

"Death first," Eleiba rasps. "Princess—go—"

I feint letting the scim fall, and in the instant that Eleiba's gaze drops to it, I punch her square in the face. She drops like a stone.

"In." I point the scim at Nikla's throat. Already, soldiers thunder down the hall toward us. "*Now*, princess."

She bares her teeth but backs into the chamber. I bar the door and ignore the shouts getting closer.

I flip my scim around and hand it to the princess. "A token of goodwill. As I said, I just want to talk."

Nikla takes the weapon with the swiftness of someone practiced with a blade—and puts the point to my throat. Distantly, alarm bells clang. Her guards will be breaking down the door soon enough.

"Well, girl," she says. "What could the Blood Shrike of a pretender possibly have to say to me?"

"I know Keris is here for an alliance, but you can't trust her," I say. "She betrayed an entire city of her own civilians to become Empress. Tens of thousands left to the mercies of the Karkauns because of her lust for power."

"I was not born yesterday. I'd be a fool to trust your empress."

My vision goes red at that word. "She is *not*," I hiss, "my empress. She is a snake, and allying with her is a grave error."

"Keris is offering me a treaty that would end the jinn attacks on Mariner villages," Nikla says. "Can you do the same?"

"I—" I need a moment to think. Just a moment. But the blade makes it hard to breathe, let alone come up with a solution to Nikla's problem. Every trick I learned in rhetoric class flees my mind. I wish, suddenly, for Elias. He could sweet-talk a stone into giving him water.

"It's Keris's men who are carrying out those raids," I say. "She's allied with the jinn. We could fight them together."

"You and what army?" Nikla laughs and lowers the scim. Not because she's tired. But because she's no longer afraid. "Do you even have enough food to get your people through the winter? You're a fool, Blood Shrike. I can't fight Keris and her supernatural allies. I can only make a deal. I suggest you do the same."

"I'd die first."

"Then you'll die." Nikla's guards bang on the door, shouting her name. "In a few seconds, at the hands of my soldiers. Or later, at the hands of your empress."

She's not my empress! "Keris is evil," I say. "But I know her. I can defeat her. I just need—"

The door splinters. Nikla observes me pensively. My words won't convince her. But perhaps threats—

At that moment, a shrill scream punctures the air. It is so deafening that I cringe and cover my ears, hardly noticing as Nikla drops the scim and does the same. The banging on the door stops as cries sound from outside it. With a great crash, the windows of the chamber shatter and glass plunges to the floor. Still, the scream continues.

My skin prickles, and deep within my body, my healing magic stirs, restless as a pup in a thunderstorm.

Laia. Something is wrong. I can feel it.

As quick as it began, the screaming stops. Nikla straightens, her body trembling.

"What—"

The door bursts open and her guards—including Eleiba—pour in.

"Keris will betray you before the end." I dart past the princess, swiping up the scim. "If you survive it, if you need a true ally, get word to me in Delphinium. I'll be waiting."

With that, I offer her a low bow. Then I race for the shattered window and fling myself out.

CHAPTER SEVEN

Laia

I am not alone. I know it even in unconsciousness. Even in this strange blue space where I have no body.

I am not alone, but the presence with me is not outside me. It is *in* me.

There is something—or someone—inside my mind.

I have always been here, a voice says. *I have just been waiting.*

"Waiting?" I say, and my words are thin in the vastness. "For what?"

For you to wake me up.

Now wake up.

Wake up.

"Wake up, Laia of Serra."

It feels as though someone pours sand in my eyes as I drag them open. Lamplight stabs at me, and five women with kohl-lined eyes stare down at the bed upon which I lay. They wear heavily embroidered dresses that flare at the hips, their hair adorned with strands of golden coins that swoop across their foreheads.

Jaduna. The magic wielders—and allies of the royal family.

Oh skies. I sit up slowly, as if addled, but my mind races toward one thought: I need to get the hells out of here.

The room appears to be on the second or third floor of a Mariner villa, and is strewn with jewel-toned silk rugs and star-patterned screens. Through an arched window, the walls of the palace glow with the light of a thousand lanterns. Their beauty is blighted by the incessant pealing of alarm bells.

Feigning dizziness, I lie back down. Then I gather myself, spring off the bed, and lunge through a gap between the women. I am past them, nearly to the open door, just a few more feet—

It slams shut in my face. The Jaduna pull me back, and when I try to scream, my voice chokes off. I reach for my invisibility, but it is gone. The Nightbringer must still be in the city, because no matter how I grasp at it, it does not come.

The Jaduna set me down in a chair, their grip still tight. I do not attempt to break free. Not yet.

"You—you were following me," I say.

"Be at ease, Laia of Serra." I recognize the woman who speaks. She gave me a book once, outside the Great Library of Adisa as it burned down. "We do not wish to hurt you. We saved you from the Meher—"

"Silence, A'vni!" An older woman glares at A'vni before turning her dark gaze on me.

"Look at me, girl," the old woman says, and though I do not wish to do her bidding, her voice compels me. What magic is this? Was she, too, touched by an efrit? As she forces my face toward her, I claw at the arms of my chair and kick out.

"Hold her!"

"D'arju—" A'vni protests, but D'arju waves her off and bores into my mind with her gaze. Her brown irises burn against the kohl rimming them. The fight oozes out of me. She's hypnotized me and I cannot break her grip.

"We mean you no harm," D'arju says. "If we did, we'd have left you for the Nightbringer."

She is not expecting an answer, but I fight through her control and force out the words. "So he could watch Keris murder me slowly?"

"He's not hunting you to kill you," D'arju says. "He's hunting you so he can crack you open and understand what lives inside you."

I try not to let my alarm show. *What lives inside me?*

"An old magic, child." D'arju answers my unspoken question. "Waiting for a thousand years for someone with the strength to wake it." The woman smiles with a fierce joy that makes me trust her a touch more. "I thought it would be Mirra of Serra. Or Isadora Teluman or perhaps Ildize Mosi. But—"

"But even the ancient can be wrong," A'vni says archly, and the other Jaduna chuckle. I expect D'arju to get angry, but she smiles. And something she said finally sinks in.

"You—you knew my mother?"

"Knew her! I trained her, or tried to. She never liked being told what to do. Ildize was more biddable, though that may have just been her Mariner civility. Isadora I never knew—but the power in that girl!" D'arju whistles. "A shame the Empire got to her before we did."

My mind spins. "Power," I say. "You mean the power efrits gave?"

D'arju snorts. "If your power came from an efrit then I'm a jinn. Silence, now. Let me work."

The old woman drags my stare to hers again, and my mind seems to bend and strain—a slow, torturous pulling, as if some part of me was immersed in a thousand-year-old swamp and is finally clawing its way into the light. When it emerges, I find I have been nudged into a back room of my own head.

"Peace be upon thee, Rehmat." D'arju's voice trembles, and I know instantly that while she might be looking at me, she is not speaking to me. "Thy servants are here. Our vow is fulfilled."

"Peace be upon thee, Jaduna. Thy duty is complete. I discharge thee from thy vow."

The words come out of my mouth. It is my lips that move. But the low voice is not mine. I have never used the word *thee* in my life. Besides which, the voice sounds nothing like me. It is not human. It is more like what a sandstorm would sound like, if a sandstorm spoke archaic Serran.

"So this is our warrior," Rehmat says, no longer so formal. "The final manifestation of your long-ago sacrifice."

"It was no sacrifice to nest you within our people, great one," D'arju says.

"A hundred Jaduna accepted my power into their very bones, child." Rehmat's deep growl brooks no disagreement. "It was a great sacrifice. You did not know how it would affect your children, or theirs. But it is done. I live now in thousands upon thousands."

"I confess, great one," D'arju says, "I did not think Laia of Serra would be the one to wake you. The Blood Shrike might have been a more fitting champion, or the Beekeeper. The smith Darin, perhaps."

"Even Avitas Harper," another of the Jaduna says. "Or the young demon killer Tas."

"But they did not defy the Nightbringer. Laia did. Rejoice," Rehmat says, "For the path is set. Now our young warrior must walk it. But if she is to defy the Meherya, I cannot live within her mind."

Meherya. The Nightbringer.

D'arju shakes her head vehemently. "She must be one with you—"

"She must choose me. If a falcon refuses to fly, can she be one with the aether?"

Now A'vni speaks up, clasping her hands together so they do not tremble. "But—but no vessel can hold you, great one."

"I need no vessel, child. Only a conduit."

Oh skies. That doesn't sound promising. I fight for control of my own mind, my body. But they both remain firmly in control of this voice. *Rehmat.* A strange name—one I have never heard of.

"Will it hurt her?" A'vni asks, and if she had not helped kidnap me, I might have been thankful for her concern.

"I live in her blood." Rehmat sounds almost sad. "Yes. It will hurt. Hold her."

"What in the skies—" For a brief moment, I return to myself and thrash against the Jaduna. A'vni winces, but pins me down with the others.

When Rehmat speaks again, it is only to me: *I am sorry for this, young warrior.*

Fire tears through me, up and down every limb, as if my nerves are being ripped from my skin and salted. If I could scream, I would never stop. But the Jaduna have gagged me, and I strain against them, wondering what I have done to deserve this. For surely, this is my end.

A vaguely human figure emerges from my body. It reminds me a little of when the ghuls took my brother's form to frighten me long ago in Serra, at Spiro Teluman's forge. But where ghul-spawned simulacrums are bits of night, this creature is a slice of the sun.

My muscles turn to jelly. All I can do is squint against the brightness, trying to make out details of the shape, but it is not a she or he or they, and it is neither young nor old. With one last flare, its glow dulls until it is bearable.

D'arju drops to her knees in front of the apparition. When it offers the Jaduna a glowing hand, D'arju's fingers pass right through it. Whatever Rehmat is, it is not corporeal.

"Rise, D'arju," Rehmat says in that same deep voice. "Take thy kin and go. A human approaches."

I try to sit up and fail. *What human?* I try to say, but it just sounds like "Whhffff."

The Jaduna file out silently, all but A'vni. "Can we not aid her?" she says. "It is a lonely battle she must fight, Rehmat."

"Your kindness does you credit, A'vni," Rehmat says. "Fear not. Our young warrior is not alone. There are others whose fates are twined with hers. They shall be her armor and her shield."

I do not hear A'vni's response. For when I blink, the Jaduna are gone. Rehmat is gone. I do not feel tired, or weak, and the pain that wracked my body minutes ago has faded to a dull ache. I am still in the villa—from the jewelry scattered on the dresser, it must belong to the Jaduna.

Was it a dream? If so, how did I get to this room? Why do I not have any marks on me from my fight with the Commandant and the Nightbringer?

Forget it. Get out of here.

Alarm bells still blare and the shouts from the street are so loud I can make them out through the shuttered window. *"Search the next street. Find them!"*

The door slams open, and a woman walks in. I drop into a crouch behind the chair, blade in hand, but the woman throws back her hood.

"Laia! Bleeding hells." The Blood Shrike has changed into Mariner sea leathers, and though her hair is still covered, she looks more like herself. "I've been looking all over for you. What happened?"

"I . . . I was—"—*taken by Jaduna, who performed some sort of rite that led to a . . . thing coming out of me, but now it is gone and I have no idea what any of it means.*

48

"I got into a fight with the Nightbringer," I say. "Escaped out a window."

The Shrike nods approvingly. "Same. The window bit, that is. Tell me what happened on the way. We need to meet the others at the gate. Guards all over the place—"

I raise my hand, for I've seen a flash of iridescence—one of Musa's wights. A moment later, a scroll appears between my fingers.

Northeast gate compromised. Soldiers everywhere. What the bleeding hells did you two do? Get to the harbor. I'll find you.

"Nice that he managed to fit in a scolding but not which harbor," the Shrike mutters.

"It'll be Fari Harbor," I say. "Where we disembarked when we first got here. But we have to get through half the city first. And if the streets are crawling with soldiers—"

The Shrike offers a grim smile. "Streets are for amateurs, Laia of Serra. We'll take the rooftops."

CHAPTER EIGHT

The Soul Catcher

The jinn tear Cain from my hands and the Augur crashes to the ground a few yards away. I'm certain the force of it will break his frail body in half. But he rises to his elbows as three jinn close in around him, blocking his escape.

"He belongs to us." The jinn in command steps between the Augur and me. Rain sluices down her heavy cowl and her flame eyes burn with hate. "Go back to your ghosts. He is not worth your trouble, Soul Catcher."

Perhaps not. But Cain knows something about the dreams. He knows about a threat to the Waiting Place. He has information I need. *Curse you, old man.*

"The Augur was once human," I say. "He is thus in my charge. He will be removed from the Waiting Place. But not by you."

One of the jinn steps forward. His hood falls back to reveal a human form, hair braided close to his head, skin a deeper brown than mine. He is vaguely familiar, but I cannot place why. He snorts. "Big words for a little boy."

My hackles rise at the mockery in the creature's voice. *No boy now, but a man, with a man's burden upon your shoulders.* The words are from my old life, spoken to me by Cain, though I do not remember when.

I do, however, remember how to read an enemy, allowing me to shift aside just in time to avoid the blast of heat the jinn leader levels at me.

My reprieve is short-lived. She strikes again and this time, I am enveloped in flame. I have no shirt or cloak to protect me. Mauth's magic rises, saving me from the worst of the attack. But there is the faintest sluggishness to the shield. *Battling a monster of his own creation,* Cain had said.

Now isn't the time to be distracted, Mauth, I shout in my mind. *Unless you want me barbecued.*

Mauth doesn't respond, but the effort to kill me appears to have tired the jinn out—at least momentarily. Regular weapons do not do much against jinn unless they are coated with salt. In any case, I only have my fists, so I throw a punch. My fist slams into solid, burning flesh, and part of me crows in satisfaction as she rears back, screaming.

"Umber!" One of the other jinn steps away from Cain to help her.

"Get back, Maro!" Umber shrieks. But Maro is too slow, and leaves enough of an opening that I can bolt through, fists flying. I move preternaturally fast and the jinns' prejudice works against them. They do not expect my competence, and I am able to sweep Cain up over my shoulder and tear away from the grove.

The jinn might live in the Waiting Place, but they are not Soul Catchers anymore. They don't have a map of the forest in their heads the way I do. They will track me. But it will take time.

As I windwalk, I slow my pounding heart, quell the part of me that thrills at the violence and simplicity of battle. *It felt good to fight,* a voice within whispers, *for you were born to it. Your body was made for it.*

I do not answer that voice. Instead I push myself faster, until I smell the salt of the sea. We are hundreds of miles from the jinn grove, not far from where I intercepted the humans earlier. Waves crash beyond the tree line, and I keep the water at my back. The jinn won't approach from there. They hate salt.

The Augur winces when I drop him. "What do you know about the visions?" I ask. "You spoke of a threat to the Waiting Place?"

When the old man hesitates, I glance pointedly over his shoulder at the forest.

"I could let them have you," I say. "I could let you rot in their jail. Talk."

Cain sighs. "I will give you what you wish for. For a price." His hands are inexorable as they close over mine. As he lifts them to his heart. "I want release, Soul Catcher. You are the Banu al-Mauth, the chosen of Death. You are one of the few on this earth who has the power to end my life. I ask that you do it quickly."

The images I saw months ago in the City of the Jinn assail me. Cain as a young Scholar king, greedy for power and magic. Cain demanding knowledge from the jinn ruler before he became the Nightbringer. Cain manipulating a kind-hearted, lovestruck jinn woman named Shaeva into betraying her people.

Shaeva, who passed the mantle of the Waiting Place on to me. Who was chained to a fate she didn't deserve because of this man.

"Why didn't you just let the jinn kill you?" I ask.

"Because they do not want to kill me," Cain says. "Not yet. When jinn die, they speak prophecy. *That* is what they want from me."

"You're not a jinn."

"I siphoned their power for a millennium, Soul Catcher." The Augur glances back to the dark line of the forest. "The Nightbringer killed the other Augurs too swiftly to learn anything from their deaths. But he's been saving me. If he hears what I have to say, it will be the end of all things. This I swear, by blood and by bone. Kill me, Elias, before he and his kin can hear the prophecy, before they can use me. Kill me and the world might yet endure."

"I'm not going to kill you."

"Body and soul!" Cain closes the distance between us and jerks my face close, until all I can see are the reds of his eyes. "Do you remember? *True freedom — of body and of soul.*"

"Lies," I say. "Like everything else you told me."

"Not lies, but hope," he says. "Hope for the future. Hope for the Scholars, my people, whom I failed. And hope for you, Soul Catcher, even when you believe your fate is written. It is not, no matter what Mauth or the Night-bringer might tell you."

That muted voice within pokes up its head. *Fight, Soul Catcher*, it says as I try to hush it. *Fight.*

In the distance, the forest glows orange. The jinn approach.

"Tell me about the dreams and the threat to the Waiting Place. And I'll take you somewhere you'll be safe from the jinn."

"I do not want safety. The killing blow is my release, Elias Veturius. And yours. Swear you will deliver it, and you will have what you wish."

"Keep your secrets, then." There's some trick here. Something he's not saying. I try to shake him off, but he holds on like a lamprey. "I won't kill you."

"Remember I'd hoped to be gentle," he whispers. "Remember that I tried, Elias, even as you curse my name. And tell them. You are my messenger here, at the end, and if you do not tell them, there will be no sky beyond the storm. No Waiting Place or ghosts or hope. Only suffering and pain."

He grabs me, sinking his fingers into my scalp like he's going to tunnel through my skull. I shout and try to pry him off. But though I'm six inches taller and four stones heavier, Cain holds me captive as easily as if I'm that six-year-old child being dragged off to Blackcliff.

"A gift from me to you, Elias," he says. "A gift for all that I have taken. The girl with the gold eyes is Laia of Serra, heir of the Lioness. I burn her name into you, and no power on this earth shall root it out—" He flares with magic and a flood of memories explodes in my mind.

—The fire in her gaze the day I met her and—

—A dark night in the Tribal desert. Whispering *You are my temple* and—

—Her tears as she shoved a familiar armlet into my hands. *Take this. I don't want it—*

"No." I try to force Cain's hands away. "Stop this."

"The woman with the crown braid"—the Augur's bloody gaze bores into me—"is Helene Aquilla, Blood Shrike and Hope of the Empire. I burn her name into you, and no power on this earth shall root it out—"

—Her hand reaching for me in the Blackcliff culling pens and—

—Her moonlit face in the steppes north of the Empire, smiling as the wind howled and—

—*Let me go, Elias* as I fled Blackcliff—

"Cain, skies." I shove him, but he won't let go. Mauth's magic pools inside me, a white-hot sizzle at my fingertips, screaming for release.

"Stop—bleeding, burning skies—" The words are strange in my mouth and I realize I haven't sworn for months. "You mad old bastard!"

But Cain is resolute. He speaks, his words a cudgel over my head.

"The woman with your eyes is your mother, Keris Veturia, daughter of Quin and Karinna, teacher and executioner. I burn her name into you, and no power on this earth shall root it out—"

—Her tired face peering down at me and—

—*Go back to the caravan, Ilyaas. Dark creatures walk the desert at night* and—

—The tattoo winding up her neck and—

My mind overflows with their names, their faces, with all we are to each other. *Laia. Helene. Keris. Beloved. Friend. Mother.*

This cannot be borne, because I have a duty and these names, these faces, are an impediment to that. Yet I can't unsee the memories Cain has given me.

Laia. Helene. Keris.

"You get these names out of my head, Cain." I want to shout, but I only manage a whisper. *Laia. Helene. Keris.* "Get them *out*—"

But the Augur tightens his grip, and fearing he will pour more memories into me, I lash out with Mauth's magic. It wraps around Cain's throat like a whip and pulls at his life force, draining him dry in seconds. The Augur collapses and I drop beside him, understanding too late that this was his intention. That this is why he gave me the memories. He's not dead yet. But he will be soon.

As I stare down at him, I can smell the cool sand of the desert and Tribe Saif's fear. I see the stars going out as he stole me from my family. From any joy I might have had.

"It was the only way, Elias," he whispers. "I—" His body stiffens like Shaeva's did, before the end. He stares into the middle distance, and when he speaks, it's as if there are many of him.

"It was never one. It was always three. The Blood Shrike is the first. Laia of Serra, the second. And the Soul Catcher is the last. The Mother watches over them all. If one fails, they all fail. If one dies, they all die. Go back to the beginning and there, find the truth. Strive even unto your own end, else all is lost."

He shudders and holds my gaze to his. "Tell them. Swear it!" He sounds like himself again, but when he claws at my arm, there is no strength behind it. His hand falls and a rattle escapes his chest.

"Elias," he says. "Remember—"

He whispers something, two words I only just catch. Then the jinn burst out of the trees and I streak away from them, not stopping until I reach the clearing near my cabin, where I know I'll be safe.

I stumble toward it, my heart thundering in a visceral reminder of my own mortality. In the forest, the ghosts wail, in need of solace. But I slam the door shut on them. My body trembles and I wait, panting, for Mauth to heal my singed skin, to take away the thoughts in my head. *Laia. Helene. Keris.*

When the magic surges through me, I want to weep in relief. But though my burns fade and my heart ceases its frantic beat, no tide of forgetting washes the memories away. They parade across my vision, sharp as knives stabbing into my brain.

Shame consumes me when I think of all those I killed as a Mask. I can't count their number anymore, there were so many. Not just strangers but friends—*Demetrius. Leander. Ennis.*

No, no. These memories are folly, for emotion has no place in my world. *Mauth,* I cry out. *Help me.*

But he does not respond.

CHAPTER NINE

The Blood Shrike

Ninth bell tolls as we reach the quay and Laia pants like she's run a hundred sprints in the dead of a Serran summer.

"Do you need a minute?" I ask. The glare she shoots me makes me take a cautious step back.

"Or ten," she wheezes. I stop in an alley that leads to Adisa's westernmost bay. Wind whistles through the wharf, but the snow has stopped and the Adisans are out in droves.

Hawkers sell steaming noodles steeped in garlic broth, fried honey-cakes dusted with sugar, and a hundred other foods that make my mouth water. Young thieves weave through the crowd, swiftly relieving victims of their coin.

And everywhere, Nikla's soldiers patrol in groups of two and four, scaled blue armor flashing.

"We need to get out on the water," Laia says. "Musa will not be on the quay. He's too well-known."

"There." I nod to where a scrawny, white-haired fishmonger shouts loud enough to wake the dead. Despite that, the old woman has few customers, situated as she is at the end of the quay. An unattended punt bobs on the water at her back.

"Just big enough for two. And maneuverable enough to get us through the night market." Lantern-lit boats ply Fari Harbor—Adisa's renowned floating merchants. "I'll take out the old woman. You get the—"

"We are not knocking out an old woman!" Laia hisses. "She could be someone's grandmother."

The Scholar girl steps out onto the quay and knifes through the teeming crowds with her elbows. The fishmonger spots us and shakes a giant pink-and-silver fish in the air.

"Winter siltfish, fresh-caught!" she shouts as if I'm not two feet away. "Chop it, roast it, put it in a pot!"

Laia glances at the barrels of unsold fish behind her. "Business rough, old mother?"

"I'm not your mother," the fishmonger says. "But I've a nice fat siltfish for you. Ten coppers and it could feed your family for a week. How many children do you—"

"We have need of your boat." I nudge past Laia. There's no bleeding time for pleasantries. Along with Nikla's soldiers, I've spotted Martial troops— Keris's men—patrolling the edges of the market. I hand the old woman a gold mark. "And your discretion."

A mark is a fortune for someone who probably makes one silver in a month. But the fishmonger tosses the coin, catches it, and hands it back to me. "Boats aren't cheap, Martial. Neither is silence."

The woman slings up her catch again. "Winter siltfish, fresh from the harbor!" she bellows, and I fight not to cover my ears. "Fry it, stew it, feed it to your barber!"

Keris stole the treasury before betraying Antium. As such, I am low on coin. But I grit my teeth and add two marks to the first. The fishmonger pockets them and nods to her punt, yelling all the while.

As Laia and I make for the boat, I give her a dirty look. "Glad we let the nice old grandmother live?"

The Scholar shrugs. "Murder is not the answer to everything, Shrike. Grab that hat. Your hood is too conspicuous."

Evening deepens as we pull away from the dock and into the traffic of the harbor. "I don't suppose you can use your disappearing trick?" I ask Laia. Far easier to have someone watching my back if no one can see her. But she shakes her head.

"The Nightbringer is in the city. I can't—" She looks over my shoulder, eyes widening. I whirl, expecting a Mask, the Commandant, a platoon of Mariner soldiers. My daggers are already in hand. But there's nothing but the fishmonger's stall and the quay.

"Sorry." Laia puts a finger to her temple, jumping when another punt bumps ours. "I thought . . . never mind." She wags her head and I'm reminded, uneasily, of her mother, Mirra of Serra, who I knew only as Cook.

Laia collects herself as I maneuver through the busy harbor. Musa went on and on about it, and to my surprise, I find he didn't exaggerate its beauty. We pass an Ankanese dhow, its blue sails adorned with a huge eye. In its wake, a dozen vessels drift by, glowing with paper lanterns and poled by Mariners peddling ice plums and siltfish, wriggling shrimp and warty blue pumpkins.

"Shrike," Laia whispers. "Mask!"

I spot him immediately—he's on the deck of a ship so massive it casts half the floating market in shadow. Beneath the cloudy sky, the mast flag is clearly illuminated. It is black, with a white *K* emblazoned upon it. Keris's flag.

Only she's altered it from the last time I saw it. A spiky crown rests atop the *K* now. The sight of it makes me want to snap my oar in half.

"That's the *Samatius*," I say. "One of the ships I left in command of Quin Veturius in Navium." Skies only know where the old man is now.

At that moment, I spot another Mask rowing through market traffic. My heart trips. This one has the good sense to dull the silver on his face, and wears a floppy fisherman's hat.

"Harper's here," I say, and after a moment, Laia spots him.

"He's alone. Do you think Darin and Musa got out?"

"I bleeding hope so," I say. We don't have enough smiths in Delphinium. As Darin is skilled enough to make unbreakable Serric steel blades, we need him. I can't take my nephew's throne back if I don't have any scims.

We make our way toward Harper, stopping frequently to buy goods so as not to call attention to ourselves. The market is beautiful—one of the wonders of the world.

But it is Antium I long for. I miss the high pillars of the Hall of Records, and the domes and arches of the Illustrian district. I miss the orderly bustle of the markets and the soaring white peaks of the Nevennes Range, visible from anywhere in the city.

I miss my people. And I fear what they must be suffering under Grímarr's rule.

"Worrying won't help." Laia gauges the tenor of my thoughts. "But talking about it might."

"Without the Mariners' help," I say, "things are only going to get worse for us. Right now we have support because the Paters of Delphinium know what happened in Antium. But in the southern part of the Empire, the Commandant's betrayal is a rumor. One she's crushed ruthlessly."

"She has the support of all the southern families," Laia says. "And she has the army. But that doesn't mean she's won. What is it you always tell me when I'm too tired to pull a bowstring? Defeat in your mind—"

"Is defeat on the battlefield." I smile at her. When I began teaching her archery, I'd expected her to give up after she realized how difficult it was.

I was wrong. When I was short with Laia, she'd work harder. Some nights I'd see her out on the archery pitch near the Black Guard barracks, practicing. She's no Mask, but she can kill a man at thirty paces.

"You're right, of course," I say. "Keris might want us dead, but I'm not in a hurry to get to the Waiting Place—are you?"

Laia's body tenses. Too late, I realize what a callous remark it is.

"I'm uh—sorry."

"It's all right." Laia sighs. "Men are a terrible waste of air."

"Utter garbage," I agree.

"Useless rubbish," she adds, grinning.

I chuckle before unwittingly glancing at Harper, camouflaged amid a cluster of longboats. Laia follows my gaze.

"He's one of the few who isn't, Blood Shrike."

"We're almost there." Harper is not a subject I have any interest in discussing, now or ever. But Laia shakes her head.

"Poor Avitas," she says. "He does not have a chance, does he? Skies, his eyes will fall out of his head when he sees you in those Mariner leathers."

My face gets hot and I feel stung. I didn't expect unkindness from her.

"No need to be nasty," I say. "I'm aware that I'm not . . ." I gesture vaguely at her, curved in all the right places.

Laia only raises her eyebrows. "I mean it, Shrike," she says. "You are very beautiful. It's no wonder he cannot keep his eyes off you."

A strange, warm feeling fills me, like after I've won a battle, or when I'm a half dozen cups into a keg.

"You—" *You really think that?* I want to say, because if Faris or Dex or even Elias told me I was beautiful, I'd stab them in the face. "You're just saying that because you're my—my—"

"Friend? Is it so hard to admit it?" Laia glances upward, ostentatiously shading her eyes. "A Scholar rebel and a Martial Blood Shrike are friends and the sky didn't fall in. Whatever shall we do?"

"Let's start by getting out of here alive," I say. "Or I'll have to make new friends in the afterlife, and we know how that will go."

Harper reaches us then, stepping into our larger boat gracefully and abandoning his punt. He passes so close that I shut my eyes to better feel his warmth. When I open them, he's at my side, staring at my mouth. His pale green eyes burn as his gaze travels down my body. I should tell him to look elsewhere. I am the Blood Shrike, for skies' sake. Laia is sitting only a few feet away. This is inappropriate.

But for just a moment, I let him stare.

"Ah—Shrike." He shakes himself. "Forgive me—"

"Never mind. Report, Harper," I bark at him, hating the severity of my voice but knowing it's necessary.

"Soldiers, Shrike."

"That's not a report—"

Harper shoves me out of the way as an arrow smacks into the mast beside me. I did not hear it amid the noise of the market. He grabs an oar as Laia cries out.

"Shrike!" The Scholar girl looks left—then right. I see the legionnaires immediately. They are cleverly disguised as merchants, making their way toward us at speed.

And they have us surrounded.

CHAPTER TEN

Laia

One moment, I am gaping at the sheer number of Martial soldiers closing in on us.

The next, the legionnaires are leaping to our boat from a dozen different punts. I barely have a chance to shout a warning before a thick, gauntleted arm is wrapped around my neck.

Our vessel pitches violently as Harper and the Shrike battle the soldiers swarming us. I kick back, landing a blow on my captor's knee. He grunts and quite suddenly, I am weightless.

I only realize he has thrown me off the boat and into the bay when water slams into me like a gelid fist.

A memory rises in my head, Elias speaking to me in Serra when I told him I couldn't swim. *Remind me to remedy that when we have a few days.*

I thrash my arms in a panic. I cannot feel my face. My legs slow, and my clothes drag at me, like hands pulling me down to welcome me to the depths of the sea.

Let go, I think. *Let go and leave this battle to someone else. You'll see your family again. You'll see Elias again.*

Let go.

A gold figure appears before me in the water, triggering a burst of memories. The room in Adisa. The Jaduna. The excruciating pain as a *thing* rose out of my body. The Jaduna had a name for it.

Rehmat—a strange name, I think as the life leaves me. The Jaduna did not say what it meant. I suppose it doesn't matter anymore.

"Hail, Laia, and listen well." Rehmat's words crack like a whip and my body jerks. "You will not let go. Fight, child."

Whatever Rehmat is, it is used to being obeyed. I windmill my arms and legs toward the glow of the floating market. I wriggle and claw until my head breaks the surface.

A swell smacks me in the mouth, and I choke on seawater.

"There!" a voice calls out, and moments later, a pale hand yanks me onto our punt.

"Ten hells, Scholar," the Blood Shrike says. "Can't you swim?"

I do not have a chance to answer. Harper points to the quay where a platoon of Martials is launching longboats.

"More are coming, Shrike," he says. "We have to get out of here."

I hear a small shriek and catch a flash of wings as a scroll drops into the Blood Shrike's lap from midair.

"Musa and Darin are waiting northwest of here," she says after reading it. "Just beyond the floating market."

"Hold on." Avitas angles our vessel toward the thick of the market and we ram into a cluster of merchants, sending baskets, fish, rope, and people flying. Curses and shouts trail us as the Martials rain down flaming arrows, not caring who they hit.

"Come on, Laia!"

With the grace of gazelles, Avitas and the Shrike leap to another boat, and then another, making their way forward as confidently as if they are on solid ground.

But I am slowed by the chill of freezing air hitting wet clothing. I lurch forward like a drunken bear, barely clearing each deck.

The Blood Shrike turns back. With one stroke of her blade she relieves me of my cloak, a sodden, woolen weight. And thank the skies I'm wearing a chemise, because with two more cuts, my short jacket gapes open and the Shrike yanks it off.

Though my teeth slam into each other, I move more lightly. The Martials are behind us for now, but that will not last. Already I see a group of them circumventing the market, cutting off our escape.

"We can't break their cordon." Avitas comes to a halt on a dinghy piloted by a terrified Mariner boy. He dives into the water to escape us. The people of the floating market pole away swiftly, buyers and sellers alike trying to avoid the melee. We have nowhere to run.

"Shrike, you'll have to swim beneath the cordon," Avitas says. "Laia—if you can use your invisibility, I'll distract them—"

The Shrike's face blanches. "Absolutely not!"

As they argue, I reach for my power. But my magic evades me. *The Nightbringer.* That monster still lurks in the city, blocking me.

"Not so, Laia of Serra." The glow manifests at my side this time, and it is so real that I'm stunned my companions cannot see it.

"Go away," I hiss, feeling insane for talking to something invisible to everyone else.

"The Nightbringer weakened your powers early on," Rehmat says. "That was before you woke me. You are stronger now. You can disappear. You can even hide those with you."

The Blood Shrike whips out her bow and picks off our pursuers one by one. But there are too many.

Beside me, Rehmat's glow pulses. "Is this where you wish to die, daughter of Mirra and Jahan?" it asks. "Imagine your power as a cloak of darkness. Take shelter there. Then pull the Blood Shrike and the Mask within."

"How do I know you aren't tricking me? That you aren't some perversion of the Nightbringer?"

"Trust me or die, child," Rehmat growls.

A longboat looms out of the dark. There is a Mask aboard and I freeze, my fear taking hold. Then the Shrike is past me, leaping onto the Mask's boat as our own dinghy lurches. The Mask bares his teeth and draws scims, meeting the Shrike's attack stroke for stroke.

Another boat of soldiers bashes into ours and now Avitas is at the Shrike's back, swift and otherworldly. They are a four-armed monster, destroying, deflecting, defying Keris's men to come closer.

"They cannot fight forever, Laia," Rehmat says. "Reach for the magic. Save them. Save yourself."

"I *tried*—"

"Try harder." Rehmat's voice, stern before, is steel now. "You are a child of *kedim jadu*, girl. Old magic. For centuries, I have waited for one of the *kedim jadu* to defy the Nightbringer. You did so, glorious and fearless, and now you quake, child? Now you quiver?"

There is an irrefutability in Rehmat's tone that rings a bell at the core of my being. It is as if the creature is simply uncovering something that has long been carved into the arc of my life. Perhaps it has tampered with my mind, or the Nightbringer has.

Or perhaps my instinct has been honed by enough betrayal that when it sings truth, I listen. Perhaps I finally believe that my victories have been because I decided to fight, when others might have given up.

The Shrike slings arrows and the boat rocks beneath me. Avitas curses as the Martials draw closer.

The world seems to slow, as if time no longer exists. It is a moment of perfect chaos, and within it, I hear my nan. *Where there is life, there is hope.*

I will not accept death. Why should I, when there is life yet burning in my veins? I will not let the Nightbringer win so easily when it is my fury that will destroy him, and my strength that will release the Scholars from the yoke of his terror.

Disappear. Power breaks over me and I shudder at the force of it. *This? This is what I can do?*

"Imagine the darkness enveloping the Blood Shrike and Avitas Harper," Rehmat says. "Quick now!"

This is more difficult, for I do not understand how to do it. I stretch the darkness that covers me, and try to toss it over the Blood Shrike. She flickers.

"Again," Rehmat urges. "Hold it this time!"

Sweat breaks out on my brow as I try again. And again. Each time, the Shrike flickers, though she does not appear to notice. The Mask she fights gapes at her in bewilderment, and she runs him through.

"Shrike!"

A long shabka—a boat with a single mast and two sets of oars—looms out of the darkness. Darin stands at its prow, and relief floods me. He, however, looks like he wants to throttle the Shrike.

"Where's Laia? *Where's my sister?*"

The Shrike parries an arrow that nearly pegs her in the heart. "Don't get your knickers in a bunch," she shouts. "She's right—"

In that moment, I cast the darkness wide enough to cover both her and

Avitas. One second, the two of them are fighting. The next, Keris's men lower their weapons, staring at an empty boat.

I grab for where I think the Shrike's shoulder is, hoping to the skies that neither she nor Avitas think to swing a scim into my neck.

"They can't see you!" I whisper. "Get into Musa's boat. Quick!"

Air rushes past me as the Shrike slides by and pulls herself up to the deck of the shabka. Harper follows, and I reach deep within, until I have cast my invisibility over a wide-eyed Darin and Musa.

"Stop rowing," I hiss to the Beekeeper. "No one move!"

The shabka drifts, even as the Martials search the darkness, all their might and numbers nothing against my magic.

The soldiers close in on our vessel, but after scanning it for passengers, they navigate around us, making for the dinghy where we were last seen, peering into the water. We remain silent as long minutes go by. When the soldiers are out of sight, Musa and the Shrike take up the oars and row as quickly and quietly as they can, until the lights of the market are a distant glow behind us. Finally, I drop our invisibility. Everyone speaks at once.

"Thank the skies you're all—"

"What the *bleeding hells* was—"

"Laia!" One voice pipes over the rest, and a skinny figure emerges from beneath Musa's seat.

He is a half foot taller than he was when I last saw him, but the brilliant smile and sparkling eyes I first encountered in Kauf Prison, while trying to free Darin and Elias, are the same.

"*Tas?*" I do not believe it is him until he comes flying at me, and I am enfolding his slight figure in my arms. "What are you doing here? You're supposed to be safe in Ayo!"

"Tas was my 'delivery,'" Darin says. "I was worried he wouldn't get to me on time or I would have told you."

"You'll have to catch up later," Musa says. "Right now, I think it's time for Laia to tell us about her invisible friend."

Rehmat. He means Rehmat. "One day"—I stare daggers at him—"your eavesdropping is going to get you into trouble that even your wights can't get you out of."

"Not today, *aapan*," he says. "Talk."

By the time I am finished telling the tale, dawn is a pale suggestion on the horizon and the snow clouds have given way to a tangerine sky. The bay is calm, the wind is with us, and we move steadily northwest, toward a river that will take us into the Empire. Musa's stowed the oars and raised the sails, and we sit in a circle near the stern of the shabka.

"So that's it," Darin says. "You've just decided it's you against the Night-bringer?"

"It feels right." I do not add that I have no earthly idea how I will destroy the jinn—or even where to begin.

"That's not a good reason to go hunting for the most dangerous creature who has ever lived. Why should it be you?"

My brother's disapproval is maddening. He knows what I am capable of. And still, I must explain myself.

I feel a fierce pang of longing for Elias. He saw my strength long before I did. *You'll find a way*, he'd said to me in Serra, as we fled the Commandant and her men.

"I do not trust anyone else to do it, Darin. Other people have too much to lose."

"And you don't have anything to lose?" For an instant, I see how Darin will look as an old man. My brother bears the weight of our dead family stoically, speaking rarely of our parents or sister or grandparents. But I know he is thinking of them now.

I do not answer his question, and Harper clears his throat. "Setting the Nightbringer aside for a moment . . ." The Mask's hand rests lightly on the tiller. "This . . . thing. This Rehmat. It was living inside you?"

"Like a parasite?" Musa says. "Or a demon?"

"Don't be so horrified," I say. "Whatever it is, it's inside you too. All of you. Or so the Jaduna said."

Musa looks down, clearly wondering if some fey beastie will burst unexpectedly from his chest. "So if one of us had lost our temper and yowled at the Nightbringer—"

"I did not *yowl*—"

"Then we'd be stuck fighting him? No offense, *aapan*, but why not one of them?" Musa nods at Harper and the Shrike. "They might get close enough to stick a knife in that fiery monster's gut."

"I've a nephew to protect," the Shrike says. "And the Empire to reclaim. Even if I wanted to hunt the Nightbringer, I couldn't."

"I'm with her," Harper says, smiling slightly at the sudden flush in the Shrike's cheeks, before he turns stone-faced again.

"It would be better," I say. "But it is not them. It is me. And Rehmat's presence does explain my disappearing. Your particular skills, Musa. And perhaps even the fact that you and I"—I look to Darin—"were never as bothered by the ghosts as Afya was."

"But if it's in all of us," Harper says, "shouldn't Tas, Darin, and I have magic too?"

"It will require an army to take the Nightbringer down, Laia," Darin says. "This might be a ploy to get you alone and vulnerable."

"Could be that Rehmat is some devilry from the Karkaun warlocks," the Shrike offers. "We've seen what Grímarr can do."

I wait for Musa's opinion, but his head is tilted as it is when he's listening to his wights.

"Maybe Rehmat is good." Tas speaks up. I almost forgot he was here, he's been so quiet. "The world's not only full of bad things, you know. And what about Elias? We should see what he thinks."

Silence threatens, but Darin fills it quickly. "Perhaps Musa can send him a message," my brother says. "In the meantime, Tas, I'll show you how to trim the sails. We'd best take advantage of this wind while we have it."

They move to the stern of the shabka, and the Beekeeper touches my shoulder. "Laia," he says. "The Martials are amassing forces off the southern coast of the Tribal lands. They're planning an invasion. The wights just brought word."

"Do the Tribes know?" I say. "They must. There have been skirmishes before."

Musa shakes his head. "This isn't a skirmish. And the Tribes don't know. Some fey magic cloaks the Martials. The wights heard a few of the generals speaking. They plan to attack at the waxing moon."

Three weeks from now. "You can warn them," I say. "That's time enough to send a message—"

"I will," Musa says. "But skies know if they'll trust it. Keris and the Nightbringer are too strong, Laia. The Tribes will fall. And she'll move north—"

To Delphinium. To finish what she began in Antium. Musa moves off to speak to the Shrike. Near the deep purple sail, Darin's smile flashes as he shows Tas the rigging. *The world's not only full of bad things, you know.*

I wish I believed that.

«««

The days pass quickly, filled with fishing, training with the Shrike, and catching up with Darin, Musa, and Tas. When the sun sets, we marvel at the brilliant sheets of violet and pink and green that light up the northern skies.

By sunrise on the fifth day, we spot the far side of Fari Bay. The rocky coast is steep, and the towering treetops of an ancient forest appear, blue beneath a clear sky and rolling westward as far as the eye can see.

The Waiting Place.

Harper speaks with the Shrike while Musa and I listen to one of Tas's stories. But we all fall silent at the sight of the wood. Whispers sound on the wind and a shiver ripples through me.

"You know"—Musa drops his voice so only I can hear—"if you could just get Elias to talk to you, he might let us across—"

"No."

"It would save us nearly three weeks."

"We're *not* going through the Waiting Place, Musa," I say. "You of all people understand what it means to have the love of your life turned into someone else. I don't want to see him again. Ever."

"Beekeeper." The Shrike's attention is fixed on the empty sea behind us. "Can we make this thing go any faster?"

I squint—but even in the moonlight, I see only whitecaps. Then an arrow cuts through the air, embedding itself in the wood of the tiller, inches from Musa's hand. He curses and the Shrike pushes past him, draws her bow, and releases a volley of shots.

"Commandant's men!" she says as a cluster of longboats comes into view behind us. "Take cover—aah!"

I hear the sick thump of steel embedding into flesh, and the Shrike staggers. I am up now, nocking and releasing arrows as fast as I can.

"Watch your left!" Musa snaps as more longboats appear to the south. And the north.

"Ideas?" I ask the Beekeeper as the boats close in. "Because I am running out of arrows."

"One." Musa glances at me, and then toward the trees of the Waiting Place. "But you won't thank me for it."

CHAPTER ELEVEN

The Soul Catcher

For a week after I kill Cain, I dream.

I stand upon a great, blackened field, flanked by familiar faces. Laia of Serra is to my left and Helene Aquilla to my right. Keris Veturia stands apart, her gray eyes fixed on something I cannot see. *The Mother watches over them all.* The scims in my hands gleam with blood.

Beyond us, a great, rabid maelstrom. It is a thousand colors, teeth and viscera and dripping claws. The storm reaches out, wraps a putrid hook around Laia.

Elias! she screams. *Help me!*

Helene reaches for Laia, but the maelstrom roars and swallows them both. When I look to Keris, she's gone, replaced by a gray-eyed, blonde child who takes my hand.

"Once," she whispers, "I was thus."

Then she, too, is consumed by the maw, while I am dragged down into the earth, into a death that never ends.

I wake covered in sweat but shivering, like when the Commandant would make us run midnight drills in a Serran winter.

It's still dark, but I stagger up, wash, and step outside into a dull drizzle. The mourning doves haven't yet begun to croon. Dawn is far.

Passing the spirits is the work of mere hours. When I am done, the storm-dulled light brushes the tops of the trees. The Waiting Place stands oddly silent and my stomach drops at the thought of the day stretching ahead, with nothing but my thoughts to keep me company.

"Right," I mutter to myself. "Jinn grove it is."

I consider taking my scims. But I think of the dream and leave them. My attachment to the armlet is troubling enough. Yesterday, I thought I'd lost it. I tore the cabin apart looking for it, only to find it in my cloak.

Laia's armlet, the voice within shouts. *That's why it matters to you. Because you loved her.*

I streak to the jinn grove and leave the voice behind, making for the dead yew. The drizzle keeps me cool as I bring down the chain — left side, right, left side, right. But the action, while exhausting, offers no comfort.

Instead, I am reminded of Blackcliff — of laughing maniacally with Helene one winter when the Commandant ordered our cadet class to train in the middle of a thunderstorm.

Why are we laughing? I'd asked her at the time.

Because laughing makes it hurt less.

"Little one."

When the Wisp speaks from the edges of the jinn grove, it is a relief. I drop the chain and go to her. There are only a half dozen or so ghosts who refuse to leave the Waiting Place. Most have been here a few weeks, and I know I will pass them on eventually.

But the ghost of my grandmother — whose name in life was Karinna — has been here for more than thirty years. I've searched for her many times since joining with Mauth. Each time, she evaded me, seeking solitude in the deepest reaches of the wood.

Now she curls around me like smoke, little more than a shiver in the air. "Have you seen my lovey?"

"I know your lovey," I say, and her head jerks up. She solidifies completely for the first time since I've seen her, so clear that I catch my breath.

She looks just like my mother. Like Keris.

"Your lovey still lives, Karinna," I say. "But in time, she too will die. She will pass easier if you are waiting for her on the other side."

Karinna is all movement again, bolting away and back in the blink of an eye. "My lovey does not live," she says. "My lovey died. But I cannot find her anywhere."

"Why do you think she died, Karinna?" I sit on a nearby stump and let her come to me. When she is close enough, I reach out with Mauth's magic to try to understand what she needs. This is the trickiest part of passing a ghost on. Get too close and they bolt. Not close enough, and they rage at you for misunderstanding them.

Karinna doesn't resist the magic. She hardly notices it. I expect that she'll ache for forgiveness perhaps, or love. But I feel only agitation from her.

And fear.

"She's gone." Karinna says, and my head spins as I try to follow her cease-less movement through the trees. "My sweet lovey is *gone*. If she still existed in this world, I would know. But she wouldn't leave without me. Never. She would wait. Have you seen her?"

"Karinna." I take a different tack. "Will you tell me how you died? Per-haps if I know, I can help you find your lovey."

Usually ghosts are still thinking about their deaths—even discussing them. But for as long as I've been in the Waiting Place, I've never heard Karinna say a word about her passing.

She turns her face away. "I thought we were safe," she says. "I'd never have gone, I'd never have taken her if I didn't think we were safe."

"The world of the living is capricious," I say. "But the other side is not. You'll be safe there."

"No. There is no safe place anymore." She whirls on me. The air crackles with cold, the rain hardening to sleet. "Not even beyond the river. It's madness. I will not go."

Beyond the river. She means the other side. "The other side is not like our world—"

"How do you know?" Her fear sharpens and settles around her, a poisonous miasma. "You have not been there. You do not sense what crouches in the beyond."

"Other ghosts pass through and find peace."

"They do not!" she shrieks. "You send them to the chasm and they do not know what awaits them! A maelstrom, a great hunger—"

The dream. "Karinna." Urgency grips me, but I do not let it show. "Tell me of this maelstrom."

But my grandmother's spirit stiffens and spins east, toward the river. Seconds later, I sense what she does—outsiders to the far north.

"Karinna—wait—" But she is gone. Skies only know when I will find her again.

My ire at the outsiders is fueled by her departure. If they hadn't breached the Waiting Place, I could have gotten some answers out of her.

I windwalk north, considering whether to kill them or simply frighten them. When I reach the River Dusk, I do not slow. To the spirits, the Dusk is a pathway to the other side. To me, it is just a river. But today, as I cross, the midmorning mist rises and brings with it a swirl of memory. The ghosts' memories, I realize. Joy and contentment, peace and—

Agony. Not physical, but something deeper. A wound of the soul.

I have never stumbled when windwalking the Dusk. Stepping across it is like hopping across a rivulet instead of a river wide enough to hold a dozen Mercator barges.

But the pain shocks me and I plunge into the freezing water. Something grabs me—hands, pulling, pressing so hard that I can feel the skin break on my arms, my legs—

Jinn! I fight my way to the surface, sputtering, and swim for the far bank. The past few months of training have made me strong and I break free, kicking violently.

A low trick, ambushing me in the water—but one I should have been prepared for.

At shore, I look back, steeling myself for another battle with the jinn. But the river is quiet, moving swift and sure. There is no sign of anything that might wish me harm. I inspect my arms, my legs.

No marks. Though I was sure I felt blood leaking out of me.

I'm tempted to return to the river, but the intruders await. I streak northeast, frost collecting on my wet clothes, my hair, my eyelashes as I travel. The wind whips against me, fey and angry until, for the second time in a week, I walk the border of the Waiting Place, prepared to drive out whoever is foolish enough to enter it.

The fools, it turns out, are manifold.

Nearly a hundred, in fact. There are soldiers in longboats, most of whom sling arrows at a group of people clustered at the water's edge, on a short spit of beach. Those few are locked in close combat with a dozen more Martial soldiers.

The beach backs to the cliffs, with a few treacherous paths leading up to my domain.

"To the woods, Tas, run!"

The man who speaks is tall and sandy-haired, his brown skin matching that of the young woman next to him. Her armor is piecemeal, her cloak in tatters. She's hooded so I cannot see her face. But I know her. I know the way she moves, and the color of her skin and the set of her shoulders.

"Laia! Watch it!" a Scholar man with dark skin and long, black hair calls out. He holds off three legionnaires with a scim, a short dagger, and—I squint—a cloud of hundreds of wights who befuddle his foes. They defend him with a vicious protectiveness that wights aren't known for. Laia, meanwhile, spins, nocks, and shoots a soldier creeping up on her.

"Get Tas out of here *now*," she shouts. The sandy-haired man grabs the child by the arm and drags him up the trail, directly toward where I'm standing.

The forest groans. Perhaps Mauth is occupied, as the Augur said. But he still feels the assault on his territory. And he doesn't like it.

"You have trespassed into the Waiting Place, the forest of the dead." I step out of the trees. Though I don't shout, Mauth's magic carries my words down to a blonde woman fighting back to back with a Mask. To the Scholar with the wights, and Laia. To the soldiers, all of whom gape at me. "You are not welcome."

One of the legionnaires spits blood onto the beach and glares at his men. "Put an arrow in that son of a—"

He grabs his throat and drops to his knees. His men inch away.

When he is flat on his back, clawing at the sand, I look to the rest, letting the outsiders feel the full weight of the Waiting Place's oppression. Then I draw away their vitality—all but the child's—until the soldiers are gasping and stumbling through the shallows back to their boats. I turn to the others, who are still struggling to breathe.

I must kill them. Shaeva was right to leave broken bodies along the border. These constant interruptions are a distraction I can ill afford.

But the child, who is crouched behind a boulder, cries out. His distress plucks at something deep within that I cannot name. I ease the magic.

The remaining outsiders drink in long, shuddering draughts of air. Those four on the beach move swiftly up the trail, away from the soldiers. The child emerges from his hiding spot, wary gaze fixed on me. His companion stalks forward, reaching back for his scim.

"You," he says. *Darin,* I think as he bears down. *His name is Darin.*

"I thought you were a decent human," he hisses at me. "But you—"

"Now, now." The tall Scholar steps in front of Darin. His cloud of wights has disappeared. "Let's not irritate the creature formerly called Elias. He is the one who has to get us out of here."

"Get *off,* Musa—"

"I will not help you." I am puzzled that they think I would. "Leave at once."

"Not bleeding likely." Helene—*no, the Blood Shrike*—appears at the top of the trail. Blood soaks her fatigues and she limps heavily. She glances down at the Martials, who have retreated—but not far. "Not unless you want a half dozen more ghosts clogging up your day—ah—"

"Careful, Shrike." The Mask catches her, and there's something about him that makes me stare, some instinct urging me to look closer at him. We mean something to each other. But what? I have no memories of him.

The Shrike stumbles. The pain in her leg is likely hitting her now that the adrenaline of battle has worn off. Without thinking, I hold her up on one side, while the Mask grabs her other arm. The feeling of her is so familiar, the rush of memory so heady that I jerk away.

"Don't let me fall, you idiot." She lists forward. "Unless you want to carry my carcass the next hundred miles."

"Wouldn't be the first bleeding time."

It's not until she grins at me that I realize my voice wasn't that of the Soul Catcher but of someone else. The person I once was. *Elias Veturius.*

"Shut it and help me find a place to sit so I can get this arrow out, would you? Laia? Do you have your kit?" The Shrike glances over her shoulder. "Harper, where the hells is she?"

Harper murmurs something to the Shrike and she glances at me, brow furrowing.

"Tend to your wounds," I say. "Then leave. Go back to the beach. To your boats. To a quick death, it matters not. But you will not enter the Waiting Place."

"He's your brother." Musa speaks up, nodding to Harper. The Mask gapes at Musa, who doesn't seem to notice.

I cock my head, surveying Harper. His hair lies flat while mine curls at the ends. He's shorter and leaner than me, and his eyes are green instead of gray. They are large like mine, but curved up at the outer corners. We have the same gold-brown skin. The same sharp cheekbones and generous mouth.

"How dare—" the Blood Shrike sputters, eyes flashing. "Musa! That's not your—"

"Not my secret? It is if it will save our lives." The Scholar turns to me. "You've been looking at him funny. Your gut's probably telling you there's a connection. Your gut is right. Same father. Different mother—thankfully for him." The Scholar chuckles to himself. "You wouldn't let your own brother die, would you? You were raised among the Tribes. Family is every-thing."

"Once, perhaps," I say. "No longer."

"Enough." The voice that speaks conjures laughter and wonder, molten honey skin and hair the color of night. She emerges from the cliff trail and for a long time as she stares at me, she's silent.

Her regard bothers me. It makes my skin feel hot, feverish, raises memories in my mind of a granite-walled school, and a dance beneath a full moon. Of a trek through the mountains, an inn far away, her body against mine—

"You will grant us passage, Soul Catcher."

"Laia of Serra." I say her name softly. "It is not your time. The forest will not abide it."

"I say it will. You will grant us passage."

There is a weight to Laia's voice that wasn't there before, and a glow manifests near her. That light feels familiar, yet I cannot recall seeing it before.

A cluster of ghosts gathers behind me, but they are silent. Laia lowers her gaze, fists clenched, and I have a sudden, strange thought. She is conferring with someone—or something. As a man used to voices in my head, I recognize when others are listening to voices too.

Nodding as if in agreement with someone, Laia steps past me, into the Waiting Place. I wait for the ghosts to howl, for Mauth to protest. But the forest is still.

The others follow her in. If I do not stop them, something will shift. Something irrevocable. Something that began with that blasted Augur giving me back my memories.

I gather up my magic, prepared to drive them out.

But Laia looks back at me with betrayal and pain in her eyes and I let the magic drain away. An unfamiliar emotion fills me.

Shame, I realize. Deep and gnawing.

CHAPTER TWELVE

The Blood Shrike

The Soul Catcher guides us away from the edge of the forest to a muddy game trail. I glance at him, searching for vestiges of my friend Elias Veturius. But other than the hard lines of his body and the sharp planes of his face, there isn't a shred of the boy I knew.

We stop in a small clearing, and he watches as Laia carefully removes the arrow and bandages my wound. At the crack of a branch behind me, I draw my scim.

"Just a squirrel," the Soul Catcher says. "The soldiers won't enter here. The ghosts would drive them mad."

My neck prickles. I know there are ghosts here, but they are quiet, far different from the screeching demons that possessed my men at the gates of Antium.

"Why won't they drive us mad?" It is the first Tas has spoken.

The Soul Catcher looks down at the boy, and his voice is gentler. "I don't know," he says. His brow is furrowed. It's the look he'd get at Blackcliff when the Commandant would send us after a deserter, and he couldn't settle on how he felt about it.

Forget about Blackcliff, Shrike. I have more important things to think about. Like getting the hells back to my nephew. Figuring out what my next steps are beyond crossing this wood for three weeks.

By the time I reach Delphinium, I will have been gone for two months. Skies know what I will find on my return.

When I mutter as much to Laia, she shakes her head.

"Not if he helps us." She glances at the Soul Catcher. He hears. He might be some otherworldly servant of ghosts now, but he's still tied to Laia, still a part of her song, whether he admits it or not.

"You'll be through by dawn," he says. "But stay close. The ghosts are not the only fey who walk the Waiting Place. There are older creatures that would seek to harm you."

"The jinn," Laia says. "Those the Nightbringer freed."

The Soul Catcher gives her a brief, unreadable look. "Yes. One human might slip through the forest undetected by them. But a half dozen? They will know you are here soon enough."

"Can't you just—" Musa puts his hands around his throat and mimes choking—referring no doubt to how the Soul Catcher can steal away breath.

"I'd rather not." The Soul Catcher's voice is so cold that Musa, who lives and breathes impudence, is silent. "I will windwalk you across," the Soul Catcher goes on. "But there are many of you, and it will take time. We will be pursued."

"But the jinn were just rampaging across the Mariner countryside," Darin says. "How—"

"Not all of them," Musa says. "The Nightbringer takes only a few on his raids. But thousands were imprisoned. And they used to live here. Do they still?" Musa glances around warily. "Do you let them?"

"This was their home before it was mine." The Soul Catcher tilts his head, and it's another gesture I recognize. His instincts shout a warning at him.

"We've tarried too long. Child—" He reaches out a hand to Tas, whose face falls at the Soul Catcher's aloofness.

I understand his grief. When Elias turned his back on me in Antium, I didn't realize what he had become. Not really. Even now, he looks the same as ever. He feels solid. Real.

But he's put duty above all things. He's put on the mask and set aside his humanity. Just like we were trained to do.

Tas takes the Soul Catcher's hand and we form a chain, Tas holding on to Harper, then me, Musa, Darin, and Laia.

"Walk as you normally would," the Soul Catcher says. "Close your eyes if you wish. But no matter what you see, do not let go of each other. Do not reach for a weapon. Do not try to fight." He looks at me when he says this and I nod grudgingly. I know an order when I hear one.

Seconds later, we are flying, the trees blurring by faster than I thought possible. It feels as if I am on a boat tearing across a wild sea with the wind at my back. Naked branches whip past, a massive oak, a clearing of frosted grass, a lake, a family of foxes.

The smell of the ocean fades, and we are in the deep woods, the canopy so thick I cannot make out the evening sky. Beneath my feet, the underbrush is soft and springy. I don't understand how the Soul Catcher can move us through such dense forest without knocking us all unconscious. But, as when he was a soldier fighting at my back, he does it with complete confidence. After an hour passes, I let myself relax.

Then Laia screams. Her hair has come loose from her braid, streaming out behind her. Beyond it, a half dozen shadows stir, each with eyes that blaze like tiny suns.

My stomach plunges, and I want my scim so badly that I nearly countermand the Soul Catcher's order and pull away from Harper. Because for a second, I think one of the shadows is *him*. The Nightbringer. The monster who demanded my mask from me, who engineered the hell rained down upon my people.

But these shapes are different. The Nightbringer is a typhoon of wrath and subtlety. These creatures are a shadow of that. Still, their anger is palpable, like the air before a lightning storm.

"Soul Catcher!" I shout.

"I see them." He sounds almost bored, but when he looks back over his shoulder, he has the flat concentration of a Mask surrounded by the enemy. He cuts north—then west again, then north, then west until my head spins and I don't know what direction we're going.

The sun dips below the horizon, and for a time, it seems as though we've outrun the jinn. The River Dusk is nothing more than a flash of blue and a rush of sound before it is past. But not long after we cross, they catch us. This time, we can't shake them. The jinn shriek madly and surround us.

Ahhh, Blood Shrike. The voice is sibilant and feels as if it's worming through my mind. *Without your sacrifice we would never have been free. Accept a token of our gratitude, a glimpse into your future.*

"No!" I shout. "I don't want—"

We see you, baby bird, not a Shrike but a small and weak thing, fallen far from safety. Parents dead, sister gone, and the other sister soon to join her—

"Stop!" I curse them, but they do not stop. The minutes are hours, and the hours are days as the jinn dig around in my thoughts. I cannot keep them out.

You do not love the child, they say. *He is your blood, but you'll see him dead and yourself upon the throne. You have always wanted it, wicked, wicked Shrike.* They pack my mind with images of violence: my nephew, sweet Zacharias, lying limp, his small face drained of life. The horror of it is worse for his innocence, for the burden of rulership that he never knew he carried.

As I cry and beg that he be brought back, Keris laughs. The scars on my face ache, a soul-deep pain. Cook speaks in my ear, poor dead Mirra, but I cannot hear what she says because now there is a great roaring, a maelstrom coming closer, and it will devour us all—

Then I hear the Soul Catcher, though he is not next to me. "Do not listen to them," he says. "They want to break the chain. They want to fall upon each of you, tear you away and consume your minds. Do not let them. Fight."

"I can't," I whisper. "I—"

"You can. It is who you are. It is what you do best."

It *is* what I do best. Because I am strong, and I dig for that strength now. I watched my family bleed out at my feet and I fought for my people and faced a horde of Karkauns alone on a hill of dead bodies. I am a fighter. I am the Blood Shrike.

You are a child.

I am the Blood Shrike.

You are weak.

I am the Blood Shrike.

You are nothing.

"I am the Blood Shrike!" I scream, and the words echo back to me, not in my own voice but in my father's and my mother's, in Hannah's and in the voices of all those lost at Antium.

Broken, unmade thing, you will lose more before the end, for you are a torch against the night, little Shrike, and above all a torch burns.

Quite suddenly, we stumble to a stop in a clearing. A dimly lit cabin rises out of the darkness. I stumble toward it, along with Darin and Harper. Laia has an arm wrapped around Tas, her teeth bared.

The Soul Catcher stands between us and the heavily cloaked jinn, who pace beyond the clearing. He has no weapon. He needs none, for in this moment, he calls to mind his mother's quiet violence.

"You will not touch these humans," he says. "Leave."

One of the jinn detaches from the others. "They are your weakness, Soul Catcher." She drips with malice, shakes with it. "You will fall and the Waiting Place will fall with you."

"Not today, Umber," the Soul Catcher says. "They are under my protection. And you have no power here."

The softer the Commandant spoke, the more dangerous she was. The Soul Catcher's voice is very low indeed, and power pulses through him. The air in the clearing thickens. The fire in the jinns' eyes pales, as if suddenly quenched.

The jinn retreat, fading into the trees, and when they are gone, my legs go weak, my wound aching. Harper is beside me instantly, shaky himself but trying to hold me up. Musa stands apart, eyes glazed. Darin is pale as he wraps an arm around Laia's trembling shoulders.

Tas is unaffected, and glances between us. "What—what happened?"

"Are you okay, Tas?" Laia pulls him close. "It wasn't real what they said. You know that—"

"They didn't speak to the child." The Soul Catcher casts an appraising look at us. "The border is close," he says. "But they will be waiting, and they are strongest at night. You are depleted. As am I. Come. They cannot hurt us in the cabin."

The cabin is large and smells of wood shavings, but it's tight as a drum and solid as Blackcliff. A stove squats in one corner, with copper pans hanging from hooks on the wall. Beside it is a shelf with baskets of carrots and gourds and potatoes. Strings of garlic and onion hang from above, along with bunches of herbs I couldn't begin to name.

There is also a table, fresh-built with a long bench on either side. A fireplace sits in the center of the room against the back wall, with a soft Tribal rug and cushions strewn about. The Soul Catcher's bed is spare, but Tribal lanterns hang above it, making it seem almost cozy.

After a moment I realize what the cabin reminds me of: Mamie Rila's wagon.

The Soul Catcher prepares a meal and though I know I should help, I do nothing, still numb from the jinns' predations. Only Tas has the energy, setting out plates and cups until the Soul Catcher bids him sit.

I always preferred Elias's cooking on long journeys. Distantly, I understand that the meal he serves us is hearty and well seasoned. But I do not taste it. From the silence at the table, no one else does either.

After, we take turns in the washroom, and though the water is ice-cold, I scrub off a week's worth of sea brine gratefully. By the time I emerge, Musa, Darin, and Tas are fast asleep on the floor. Harper has lain down on his roll too, his eyes shut. But if he's asleep, then I am a walrus. I wonder what the jinn said to him. I do not ask.

Instead I sit beside Laia, who is cross-legged before the fire. She runs a comb through her long hair, pointedly ignoring Elias as he cleans. His sleeves are rolled up, big hands carefully scrubbing out the stew pot with sand. His hair is longer, curling at the ends, but other than that, he looks like he'll turn to me any moment with a smile on his face and a tale that will have me in stitches.

"The last time the three of us were in a room together, I was about to kill you," I say to Laia. "Sorry about that."

"I'll forgive you—one day." Laia smiles, but her eyes are sad. "Do you want to talk about it?"

I shake my head. After a moment, I realize she might have asked because she, too, is haunted by what the jinn said to her.

"Do—do you?"

She wraps her arms around her legs and makes herself small. "I was alone," she whispers. "Everyone was gone. The Nightbringer had taken Darin. You. Tas. Afya Ara-Nur. Even E—the Soul Catcher. And there was this—this storm. But it was alive and—"

"Hungry," I say. "A maw, wanting to devour the world. I felt that too."

The Soul Catcher turns toward us. We lock eyes for a moment, until he shifts that cold gray gaze to Laia.

"You spoke of a hunger, Blood Shrike," the Soul Catcher says. "What did it feel like? Look like?"

I consider. "It was a storm. Massive. And it felt—skies, I don't know—"

"Why are you asking, Soul Catcher? Do you know of it?" Laia says, and at his silence, she leans forward. "You've seen it too. Where?"

But the Soul Catcher shakes his head. "In dreams," he murmurs.

"You must know something," I say. "Or why ask us the question?"

He joins us before the fire, putting a good distance between himself and Laia. "The Augur spoke of it," he finally says.

"Augur?" I say. The Augurs haven't been seen since the jinn were released. "Cain? What did he say? Is he here in the Waiting Place? Has he been here all this time?"

"He's dead," the Soul Catcher says. "The Augurs are all dead. The Night-

90

bringer killed them when he set the jinn free—all but Cain. He died a few days ago. I . . . was there."

"Dead?" I cannot fathom it. The Augurs are immortal. As much as I loathe them, their power is staggering.

But if they *are* dead, what does it mean for Zacharias? The Augurs named Marcus the Foretold—*the Greatest Emperor, scourge of our enemies, commander of a host most devastating.* They legitimized his dynasty. Their support was vital.

"Why would the Nightbringer kill them?" I ask.

"Because of what Cain—and the Augurs—did to the jinn."

At mine and Laia's twin looks of confusion, the Soul Catcher considers us. Then he tells of Cain's invasion and betrayal of Shaeva. Of the Nightbringer's desperation to protect his kind. That part of the story is so familiar that I clench my fists in sympathy. I know what it is to fail my people.

When the tale is over, my questions flee my mind. All I can think of is what Cain said to me before Antium fell.

The Nightbringer is no monster, child, though he may do monstrous things. He is cloven by sorrow and thus locked in a righteous battle to amend a grievous wrong.

"So the Augurs were Scholars." Laia sounds as numb as I feel. "The first time I met Cain he told me—but I did not understand. He said he was guilty. That all of the Augurs were guilty."

"He knew he was going to die," I say. *"The time to atone for our sins approaches,* he said. I remember because I couldn't stop thinking about it."

"Jinn speak prophecy at death." The Soul Catcher lifts his hands to the fire, and I find I'm surprised. I wouldn't think he'd feel the cold.

"When the Augurs stole jinn powers, the theft backfired," he says. "The

Augurs were left in a state of living death. They could not sleep or rest or die. But they could see the future—far more clearly than the jinn ever could. In those visions, there was only one path to freedom."

"Freedom for them," Laia says. "What about the rest of us? He called you and me embers in the ashes, Soul Catcher. He said the Shrike was—"

"A torch against the night. If I dared to let myself burn." Skies, I was naive. "Lies. For them, we were just a means to an end."

"Perhaps," the Soul Catcher says. "In any case, the Augur had a message for you. For both of you."

Laia's dark brows shoot up. "When were you planning on telling us?"

"I'm telling you now." The Soul Catcher's composure is grating and Laia's nostrils flare.

"Before he died, Cain, too, spoke prophecy," the Soul Catcher says. "*It was never one. It was always three. The Blood Shrike is the first. Laia of Serra, the second. And the Soul Catcher is the last. The Mother watches over them all. If one fails, they all fail. If one dies, they all die. Go back to the beginning and there, find the truth. Strive even unto your own end, else all is lost.*"

He speaks like a scribe reading off a page, like he isn't delivering the last words of a creature that helped to cause untold destruction and death.

"That was all," he says after a pause. "He died just after."

"The first—the last—?" Laia shakes her head. "It makes no sense."

"The Augurs are not known for their perspicuity," the Soul Catcher says. "Before . . ." He shrugs. "I could never make sense of them."

"Curse them," Laia spits. "The jinn are murdering innocent people. The Nightbringer has a fleet headed for Sadh under Keris's flag. The Tribal lands will fall unless they are stopped. We do not have time for Augur riddles. Though—" She considers. "He did get one thing right. I *will* strive to the end. I will not give up. Not until the Nightbringer is dead."

"The troubles of the human world are not my concern," the Soul Catcher says, and the finality of his words is chilling. "The Augur asked that I relay the message. He was dying, and I didn't wish to deny his last request."

He rises and makes for his bunk, carelessly stripping off his shirt as he goes. I'm silenced at the sight of him, at that stretch of golden skin, the planes of hard muscle, the ridges and runnels of scars across his wide shoulders, a mirror of my own.

If he was still Elias, I'd have thrown a pillow at his head for being so obvious about showing off his attributes. Now the sight just makes me sad.

Beside me, Laia plucks at the knots on her bedroll, then dashes her hand against her eyes. What can I say to her? It is torment to love someone hopelessly, with no chance of requital. There is no salve for it, no cure, no comfort.

I undo the knots and lie down with my back to her, so she can mourn in peace.

The fire dims and I try to sleep, but the jinns' words scream through my head. *You'll see him dead and yourself upon the throne.* If Zacharias dies, it will be because I did not protect him. I could not live with myself if I did not keep my baby nephew safe.

Without Marinn's backing, the task will be difficult. Keris wants Zacharias and Livia dead. Grímarr lurks in Antium, tormenting my people and choking off my supplies. The Delphinium Paters lose faith. Our weaponry and soldiers are limited. Our food is running out. And the Commandant— she has all of those things. Along with a horde of jinn at her back.

My gaze falls on Harper. Other than Laia, everyone is asleep. No one would see if I let myself look at him. If I considered his beauty and his strength. But I make myself look away.

You are all that holds back the darkness. I draw on my father's words, spoken just before he died. Those are the words I will live by. The words I will chant to myself.

I will find allies. I will protect my family. I will buy, borrow, or steal weaponry. I will recruit soldiers.

I will see my nephew on the throne. Even unto my own end.

CHAPTER THIRTEEN

Laia

The fire in the cabin burns low, and the Blood Shrike eventually falls into slumber, but I cannot sleep. A thousand worries march through my head, and finally I slip outside so my tossing and turning do not wake everyone up.

The night is freezing, the sky aglow with the spill of the galaxy. A comet streaks across the empyrean and fades into the dark, and I remember a night like this a year ago, when I stood outside a different cabin with Elias, just before he finally kissed me.

We laughed together that night, and on many nights after. Mauth gave Elias a splitting headache every time we kissed, but we'd steal a few hours, sometimes.

Once while Darin was recovering from Kauf, Elias and I hiked to a waterfall a few miles from the cabin. He was supposed to teach me to swim, but we learned other things about each other that day.

And after the requisite jokes about Mauth wanting to keep Elias chaste, we stuffed ourselves with cold pears and cheese and skipped stones on the water. We spoke of all the places we wanted to see. We fell asleep in the sun, fingers intertwined.

Part of me wants to sink into that memory. But most of me just wants to leave.

Every moment in the Soul Catcher's cabin has been torture. Every second of staring at that dead-eyed *thing* in the body of the boy I loved makes me want to burn the place down. Shake those big shoulders. Kiss him. Hit him. I want to make him angry or sad. Make him feel *something*.

But none of it would matter. Elias Veturius is gone. Only the Soul Catcher remains. And I do not love the Soul Catcher.

"Laia?"

Tas pads out of the cabin, shivering in a thin nightshirt, and I drape my cloak around him. We stare out at the treetops of the Forest of Dusk, mist-cloaked and purple this deep in the night.

The Nightbringer is somewhere beyond the borders of this place, raising hell with his jinn. Keris is out there with her army. To the west, Grímarr and the Karkauns torment the people of Antium.

So much evil. So many monsters.

Tas snuggles deep into the cloak. "This is new," he says. "Warmer. But I liked the one you used to wear. It reminded me of Elias." Tas looks up when I do not respond.

"You've given up on him," he says.

"I've given up on the idea that there will be an easy answer to any of this," I say.

"Why?" Tas asks. "You didn't see what they did to him in Kauf. What the Warden did. They tried to break him. But he wouldn't break, Laia. He never gave up. Not on Darin. Not on me. And not on you. Elias fought. And he's still in there somewhere, trying to escape."

I hoped that was the case, once. No longer. *We are, all of us, just visitors in each other's lives.*

"I thought you were different, Laia." Tas shrugs off my cloak. "I thought you loved him. I thought you had hope."

"Tas, I do—" But as I say it, I realize it's not true. All has been dark for so long. To hope is a fool's errand. "Elias as we knew him is gone."

"Maybe." Tas shrugs. "But I think that if you were the one who got chained up in the forest, Elias would never give up. If you had forgotten how much you loved him, he'd find a way to make you remember. He'd keep fighting until he brought you back."

My face burns in shame as Tas returns to the cabin. I want to call out after him, *You are only a child. You have no idea what you speak of.*

But I do not. Because he is right.

«»«

The Soul Catcher wakes me at dawn with a hard tap to my shoulder. It is the first time he has touched me in months and so perfunctory that I wish he had woken me with a curse and a kick to the heels, as Cook used to.

"Time to leave." He drops my pack—already buckled shut—by my head. The others are up and ready moments after me. Tas looks hopefully toward the stove, but it is cold and barren.

Just as well.

"You all right?" Darin lifts my pack as I pull on my boots. "That's a dumb question, isn't it?"

He looks so rueful that despite everything, I smile. "I am fine," I say. "In a way I'm glad I saw him like this. I needed to be reminded that Elias is gone."

It takes mere minutes to reach the border of the Waiting Place. Beyond the tree line, the land slopes down into gentle rolling hills, their yellowed grasses poking through old snow. The presence of the Empire settles over me like an iron mantle.

The Soul Catcher does not step beyond the trees. He holds something in his hand, examining it absently. My heart leaps when I realize what it

97

is: my armlet. The one he made me months ago. The one I gave back to him.

He's still in there somewhere, trying to escape.

"The jinn will sense your departure," the Soul Catcher says, armlet still in hand. "By nightfall, they could come after you. Move swiftly. I do not wish to welcome any of you to the Waiting Place."

He turns his back and a small hand reaches out to stop him.

"Elias," Tas says. "You don't remember me, do you?"

The Soul Catcher looks down at the boy, and I think of how he spoke to Tas after we escaped Kauf, by dropping to a knee so they were eye-to-eye.

"My name is Soul Catcher, child."

I step forward to draw Tas away. But he holds tightly to the Soul Catcher.

"I'm Tas," he says. "You gave me my name. In Sadhese, it means—"

"Swift," the Soul Catcher says. "I remember."

Then between one blink and the next, he is gone, leaving a heavy silence in his wake.

The Blood Shrike turns west. "There's a garrison ten miles away," she says. "We can get horses there, and replenish our supplies before heading to Delphinium."

Everyone moves off behind her, even Tas, but I find myself lagging. My legs feel like lead, and every step is labored. *What in the skies?* When a glow blooms at the edge of my vision, relief floods me.

"I'd wondered where you went," I say to Rehmat. "Is this you?" I gesture to my stubborn feet. "Can you stop it? I need to catch up with the others."

"Your unwillingness to travel a road you should not travel has nothing to do with me," Rehmat says. "The heart knows what it knows."

"Well, *I* do not know what it knows, so please enlighten me."

Rehmat does not say anything for a moment, but when it does, it is with a note of censure. I think of Pop's face when Darin was being particularly obstinate.

"The fate of millions rises or falls with your strength, Laia of Serra," Rehmat says. "You challenged the Nightbringer. You woke me. Together, we must stop him from the apocalypse he wishes to inflict upon the world. Such willful ignorance is beneath you. You do not wish to abandon Elias Veturius. Accept it."

I feel suddenly exposed and cowardly. "I am not—I *will* fight the Nightbringer. I will destroy him and not because you tell me to. But Elias—the Soul Catcher—he has nothing to do with this."

"He does and your heart knows it. Go against its wishes at your own peril."

"My heart"—I draw myself up—"fell in love with a murderous jinn. It cannot be trusted."

"Your heart is the *only* thing that can be trusted." With that, the creature disappears and I stand there, ankle-deep in frozen grasses, my mind pulling me forward while my skies-forsaken heart yanks me back.

Darin, noticing that I've fallen behind, jogs to me. Skies, what will I say to him? How will I explain this?

"I can't change your mind," he says when he's within earshot. "Can I?"

"You—" I sputter. "How did you—"

"You're more like Mother than you'll ever admit."

"I cannot abandon him, Darin," I say. "I have to at least *try* to break through." The more I think about what I want to do, the more it makes sense. "I'll head south. Months ago, a Tribal *Kehanni* tried to tell me of the Nightbringer. But wraiths killed her. The Nightbringer wanted his past hidden.

Which means there must be something about him worth knowing—secrets, weaknesses—information I can use to destroy him. Maybe that *Kehanni* is not the only storyteller who knows the Nightbringer's tale. Maybe there is another who will tell it."

"Right, well, I'm coming with you." Darin turns to hail the others, but I stop him.

"Our people need you," I say. "They need Musa. They need a voice in the Emperor's court. The Shrike means well, but the Empire is her first priority. Not the Scholars. Besides." I look to the forest. "Talking to the Soul Catcher—getting through to him—it will be difficult enough. I do not want any distractions."

Darin argues with me for several long minutes, and far ahead, the others stop to await us.

"Skies, but you're stubborn, Laia," he finally says, running a hand through his hair, making it stand on end. "I hate this. But if you're set on it, I won't tell you what to do. Not that I ever could." He digs around in his pack, pulling out a lumpy package.

"This was supposed to be a surprise for when we made it to Delphinium." He offers it to me. "Don't—" He stops me when I go to untie the twine. "Don't open it," he says. "Wait until you're out on the road."

I consider calling out to the others. But a nearby flash of wings tells me Musa will know about my decision in a moment anyway. Tas and Harper will understand. And while the Shrike's friendship has been a pleasant surprise these past months, her first loyalty is to the Empire. The Empire would want Laia of Serra in Delphinium, sustaining an alliance between Scholars and Martials.

"Will you be all right?" I look up into my brother's face, the first real stirrings of anxiety pulling at me.

But he flashes me Mother's cavalier smile. "We fight less when we're not in the same city. And I won't miss you stealing my food or bossing me around like you're my nan instead of a wittle cwicket—"

I bat him away, laughing as he pinches my cheeks like I'm an infant. "Oh, *piss* off—"

He pulls me into a hug, and I yelp when he lifts me up. "Be safe, little sister," he says, and there is no laughter in his voice anymore. "It's just us now."

PART TWO

THE REAPING

CHAPTER FOURTEEN

The Nightbringer

As a young jinn, I drifted through the trees in awe of the silence and the sound, the light and the redolent earth. In my ignorance, I set the forest alight. But Mauth's laughter was gentle, his instruction patient. He taught me to dance from shadow to flame, to step lightly so as not to disturb the small creatures with whom I shared the Waiting Place.

After I had learned the swell of the forest and the curves of the river, after I stalked with the wolves and rode the winds with the falcons, Mauth guided me to the border of the Waiting Place. Beyond, fires burned and stone clashed. The children of clay laughed and fought and stole life and brought it forth with joy and blood.

"What are they?" They mesmerized me. I could not look away.

They are your charges, *Mauth said.* Fragile, yes, but with spirits like the great old oaks, long-lived and strong. When their bodies are finished, those spirits must pass on. Many will do so without you. But others will require your aid.

"Where do they go?"

Onward, *he said*, to the other side. To a twilight sky and a peaceful shore.

"How do I care for them? How do I help them?"

You love them, *he said*.

The task seemed like a gift. For after a few minutes of watching them, I was half in love already.

Keris Veturia leaves Marinn with grain, leather, iron, and a treaty that includes the expulsion of every Scholar who walks the Free Lands. Though not their sale, much to her irritation. Still, after days of negotiations, it is a victory. She should feel satisfied.

But for all of her cunning, Keris is still human. She seethes over the Blood Shrike's escape, over the fact that I forbade her from personally hunting the Shrike down.

The Empress finds me on the garden terraces that overlook Fari Harbor, her expression unreadable as she surveys the delicate arched bridge and mirror-clear pond of the terrace below. A young family crosses the bridge, a father holding one giggling child under each arm, while their mother looks on with a smile.

"The sea efrits will speed your ships to the Tribal lands, Keris," I say. "Drop anchor outside Sadh. In a fortnight, we will commence the attack."

"And Marinn?" Keris wants the Free Lands. She wants this city. She wants Irmand's throne and Nikla's head on a pike.

"A reprieve." I follow the family's progress down a neatly cobbled path to a gazebo. "As we promised."

Keris inclines her head, gray eyes glittering. "As you will, my lord Nightbringer."

I smooth the Empress's edges as she departs, nudging her mind toward strategy and destruction. When she is out of sight, a cold wind whips at me, depositing two flame-formed jinn to the earth at my side.

"Khuri. Talis." I welcome them with a flare of warmth. "Your journey was swift?"

"The winds were kind, Meherya," Khuri says.

"What news of our kin?"

"Faaz cracked a river boulder yesterday." Khuri's voice betrays her pride in her brethren's skill, and I smile to hear it. She was barely a century when the Scholars came. She lost her younger siblings in the war, her parents to grief. "And Azul sent a snowstorm to Delphinium two days ago."

"Talis?"

"My power was ever a struggle, Meherya," he says quietly.

"Only because you fear it." I raise my hand to his face and he takes a shuddering breath, letting the calm of my years flow through him. "One day, you will not."

"The girl—Laia—" Khuri spits the name. "She and her companions entered the forest. We gave chase but—but she escaped, Meherya."

Below, the Mariner woman exclaims as her son offers her some small treasure he's found in the garden.

Khuri's flame deepens at the sight, her fists clenching as the children shriek in joy. "If you would only tell us *why* the girl must live, Meherya? Why can we not simply kill her?"

I feel the barest touch on my mind. A sudden urge to answer her question.

"Khuri," I chide her, for her power is compulsion. I trained her myself, long ago. "That was unnecessary."

A moment later, she screams, so high no human could hear it. A flock of starlings explodes from the trees behind us. The young family below watches the birds, exclaiming at their murmurations. Talis cringes and tries to retreat, for when he let that sorry creature Cain die, he, too, was punished. I hold him still with my magic. I do not let him look away.

Khuri collapses, looking down in horror at her wrists, which are encased in thin chains the color of clotted blood.

"I destroyed most of them after the fall," I say of the chains. "I never liked having them in our city, but our guard captains insisted."

"F-f-forgive me—please—"

When Khuri's fire has flickered to ash, I remove the chains and put them in a sack, offering them to her. She trembles uncontrollably, cringing back.

"Take it," I say. "Talis will join me in the south. You have a different task, Khuri."

I explain what she is to do, and there is no doubt in the flicker of her flame. As she listens, sorrow grips me. Sorrow that I had to hurt her. Sorrow that I cannot tell her and Talis the truth. The truth, I know, is not something they could bear.

After they leave, I wander to the edge of the terrace. The father unrolls a cloth and begins doling out morsels of food to his family.

I smile, remembering two tiny flames from long ago, and my queen laughing at me. *You spoil them, Meherya. So many sweets will dim their fire.*

In the end, of course, humans took their fire, crushed it out with salt and steel and summer rain.

I turn my back on the Mariner family and spin into the sky on an updraft. A moment later, the father shouts, for his wife clutches her throat, suddenly unable to breathe. Just after, his children are also gasping, and his cries transform into screams.

The guards will come. They will try to breathe life into the children, the mother. But it will do no good. They are gone, and nothing will bring them back.

CHAPTER FIFTEEN

The Soul Catcher

After Laia and her companions depart for the Empire, my days are quiet.

Too quiet. Death stalks the land. Food shortages in Delphinium. Wraiths murdering the Scholars who flee from Marinn. Efrits softening up the Tribes to weaken them before Keris Veturia's invasion.

I should be losing sleep with all the ghosts I must pass.

But the Waiting Place remains stubbornly empty, other than a few spirits drifting through. The rustle of bare branches and the pattering of winter's creatures are nothing against the silence of the place. It's in this silence, as I scour the trees for ghosts, that I notice the rot.

The smell hits me first. It is the stench of a decaying animal, or fruit left to insects. It emanates from an evergreen near the River Dusk, one so wide that it would take twenty men standing fingertip to fingertip to encircle it.

On first glance, the behemoth appears healthy. But deep in its branches, needles that should be a rich green are a sickly orange. The earth at its base is spongy, leaving the tree's roots exposed.

When I kneel to touch the soil, pain tears across my spirit. It's raw and corrosive, every regret I've ever dwelled on, every mistake I've made. Beneath the pain is the hunger from my nightmares. It envelops me in blinding whiteness. I'm thrown back, and when I sit up, the feeling is gone, though my body still shakes.

"What the *bleeding* hells?" I gasp, but there is no one to hear me. I crawl back to the tree, touch the dirt. Nothing happens. The soil around the evergreen is as lifeless as the salt wastes west of Serra. Small carcasses litter the ground—beetles on their backs. Spiders curled into balls. A fledgling jay, its neck broken.

I don't bother calling out to Mauth. He hasn't spoken since the day Cain returned my memories.

Perhaps the memories caused this. Eating away at the forest the way they eat away at me. But I've had them for days and this rot is new.

"Little one." I nearly jump out of my skin, but it's only the Wisp.

"A girl walks the trees." The Wisp tilts her head, as if wondering why I'm on the ground. "A human, near the western border. Do you think she knows where my lovey is?"

"A girl?" I scramble to my feet. "What girl?"

"Dark of hair and gold of eye. Heavy of heart and burdened by an ancient soul. She was here before."

Laia. I reach for the map of the Waiting Place and find her quickly, a glowing dot due west. She must've just entered the wood.

"Karinna," I say, not wanting to lose track of the spirit yet again. "Will you wait here for me? I'll be back soon—we can talk."

But Karinna fades into the trees, muttering to herself, lost once again in her search for her lovey.

I turn toward the setting sun. The girl's presence might explain why there's rot in the Waiting Place. If she's harming the forest, I'll need to persuade her to leave.

By the time I find her, the sky is thick with stars, and the treetops dance in the wind. She's lit a fire. No ghosts watch her and there is no decay in the forest near her. She seems for all the world like a normal girl traversing a normal forest.

A memory seizes me. Her face hovering above mine in the Serran desert as rain poured down around us. I was poisoned—raving. It was Laia who kept me from drifting away, who tethered me to reality with her quiet, indomitable will. *Stay with me.* She put her hands on my face. They were gentle and cool and strong.

You are not welcome here. The words are on my lips, but I don't speak. Instead I watch her. Perhaps if I look at her for long enough, I'll see that ancient soul that the Wisp spoke of.

Or perhaps she's simply beautiful, and looking at her feels like sunlight flowing into a room lost to the darkness for too long.

Stop, Soul Catcher. I shake myself and approach loudly, so as not to startle her. But even when I'm certain she's heard me, she doesn't look up. Her hair is thrown into a long braid beneath a black kerchief, and she stares fixedly at a simmering pot of water.

"I wondered how long it would take." She removes the pot, adding cooler river water to it. Then she unhooks her cloak and starts pulling off her shirt.

I'm dumbfounded until I realize she's bathing and I turn away, my neck hot.

"Laia of Serra," I say. "You have trespassed into the Wa—"

"I swear to the skies, Elias, if you finish that sentence, I *will* tackle you. And you wouldn't like it."

Something twinges within, low in my body. A sly voice in my head urges me to say, *Maybe I would.*

"My name is not Elias."

"It is to me."

Her emotions are veiled, so I reach out with my magic. For a second, I get a sense of her. Sadness, anger, love, and . . . desire. She suddenly goes blank, as if a part of her is shoving me away.

"Do not do that to me." Her voice vibrates with anger. "I'm not one of your ghosts."

"I only want to understand why you are here. If you need something, I can give it to you, and you can go."

"What I want, you cannot give me. Not yet, anyway."

"You desire me," I say. The quiet splash of water ceases. "I can satisfy you if that's why you're here. It's easy enough and if it means you'll leave, then I'm willing to do it."

"Satisfy me? How kind of you." She laughs, but it doesn't sound joyful.

"Desire is simple. Like the need for shelter or warmth. And it won't be unpleasant."

I hear a soft step and turn, forgetting that she has stripped down to very little. I catch a glimpse of skin, curved and golden and tapering to the swell of her hips. She's piled her hair on top of her head and her expression is preternaturally calm.

Shouldn't have looked. I direct my gaze up toward the treetops, which are infinitely less interesting.

"You really think it will be so easy?" She runs a slim finger along my shoulder blades, before her hand settles in my hair and she comes around to face me. She rises on her toes and tugs me close, stopping before our lips touch.

"For me, Elias, desire is not simple. It is not shelter. It is not warmth. It is a fire that offers no light, only heat, ruinous and consuming. The longer you deny it, the hotter it burns. You forget shelter. You forget warmth. There is only that which you want and cannot have, and the desolation that follows."

Her lashes, I note, are unusually long, but it's the cool challenge in her eyes that makes me wonder why she doesn't have the world in her thrall.

My hands move to her bare waist and I pull her closer. But doing so is a mistake, for I don't expect her skin to be so soft, nor for the press of her body to evoke a cascading wave of heat in my own.

"Is that a yes?" *Say yes.* "If I satisfy you, you'll leave?"

I know her irises are gold, but in the darkness, they appear almost black as she searches my face. She sighs so quietly I nearly miss it.

"Never mind." She backs away, and I don't need Mauth's magic to sense her sadness. "No matter what *you* do, Soul Catcher, it will not satisfy me. Turn around, please."

I do as she asks, though disappointment lashes at me. I don't let myself dwell on why.

"In that case, I will escort you from here. Your presence disturbs the ghosts. And there is rot near the river."

"There are no ghosts, Elias," Laia says. "You're doing an excellent job. I do not know anything about the rot. The river is hundreds of miles away, and I entered the Waiting Place just this afternoon. If something is wrong with the river, I suggest you look elsewhere for the culprit."

Water drips from her washcloth as she returns to bathing, and the scent of her soap wafts toward me, light and sugary, like summer fruit. I used to wonder at that scent. How it clung to her even when we traveled through the muck of the Southern Range, even when all we had to wash with was days-old rainwater.

"Why are you here?" My curiosity gets the better of me. "Why are you traveling through the forest?"

"I need to get to the Tribes," Laia says. "To the encampments near Aish. I traveled alongside the Waiting Place for a few days, but decided it was safer in the forest than in the Empire. Keris's patrols still hunt for her enemies."

"The Tribal lands are soon to be a war zone. And I don't wish to welcome your spirit here."

"Your wishes do not matter much to me," she says. "In any case, Tribe Saif and Tribe Nur are there. I need to find Mamie and Afya Ara-Nur. See if they can help me learn something about the Nightbringer."

"You can't linger here. The jinn walk this wood. You saw what they can do."

"You said they would not sense one human walking alone through the forest," she says. "And they haven't. Not yet anyway. You can turn around now."

She pulls on a shirt and unbinds her hair, which falls in a spill of loose ebony curls across her back. Another memory hits me. An inn, far away. A wall. A bed. Her legs tight on my waist. Her skin smooth and giving beneath my lips, and the sheer joy of getting more than a stolen moment with her. The feeling of rightness—of home.

I shove the memory to the back of my mind. "Let me take you south," I say. I could leave her at the border, near the Duskan Sea. If she is causing the rot, it will fade when she leaves.

"I'm not windwalking with you," she says. "Besides, I thought I could speak to the ghosts as I traveled. Maybe they know about the Night—"

"No." I close the distance between us. She gasps at the suddenness of it. But then her face hardens and I feel steel against my throat.

"You will not touch me," she says quietly. "You will not even think about taking me anywhere without my leave."

She's a little breathless, but she holds the blade steady. I do not tell her that it would do no good. That if she plunged it into me, Mauth would heal my body.

"If you so desperately want to keep me out of trouble," she says, "walk with me. If the jinn come, I give you leave to take me where you like."

Mauth's magic twinges, a somnolent snake stirring, sensing a distant threat.

I nod once, in agreement. *I give you leave to take me where you like.* The way she regards me is—fixed. Yet there is a warmth to it. A sultry heat underlying her determination. What is she thinking, when she looks at me like that? Where *would* I take her if I could?

The voice imprisoned within answers: *Somewhere peaceful. Rain drumming above and a fire crackling, a soft bed and hours and hours ahead.*

I turn my back on that voice, and on her.

"I'll be nearby," I tell her. "No need to come looking for me."

Then I windwalk far enough away to collect myself, before she makes me feel any more.

CHAPTER SIXTEEN

The Blood Shrike

By the time we reach Delphinium, my arrow wound has reopened and bleeds freely down my thigh. I grit my teeth against the pain as my men drag open the ancient wooden gates, which dump a small avalanche of fresh snow onto my head. When I dismount before the decrepit castle that is the new seat of the Emperor, my legs nearly give way.

"Harper," I say. His brows are furrowed, his hand half-extended toward me, but I shoo him into the castle. "See that Musa, Darin, and Tas are well settled. I must find Livia."

The Gens Aquilla flag flies high atop the castle's steeply pitched roof, as does the hawk-and-hammer flag of my nephew. Delphinium has never felt like the rest of the Empire. It lacks the domes and columns of Antium, or the vast orchards of Serra.

Instead it is a city of thatched roofs and cobbled lanes, tucked into the massive Nevennes Range. The residents are tough and boisterous and less concerned with class than the rest of the Empire. Taius the First was born here five hundred years ago, when it was nothing but a trading post for trappers selling furs and fish.

I listen to the drum messages as I ascend the steps. *Supply train attacked north of Estium, thirty dead. Warlock Grímarr spotted in Strellium barracks raid. Seventy dead.*

My time away has emboldened Keris and her cronies. I must find a way to wrest the balance of power back.

The men at the front gate salute, and I barely wave them at ease before turning toward Faris, who strides out of the keep to greet me. "The Emperor?" I say.

"Charming petitioners with the Empress Regent." He glances down. "Shrike, you're bleeding all over the steps."

"A scratch," I say, and when he rolls his eyes instead of smothering me with concern like Dex or Harper would have, I'm thankful he understands me. "The Emperor shouldn't be so visible. Why is Livia seeing petitioners with him?"

"You can take that up with her." Faris puts his hands up. "She won't listen to Rallius, or me. Says the people need to see their emperor."

Of course Livia would say that. She doesn't realize how many assassination attempts we've foiled.

Dex appears from the hallway behind Faris, in his usual Mask's armor, but for a blue-and-gold cloak that marks him as Livia's steward.

"Security is the least of our issues, Shrike," he says. "There are a dozen Paters making noise about the recent attacks on supply trains. The Empress Regent is to meet with them in an hour, but they might take greater heed of her if you—and your scim—were present."

"I'll be there," I say. Delphinium welcomed us with open arms five months ago. The people here welcomed the Scholars too.

But then Livia freed the Scholars. The Commandant sent assassins for our allies and my nephew. The troops haven't been paid in weeks. We began rationing to prevent starvation, as Keris has a chokehold on all the roads south of the Argent Hills.

And I bear more bad news.

As I pass him, Faris peers behind me. "Where's your little archer?"

I know who he's speaking of. Laia's sudden departure from our group stung. Part of me respects her lack of sentimentality. She had a mission. She did what she had to do.

Still, I wish she'd at least said goodbye.

"Little archer? She has better aim than you, you ass." I punch Faris in the arm, and he winces. "And she's braver. I didn't see you delivering a baby in the middle of a siege. As I recall, you were trying not to faint. Dex, catch me up."

Dex slows his stride to match my limp. "Grímarr attacked three more supply trains. Burned them down to the axel. His men were screaming the same thing they've shouted during every raid."

"*Ik tachk mort fid iniqant fi.* Have you found anyone to translate it?"

"It's archaic Karkaun," Dex says. "I'll keep working on it. I do have good news: My uncle sent word that he'll be here in a week. He brings a thousand men."

"Thank the skies." That will swell our numbers to a little more than ten thousand, and that's with the Scholars fighting. It's nothing against the hundreds of thousands of men Keris commands. But she's the one who taught me that there are many ways to win a war. Not all of them rely on superior numbers.

"We'll have to cut rations again," Dex adds.

"Gens Lenida is sending us grain, potatoes, and apples from their reserves," I say. "Dispatch a platoon of guards to meet it. That shipment will buy us time."

"Time for what, Shrike?" Dex says. "What's our play? The Paters will ask you the same question. Are you ready to answer it?"

Apparently not. "Anything else?"

"A request from the Scholar council. And—" He considers his words.

"The Ankanese have sent an ambassador. No escort, no horse even. Just appeared at the gates this morning out of thin air. Said you'd be back by midday and that he'd see only you."

My father visited Ankana long ago. *They think we're barbaric,* Father told me upon his return. *They are so far beyond us that I'm surprised they agreed to see me.*

"Shall I have him wait until the Empress Regent can see him too?" Dex asks.

I shake my head. Livia has enough to deal with. "Send him to my quarters. Immediately."

"Perhaps a physician first?" Dex's brow furrows at my limp. "Lieutenant Silvius arrived from Navium while you were away. Rode with your uncle Jans." Dex lingers a moment on the physician's name, and I hide a smile. At least there's still some joy left in this world.

"I heal quickly," I say. "But give Silvius quarters in the castle. In Navium, he made do with limited supplies, as I recall. We need that kind of skill. And get me that translation. Look into Karkaun customs and rites—it felt more like a chant than a war cry."

By the time the Ankanese ambassador knocks at my door, I've washed the road off and changed into my ceremonial armor. Most of my shallow wounds have healed, and the hole in my leg has stopped bleeding.

"Greetings, Blood Shrike." The man is my height, with deep brown skin and curly gray hair. He speaks Serran with the barest trace of an accent. His slippered feet allow him to walk silently, but his blue tunic, heavily embroidered with silver animals and flowers, rustles as he bows.

"I am Ambassador Remi E'twa." Despite the fact that he has no weapon, there's power in the breadth of his shoulders and in his purposeful gait. He is a fighter.

"You have the look of your father," he says as I close the door. "I met with him, long ago. He was a good man. Open to our ways. I taught him the words of parting. *Emifal Firdaant.*"

"What do they mean?" I ask.

"'May death claim me first.'" At my expression, Remi smiles. "Your father was confused too. But then he spoke of his wife and daughters, and he understood. I felt great sorrow at his death."

I gesture for the ambassador to join me in my sitting room. "Your people have long avoided dealings with the Empire. What has changed?"

The ambassador appears surprised at my bluntness, perhaps used to pleasantries.

"You have outlawed slavery, Blood Shrike," he says. "A requirement of any dealings with our nation. If you can swear that it will remain so, I am here to open trade between Emperor Zacharias and Ankana, and negotiate an agreement. As a token of our goodwill, I have brought a dozen Ankanese sappers—"

We have army engineers, I nearly say, but bite my tongue. Among all of my men, I can likely count a half dozen sappers. Keris has the rest.

"And portable trebuchets," he says. "Smaller and lighter than what you had at Antium, but just as powerful. You will need them, I believe, for the coming battles."

His presumption rankles me, but considering I have few sappers and no trebuchets, I swallow my annoyance. "You see the future," I say. "Like the Augurs."

"Our gift is not stolen." Remi is pointedly neutral. "It is earned after long years of study. We see impressions. The Augurs saw details."

"When you look at me, what do you see?"

It is not the question I mean to ask. But it is what I have wanted to know from the moment Dex told me the ambassador was here.

"When I look at you now, I see *Dil-Ewal*," he says. "She who heals. When I look at your future, I see —" He pauses and shrugs. "Something else."

He transitions smoothly into the trade agreement, laying out what he wants in return for the sappers and trebuchets. I agree to sell him grain and livestock—skies knows where I will get them from—and tell him the crown will consider the sale of scims, which appears to satisfy him. After he is gone, a knock sounds at my door.

I open it to find my sister's head bent at an awkward angle. Zacharias clutches a hank of her hair and pulls at it with happy vigor.

"What madness possessed you to leave your hair down?" I tickle Zak's foot and he releases Livia and flops toward me with a "ba!"

Livia says he's too young to be speaking. But I think he knows who loves him best. When I take him, he reaches for my braid, but only gives it a light pat before grabbing my face instead.

"Traitor child." My sister smiles. Zacharias is as beautiful as she was as a baby, with soft brown curls and cheeks that want a pinch. His coloring is a mix of Livia's and Marcus's, a glowing golden-brown, and he watches me with the pale yellow eyes of the Farrar family.

"He missed you." Livvy settles herself into the spot I vacated. "Refused to sleep properly without Auntie Shrike to give him a cuddle. But I told him you were off doing something very important."

I glance at her ladies-in-waiting, Merina and Coralia Farrar. They're

Marcus's cousins—and nothing like him. They love my sister and Zacharias with a fierce protectiveness, but they do not need to be party to matters of state. Livia dismisses them, and they take the Emperor from me, escorted by a sober-faced Captain Rallius and three other Masks.

After I tell Livia everything that happened in Marinn, she rises in agitation.

"We knew the Commandant would play dirty," she says. "The jinn attacks were meant to bring Marinn to its knees just in time for her to demand a treaty." My sister paces the room. "Sometimes I want to leave all of this. Take Zacharias and go far away, to some warm southern land, where no one will know us. Where he can have a normal life."

"Your people need you," I say. "And they need him. He is the child of a Plebeian and an Illustrian, brought into this world by a Scholar. He is a symbol of hope and unity, Empress Regent. A reminder of what the Empire could be."

"Thank the skies you've finally come around." Livia smiles. "A few months ago, you wanted to throttle me for setting the Scholars free."

"But you did it anyway," I say. "You're brave. And wise. You just have to be patient too."

By the time Livia and I enter the throne room, a wood-beamed dining hall with too many cobwebs, two dozen Paters have gathered. My uncle, Jans Aquillus, is also there, and nods when I enter. He will be one of the few Livia and I can count on to stand with us.

I offer a greeting, but step back, a hand on my scim, to allow Livia to speak. For the thousandth time, I wish for my mask. Its silver reminded me of who I was. What I was capable of doing. It reminded everyone else as well. Too often, the Paters forget.

"Wine, soldier," Livia calls to the aux at the door. He disappears and Pater Cassius snorts.

He's a tall, slope-shouldered fellow with a thick head of gray hair and parchment-pale skin. "He'll be hard-pressed to find it," Cassius says.

"A by-product of war, Cassius," Livia says. "We're not having a garden party."

"No, we are not." Pater Agrippa Mettias speaks up. He is clever, blunt, and an excellent fighter—a quintessential Northman. Though only in his late twenties, he's successfully guided his Gens since the age of sixteen.

With his deep brown skin and high cheekbones, he is also exceedingly handsome. The grizzled old Paters tease him for it, but he doesn't seem to mind. His self-assurance makes me like him more. He's a good ally. I would hate to lose his support.

"Keris seized Gens Mettia's southern estates," he says. "Declared me a traitor. Most of my family escaped—but those who did not were beheaded. She has offered my lands as a reward for the Emperor's head. And an additional ten thousand marks for mine."

Bleeding skies. Every assassin from Antium to Sadh will be on their way here for a bounty like that.

"I am deeply sorry for your family's suffering, Pater," Livia says. Perhaps I imagine it, but his face softens, ever so slightly.

"That is the cost of loyalty, Empress Regent." Mettias glares at Pater Cassius. "I am willing to pay it, even if others are not."

"Hear, hear," Uncle Jans mutters, half of the Paters joining him.

"But"—Mettias fixes his flinty gaze on me—"we need a plan. Keris chips away at us bit by bit. An assassin was found on the castle grounds a week ago.

And in every city she has visited, the people have proclaimed her Imperator Invictus."

My fist tightens on my scim. *Supreme Commander.* It is an honorary title for an Empire's ruler, but when bestowed by the people, it carries far more weight. Before Taius was named Emperor, the Martial clans dubbed him Imperator Invictus. When his sons vied for the throne after him, his second-born won the title—and the throne—because of his prowess on the battlefield.

"How?" Uncle Jans paces the room. "How, when she left our people to suffer and die?"

"Those in the south don't know—or want to know—what really happened in Antium," Livia says. "Not when she's promising them wealth and slaves from the Tribal lands."

A side door opens and I turn, expecting the aux with the wine. But it is Faris who hovers at the threshold.

"Shrike." Faris is so pale that I wonder for a moment if he's been injured. "A word."

I step out into the hall, where Faris waits with half a platoon, three of whom are Masks.

"Something's happened in the kitchens." He gestures for the soldiers to stand guard and hurries down the corridor.

If an assassin has gotten in, I'll bleeding break something. Even if the killer is dead—which he must be, or we'd be walking to the dungeons—another breach is not something the Paters will tolerate.

Four legionnaires flank the entrance to the scullery. With them is the aux Livia sent for the wine, his face an unsavory green.

"I have two more guards at the exits. Shrike . . ." Faris is at a loss, and I am suddenly unsure of what I am about to see. I shove through the doors and stop short.

For it is not a dead assassin I find, or even a live one. It is a bloodbath. A wretched stillness blights the air, and I do not need to look at the ravaged bodies to know everyone is dead. One of the faces is familiar. Merina— Livia's lady-in-waiting and nurse to my nephew.

"Merina came down to get tea for the Empress Regent," Faris says from behind me. "The aux you sent for wine found them."

I clench my fists. Both Plebeians and Scholars worked in these kitchens. It was one of the places they got along just fine. All were survivors of Antium. All loyal to the Emperor.

And this is what they got for their loyalty.

"The assassin?"

"Killed himself." Faris nods to the wall behind me. "But we know who sent him."

I turn. Splashed across the stones in blood is a symbol that enrages and sickens me, all at once.

A *K* with a crown of spikes atop it.

CHAPTER SEVENTEEN

Laia

Winter falls harsh on the Forest of Dusk. The thick evergreens protect me from the worst of the wind. They do not, however, protect me from Elias's frosty countenance.

The first day after he finds me, I try walking beside him—talking to him. He bolts so far ahead I can barely see him. For the rest of the day, I walk alone, missing Darin, Musa, Tas—even the Blood Shrike. At one point, I call out to Rehmat, thinking I can finally ask it questions about its origin. But it does not respond.

Later that night, when I pull out a meal of desiccated dates and flatbread, Elias disappears, returning a quarter hour later with a steaming bun stuffed with minced fowl, raisins, and almonds.

"Did you steal this?"

At his shrug, I bristle. "This is someone's hard-earned labor, Elias."

"Soul Catcher, please."

I ignore that. "I will not eat it if you stole it."

"You wouldn't, would you?" His glance is fleeting and I cannot tell if he is mocking me or making an observation. "I always leave a gold mark," he says flatly. "Bakers are less likely to lock their doors that way."

I am about to respond when I notice the stiffness of his shoulders. How he clenches his fists.

When Elias and I traveled through the Serran Range after escaping Raider's Roost, I did not wish to talk, for I had taken my first life—a Tribesman who tried to kill us both.

Elias was so careful with me then. He spoke to me—but he did not rush me. He gave me time. Perhaps, with his mind so deeply entwined with Mauth, I must do the same.

The next day, I do not speak and he relaxes a touch. In the evening, when we've stopped, I break my silence.

"I saw your mother, you know," I tell him. "She's as charming as ever."

He pokes at the fire with a stick.

"She tried to kill me," I go on. "But then *her* master and *my* former lover showed up. The Nightbringer—you remember him. He was in full Keenan regalia. Red hair, brown eyes, those freckles . . ."

I sneak a look at Elias. But other than a slight tightening of his infuriatingly square jaw, he does not react.

"Do you ever think of Keris as your mother?" I ask him. "Or will she always be the Commandant? Some days, I cannot believe Cook and my mother were the same person. I miss her. Father and Lis too."

I yearn to speak of my family, I realize. To share my sadness with someone.

"I dream of them," I say. "Always the same nightmare. Mother singing that song and the sound of their necks br-breaking—"

He says nothing, only rises and melts into the night. The space he leaves is vast, that gnawing loneliness of showing your heart to someone only to find they never wanted to see it. The next day, he is silent. And the next. Until three days have passed. Then ten.

I talk about everything under the sun—even Rehmat—and still he says nothing. Skies, but I have never known a man so stubborn.

After a fortnight, we make camp early, and Elias disappears. Usually when he leaves, he windwalks and I cannot follow. But this time, he stalks into the forest and I find him in a clearing, lifting a small boulder above his head—then slamming it down. Lifting it, slamming it down.

"Easy," I say. "What did that poor rock do to you?"

He does not appear surprised by my presence, even though he was engrossed in his strange ritual.

"It helps when—" He gestures to his head and lifts the rock again. This time, when he drops it, I sit on it.

"You need a pet, Elias," I say, "if you are turning to rocks for company."

"I don't need a pet." He leans down, grabs me by the waist, and throws me over his shoulder.

I yelp. "Elias Veturius, you—you *put* me down—"

He drops me at the edge of the clearing—not ungently—and goes back to his boulder.

"You do need a pet." I settle my breath, which has gone a bit shallow, and circle him, considering. "Not a cat. Too solitary. Maybe a horse, though with your windwalking you would not have much use for one. An Ankanese jumping spider, perhaps? Or a ferret?"

"Ferret?" He looks almost offended. "A dog. A dog would be fine."

"A small one." I nod. "One that barks incessantly so that you have to pay attention to it."

"No, no, a big one," he says, "Strong. Loyal. A Tiborum shepherd dog, maybe, or a—"

He stops short, realizing that he is engaging in actual conversation. I smile at him. But he makes me pay for my victory, stepping into a windwalk and vanishing, muttering about seeing to the ghosts.

"Why?" I mutter to the trees hours later, unable to sleep. "Why did I have to fall in love first with a vengeance-obsessed fire creature, and then with a noble idiot who, who—"

Who gave up his freedom and future so Darin and I could live. Who chained himself to an eternity alone because of a vow he made.

"What do I do?" I mutter. "Darin—what would you do?"

"Why do you ask the night, child? The night will not answer."

Rehmat's voice is a whisper, its form a scant shadow limned in gold.

"I thought I'd imagined you." I offer it a smile, for imperious as the creature is, its presence leavens my loneliness. "Where have you been?"

"Unimportant. You wish to speak to your brother. Yet you do not. Why?"

"He is hundreds of miles away."

"You are *kedim jadu*. He is *kedim jadu*. And he is your blood. If you wish to speak to him, speak to him. Still your mind. Reach."

"How—" I stop myself from asking and consider. Rehmat was right about my disappearing. Perhaps it is right about this too.

I close my eyes and imagine a deep, quiet lake. Pop did this with patients sometimes, children whose bellies ached for reasons we could not see, or men and women unable to sleep for days. *Breathe in. Let the air nourish you. Breathe out. Expel your fears.*

I sink into the stillness. Then I call out, imagining my voice stretching across the miles.

"Darin. Are you there?"

At first, there is only silence. I begin to feel foolish. Then—

Laia?

"Yes!" I nearly leap up in my excitement. "Yes, it's me."

Laia, what is this? Are you all right?

"I'm fine," I say. "I—I am in the Waiting Place."

Is Elias with you? Is he still being an idiot?

"He is not an idiot!"

Figured you'd say that. I wanted to make sure it was really you. Are you sure you're all right? You sound—

Rehmat appears so suddenly that its glow blinds me. "Fey creatures! Approaching from the west. They must have heard you, Laia. Forgive me—I did not sense them. Arm yourself!"

The gold light fades as quickly as it appeared, and I am left alone in the inky murk. I scramble to my feet, dagger at the ready, my pulse pounding. A cricket chirps nearby and the wind whispers through the branches. The forest is quiet.

And then, in an instant, it is silent. Shapes flit between the trees, too fast to track. Jinn? Efrits?

I scuttle back, trying to use the night to my advantage. *The darkness can feel like an enemy,* the Blood Shrike said once, insisting I wear a blindfold while she trained me in hand-to-hand combat. *Let it be a friend instead.*

The shadows draw closer. Where in the skies is Elias? Of course, when he and his big fists and murderous demeanor might actually come in handy, he's not here.

Something cold brushes past me, and I feel as if my neck has been plunged into pure snow. I dart around the fire—kicking at it to get air on the embers. They flare for a moment, then fade. But not before I see what hides in the dark.

Wraiths.

Stay calm. Elias and I fought these things out in the desert east of Serra. Taking off their heads kills them. Too bad I have a dagger with no reach instead of a scim.

Invisibility will not fool them. All I can do is run. I kick the embers into the faces of the wraiths, and as they screech, I bolt through an opening in the trees. I feel them behind me, all around me, and lash out with my dagger. They fall back—and I have a few more inches, a few more seconds.

Did the Nightbringer send them? *You fool, Laia. Did you think he would just let you get away?*

Through the gasps of my breathing and the crunch of brush beneath my boots, I hear a creek. Most fey creatures hate water. I tear toward the sound, slipping on the wet rocks, only stopping when I am midstream, with the water at my knees.

"Come out, little girl." The wraiths speak as one, their words high and reedy, as if a winter gale out of the Nevennes has been given voice. "Come out and meet your doom."

"Why don't you come in here?" I snarl. "You ragged bastards could use a bath."

The blue starlight throws the shadows emerging from the woods into sharp relief. A dozen wraiths, at first. Then two dozen. Then more than fifty, their shredded clothing fluttering in a nonexistent wind.

They could have rushed me in the woods. Ambushed me. But they did not. Which means they want me alive.

Think! There is a reason the wraiths are here and it is not to kill me. *Brazen it out, then, Laia. And hope to the skies you aren't wrong.* Without warning, I sprint through the water toward them.

I expect them to move. Instead they catch me and squeeze. *Bad idea, Laia. Very bad idea.*

Impossible cold lances through me and I scream. The chill is all-consuming, and I am certain that this will be a slow death, like being bricked away and knowing you will never escape.

My body seizes, my vision flashes to a vast sea, dark and teeming. Then to the River Dusk. I see it from above, the way a bird would. I follow its serpentine path through the Waiting Place. But there is something wrong. The river disappears, rotting at the edges. There are no ghosts winding among the trees. Instead, screams echo in the air and there are faces in the water. Thousands of them, trapped. The air grows ponderous, and I turn to face a maelstrom of teeth and sinew, obscenely violent. A maw that is never satisfied.

But it will not have me. *No!* Though the images I saw still reverberate in my skull, I have enough sense to lash out with my blade, dodging the shadows as they reach for me.

They want my screams, I realize. They want my pain.

"You cannot have it," I roar at them. "You can have my wrath instead. My hate."

"Laia—" Elias's voice calls from somewhere on my right, and the wraiths chitter and draw back.

"She doesn't belong here, Soul Catcher," they say. "She is not dead."

"Neither do you." Elias's words make me shudder, for they are delivered in the flat, cold voice of the Soul Catcher. Of a Mask. "Leave."

He gathers his magic—I feel the air tighten around me. The wraiths recoil and I dart through them.

"Go, Elias!" I shout when I'm within reach of him. "Windwalk! Now!" His arms close around me and we are away.

I shiver from the cold still in my bones and press into him, desperate for his warmth. He moves so quickly that I close my eyes so I am not sick. The maelstrom circles in my head, ever devouring, and I have to tell myself that I am safe.

Safe. Safe. Safe. I chant the word to the throb of Elias's heartbeat. The rhythmic thud is a reminder that despite his vow and his magic, his detachment and his distance, he is still human. By the time he slows, I have the sound memorized.

The scent of the Duskan Sea cuts through the air first, and then the dull roar of the waves. Seagulls call out, and far to the east, the sun burns away a heavy cloud bank.

We have traveled hundreds of miles. He got what he wanted after all—me out of his territory. As soon as we are free of the trees, he releases me. I crash to the earth, scraping my hand on a tree trunk trying to get my balance.

"The wraiths are far away." Elias looks northwest, where a Martial guard tower looms atop a hill of dead grass. "But they might track you. Get to a human settlement quickly. When it's full light, you'll be safe to travel again."

"I saw something, Soul Catcher," I say. "An ocean filled with—skies, I do not know. And faces. Trapped faces within the River Dusk. I saw that—that maelstrom, and it wanted to devour me and you and—"

"And everything else." Elias glances down at me, and those pale eyes I learned to love darken. Some unfathomable emotion flickers across them, an echo of who he was.

"We can travel together." I touch his arm, and he starts at the spark that jumps between us. *He's still human. Still here.* "We can speak to the *Fakirs*, the *Kehannis*. You could ask—"

At the chill in his gaze, I cease. I keep trying to appeal to his humanity. I might as well throw myself against a stone wall. He does not give two figs about me. He cares about the Waiting Place. He cares about the ghosts.

"How many ghosts have you passed, Elias? How much rot have you seen?"

He tilts his head, contemplating me.

"It's not because of me," I say. "Something is *wrong*. What if it is the Nightbringer's doing? You are dedicated to protecting and passing on the ghosts. The Tribal *Fakirs* are also dedicated to the dead. They might know where the rot is coming from."

Stay with me, I think. *Stay with me so I can remind you of who you used to be.*

"A rider approaches." Elias glances over my shoulder. The sky pales enough that I can see foam on the waves, and I squint toward the western horizon, searching.

"Tribespeople," I say. "Musa told them I was coming. They must have scouts watching the forest."

"Not the Tribes. Someone else." Elias takes a step back. "The voice in your head, Laia," he says, and I remember then that I told him of Rehmat. "Beware of it. Such creatures are never quite what they seem."

I stare at him in surprise. "I did not know you were listening."

Hooves thunder from behind me. A quarter mile to the northwest, a band of men and horses appears atop a hill. Even at a distance, one of the forms flickers strangely. It swings its head toward me.

Two sun eyes penetrate across the distance, pinning me like an insect on a wall.

"Elias," I whisper. "Elias, it's a jinn—"

Silence. I turn to him, to ask him to windwalk us away. But as I scan the tree line, my stomach sinks. He is gone.

CHAPTER EIGHTEEN

The Soul Catcher

The dead yew in the jinn grove bears the brunt of my frustration, the trunk creaking as I slam the chain into it again and again and again.

The girl will be fine. She's swift and clever. She possesses magic.

She will survive.

She's not "the girl." She's Laia. And if she dies, it's your bleeding fault.

"Shut up," I mutter, delivering a particularly savage blow to the tree. A nearby crow squawks and flies into the clear winter sky.

You're a fool, the voice hisses, deriding me as it has for the past week, ever since I left Laia at the edge of the Waiting Place.

My exhaustion is bone deep, a product of sleep riven with nightmares and waking thoughts consumed by her. I lift the chain, seeking that sweet oblivion that takes over when my body screams that it cannot go on.

Oblivion doesn't materialize. As Cain promised, Laia remains in my mind. Every story she told. Her shaking body as we escaped the wraiths. Her hand against my arm as she tried to persuade me to see the *Fakirs* with her.

And her questions. *How many ghosts have you passed, Elias?* Since she left, I have scoured the Waiting Place for spirits, encountering a mere half dozen in as many days. *Something is wrong.*

I hear a low, animal moan, and turn to find a spirit reeking of death and wringing her hands at the edge of the jinn grove. Immediately, I move toward her. Mauth's magic allows me to dip into her memory, and I see a fleet of ships off a fair gold coast. Invaders wearing Keris Veturia's sigil. Sadh's silver domes and slender white spires burning and falling. Its people fleeing and dying.

Speaking Sadhese, the spirit tells me her story in bits and pieces and I usher her slowly toward the river. Focusing on her calms my mind. This is my purpose. Not night after night of oneiric hauntings. Not helping a girl cross the forest. Not talking to a *Fakir*.

"My children," the ghost says. "Where are they?"

"He leaves them," I tell her. "They'll find their way to the nearest settlement. Do not fear for them."

"Did they see it?" The spirit belongs to a Tribeswoman, and she turns her dark eyes toward me. "The storm?"

"Tell me about this storm," I say. "Release your fear."

The ghost shudders. She holds too tightly to her suffering. I let my magic curl around her like smoke and try to ease her pain from her. But she will not let it go.

"It was vast. And hungry. It wanted to devour me."

"When did you see this?" If she did get a glimpse of the storm, she will be the first ghost to mention it other than Karinna. My neck prickles. "Where?"

"When the Nightbringer came for me. He lifted his scythe. Our *Kehanni* said if you look into a jinn's eyes, you see your future, so I tried not to look. But I couldn't help it. Is that what will happen to me when I cross over? I will be devoured?"

"No," I say. "It's not." But I do not speak with conviction. Before, I knew in my bones that the ghosts were moving on to something better. Now I am not so sure.

"Something took the other spirits," the ghost says. "But I escaped. I don't know where they went. I don't know why."

"You don't have to worry about that anymore." I force myself to believe it, for if I do not, how will she? "The other side waits for you, and with it, peace."

She goes, finally, and when the next ghost appears, it, too, is from the invasion of Sadh. "I don't want to go," it screams. "Please—it's waiting for me. It will devour me!"

For the next three days, every ghost who passes through speaks of the maelstrom. I expect more spirits, for it is clear Keris Veturia takes no prisoners. But then, Tribal ghosts have always been rare in the Waiting Place. Their *Fakirs* usually pass them on without any intervention from the Soul Catcher.

Those ghosts who do enter the wood grow progressively more difficult to handle. Day after day I hear the same story. I hold and painstakingly extract the same terror. A sinking feeling creeps over me—that I am doing something terribly unjust by passing the spirits.

Then, after passing a boy who is far younger than the Nightbringer's usual victims, I go to swim in the River Dusk, to cleanse my mind of worries.

And I find that the rot has spread.

It smells worse than before, like the aftermath of a battle. The trunks of dozens of trees are crumbly with decay. The earth is raw and smoking, as if scorched, and dead fish lay stinking along the river's banks. I taste the river water and spit it out almost in that same instant. It savors strongly of death.

Laia was right. Something is deeply wrong with the Waiting Place. And I can ignore it no longer.

CHAPTER NINETEEN

The Blood Shrike

We try to keep word of the massacre in the kitchens from leaking out. But it's impossible. Within a week, the news is all over Delphinium.

"If she can get to the kitchens, she can get to anyone." Pater Cassius paces the throne room. Sleet hammers the roof, and though it's early afternoon, the storm clouds are so thick it looks as if night has fallen. We'll have snow by morning. I can smell it.

A dozen men nod or grunt in agreement with Cassius—nearly half of our advisory council. Musa and Darin, here to represent the Scholars, exchange a glance.

"She hasn't yet gotten to the Emperor." Livia straightens upon the ornate seat that serves as a throne. "Not even close."

"Because she's distracted by her campaign in the Tribal lands," Cassius says. "We must consider a truce. Ask for clemency—"

"There will be no clemency from the Commandant," I say. "I trained with her for fourteen years. She doesn't understand mercy. If we give in, we die."

"Do you not remember what she did to Antium?" Darin, quiet until now, stares down Cassius. "Thousands of your people were slaughtered. Thousands of mine too."

"Silence, Scholar! You think because that fool Spiro Teluman trained you—"

"Do not invoke his name." The steel in Darin's voice reminds me of his mother. "Spiro Teluman was ten times the man you are. As for silence—we are done being silent. Without us, you can't hope to ever take the Empire back from Keris. You need the Scholars, Pater. Keep that in mind."

139

Cyrus Laurentius, a diplomat like my father, steps in. "Keris betrayed Antium to the Karkauns. She is the real enemy, Cassius. Skies only know what our people are suffering."

"And what have we done to help them?" Pater Cassius glares at me.

His censure rings in my head as the argument rages. I circle the room, ignoring the Paters. *And what have we done to help them?*

Zacharias must take the throne. But he is a child with no power, and there is nothing any Martial respects more than power. Keris wields hers like a blade. It is why she insisted she be hailed as Imperator Invictus, instead of merely as Empress. It is why she is fixated on conquering and plundering the Tribal lands.

We need a victory just as resounding. One that will send a message of strength not only to the Paters of the Empire but to our people.

"Blood Shrike," Harper murmurs from my shoulder. "What are you thinking?"

I answer him loud enough that the room can hear. "Pater Cassius is right about one thing. Our citizens in Antium have waited for liberation long enough."

"How the hells do we take on the Karkaun army when we barely have enough men to hold Delphinium?" Pater Cassius asks. "I thought you studied war theory, Shrike."

"We don't use the army we have. We recruit the one in the city. There are fifty thousand Karkauns in Antium." The shape of a mission coalesces as I speak. "To quell a population of well over four times that. Many women and children yet live. I know our people, Paters. If we can remind them that they are not alone, they will rise up. And if we take back the city, we can show Keris's allies our strength—and win them over to our side."

140

Pater Mettias, who until now has observed the proceedings from beside the fire, looks at me askance. "How can women fight against those monsters? How will you arm them?"

"Have you forgotten that the Shrike is a woman, Mettias?" Livia examines the young Pater with enough asperity to make him fidget. "Do not bore us with old prejudices. You are a better man than that."

"We have weapon caches hidden in the city." I glance at Dex, who nods. "Our spies tell us that Grímarr's men have not discovered them all. And Darin here can make Serric steel."

A scuffle at the door has all of us turning at once. A guard flies into the room, and scim rings against scim. I grab Livia, shoving her down beside the throne as the Paters close ranks in front of us.

"Don't you dare tell me I need to prove my identity to you, boy," a voice rings out. "I was wearing Karkaun finger bones for a necklace before your dog of a father ever made eyes at your mother."

A tall, broad-shouldered figure marches into the throne room, and I release my weapon. His armor gleams, he has not a hair out of place, and he looks as if he's just come from a military inspection instead of what was likely a multi-month trek.

"Greetings, Shrike." Quin Veturius strolls toward me, nodding imperiously at the other Paters. "What's this I hear about stealing allies from my daughter?"

«« «

The Paters are skeptical of my plan. But in the end, I give them no choice. We won't take the capital back in a day. But this mission is a first step. It will allow us to let the people know that we have not forgotten them. That they must be ready to fight.

As I leave the meeting chambers, Harper follows me out, jogging to keep up as I stride through the busy hallways toward my quarters.

"Bring me the spy reports out of Antium," I say. "And get word to our people in the city. I leave in three days."

"Will we go via the Nevennes?" Harper asks. "Or the Argent Hills?"

"The Nevennes. A small force. Very small. Find me two men—your best. And get Musa—"

"I'm already here, Shrike." The tall Scholar has followed us out. "I needed to speak to you a moment." His handsome face is taut—strange, as he usually appears to be laughing at everyone else. "I sent a score of wights to Marinn to keep an eye on things," he says. "They have not returned. Not a one."

"Well, it is a long journey—" Harper begins, but Musa shakes his head.

"They can make that journey in a day. Two days if they get distracted. I sent them the moment we arrived in the Empire. Weeks ago now. Do you have spies in the kingdom, Shrike?"

"A few," I say. "But they've been quiet. I'll have Dex check in. We'll get you some answers. In the meantime, I could use you in Antium."

He looks between me and Harper, eyebrows raised. "Don't you have a second for that?"

"Harper will remain here to protect the Empress Regent." I ignore Harper's stiffening posture, the disbelief rolling off him. "Scholars should be represented on the mission. Laia says you're handy with a blade. And your little friends might be helpful."

Musa assents with a nod, and the moment he's out of earshot, Harper turns on me. "My place is with the Blood Shrike—"

"The situation here is too precarious, Harper." I resume my quick pace, through a courtyard and into the dim stone hall that leads to my quarters. Not a moment too soon. I need to get away from him. He's too close. Too angry. I like emotionless Harper. Cold Harper.

Fiery Harper—the Harper who looks at me like I'm precious to him—that's the Harper I need to avoid.

"I need someone I trust guarding the two most important people in the Empire."

"You trust Dex. You trust Quin. You trust Faris."

"Dex will remain too. The Empress Regent requires her steward. But Faris will come with me. I need his brawn. And Quin will insist on accompanying us."

Harper steps close enough to me that I am forced to stop. I glance up and down the hall, but there is no one. Even if there was, I doubt he would care. He is clench-jawed and furious, fighting to keep control.

For the thousandth time, I wish for my mask back. Its presence would have made facing Harper so much easier.

"Why don't you want me to come, Blood Shrike?" His voice is low and dark, the way I have never heard it. When I meet his green eyes, they flash with frustration, yes, but something deeper that strums a chord within me.

I step back from him and he shakes his head.

"You are the Blood Shrike," he says. "And I am sworn to protect you."

"I'll assign you somewhere else," I say, but my words lack anything resembling conviction. We both know I don't trust anyone as much as him. "I don't need . . . this."

"I know what you need, Shrike." He runs a hand up my arm, so careful despite his anger. "I want you to ask for it."

I need you to disappear. To never leave. I need to have never met you or felt you. You. You. You. I need you.

"I need you to stay here," I say. "And keep my sister and the Emperor alive."

I back up to my door and slip in, then close it in his face. For a long moment I am frozen, staring at it. He's just there on the other side. Maybe his heart thuds like mine. Maybe his hands shake like mine.

Or perhaps I've finally driven him away for good. I know which one I'd prefer. And I hate myself for it.

«««

Ten days later, I enter Antium to find it a broken city. I know it from the sights—the shattered streetlamps and chug of pyre smoke that hovers over everything. I know it from the sound—a horror-struck silence punctuated by the occasional scream. And I know it from the stench. Rot and refuse and burning flesh.

But it is still my city. The Karkauns can befoul the streets but they cannot bring down those massive granite walls. They can rage and kill and torture, but they cannot crush my people.

Quin, Musa, Faris, and I all crouch in the ruins of an old market, silks and pots and satchels scattered as if a tornado ripped through. The moon is bright above us, and I scowl at it. Under normal circumstances, I would never conduct an assassination mission on a night so bright.

But this cannot wait. Grímarr is one of Keris's strongest allies. He is the monster behind the despair in this city. He must die.

Behind us are the Masks who Harper picked to accompany us. Ilean

Equitius is a decade older than me, and cousin to my old friend Tristas, skies rest his soul. Septimus Atrius is from Dex's Gens, and around Musa's age. Neither of them so much as twitch at what they see. They both survived the Karkaun siege. They know the cost if we fail tonight.

I do not have to give them orders. We have gone over the plan—along with the backup plans Quin insisted on—a hundred times in the week it took us to trek here.

Deep in the city, a bell tolls twice.

Quin, Ilean, and Musa rise. The old man turns to me. "Fifth bell," he says, and then the three disappear, leaving Faris, Septimus, and me to wait.

And wait.

What if they can't clear the guards? What if we were betrayed? We have few sources in the city. Trusting them is a risk. They might have been tortured into giving our plan away. Or Quin, Ilean, and Musa might have been overwhelmed. In my mind, each scenario is worse than the last, until I am clutching the hilt of my scim, knuckles white.

"It's Quin Veturius, Shrike," Faris whispers. "That old bastard will outlive us all. Having him at our side is almost like having Elias back again."

A barn owl hoots from the street beyond the market. The signal. Faris and Septimus follow me out through Antium's Mercator Quarter and into its red-light district.

Here, the streets offer some of the only signs of life in the city. For all their hatred of "heathens," the Karkaun swine still want their whores.

Grímarr is no different. Our spy, Madam Heera, who ran one of the finest brothels in Antium, told us as much in her coded missives. In the months that Grímarr's been in the city, he's murdered six of her girls.

He kills them slow, in Taius Square. He chooses the nights with a full moon, *so everyone can see. One person from each household must attend, or the entire household pays the price.*

I grit my teeth at the sounds coming from the brothels and move quickly. The cool night wind muffles our footfalls. Soon enough, we stand across the street from Madam Heera's. Nothing's left of the Karkaun guards but a few bloodstains on the cobbles.

The brothel is dimly lit. An upper window hangs open. Within, someone weeps. Underlying the sound is an eerie chanting that can only be the Karkauns.

Faris, Septimus, and I scuttle across the street and make our way to the side of the building, toward a window that should be unlocked.

I wedge my blade beneath the sill and angle up. The window does not budge.

The chanting above intensifies, a low droning that raises the hair on my arms.

"*Ik tachk mort fid iniqant fi. Ik tachk mort fid iniqant fi.*" Dex never found a translation—though he did share far too much about the Karkauns' chilling blood rites.

"Break the window," Faris whispers. "We don't have a choice, Shrike."

I nod and wait long moments for the third bell. When it rings out, I wrap my hand in my cloak and punch through the window.

The glass shattering is the loudest sound I have ever heard, even with the bells. I wait for a warning cry, but it does not come. The only sound is that infernal chanting.

When I'm certain no one has heard us, I shimmy through the window and into a dirty room with stains on the walls and a sagging bed.

"Come on—" I hiss at Faris and Septimus, but the window is too small for them.

"Back door," I whisper. "I'll unlock it."

"Shrike," Faris hisses. "This isn't the plan."

But I'm already through the room and in the hallway beyond, slipping along the darkened corridor. I unlock the door Faris and Septimus will use and move past a refuse-strewn staircase.

"Sh-Shrike."

I jump at the whisper, and scan the darkness to see a figure hunched against the side of the stairwell. Heera. Her hands rest limply on either side, each in a bowl filled with liquid.

Blood for the Karkauns' rites.

I am at her side instantly. "It's okay, Heera." I glance behind me, my nerves screaming a warning. She's the madam of the house, the woman who can procure their pleasure for them. The Karkauns would not kill her unless they wanted her—or her body—to be a message.

"He knows, Shrike," Heera whispers. "Grímarr. He knows you've come to kill him. He wants you. Your blood. Your bones. He's—he's waiting—"

If she says more, I don't hear it. To my right, from behind a closed door, a board creaks.

Then the door bursts open, and an army of Karkauns pours out.

CHAPTER TWENTY

Laia

The jinn is hooded and cloaked, but I can tell it is not the Nightbringer. The air around the creature is not curdled or twisted. The humans who ride with it do not cringe away.

My mind races. Nothing blocks their line of sight and the sun rises from the sea at my back. A shout of alarm confirms that they have seen me. Skies only know how they found me.

Rehmat's voice sounds from beside me, though the creature does not manifest. "Why do you stand there like a moonstruck doe, child?" it demands. "If they catch you, they will kill you."

"They are in bow range. If they wanted me dead, they'd shoot me." I consider the advancing soldiers, and though my courage falters when I spot the silver glitter of a Mask, I remind myself that if I need to disappear, I can. "What if I let them catch me? There's a jinn with them. I could trick it into giving me information about the Nightbringer."

"You cannot trick a jinn." I hear a long sniff. "And I smell devilry in the air."

"I need to learn about the Nightbringer," I say. "What better way than from his kin?"

"I cannot help you if you are with the jinn," Rehmat warns me. "I cannot be discovered."

Rehmat hasn't mentioned this before. "What happens if they discover you?"

But the soldiers crest the rise of a nearby hill and thunder toward me. The jinn, cloaked and hooded with her face in shadow, leads.

If I just stand here, she will realize something is amiss. So I run. The

Nightbringer has likely told the jinn I cannot use my invisibility around their kind. If she tries to kill me, or if I fail to get information from her, I can simply disappear. The Tribal lands are not far, and there are plenty of gullies and gulches to hide in.

I call on my magic and then let it falter, as if it is beyond me. The jinn surges forward eagerly—my deception worked. As the soldiers close in, I turn west, toward the grassy foothills that slowly flatten into the Tribal desert.

"Spread out!" The jinn's voice is as crisp as the first breeze of winter, and instantly, the soldiers obey. "Do not let her past."

I drop low to the ground, do my best to look terrified, and make a run for it. A blast of heat singes my back and a burning hand closes on my arm, tighter than a Martial torture cuff.

The jinn turns me around to face her. Despite the wind, her hood remains low, and all I can make out are the flames burning in her eyes.

"Laia of Serra," she says. "The Meherya will be pleased to see you, vermin."

The jinn nods to the Mask, who pulls chains from a pack mule. They are made of some glittering black metal I do not recognize. When the Mask claps them on me, an unpleasant tingle runs up my arms.

I smell devilry in the air.

On a hunch, I try to conjure my invisibility. But despite Rehmat's assurances that its presence has strengthened my power, the magic does not respond.

"An extra precaution." The jinn rattles my chains. "One cannot be too careful around humans." She curls her lip at the last word and turns away.

My plan to mine information from her suddenly seems like the scheming of an idiot child. I do not even know what she can do. The Nightbringer is the first jinn, and thus possesses a panoply of powers: riding the wind; foretelling the future; reading minds; the manipulation of air, water, fire, and weather. This jinn might possess all of those skills—or a type of magic I have never heard of.

Whatever her power, I am now vulnerable to it. Rehmat said the jinn could no longer use their powers to tamper with me. But it said nothing of magic-suppressing chains.

"You were right," I whisper to Rehmat. "I was wrong. *Please* help me get the hells away from here!"

But Rehmat does not reappear.

"Where are you taking me?" The jinn remains silent and I wish I had something to throw at her. Ultimately, all I can do is glare. I turn to the Mask. "Where are we going?"

"We're heading—"

"Silence, Martial," the jinn says, and her animosity for him is no less than it is for me. To my surprise, the Mask ceases speaking, though his glare is a soliloquy unto itself.

"You too." She glances over, and though a retort hovered on my lips, I find I cannot say it. *Oh skies.* This jinn's power, it appears, is compulsion. And I have no defense against it.

Panic licks at my mind, for if she has stolen my magic and laid me bare to her own, I am lost. I can get no information from her. I can only serve her until she is satisfied.

Fear is only your enemy if you allow it to be. Think, Laia. The jinn's power must have limits. For instance, can she control the animals we ride? Or only humans?

I watch her from the corner of my eye as we turn southeast toward the

Tribal lands. The brown mare she rides moves as if it's part of her, calm and fluid. When drums thud out a message from the nearby garrison, hers is the only animal that doesn't even twitch.

I drive my legs into my horse's flanks, to see if it will react. It jerks, but continues at a steady pace. The jinn glances back.

"Stop it, girl," she says. "The creature will not obey."

The Mask rides at my side, stone-faced. He's a lean, dark-skinned man who looks a bit older than the Commandant. The fine cut of his shirt and intricate plating of his armor indicate that he's high up in the Martial pecking order. But he grips his reins as if they are his only purchase on this world.

I open my mouth to ask him if he has ever broken free. But when I do, no sound comes out. She has silenced my voice too.

My movement catches the man's attention and he meets my stare. Beneath the silver mask, his pale blue eyes spark a desperate sort of fury. He hates what is being done to him as much as I do.

Which means that even though he is a Martial and a Mask to boot, he could be an ally.

I nod to my hands and, very slowly, spell out my question. *Have you ever broken free?*

For nearly a minute, he does not so much as twitch. Then he nods, once.

But the jinn turns, eyes on the Mask as if sensing his internal rebellion. She narrows her eyes and he jerks his head forward like a puppet, lips sealed tight.

We ride for hours without stopping, the only sound the clip-clop of the horse's hooves and my own ragged breathing. The animals eat away at the miles more swiftly than is natural, aided no doubt by the jinns' inborn skill with the wind. Every now and then, distant Martial drums beat a message.

I try to make sense of them, but despite the Blood Shrike's attempts to teach me how to understand them, I can only make out a few words. *Sadh. Enemy. South.*

The jinn cares as little for us as she would for a pack of animals. When we stop, she orders me to relieve myself behind a boulder, as if I am a hound she is walking. But my body obeys her and I burn with shame. And hatred.

That first night, we camp at a tiny oasis. She adjusts my chains and lashes me to a date palm.

"You will not consider escaping, girl." She turns to the Mask. "Novius, is it? You will keep your men away from her, feed her, and see to any wounds. Rub a salve into her wrists for the chafing. You will not speak to each other. You will not set her free or aid in her escape." At Novius's nod, the jinn disappears into the desert.

Mask Novius does as he's told, and when I try to capture his attention again, he looks furtively out at the dark, before focusing in on my hands.

Where to? I spell out.

Novius shakes his head. Either he cannot respond, or he does not wish to. I try again.

Weaknesses?

The Mask glances over my shoulder. Swiftly, he spells out:

Pride. Anger. Weakest at noon.

That aligns with what Elias said about the jinn being strongest at night. I consider my chains. The jinn wears the key around her neck. But other than its strange luster, the lock appears as any other.

Lock picks? I ask. Elias taught me to pick locks when he, Darin, and I were raiding Martial ghost wagons and freeing Scholars. I haven't practiced in months, but Elias insisted it was like learning to swim. Once you know how, you never forget. He also said Masks always carry a set of picks.

But Novius only looks away.

At midnight, when the soldiers are sleeping and Novius has taken up a watch, the jinn materializes out of the desert and sits beside me. The moonlight tinges the flames of her eyes blue, and there is an emptiness there that makes me shrink back.

"Tell me of yourself, girl." She settles herself just out of reach. "I allow you to speak."

At first, I try to keep my mouth closed. But she presses her lips together and the compulsion to talk is overwhelming. *Small truths, Laia,* I tell myself. *Don't give anything away.*

"My name is Laia of Serra," I say. "I am nineteen years old. I have a brother—"

The jinn waves my words away. "Tell me about your magic."

"I can disappear."

"When did you encounter this magic? Where did it come from?"

"A year and a half ago," I say. "When Martials broke into my home and I was trying to escape them. I didn't realize I had it." I pause, for I cannot say the magic came from Rehmat. The creature seemed adamant that its existence not be revealed.

"I—I thought I got it from an efrit I encountered when I was escaping Serra—"

The jinn's jaw tightens. "Efrits," she says. "Traitors and thieves. No efrit should have bestowed power upon you."

I relax marginally—and far too soon.

"What of the darkness within?" She leans forward. "When is the first time you felt that?"

I lick my lips. *Rehmat?* But the creature cannot risk appearing. It made that clear.

My silence has irked the jinn. "Speak!"

"The first time was near Kauf Prison," I say. "After I gave the Nightbringer my armlet."

"*Our* armlet," she informs me, a tightly leashed wrath stiffening her shoulders. "The Star was never yours, human."

At the edge of the clearing, Novius turns and looks at us for a long moment. His hands fall to his scim, and the jinn swings her attention toward him. Almost immediately, he twists back around, his spine pulled unnaturally upright. *Pride*, he'd told me when I asked for the jinn's weaknesses. *Anger.*

I try to memorize her movements, the play of emotion in her body. If the Nightbringer sent her after me, she must be close to him. But there is something about her that's barely restrained. A volatile hatred for us that she's not bothering to hide.

"Has the darkness within ever spoken to you?"

"Why—why would it speak to me?" When she doesn't respond, I go on. "What is it? Did the efrits put it in me?"

"I ask the questions, girl," she says. "Can you summon the darkness?"

I am thankful then that Rehmat has not responded to my appeals, because I can answer honestly. "No," I say. "I could summon my magic if you took off these chains."

The jinn smiles the way a hyena grins at its prey before it tears out its throat. "What good would that do you?" she says. "Even without the chains, your magic is weak. I would feel your presence, and hunt you as easily as a Mask hunts a wounded Scholar child."

154

The image is a cruel one and I glare at her. She snorts dismissively.

"Bah, your knowledge wouldn't fill a wight's thimble. But no matter. In two nights, we will be in Aish. The Meherya will open you up. Dig the truth out of that weak mind of yours. And it will hurt, girl."

"Please." I let a bit of desperation enter my voice; I have an idea. "Don't take me to him. Let me go. I will not attack you, I swear it. I would not harm you or kill you or use steel or summer rain against you—"

"Harm!" She laughs, but with that same cold fury. "Kill? Can a worm hurt a wolf, or an ant kill an eagle? We do not fear summer rain, and no blade forged by human or efrit, wight or ghul or wraith, nor any object of this world may kill us, rat. We are old creatures now, not soft and open as we were before. No matter how badly you want us to die, we cannot."

She sits back, attempting composure. But her body trembles and she purses her lips. I consider what she said. It is not true. It is not true because—

"You will forget the words I just spoke."

My mind blurs, and I find I am staring at the jinn, bewildered. She said something, I think. Something important. But the words slip away like sand through my fingers. *Remember,* some part of me screams. *You must remember! Your life depends on it. Thousands of lives depend on it!*

"You—" I put a hand to my temple. "You said something—"

"Sleep now, girl," the jinn whispers. "Dream of death."

As she rises, darkness closes over me. Mother walks through my nightmares. Father. Lis. Nan. Pop. Izzi. *Remember,* they say. *You must remember.*

But I cannot.

CHAPTER TWENTY-ONE

The Soul Catcher

Leaving the Waiting Place used to anger Mauth. But once he joined with me, he loosened the leash. Which is useful now, for Tribe Nasur trades in Aish, well south of the Waiting Place's border. Their *Fakira*, Aubarit, is one I trust completely. She may know something about the rot plaguing the forest.

As I windwalk, a howling gale sweeps through the long stretches of parched land, peppered with dirt devils and the occasional dust storm. The last time I dealt with weather this unnatural, the Nightbringer was behind it. I have no doubt that he and his ilk are behind this too. Only a day after I set out, I must take shelter.

It's been years since I traveled with a caravan, so I force myself to sift through my recollections of the Blood Shrike. We had plenty of hidey-holes out here when we were Fivers. One memory stands out: she dared me to burgle a massive pot of rice pudding bubbling in the middle of a Tribal camp. It was a stupid dare, but we were hungry and it smelled good. We escaped the Tribesmen who came after us only through sheer luck; we stumbled on a nearby cave and hid for three days.

As I make for that same cave now, I think about how, to this day, I've never tasted anything as good as that rice pudding. *It's sweeter because you almost died stealing it*, Helene said, grinning as we stuffed our faces. *Makes you appreciate every bite.*

The cave was near a massive escarpment several hours north of Aish, and I'm relieved to find that not only is it still there, but that the stream nearby runs high. I don't like being stuck—I don't like anything that will keep me from carrying out my duty. But at least I won't suffer from thirst.

I start a small fire just outside the cave and take in my reflection in the stream—my face, hair, and clothes are all a pale, sand-blasted beige.

"You might well be one of us, Banu al-Mauth," a deep voice says. "Though we would not be fool enough to ride winds such as these."

A diaphanous figure steps into the firelight. At first, I am confused, for despite its shape, it cannot possibly be human.

"Rowan Goldgale," the figure says. "We have met before."

I recognize the name. "Yes," I say. "You tried to murder my friend and me during the Trials. Now you and your fellow sand efrits are burning Tribal wagons and ransacking villages."

"All are actions we have been forced to take." Rowan steps closer, and I look behind him, wondering if he's brought his marauding fellows with him. But he shakes his sandy head.

"I come alone, Banu al-Mauth, in humility and sincerity, in the hopes that you might hear my plea."

I bid him sit and he crosses his legs on the floor of the cave, his form growing solid enough that I can make out a beak-like nose and thin lips.

"The Nightbringer moves against the human world." As Rowan speaks, he gestures. The sand on my face, hair, and clothes drifts into a cloud, dropping into a neat pile, leaving me looking marginally more human. "He has enslaved my kind and sworn us to silence, but his plans—"

The king of the sand efrits shudders and I lean forward. Efrits have always struck me as having a sort of malicious mischievousness. But Rowan couldn't be more serious.

Human world. I think of Laia, of the Blood Shrike, and my curiosity gets the better of me.

"What are his plans? He's already killing at will."

"My vows prevent me from sharing his plans, but—"

"That's convenient," I say. "Then why mention them?"

"Because my people read the desert winds as the Augurs read their dreams. They see a great commander who—"

"Do they see anything about the Waiting Place?" I ask. Rowan appears taken aback. I suppose kings rarely get interrupted.

"There is rot in the forest and I need to know why. Do your wind prophecies mention it?"

"Nay, Banu al-Mauth. But—"

"If you have nothing to tell me about the Nightbringer's plans or the Waiting Place," I say, "then I'm uninterested in what you saw." I stand, and the efrit, startled, rises as well.

"Please, Banu al-Mauth. You are destined for more than this—"

"Don't make me sing, Rowan." I think of a tune someone crooned to me long ago. *Efrit, efrit of the sand, a song is more than he can stand.* "I have a rubbish voice. Like a cat getting strangled."

"You will wish—"

"Lady Cassia Slaughter was a wrinkled old hag," I sing, "but it's said that her daughter was a mighty fine sha—"

The foul little sea shanty is the first song that comes to me, and before I finish the verse, Rowan howls and disappears, leaving only a cloud of dust in his wake.

When the cave is silent again, I turn to my dinner. The efrit was likely a ruse sent by the Nightbringer to distract me from my mission. The creatures cannot be trusted. It was efrits, after all, who tried to kill the Shrike and me during the Trials. Efrits who burned down Shaeva's cabin.

Still I feel uneasy. What if Rowan wasn't a ruse? What if I should have heard him out?

For a long time, I do not sleep. I sit by the fire, carving shapes into Laia's armlet. When I lay my head down, Mauth's magic finally stirs and smooths the unease away. By the time I wake, the efrit and his warning are forgotten.

«««

I reach Aish the next night, well after sunset. I haven't been here in years— not long ago it was nothing but a seasonal trading post built around an oasis. But since I came here as a Blackcliff Fiver, Aish has burgeoned into a permanent settlement.

Like most Tribal cities, its population is fluid. But the Commandant's assault on Sadh has swelled the city with refugees. The whitewashed buildings, built three and four stories high, are lined with archers. The many gates are flung open, each more crowded than the last with some people seeking shelter and others fleeing.

North of the walls, the Nasur encampment is in disarray. A steady stream of wounded trickles in—mostly women and children—all speaking of the fall of the city of Sadh.

"The Martials take no slaves, nor prisoners," a white-haired woman tells the Nasur *Kehanni*. "They just kill."

Briefly, I wonder if Laia ever arrived here. She was headed for Aish. *You're here for Aubarit, Soul Catcher. Not Laia.*

Tribe Nasur is not the only one taking refuge north of the city gates. I recognize the green and gold wagons of Tribe Nur, and the green and silver of Tribe Saif. As I survey the vast encampment, searching for the *Fakira*'s wagon, a familiar, dark-haired figure hurries past.

She holds two injured children, and at the sight of her, I nearly call out. I should know her from my own memories, but instead it is the memories Cain gave me of Laia and Helene and Keris that tell me who she is.

Mamie Rila. My adoptive mother.

She hands the children over to a Tribal healer and hurries back the way she came. Then, quite suddenly, she stops short. Tentatively, she searches the darkness.

"E-Elias?"

"Banu al-Mauth now, Mamie Rila." I emerge into the light.

She stiffens and bows her head. "Of course." Her voice is low, but it cannot hide her bitterness. "Why are you here, Banu al-Mauth?"

"I must speak with Aubarit Ara-Nasur."

She considers for a moment, then nods. "If any here see you . . ." She sighs. "They will think you are here to help. Come."

Mamie avoids the chaotic center of the camp and heads to the outer circle of wagons. The warriors of Tribe Nasur stand guard in the empty spaces, glaring out at the dark, waiting perhaps for the shine of a Martial blade, or worse, the swift-moving flames that herald approaching jinn.

"There." Mamie nods past the guards, to a wagon nestled in the shadows of Aish's wall.

"Thank you." I leave her, slipping past Tribe Nasur guards and toward Aubarit's wagon. Multicolored lamps twinkle brightly within, and when I rap on the door, it opens almost immediately.

"Banu al-Mauth!"

Aubarit holds a shroud in her hands, upon which she has sewn the geometric patterns of her tribe, traditional for a burial. She drops into a curtsy, flustered at my sudden arrival, and moves aside to let me in. "Forgive me, I did not know—"

"Sit, *Fakira*." I take salt from the bowl beside her door and put it to my lips. "Be at ease."

She sits at the edge of her bench, fingers twisted deeply within the shroud, the exact opposite of "at ease."

"Would you like some—" She gestures to the hot tea on a table beside her bench, pulling another cup from the cupboard above, but I shake my head.

"Aubarit, I need to know if you—"

"Before you begin, Banu al-Mauth," the girl says, "you must forgive us. There have been so many dead—but there are not enough *Fakirs*. You must be inundated, but the war—"

"How many dead since yesterday?"

"We've buried two dozen," she whispers. "I was only able to do rites for half. The rest—their souls were already gone. I—I did not want to send you so many—"

The import of her words turns my blood to ice.

"The Waiting Place doesn't have too many ghosts, *Fakira*," I say. "It has too few. I passed only a dozen ghosts in the last week. I thought you and the other Fakirs had passed on those killed in Keris Veturia's assault. But if you only did the rites for half, and if the other *Fakirs* are similarly inundated, then there should be hundreds of ghosts pouring into the Waiting Place."

The *Fakira* nearly drops the shroud, her fear palpable. "The wall—"

"It holds. The ghosts are not escaping into the human world. If what you say is true, they are not arriving at all. Those who do enter don't wish to move on. Not because of the suffering they endured in life, but because they fear what lies on the other side."

A brief terror shines in Aubarit's eyes, but I don't have time for her fear. "They speak of a great maelstrom," I say. "A hunger that wishes to devour them. What do the Mysteries say of this maelstrom? This hunger?"

Aubarit's dark skin pales, her sprinkling of freckles standing out starkly. "I have heard of no maelstrom in the Mysteries. There is the *Sumandar a Dhuka*, the Sea of Suffering—"

"What is that?"

"I—I—"

At Blackcliff, our Centurions would slap us when we were too gripped by fear to carry out an order. Now I understand why.

"Speak, *Fakira*!"

"*And though the Sea of Suffering churns, ever restless, verily does Mauth preside, a bulwark against its hunger.*"

Laia's voice whispers in my mind. *I saw something, Soul Catcher. An ocean filled with—skies, I do not know.*

"What else do you know about this sea?"

"It is the repository of human suffering," Aubarit says. "All the sorrow and pain you take from the spirits and give to Mauth—it goes into the Sea. As you stand guardian between the ghosts and the world of the living, Mauth is the sentinel between the Sea of Suffering and our world."

Aubarit puts down her tea, more agitated with every word. "But the Mysteries are vast, Banu al-Mauth. We have no magic to aid us in their learning, only words passed down through the centuries. We do not even know their source. Your answer might be in a part of the Mysteries called the Signs—but I never learned them. My grandfather died before he could teach me."

162

Him and a dozen other *Fakirs*. The Nightbringer's handiwork.

"Are there any *Fakirs* who know the Signs in their entirety, Aubarit?"

"*Fakir* An-Zia," she says. "I do not know if he escaped Sadh."

"There must be some way—" I stop at the sound of a hurried knock at the wagon door.

"*Fakira*." I recognize Mamie's voice from outside. "Banu al-Mauth, come quickly."

I pull open the door. "Return later," I bark, but she blocks the door before I can shut it.

"Fire on the horizon," she says. "We must flee, or else take shelter in Aish."

Aubarit clutches the shroud close. "Fire—"

"Jinn, *Fakira*." Mamie grabs the girl's arm and pulls her from the wagon. "The jinn are coming."

CHAPTER TWENTY-TWO

The Blood Shrike

Thank the skies for Heera's warning, for when the first fur-clad Karkaun comes roaring toward me, my daggers are unsheathed and sinking into his gut before I can get a good look at his face. The next impales himself on my waiting scim, and if this is all they have, I will fight every Karkaun in this city until Madam Heera's brothel splits at the seams from their eviscerated corpses.

I kick the bowl with Heera's blood. Curse those bastards for thinking they could use her so. Skies know how long she had to suffer before delivering her warning.

"Back, you filth!" Faris bellows from outside.

The barbarians have found him and Septimus. As Karkauns spill from the bedrooms and hallways, I make my way back to the stairs. These are not their best warriors. Just the vanguard sent to try to kill us, to overwhelm us with sheer numbers.

"Ik tachk mort fid iniqant fi! Ik tachk mort fid iniqant fi!"

Above, the chanting quickens, and Grímarr's voice rises above the others.

The back door splinters and bursts open, and a dead barbarian comes flying through. Faris's giant frame fills the doorway and he stalks in, shoving aside Karkauns until he's beside me.

"What in the hells is this, Shrike?"

"Grímarr is preparing a rite," I say above the din. "I'm his guest of honor. Where's Septimus?"

A tall Karkaun rushes me. "You dare wield steel, Martial whore!" he screams, scim held high. Too high. I run him through and then take off his head.

"Outside picking them off." Faris kicks the Karkaun's head to the side, his scims flying at the enemies still pouring into the hallway and down the stairs. "They have us surrounded."

"We need to get up there," I say. "He's just biding his time until he's done with this skies-forsaken chant."

We fight our way back toward the stairs. But the barbarians keep coming, slipping on the blood-slicked ground, the deaths of their fellows only feeding their furor.

"Front door, Faris," I scream at him. "Break a bleeding path!"

He barrels through the Karkauns and I follow in his wake, stabbing and slashing until we spill out into a street littered with bodies—Septimus's handiwork. Through the open window above, Grímarr's chanting reaches a fever pitch. *"IK TACHK MORT FID INIQANT FI!"*

"Tell me you have a grappling hook."

Faris shakes his head, gasping for breath. I hope to the skies that his clothes are sticking to him because of all the Karkauns he's killed, and not because he's about to die on me.

"We'll have to jump." Faris nods to a pale stone building behind the brothel, with a balcony a dozen feet from the brothel's roof.

"Go, Shrike!" Septimus calls from a sniper's nest somewhere above us. An arrow whizzes past, thudding into the chest of a Karkaun creeping up on me. "I'll cover you!"

I bolt away from the brothel and double back down an alley. As I do, I get an impression of faces—watching us. Women and children mostly, for the men have been gone for months. The only boys left are those who will grow up to be sacrificed by the Karkauns.

Unless I stop them.

Yells echo behind us, and a band of Karkauns appears. Three of them fall upon Faris, and one leaps at me, knocking me off my feet. My scim clatters to the ground and my attacker pins my body, his weight and stench stealing my breath. His meaty hands close about my throat. I twist and claw at him, but he just laughs, spittle dribbling into his pale beard.

Suddenly, his hands loosen and blood spurts from his mouth. He topples over, and a dark-skinned, curly-haired Martial woman steps forward and yanks her kitchen knife from the Karkaun's throat.

"Blood Shrike." She offers me a hand. "I'm Neera. How can I help?"

"Get us to that balcony." I point, and Neera is off and running.

Faris and I both grab shields from the fallen Karkauns, and in half a minute, we have reached the balcony across from the brothel.

The distance between the buildings seems greater now—looking down makes me ill. *Don't think about it.* I back up, run, and leap, landing so heavily on the brothel's roof that, to my horror, I slip off. But then Faris is there, pulling me up with a grunt. More Karkauns approach, and we skitter across the roof until we are directly above an open window that rattles from the force of Grímarr's chant.

"Ready?" I ask Faris.

He swings down from the roof through the open window, and bowls over a pair of guards. I follow to find myself in a sprawling room cleared of furniture with a door at one end. Grímarr stands over a larger brazier that emits clouds of choking white smoke. He is stripped to the waist and painted in woad, his eyes rolled into the back of his head.

A line of Grímarr's guards, all armed with crossbows, stand in front of him, facing the window. All at once, bolt after bolt hits my shield and Faris's.

"Bleeding hells!" Faris lurches back, his shield cracking. Mine splits down the middle, and he flings me behind him, covering me until the Karkauns run out of bolts.

The crossbows drop—and the guards have no time to reload before we are upon them.

As I take out one Karkaun, and another, and another, bootsteps sound from outside Heera's quarters.

"The door, Faris!"

He gets there just as it bursts open, and falls beneath a wave of fresh attackers.

"I was wrong about you, Blood Shrike." Grímarr does not appear at all alarmed that the men protecting him lie dead. He grins, blood in his teeth. "I thought you were but a woman, but you—"

He barely ducks the throwing knife I fling at his throat. I shake my head. Men and their skies-forsaken bleating. They think words matter in a fight when really, they're just a distraction.

"Fight, then, girl, fight!" He roars and beckons me toward him. "The heat of your fresh-spilled blood will be as ambrosia on my lips."

Would that I could issue a Karkaun blood challenge. From what Dex told me, they are not complex. One must spill one's own blood, cast all blades aside, and fight without weaponry to the death. The loser's body is desecrated, their name, deeds, and history obliterated. It would be a just end for Grímarr.

But right now, I just need to kill the bastard. Quickly.

Faris is on his feet, beating back the onslaught of Karkauns at the door, and I cut through the three who stand between me and Grímarr. As they fall, I ram into the warlock, knocking him to his knees. But he bats away the blade I try to shove into his heart, and wraps an arm around me, pulling me into a choking embrace. I cannot breathe, only claw at him as he rips my armor back and bites into my neck like a rabid wolf.

I draw a dagger from my belt and stab him in the thigh. His arm loosens and I punch him, the first blow breaking his nose, the second sending blood and teeth flying. He reels back but rolls to his feet immediately, and I draw my scim. Blood pours down my neck, making my fury burn hotter.

Grímarr is too fast to leave himself exposed to a mortal blow, but I open up his milky skin with a half dozen quick slashes, just deep enough to slow him down.

"Shrike!" Faris is on one knee, still fighting, but fading quickly. *Now or never, Shrike.*

"You cannot kill me—" Grímarr advances, a shield on one arm. "*Ik tachk mort fid iniqant fi.* Your blood is the conduit by which—"

"Again with the talking!" I pivot a half step back and feint with the dagger in my right hand. He comes within range of my scim, and I whip it up, intending to take off his head.

But one of his lackeys bull-rushes me. I drive the dagger into the bastard's guts and slash up with my scim, cutting clean through Grímarr's arm.

He screams, a brief, high-pitched sound. Then his men are abandoning the fight with Faris, surrounding Grímarr and dragging him away from us, out the door, and down the stairs.

"Come on!" Faris grabs my hand and pulls. "There are too many, Shrike."

"Wait—" I sweep up the severed arm and take it with me—out the window, down the balcony, and into the street. Here, it is quiet, the Karkauns who had set upon us either dead or fled.

"Septimus!" I call out, but there is no answer from the Mask's perch, on the fourth story of a building across from the brothel.

"He's dead, Shrike. A Karkaun arrow took him out." Neera appears from the doorway of what must be her home, gesturing us in as the thud of boots echoes from close by. Once inside, she hands me a cloak.

"For the, ah—" She nods to Grímarr's arm, dripping blood all over the floor.

"Sorry for the mess." I tear a few strips off the cloak for Faris to bind his wounds, and wrap the arm quickly. "We need to get to Taius Square."

I was supposed to hang Grímarr's headless body in the square. His arm will have to do.

Neera nods to her back door. "It's the rooftops or the houses." She glances at Faris, who is ghastly pale, and then at the seeping bite wound on my neck. "Houses, I think."

Two children peek out at me from behind her skirt. "You've done enough," I say. "Get out of here. Take your children. If anyone tells the Karkauns you took us in—"

"No Martial would say a word." Neera's voice is hoarse with emotion. "Nor the Scholars. There are no traitors here, Shrike." Her eyes are fierce. "We've been waiting for you."

"Come morning," I tell her, "there will be a message in Taius Square. Tell as many as you can."

We hurry into her courtyard, where one of her neighbors waits and ushers us through a door. There, another woman, this one a wizened old Scholar, guides us to the next house. And so we make our way through the city. At each house, we whisper the message.

The Shrike has come. She's struck at the heart of the Karkauns. When she comes again, it will be time to fight.

Seeing the fervor in the eyes of my people makes me wish I could lead the attack now. But we need time to shore up our supply of weapons and smuggle them into the city. We need time for the message to spread so that when we do attack, the women will be prepared to fight.

Fifth bell has long since tolled when Faris and I emerge from a shuttered clockmaker's shop into Taius Square. The sight of it—of the pyres and what still smokes upon them—should make me angry. But mostly, I feel sick, numb and bleeding from a dozen wounds, and nauseous from the stink.

"Bleeding hells, girl." Quin appears out of the shadows. "You're late." His armor is splashed with blood, but he doesn't appear to have any wounds. Musa materializes behind him, limping.

"Good in a fight." Quin nods to the Scholar approvingly. "Better luck than Ilean anyway. He's dead." The old man looks me over. "I don't see a body, Shrike."

"Grímarr got away." Saying it makes me want to scream. "He knew we were coming—flooded the brothel with his fighters. We'll have to make do. Is the square cleared out?"

"We got most of the guards," Musa says. "But more are coming. You have a few minutes."

"Good," I say. "You two get the hells out of here in case I cannot."

"Come with us, Shrike," Musa urges. "The Karkauns got the message—"

"The message isn't for them. Go."

When Marcus was Emperor, he hung bodies on a whitewashed wall at the south end of the square. I make for that wall, Faris following. As we reach it, I hand Grímarr's stinking arm to my friend. He grins and impales it high up with a spear from one of the fallen guards. I take the blood-sodden cloak and, beneath the arm, leave my message. *LOYAL TO THE END.* It is a call to arms and a reminder that I have not forgotten my people. That we will fight.

"*Ikfan Dem!*"

The shout comes from yards away. The Karkaun patrol.

Faris hauls me from the wall and I wince, putting a hand to my neck where the bite wound still bleeds. Arrows ping near my head.

"Come on," he says. "There's a grate on the other side of the square. Leads right to the tunnels. We can make it if we're fast."

We weave swiftly through the pyres. But there are too many barbarians, and there is too little cover.

"Shrike!" Faris calls a warning just as an arrow slices through the air. My back jerks as the shaft cuts through my soft clothing and into my shoulder. Within seconds, my shirt is soaked with blood. Another arrow lances me through the thigh.

"F-Faris." I drop to my knees, and though he has arrows sticking out of his arm and shoulder, he hauls me up and we stagger, step by torturous step. Twice more, his body jolts as he's struck. But he keeps going, dragging me with him past the pyres, across an open stretch of cobblestone, and into a narrow street littered with bones and glass and rubbish.

"There." I see a dull disk of copper embedded into the stones just ahead. "The grate." I collapse, pawing at it. My head spins. I'll survive this, if only I can get away. Get somewhere I can heal.

"Can't—open it—"

Faris grabs the grate and wrenches it up. The howls of the Karkauns close in.

My friend glances toward the square, then at me. If we go down this grate together, they will follow us almost immediately, and they will catch us.

"Shrike," Faris says. "Listen to me—"

"Don't say it," I tell him. "Don't you *bleeding* say it, Faris Candelan."

"We can't both survive," he says. His skin is blanched whiter than bone, body shuddering from loss of blood. "They'll be here in seconds. But if I stay, I can give you the time to get away."

"I'm hit too. I might not make it." My head feels fuzzy, and the shouts are louder now. Too loud.

"You'll make it. Go."

"Captain Faris Candelan, I order you to get down into that tunnel, *now*—"

"I'm done," he says. "I've got one good battle left in me. Let me fight it. The Empire needs its Shrike. It doesn't need me." His pale eyes bore into me, and I cannot speak.

No. *No.* I've known Faris since we were six, starving in Blackcliff's culling pen. It's Faris who could make Elias laugh in his darkest moods, who helped keep me sane when Marcus ordered us to hunt him. Faris who took me to Madam Heera's for the first time and who protected my sister. *Not Faris. Please, not Faris.*

"I said, I *order*—" I do not finish. He grabs me by the straps on my armor and shoves me down the grate. I land heavily, knees buckling.

"Faris, you *idiot*—"

For a moment, his silhouette is all I see, backlit by dawn breaking above.

"It was an honor to serve by your side, Helene Aquilla," he says. "Give my best to Elias, if you see him. And for skies' sake, put Harper out of his misery. Poor bastard deserves a roll in the hay after all you've put him through."

I burst into wild laughter, my face wet with salt or blood, I know not which. The Karkauns bay like hounds, and Faris lifts his scim and shoves the grate closed with his boot. Blades clash, and I hear him roar a battle cry as he fights his last.

"Loyal to the end!"

I stumble toward a torch flickering just ahead. Where did it come from? *Who bleeding cares. Get to it.* Just as I reach it, the sounds of fighting above cease. I listen for long minutes, hoping the grate will move. Hoping my friend will appear.

But he doesn't.

He's dead. Bleeding hells. Faris is dead. Dead because of me, like my parents and sister and Cook and Demetrius and Leander and Tristas and Ennis, and I do not deserve to live when they all died.

Perhaps death will find me too, down here in the dark veins of a city that I should have saved.

But no. I cannot die. Too much is at stake. And too much has been lost already. The Karkauns will find their dead countrymen. They will find Faris. They will come after me.

The Empire needs its Shrike. The last thing I want to do is move, but I drag myself to my hands and knees. I hold my bleeding body and crawl, hoping to the skies that my friend did not just give his life for nothing.

CHAPTER TWENTY-THREE

Laia

On the second day of my captivity, the jinn aims us south, and within hours, the Duskan Sea is lost to view. Soon, we are deep within the Tribal desert. Eerie rock formations rise into the sky, each a hundred wind-blasted shades of the sun. Purple rain clouds lay heavy on the horizon, and the freezing wind carries the sharp, almost medicinal smell of creosote.

Every few hours, the jinn ranges ahead on her mount. Before she goes, she reinforces the compulsion she's already placed upon us by again demanding silence.

But on the morning of the third day, she forgets.

Most of the soldiers do not notice, and ride onward with dead eyes, bodies swaying to the clip-clop of the horses' hooves. Only Mask Novius, riding beside me, jerks his head up as she leaves. A muscle pops on his jaw as he strains against the jinn woman's control.

I watch him surreptitiously. His mask gleams in the dreary winter sunlight, and though he stares straight ahead, I sense he is aware of my every move.

Rehmat will not or cannot help me. I have no magic. I tried to contact Darin—to no avail. We travel at unnatural speeds. If I do not act soon, I will be in Aish—and the Nightbringer's hands—by nightfall tomorrow. Skies only know what he will do with me. Not kill me, perhaps. But there are things worse than death. My mother's fate as the Commandant's slave taught me that.

Far ahead, the jinn is a distant silhouette on the horizon. With utmost care, I rest my left palm where Novius can see it.

Help, I trace slowly. *I have a plan.*

A minute passes. Then another. *You will not set her free or aid in her escape.* He cannot break free of the jinn. Perhaps I was a fool to think that any of us could.

After a few minutes, though, I hear a strange sound. Like a roar through a mouth with a hand held over it.

Novius looks at me now, fury etched into every crag of his face. I realize that it is he who has made the sound. That he has broken free, at least a little bit, from the jinn's control.

Quite suddenly, he drives his horse into mine. If I could, I would cry out. My mount stumbles, throwing its head back in agitation, lifting its front legs. I grab for the pommel, but it slips out of my fingers. My back meets the desert floor with such force that I nearly bite through my tongue.

The Mask might hate being controlled, but he's a Martial, through and through. I glare at him and he meets my gaze with that same barely quelled rage. He dismounts, grabs me by my bound arms, and shoves me toward my horse.

In the distance, the jinn wheels her steed around and gallops back toward us.

"What is this?" Her beast whinnies in complaint as she yanks him to a halt. "What happened?" She looks at me. "Speak, girl! And you will not deceive me."

"I—I fell off my horse."

"Why did you fall off your horse? Was it on purpose? A distraction? Tell the truth!"

"Not on purpose," I say honestly. "I lost my balance." Unwillingly, I glance over at the Mask. The jinn narrows her eyes.

"Did Novius speak to you? Are you two planning something?"

"No," I say, thanking the skies that the Mask's muffled bellow could hardly be called speech.

The jinn observes me for long moments before turning away. Novius helps me back onto my horse, and the jinn rides ahead again, remaining close enough that I cannot write a message to Novius.

But far enough that I can hide the scroll he slipped me into my sleeve.

«««

I do not get a chance to read the scroll that night—the jinn watches too closely. The next morning, a powerful, dry gale churns up a dust storm. The jinn urges the horses onward, until visibility is so poor that they groan and snort. She forces them toward an outcropping of rock, where we settle down to wait. An hour later, with the sun a rusty disk overhead, the sandstorm has not abated.

The jinn appears wan, almost sickly as she crouches beside a boulder. The rest of the soldiers stand beside their horses, unnaturally still, like Mariner windup dolls frozen in place.

As the wind blasts us, the jinn's blazing eyes remain fixed on me. I distract myself by thinking of the last time I traveled this desert. Izzi was still alive. It's been so long since I thought about my friend—her gentle manner and quiet rebellion. The way she loved Cook like a mother. She was another sister, even if not by blood.

I miss her.

"Girl." The jinn woman's voice brings me back to my predicament. "You've walked these lands before. How long do these storms last? Speak."

176

"A few hours at most." My voice is a croak. "We'll need to clean the horses' eyes before setting off again. Or they'll go sand-blind."

The jinn nods, but does not silence me again. Perhaps she is too tired from so many days of using her power on us. Or perhaps, as Novius suggested, she is at her weakest.

To my relief, she stops staring at me and rises to walk among the soldiers. So slowly I am hardly moving, I reach for the scroll. Then I bend my head into my knees, as if shielding my eyes.

I dare not give myself more light, so it takes me a minute to read the cramped writing. And once I've read it, I am baffled. I'd expected instructions on how to get the Mask's lock picks. The outlines of a plan to break free.

But of course, he couldn't give me that. The jinn ordered him not to help me. Still—this makes no sense.

No blade forged by human or efrit, wight or ghul or wraith, nor any object of this world may kill us. No matter how badly you want us to die, we cannot.

What do the words mean? Why would he—

The memory comes rushing back so quickly that I am dizzy from it. She spoke these words to me before—and ordered me to forget them. But the Mask was listening too, and she gave him no such order.

The jinn is still among the soldiers, so I read the scroll one more time to commit the words to memory, and then let the wind carry it away. The second part of what she said is a lie. Jinn can be killed. I saw it with my own eyes.

The Nightbringer killed Shaeva with a blade. And she was at least as old as the jinn locked in the grove. Perhaps older.

I close my eyes and try to remember what the blade was. A black sickle that glittered like diamond, wickedly curved and attached to a short hilt. It was a strange metal—one I hadn't seen before.

But I have seen it since, I realize, staring down at the glittering chains binding me.

No blade forged by human or efrit, wight or ghul or wraith, nor any object of this world may kill us.

Jinn-forged then. Created out of a metal only they can access.

Or perhaps the sickle has no special properties. Perhaps the Nightbringer used a weapon to stab Shaeva, but magic to kill her.

But no—at the very least, these chains suppress my magic, and I am a mere human. What would they do to jinn, who are born of magic?

I am so consumed with thoughts of the sickle that I do not notice the storm has passed until the jinn kicks me and orders me to my feet.

It is early evening when I spot the strange dark splotch on the horizon. It looks to be a large lake of some kind, its currents flashing silver in the fading light. Then the wind carries the sound of horses, the smell of leather and steel. And I understand that it is not a lake but an army, that the flashes are not waves but weapons.

The city of Aish is under attack.

The jinn gives Novius orders to lead us toward the city before putting boot to flank and ranging ahead. A moment later, a whisper tickles my ear.

"Laia." Rehmat does not appear, but it sounds as if it is right next to me. "Let us get you free of those damnable chains."

"I thought you could not help," I whisper back.

"Khuri goes to speak with her kin. We have a few moments. First, you need your weapon—"

"How do you know her name?"

"I know many things you do not, child. Novius has your blade. Once you are invisible you can take it from him. Now—these chains. I think you can—"

"The Nightbringer"—I cut Rehmat off—"used a sickle to kill Shaeva. Do you know anything of it?"

"I know what lives in your memories."

I flush, thinking about the other things it's probably seen in my memory, but then push my embarrassment aside. Rehmat's answer was . . . careful. Too careful.

"Did Shaeva die because of the blade?" I ask. "Or the Nightbringer's magic?"

"The blade."

The Mask glances over and I realize I probably look mad, gabbling to myself. I lower my voice. "If all you know of the blade is what's in my memory, how do you know it can kill jinn? And why the skies did you not tell me about it?"

"The weapon will be impossible to take from the Nightbringer, Laia," Rehmat says. "And it is not guaranteed to destroy him."

"But the sickle can kill *other* jinn." I want to shout, but settle for a furious whisper. "The ones rampaging across the Tribal desert, leaving death and terror in their wake. The ones out there." I nod toward Aish and the army inching ever closer to it.

"Laia." Rehmat flickers in agitation and I wonder if the creature is not an "it" but a "he," for there is something irritatingly male about its obduracy. "We need to understand the Nightbringer's weaknesses if we wish to stop him. We need his story. Your plan to find the Tribal *Kehannis* was a wise one. But to carry it out, you must escape. That is a war you ride toward."

"It is indeed," I say, and the idea that comes to me is one Afya would approve of, as it is utterly mad.

"Come, child. Do not be a fool—"

"Why are you afraid?" Until now, Rehmat has seemed wise if a bit high-handed. I have never sensed its alarm, like I do now. "Because you think the Nightbringer will discover you? Destroy you?"

"Yes," Rehmat says after a long hesitation. "That is what I fear."

No, it is not. I know this immediately. The creature lies. Conceals. This is the first time I've felt it for certain, and an odd pang goes through me. Rehmat is like no one I have ever met or even heard of, but I have grown to trust it. I thought it was my ally.

"Let me help you, Laia." Rehmat modulates its tone at the last instant so it sounds calm and level-headed, instead of like an overlord. "You must not fall into the Nightbringer's hands in the midst of a war—"

"Falling into his hands in the midst of a war," I tell the creature, "is exactly what I have to do."

CHAPTER TWENTY-FOUR

The Soul Catcher

A horn trumpets from the southern buildings of Aish, echoing from guard tower to guard tower, a frantic blare. The wind picks up, carrying the stench of singed earth and blood.

The Tribal encampment is in chaos. Men and women throw children into wagons and sweep up belongings. Cookfires spark. Camels and horses groan as their masters work frantically to buckle saddles and harnesses.

But when the Tribespeople see me, many of them stop what they are doing, hope dawning in their eyes.

"Banu al-Mauth! Are you here to aid us?"

"Will you destroy the jinn?"

I ignore them as Tribe Nasur's guards converge on Aubarit's wagon. "*Fakira*," one of them says. "We must take shelter in the city before the gates are closed."

The Tribe's silver-haired *Kehanni* follows them, frowning. "Better to flee into the desert," she says. "The Martials will be occupied with Aish. They will not hunt us."

"Tribe Saif will flee," Mamie Rila speaks. "Even if they pursue us, we can evade them."

She turns to me. "Help us, Banu al-Mauth," she says. "There are too many jinn. Too many Martials. And a city filled with innocent people who did nothing to invite this invasion. You could use your magic to defeat the enemy—"

"That is not how the magic works, *Kehanni*."

"But if you helped, fewer would die." Aubarit grabs my arm, holding on

181

to me even when I attempt to shake her off. "There would be fewer ghosts to pass—"

But I do not seek fewer ghosts. I seek to understand what is happening to them.

What if it is the Nightbringer's doing? Laia's words echo in my head. The few *Fakirs* who could have answered my questions were murdered by the Nightbringer. In the battles he has fought, where hundreds of ghosts should flow into the Waiting Place, none arrive.

Perhaps this is an opportunity to see why.

"Make for water." I raise my voice, and the Tribespeople nearby fall silent. "The jinn hate it."

"The only water is in Aish's wells," Mamie Rila says.

"The Malikh escarpment has water." The information costs me nothing. "Stream is running high."

The horns of Aish call out again, a low thrum that elicits cries from across the encampment. The approaching fire is distant no longer. The jinn are here.

Aubarit and Mamie's questions fall upon the unfeeling wind as I stream away, past the Tribespeople scrambling to get into the city, past the refugees from Sadh looking for shelter where there will be none. Keris Veturia's army will pour through Aish's many gates. The wide streets that are perfect for Tribal caravans, open markets, and traveling players will become killing fields.

Such is the world of the living.

I pull up my hood so no one recognizes me and scan the horizon. Screams echo from the south, and flames light up the sky, moving like whirling typhoons. Jinn. The fear of the Tribespeople curdles the air, turning the cold night bitter.

A rooftop will offer a better view, and I spot a trellis I could climb. But it is blocked by a wagon with an old man and two little children inside. A woman struggles to hitch her horse to it while her daughter, barely tall enough to reach the harnesses, tries to buckle them.

I look around for another place to climb. Finding none, I lift the child into the wagon and buckle the straps for her. The girl peers at me, and then offers me a brilliant smile. It is so incongruous with the panic around us that I freeze.

"Banu al-Mauth!" she whispers.

I put my finger to my lips and secure the wagon shafts. The child's mother sighs in relief.

"Thank you, brother—"

"Make for Nur," I tell her, keeping my hood low. "Warn them of what's coming. Tell others to do the same. Go."

The woman climbs into the wagon seat and snaps the reins. But only yards away, she is slowed by people cramming into the streets. Her daughter looks back at me, hopeful, like I will clear the way for them.

I turn from the child, climb the trellis, and head east, toward the sound of thundering Martial drums. A distant, unified shout follows: *"Imperator Invictus! Imperator Invictus!"*

Keris Veturia has arrived. With her, an army to do the murdering and pillaging after the jinn weaken the city. Her forces are still a good distance away. But a vanguard of riders ranges out from the main force to cut down those Tribespeople who are unfortunate enough to be in their way.

My mother leads them. She is easy enough to recognize, distinctive for her diminutive size—but more for the brutality with which she kills. She wears steel-and-leather armor and wields a long spear that allows her to impale easily from atop a swift-footed white mare. As I watch, she kills two women, an elderly man, and a child who stands paralyzed as she thunders toward him and mows him down.

I should feel nothing. Emotion is a distraction from my duty.

Yet my mind recoils at the sight of my mother blithely murdering a child. Though I rarely wonder about my father, I think of him now. Perhaps he, too, loved to cause pain. Perhaps that is why I care so little for the living. Perhaps my parents' lack of humanity is why I was able to become the Chosen of Death.

Suddenly, Keris wheels her horse about and scans Aish's skyline. Her gaze settles on me. Strange. I could be an archer. A soldier. Anyone.

Yet somehow, she knows it's me. I feel it in my bones. We gaze at each other, connected by blood and violence and all our sins.

Then she pulls her horse back around and disappears into the band of soldiers returning to the main army. Shaken, I turn away and windwalk the roofs toward the jinn-spawned flames inking the southern sky. I streak past cookfires and rope beds, over pigeon coops and squawking chickens. The sounds of war fill my ears.

I reach for my scims, forgetting that they've been in my cabin for months. I want to fight, I realize. I want a battle that isn't in my head. A battle that can be won based on physical strength and training and strategy. I could find a weapon. Fight with the Tribespeople. It would feel good to do it.

The slow weight of Mauth's magic pulls at me, a reminder, and I shake myself. Battles mean death. And I have dealt out enough death. *Nightbringer. Find the Nightbringer.*

The closer I get to the southern edge of the city, the worse the flames are, until I have to stop at a water pump to soak a kerchief.

Screams echo from below me, and a building crumbles to dust before my eyes, a cloaked jinn man staring at it fixedly before turning away and bringing down another. Behind him, a fire-formed jinn hovers in the air as if it's her own chariot. An unnaturally dry wind follows her, fanning the flames.

Stalking the streets below is a jinn in full flame, her body pulsing with hatred. I recognize her instantly. Umber. Her glaive spins as she cuts down any who block her path, and others who are desperately fleeing from her. As I watch, she lifts one man in the air and crushes his windpipe—slowly.

His spirit leaves his body and, for a moment, hovers near it. Then the air shimmers like a cat's eyes flickering in the shadows. The spirit disappears.

It does not go to the Waiting Place. Or the other side. I would feel it, if that were the case—I would know in my bones. So what in the ten hells am I seeing?

I skulk along the rooftops, following Umber, watching as she kills. The air around her shimmers and flickers as soul after soul vanishes. Each disappearance leaves behind an emptiness, a void that weighs heavy on the air.

Before Umber spots me, I windwalk away, making for Aish's tallest building, the Martial garrison. Never have I wished more for Shaeva. For her cool competence and vast well of knowledge. She would know what is happening. She would know how to stop it.

But she is not here, so I must make sense of this alone.

To the Nightbringer, Scholars—and their allies, the Tribes and Mariners—are the enemy. Prey. Meant to be destroyed. And yet, despite freeing thousands of his kindred from the jinn grove, he is primarily using a Martial army to carry out all the murder. The only logical conclusion is that the jinn cannot fight humans head-on.

Perhaps they have been weakened by their imprisonment. Perhaps their magic is limited. All magic comes from Mauth and even I have noticed a dip in Mauth's strength, a torpidity.

So what, I argue with myself. *The Nightbringer is stealing ghosts to fuel his magic?*

It is as good an idea as any. If Mauth is the source of all magic, and he is Death, then it would follow that ghosts might be linked to that magic.

If I could get to the Nightbringer himself—I might be able to test the theory further. I reach the garrison's flat rooftop and drop out of my wind-walk, shading my eyes. The buildings all around are engulfed in flame. I won't be able to see anything from here.

As I make to leave, something gleams in the air. A figure appears out of the smoke billowing across the roof, cloaked and flame-eyed, with a wickedly curved scythe held loosely in one hand. It is attached to a long handle and its dark shine is familiar.

The scythe, I realize, used to be a sickle. A sickle that the Nightbringer used to kill Shaeva months ago.

"Have you come to thank me, Usurper?"

The Nightbringer speaks softly, but his voice no longer makes my skin crawl. Nor do I feel apprehension when I look at him. He is but a living creature, who loves and hates, desires and mourns. A creature who is interfering with my work in the Waiting Place.

Mauth's magic rises, sensing the threat. "You tamper with the spirits, jinn," I say. "You tamper with Mauth. You must cease."

"Then you are not here to thank me." The feigned surprise in the Nightbringer's voice grates on my nerves. "I cannot think why. There is so much less work for you, now that you have no ghosts to pass."

"What are you doing with the spirits?"

"Silence, worm!" Umber appears out of the flames beside the Night-bringer. "You dare to speak to the Meherya thus? Faaz! Azul!" Two jinn materialize from the flames. "Khuri! Talis!"

"Peace, Umber." The Nightbringer sheaths his scythe and four more jinn appear. The first two—Faaz and Azul—I saw breaking buildings and altering the weather. The third—Khuri—is in her shadow form. The last, whom I assume is Talis, wears his human face, and I recognize his dark eyes and compact body. He accompanied Umber after I killed Cain.

And he was the jinn who cast thoughts into the minds of Laia and the others. He brought their deepest fears and darkest moments to life.

The Nightbringer glides closer. Shadows seethe around him, deeper than before and eerily alive. They writhe with some fey devilry that drags on him like a weight. Despite that, his power is unaffected. If anything, he appears stronger.

The air flickers behind the Nightbringer. Another jinn. One Umber did not call to. I squint—what is he doing? I take a single step toward that jinn, for there is a whiff of ghost about him, a sense of the dead nearby.

That is as far as I get. The Nightbringer snaps his fingers and Khuri steps into the shadows, reappearing seconds later with a limp human figure.

"You are Mauth's creature now, boy. So dedicated to your duty," the Nightbringer says. "Shall we test that dedication?"

The figure is bound with chains made of the same sparkling metal as the Nightbringer's scythe. Her clothing is dark, and her long hair obscures her face. But I know who it is. I know her shape and her grace because the Augur put her in my head and I cannot get her out.

The Nightbringer grabs Laia's hair and yanks her head back. "If I slit her throat, Soul Catcher, would you care?"

"Why are you taking the ghosts?" I force myself to ignore Laia. "To strengthen your jinn? Yourself?"

"Not a single word for the woman you used to love," the Nightbringer says. "And your kind think that I am cruel. Do you even remember those you've killed, boy? Or are there so many that their faces fade together? The latter, I think. That is how humans go through this life. Murdering and smashing and forgetting. But—" He looks at the city around him.

"I understand every death caused in service of my purpose. I do not take them lightly. Am I not kinder than you and your ilk, who cannot recall face or form of your foes? Your homes and lives and loves are built upon the graves of those you never even knew existed—"

Laia, who hangs limply from the Nightbringer's hand, suddenly comes to life. Her chains go flying toward Umber, who screams when they touch her. I expect Laia to disappear. To escape.

Instead, she lunges for the Nightbringer.

For a moment, they tumble back in a tangle of shadow and flesh. But when he rises, he has Laia's wrists caught in one of his hands.

"You cannot kill me, girl," he sneers at her. "Have you not learned?"

"So everyone keeps saying," Laia gasps, glaring at him, at the other jinn. "But you are all monsters. And monsters have weaknesses."

"Monsters?" He twists her around until she faces me. "There stands a monster. Walking through a city burning, ignoring the screams of his own kind. Without a care for anything but his precious ghosts. He will not mourn you if I kill you slowly."

"Can't kill me," she gasps. "Star—"

"Perhaps I've overcome that little hiccup," the Nightbringer says. "What of it, Soul Catcher? Would you like another ghost for your kingdom? Or maybe I will reap her soul too. Would you let her die, knowing her spirit will never cross the river?"

My attention flicks again to what's happening behind the Nightbringer. The girl thrashes, clawing at him.

But she's not "the girl." Cain made sure she never would be again.

If she let herself be cowed, I could look away. Instead she defies the Nightbringer, kicking and fighting even as he squeezes the life out of her.

A memory surfaces—a day long ago at Blackcliff, the first time we saw each other. Skies, the determination in her, the life. Even then, she was an ember ever burning, no matter how much the world tried to quench her fire.

Our eyes meet.

Walk away, Soul Catcher, I tell myself. *Look to the jinn behind the Nightbringer. Figure out what he is doing. Save the spirits from whatever skies-awful fate he is inflicting upon them.*

Walk away.

But for a moment, just a moment, the wrathful, imprisoned part of me, the old me, breaks free.

And I cannot walk away.

CHAPTER TWENTY-FIVE

The Blood Shrike

The dark stone tunnels beneath Antium are laid out in a grid, meant to allow ease of movement when the weather is wretched. If you know the tunnels, traversing them is child's play.

For me, they are a nightmare, stinking of mold and death, littered with the detritus of our flight from Antium months ago. Clothes and shoes. Blankets and heirlooms. And now my blood, a trail of it that any tracker could follow.

My ragged breathing is punctuated by the occasional skittering of rodents, their eyes flashing in the dark from afar. *Move. Keep moving.* I drag myself across the damp rock for hours. Pick my way through an unending reminder of what the Karkauns did to us.

No, I think. *What we did to ourselves.*

When the blood has all drained out of me, when I know that my healing power will not save me, I stop. My torch has burned down to almost nothing. *You are a torch against the night—if you dare to let yourself burn.* Cain said that to me.

Only it's not true any longer. The Augurs are gone. There is no light in this place. Only my pathetic life, finally at its end, and everyone and everything we left behind.

I wait for pursuit but it does not come. I wish it would. I wish the Karkauns would just kill me quickly.

My eyes adjust to the darkness, and I realize I am staring into the face of a skeleton. It is picked clean, for there is life in these tunnels even if it isn't human.

The skeleton is not large. A child, a wooden horse clutched in his shriveled hands. Injured in the attack and left here, perhaps. Or maybe separated from family and abandoned to fend for himself.

The horse appears to stare back at me. It reminds me of something. As I am waiting to die, I might as well try to remember. It feels important, suddenly. Where have I seen that horse before?

I haven't, I realize. But I saw one like it. Long ago, after Marcus ordered me to hunt Elias, and Cain took me to the ashes of an Illustrian home. He told me a story of a family who lived there. A boy. What the bleeding hells was his name? *Remember. He deserves to be remembered.*

But it is the Scholar slave who I remember—Siyyad. He carved the horse for the boy because he loved him like a son. And he went back for the boy, though it cost him his life.

I cannot remember the child's name, though. And I won't ever know this child's name either. Is it a Scholar child? A Martial? A Mariner or a Tribal child, caught in the chaos?

It doesn't matter. The knowledge rolls over me like an ocean wave after an earth tremor, ruthless and unending. It doesn't matter because it was a life cut down too early. Even if he was a Karkaun child, he would still be worth mourning, because at this age, he would have been tender and soft, not yet molded by the violence of his elders.

Whoever he was, he did not deserve any of this. Adults brought this upon him. I brought this upon him. The Commandant. All of us striving for power and control, and destroying any who got in the way.

Laia of Serra knows this. Of course she does, for she has lived it. All her pent-up rage at what was done to her people—and I never understood it until now. I thought I served a great cause: protecting the Empire. But all I did was protect people who were never in any danger.

Maybe this is what Elias learned from Mamie and her stories. The ones where I never understood who the villain was and who the hero was. Maybe all of us need more stories like hers.

"S-s-sorry," I whisper to the skeleton. "I'm so sorry."

Skies, I hurt so many. And I only realize it now, at the end, when I am a torch no more, but an ember with no air, the great dark closing in forever.

Too late to say sorry, Helene. I think my own name for the first time in months. *Too late to fix anything.*

At least I saved Harper. At least he did not come with me. I let myself drift in thoughts of our kiss. It was months ago, but I remember every second. How he tasted of cinnamon, and how his eyes fell closed as he pulled me toward him, and how—

Ping. Ping. Ping.

The sound jars me from my thoughts, and I stare at the skeleton, listening. *Greetings, Death,* I think, and strangely, it is a relief. *You come to claim me at last.*

But all is silent, until, after a few minutes—

Ping. Ping. Ping.

I let myself drift into the dark. I want sleep now. I want to fall away with thoughts of Avitas Harper in my mind.

Ping. Ping. Ping.

What the *bleeding* hells is that noise? I try to turn, but I cannot. And then in the darkness, a voice.

"Rise, Blood Shrike, for your people have need of you yet. Loyal to the end, remember?"

"F-father?"

"Father and mother. Sister and brother and friend. Rise."

Hands come under my arms, lift me to my feet, but when I turn to look, there is no one there, and I think perhaps there were no hands. I stagger forward, leaning against the wall, one tiny step at a time.

Ping. Ping. Ping. Ping.

That was four. The last few were only three. There's a rhythm to the sound too, like music. Like something only a human could make.

It could be the caves. When I came here before the siege on Antium, I heard a sound just like this one. *Just the caves singing their stories*, Cain had said.

If that's a song, what the bleeding skies is it saying? It won't stop and it keeps changing. I just want to die, but it won't let me.

"That's it," the voice that spoke before says. "Keep going. Find that sound."

Soon, the sound is not a *ping* but something deeper, like the ringing of a bell. But no — it is too flat and short to be a bell. It is not joyous or gentle like a bell. It is cold and hard. Like me.

Ahead, I make out light and drag myself toward it, my vision clearing. The light grows brighter until I stumble into a room lit with torches and hot from an unnaturally blue-green fire. It burns in a furnace that creates no smoke.

PING. PING. PING.

A man I've never seen before looks up from an anvil. His head is shaved, and his dark skin is covered in tattoos. He is perhaps a decade older than me. In one hand, he holds a hammer, and in the other, a helmet that glows with a strange, silvery light.

"Blood Shrike." The man appears entirely unsurprised as he walks to me, puts an arm around me, and helps me to a bed in the corner. "I'm Spiro Teluman. I have been waiting for you."

CHAPTER TWENTY-SIX

Laia

The Nightbringer grabs the back of my head and squeezes. I suppress a scream, for I will not give him the satisfaction. Tears leak from my eyes, and I lash out at him. *Fight, Laia, fight!* I stole my dagger from Novius, picked the lock on my chains, and feigned weakness and defeat with Khuri—all for this moment. I cannot fail now.

As he looks at the Nightbringer, Elias cocks his head. He is otherworldly, eldritch as the jinn themselves. There is no empathy in his gaze. No trace of the man he was.

And though this is part of my plan, though getting captured by the Nightbringer means getting closer to the sickle—now a scythe—I wish I did not feel so desperately alone in my battle against the jinn.

Unwillingly, I look at Elias, knowing I will only be met with the Soul Catcher's icy regard.

Instead, I see vitality in his gaze, and my body jolts in surprise. This is the Elias I met at Blackcliff. The Elias who escaped Serra with me, who exploded out of the depths of Kauf, my brother in tow.

The Elias I thought Mauth had crushed.

He blurs into motion, not attacking the Nightbringer, but moving for the jinn with the long spear—Khuri called her Umber. He disarms her with two quick thrusts of his hands, and then knocks her back into Azul.

Khuri jumps in front of Elias, glaring at him, no doubt trying to manipulate his mind. But he shakes off her magic, whipping the spear toward her too fast to follow. She crumples to the ground, stunned by the blow.

The Nightbringer flings me to the rooftop and streaks toward Khuri, who is already rising, her flame eyes scarlet. *Run*, every part of me screams. *Escape, Laia!*

I do run. After the Nightbringer, lunging for the scythe just as he reaches his precious kindred. This is it. Either I die or this scythe comes with me. There is no middle ground. I wrap my fingers around the handle and I pull with all my might. *Please!*

It does not budge.

The Nightbringer half turns, but I've drawn my dagger and I slice through the leather strap holding the scythe to the jinn's back. It comes free, and for a moment, I am too stunned to move.

"Hold on to me."

Elias appears beside me and pulls me to his chest, spinning me across the rooftop. We are away and my blood rises with the victory of the moment. I have the scythe. Elias is here with me. *Elias*, not the Soul Catcher.

I catch sight of a deep red flame—Umber. We lurch to a sudden halt and Khuri is there, her mouth curled in a snarl as she attempts to wrest the scythe from me. Elias shouts as Umber attacks, snatching back her spear and bringing it down on his shoulders. Though his magic must dull the spine-breaking blow, it does not stop it, for Elias gasps, on his knees.

"This," Khuri says with an unnatural calm as she slowly pries my fingers from the scythe's handle, "does not belong to you, human." I feel her influence, her compulsion.

"Khuri!" The Nightbringer's shout is low as a roll of thunder, laced with a terror I've never heard from him before. "No!"

She turns to him, startled, and I level a vicious kick at her knees. The handle of the scythe comes loose from her grip. Her legs buckle as she lurches forward, fingers crooked at me. I thrust her away, the scythe in hand, and the blade cuts through her like she's flesh and blood instead of fire and vengeance.

Flames pour down my wrists, and I flinch back, my skin burning. Khuri scrabbles at her throat, but her strength is gone, and she slumps to the ground. She speaks then, her voice layered as if there are dozens of Khuris within her.

> *The son of shadow and heir of death*
> *Will fight and fail with his final breath.*
> *Sorrow will ride the rays of the day,*
> *The earth her arena and man her prey.*
> *In flowerfall, the orphan will bow to the scythe.*
> *In flowerfall, the daughter will pay a blood tithe.*

Tears spring to my eyes at the sight of the fallen jinn. She bursts into flame, just as Shaeva once did, her ashes caught on the wind. And though she was my enemy, I can take no joy in her passing. For as she dies, the Nightbringer screams.

"Khuri!" The sorrow in his keen turns my blood to ice, for I have heard such pain before. His cry is my father moaning in his jail cell and my sister's neck snapping. It is Nan stifling her wails in her fist as she mourned her only child and Izzi telling me she was scared as she breathed her last. It is every death I've ever suffered, but so much worse, for he had only just gotten Khuri back. He had fought a thousand years to get her back.

"I'm sorry." The scythe falls from my nerveless fingers. "Oh skies, I'm so sorry—"

The air near me glows the faintest gold. "Flee, Laia of Serra," Rehmat whispers, its sadness palpable. "Flee, lest he burn you to ash."

I do not know if Elias heard Rehmat, or if he simply senses the Night-bringer's rage building like a tempest over a warm sea. It does not matter. As my eyes meet those of the jinn, the Soul Catcher's arm comes around me, and seconds later, we are on the wind.

CHAPTER TWENTY-SEVEN

The Soul Catcher

The soldier in me tallies up the jinns' weaknesses: Umber succumbing to my magic as I siphoned away her life force; the glaive wounding Khuri; the scythe killing her.

The Soul Catcher in me yearns for the Waiting Place, rattled by Khuri's prophecy. I need the peace of the trees, the focus that the ghosts give me. I need Mauth to ease my mind.

And the human in me marvels at the feel of this girl in my arms—that she lives, that she not only survived the Nightbringer but wielded his weapon.

"I had it in my hands," she whispers as we windwalk. "I had it and I lost it."

When we stop, it is with a crash at the top of a dry gully choked with scree and spindly trees. I take the brunt of the fall, wincing at the rocks slicing through my clothing. Branches groan in the fierce wind tearing across the desert, and Laia tucks her head into her arm, shielding her eyes from the sand.

"Elias, are you all—"

"Fine." I lift her off me quickly, then back away a few feet. The sky above is ablaze with stars and we are so far from Aish that it isn't even a glow on the horizon.

It's hard to make out Laia's face in the dark. But that's a relief. "The foretelling we heard," I tell her. "Those first two lines were about me."

"You?" She gets gingerly to her feet. *"The son of shadow and heir of death—"*

"Will fight and fail with his final breath." I pause for a long moment. "You know the cost of my failure. You've seen it firsthand."

"It is just a foretelling," Laia says. "Not all foretellings are real—"

"Shaeva's foretelling came to pass," I say. "Every line of it. And she, too, was a jinn. You were right, you know. The Nightbringer *is* doing something to the ghosts. I nearly found out what it was. But—"

"But you saved me instead." Laia looks at me like she knows my insides. "Elias." Her voice is strained. "I'm not sorry. You came back to me—I've missed—"

"You'll have to make your way back to wherever it is you're going," I say. "I've been away from the forest for long enough."

She closes the distance between us, grabbing my hand before I can windwalk away. Her fingers are twined between mine, and I think of the night she spent with me in Blackcliff. Before she left, she tried to give my blade back. The words she spoke carry layers of meaning now that they did not have then.

You have a soul. It's damaged, but it's there. Don't let them take it from you.

"Talk to me," she says now. "Just for a moment." The gully is filled with scraggly trees that are blue in the starlight. But she finds a long, flat rock and sits, pulling me down with her.

"Look at me, Elias." She takes my chin in her hand. "The Nightbringer baited you. And I gave him the perfect bait. He knows you, like he knows all humans. He expected you to help me and knew you would later feel guilty about it. He's always a step ahead of us. But the cost this time is thousands of lives—tens of thousands—"

"The concerns of the human world are not—"

"He's playing a tune and you are dancing to it. That is your concern. The Nightbringer wants you chained to the Waiting Place. It serves his purposes perfectly. Because if you are trying to control things there, you are not fighting out here."

"If I am chained to the Waiting Place, it is because of my own choices—not because of the Nightbringer."

"You're chained because of me." She releases me, her face in her hands. Seeing her this way feels wrong. *No*, I realize. It feels wrong to see her this way and not give her comfort.

"You died, Elias, and still you could not let yourself fail. You promised to save Darin and so you did, though it led to your own imprisonment. You promised to serve Mauth and so you do, though it will lead to the destruction of my people. You are so—so—" She throws up her hands. "So stubborn! And the Nightbringer *knows* it! He is counting on it, for it allows him to wreak havoc in the human world without anyone to stop him."

Laia's disquiet swirls around her, a weight too heavy to carry alone. "You said yourself the forest is sick. The ghosts are not coming through. I tell you, the source of these ills is the Nightbringer. If you want to fix the Waiting Place, you must stop him from tampering with the spirits."

Though I'm certain I had the good sense to put a foot of space between us, our knees touch. She pulls my hands to her heart, and my pulse judders in response.

"Thank you for helping me," she says. "I know it cost you. But if you hadn't helped me—"

"You'd have been fine." This, I know. "You're tough and smart. You're a survivor, Laia. You always have been."

She smiles and looks down, her hair falling into her face. "It is sweet to hear you say my name," she whispers.

A desert wind gusts through the gully, and I breathe in the scent of her, sugar and sweat and something unknowable that makes my head spin. I push her hair back from her face, and find my thumb lingering on her cheek. It is flushed, though the night is cold.

Laia looks up at me as if she is going to speak, and her fingers press into my forearm. My own desire stirs at the depth of hers, and I imagine her fingers digging into my back, her eyes on me like they are now, her legs around my hips—

Stop. You are the Banu al-Mauth.

But the voice fades when she rises to her knees on the rock and brushes her lips against mine. She is careful, like I might flee. But her wildly thudding pulse matches mine, and I drop my hands to her waist and pull her close, my lips parting hers. Closer still when she moans, her nails grazing my neck. The sound that it elicits from me is nothing close to decent.

She pulls away, smiling, and I wish she had not, for in the space that opens between us, tumult takes hold, the cold reality of my present sweeping over the horizon of my mind.

I am a fool. Holding Laia, kissing her, touching her, letting myself want her. All I've done is given her hope.

She must sense it, for she tilts my face toward hers. "Elias—"

"That's not my name." I pull away and stand, grasping for the coldest version of myself: Mask, Soul Catcher, Chosen of Death. I think of the thousands of ghosts I created, the thousands who died because of me—friends and enemies and people whose names I never even knew.

The Nightbringer was right about humans. *Murdering and smashing and forgetting.*

"Please," I tell her. "I could not live with myself if more suffer because of me. Stay away. Leave me in peace. Find someplace safe to—"

"Safe?" Laia laughs and it is a terrible sound. "There is no safe place for me in this world, Elias. Not unless I create it for myself. Go then to your duty. I will go to mine."

Before she turns her back on me, I am gone, windwalking east, flying faster and faster until sand turns to scrub and scrub to trees. I do not stop until I am at my cabin. There, the only sound is my ragged breathing. And once it slows, the silence settles in. I am so used to hearing the soughing of the ghosts that their complete absence is unnatural.

A small figure emerges from the trees. She looks around with innocent curiosity, and I know her immediately. The child from Aish who recognized me. *Of course.* She and her family could not have survived the assault.

"Welcome to the Waiting Place, the realm of ghosts, little one," I say to her. "I am the Soul Catcher, and I am here to help you cross to the other side."

"I know who you are," she says. "Why didn't you help us? I looked for you."

"You must forget the living," I say. "For they can hurt you no longer."

"How can I forget? That silver woman killed Irfa and Azma at the same time. Azma was only four. Why did she do that, Soul Catcher? Why didn't you help?"

The child is but one ghost, but it takes me hours to pass her on, for how do I answer her queries? How do I explain Keris's hatred to an innocent?

When it is done, when I have finally answered every question and heard every hurt, small or large, she walks into the river. I wait for the old sense of rightness to fill me. All the way home I wait. It does not come, not even when I enter my cabin and light the lamps.

Home, I tell myself. *I am home.* But it doesn't feel like home anymore.

It feels like a prison.

CHAPTER TWENTY-EIGHT

The Blood Shrike

Something sits on my chest.

The fact sinks into my consciousness slowly and I don't move a muscle. Whatever it is, it's warm. Alive. And I don't want it to realize I'm awake.

The weight shifts. A drop of warm water plops onto my forehead. I tense. I've heard of Karkaun water torture—

"Ha! Ba-ba-ba-ba."

Two small hands dig into my face and pull the way one's face simply shouldn't be pulled. I open my eyes to find my nephew sitting atop me, drooling happily. When he sees I am awake, he smiles, revealing one perfect, pearly tooth that was not there when I left.

"Ba!" he declares as I sit up gingerly.

"I thought if anyone could wake you up"—Livia offers me a handkerchief from her seat beside my bed—"it was the Emperor."

I wipe off the baby drool and give Zacharias a kiss, carefully untangling his fingers from my jaw and swinging my legs out of the bed. Snow flurries swirl outside the mottled glass windows of my room, and the blazing fireplace does little against the chill in the air. I feel hollowed out, like someone has taken a shovel to my insides. I edge away from the feeling, focusing instead on standing up.

"Easy, Shrike." Livia takes Zacharias from me. "Spiro Teluman carried you through the tunnels, and you've been in and out of consciousness for the last two days. That bite on your neck was infected. You were raving when he first got here."

203

And it must have taken at least five days to get out of the tunnels. Bleeding skies. A week. I have to pull together a strike force for Antium. Convince the Paters of my plan. Make sure we've enough weapons and food and horses. Alert those resisting within the capital. So much to accomplish and I've been asleep.

"I need my scims, Empress." My vision goes funny when I stand, and my leg aches something vicious. But I thank the skies for my healing power, for without it, I'd have died before even reaching Teluman. I limp to the dresser and pull on a clean set of fatigues. "Where's Teluman?"

"The Paters wanted him in the dungeons, but I thought that would be poor thanks for the man who brought back our Shrike," Livia says. "He's with Darin and Tas at the forge. Speaking of—I've made young Tas a little bed in Zacharias's room. The child doesn't seem keen on smithing, and I thought he could be companion to the Emperor instead."

"The Paters won't like—"

"The Paters won't notice. To them, he's just a Scholar. But he's clever and kind-hearted. He likes Zacharias. Perhaps Tas could be a friend to him." My sister's face clouds. "Something normal in all of this madness."

I nod quickly, because the last thing I need is Livia again musing about running off with the Emperor to the Southern Lands. "If Tas wishes it, I have no objection."

"Good." Livia beams at me. "And there's something else I wish to discuss with you."

Dread knots my belly, because she has that look on her face. The one she'd get before challenging my father on Martial jurisprudence. The one she had before she sent me to Adisa.

"Keris named herself Empress and the Paters accepted it," Livia says. "You could do the same."

In my shock, it takes me a moment to find the appropriate response. "That's—that's *treason*—"

"Oh, rubbish. He's my son, Shrike." She looks down at Zacharias, and smiles when he babbles at her. "I would never harm him. I want what is best for him, and this life is not it. You saved thousands of Martials and Scholars. The people love you—"

"There's more to ruling than popularity." I hold up my hands. "I'd need to be as diplomatic as Father, as clever as Mother, and as patient as you. Can you imagine me trying to make peace between Paters? Most of the time I just want to punch them. Having to meet ambassadors and make small talk—"

"You met with the Ankanese ambassador and now we have a treaty."

"He was a warrior, like me. Easy to talk to. I was made to fight, Livia. Not rule. In any case, the Augurs named Marcus our emperor. Zacharias is his son and the skies-chosen heir—"

"The Augurs are dead." My sister's lips thin, as does her patience. "Everyone knows. Keris and her allies are using it as a reason to question Zacharias's legitimacy as Emperor."

"Then they are fools and we will fight—"

A knock sounds on the outer chamber, and never have I been so relieved to be interrupted. An unfamiliar voice speaks.

"Empress?"

My scim is in my hand in an instant. "Who the bleeding hells is that? Where's Far—"

Then I remember.

Loyal to the end, he had cried. The mantra of my Gens. My scars ache and the hollowed-out feeling in my chest makes sense.

"That's Deci Veturius." Livia looks at me like I might break, and it makes me want to snarl at her. "Faris's replacement. Harper cleared him."

"Empress," Deci says again. "Forgive me. Captain Harper is here to see the Blood Shrike."

I look around the room for an escape. The closet has a passageway. It's guarded. But not by anyone who would dare to talk.

"She's—ah—" Livia calls to Deci as I walk through the doorway to the closet. "She's indisposed."

"Very good, Empress."

Livia scurries after me, ignoring Zacharias chewing on her knuckles. "Harper's been worried sick." She gives me a reproachful look. "I don't think he's slept since Quin came back."

My heart twinges a little at that, fool that it is.

"Empress." I feel for the passage entrance, and it opens silently. "If we are to solidify the loyalty of the Paters and lure over Keris's allies, then we must win Antium for the Emperor," I say. "I have much to do. By your leave."

My little sister sighs, and Zacharias regards us solemnly, as if waiting to be let in on a secret.

"One day, sister," Livia says, "you'll have to reckon with all the things you try to hide from yourself. And the longer you wait, the more it will hurt."

"Maybe," I say. "But not today."

I slip through the passageway and into the castle, which is as damp and chilly as ever, though humming with courtiers and soldiers and servants.

"It's good to see you up and about, Shrike." A Martial woman in a maid's uniform smiles as she passes, a Scholar soldier at her side.

"Heard you gave Grímarr hell, sir," he says. "I'm sorry he's still alive, but I hope to be by your side when you kill him dead."

All the way to Darin's smithy, people call greetings or stop to talk to me about Antium.

"When are we taking back the capital, Shrike—"

"I knew you'd be back on your feet—"

"Heard you took down a hundred of those Karkaun thugs—"

The more people approach, the faster I walk. *The people love you,* Livia said. But it is the Emperor who they must love. The Emperor who they must fight for.

My injuries pain me, and it takes me longer than I anticipate to get to Darin's smithy, a half-covered courtyard in the middle of the castle. The Scholar is stripped to his waist despite the chill, muscles rippling as he plunges a scim into the forge while Spiro Teluman works the bellows. As I step through one of the peaked archways into the courtyard, I notice a Scholar healer named Nawal watching Darin, steeling herself to approach.

"Not hard to look at, is he?" I jump at the voice next to me, my scim half-drawn. It is Musa, one hand gently nudging my blade back to its scabbard. He has a dozen bruises and as many cuts, most half-healed.

"So jumpy, Shrike. One would think you'd only just escaped a band of Karkauns by the skin of your teeth." He chuckles darkly at his little joke, but his smile doesn't reach his eyes. "Forgive me," he says. "Laughing hurts less than facing what happened. I am sorry about Faris. I liked him."

"Thank you," I say. "And your joke was terrible, so naturally, Faris would have loved it." I offer the Scholar a smile. "You're no worse for wear, I hope?"

He pats his face, preening. "Everyone says I'm even more dashing with scars."

"Piss off, you." I shove him, surprised to find myself laughing, and move for Darin.

"How go the blades?"

Laia's brother jumps, so immersed that he hadn't noticed me.

"We've made two hundred since you left for Antium," he says. "No beauty to them, but they won't break."

Spiro joins us, wiping melted snow off his shaved head with a rag. "The work goes more swiftly now," he says. "You look better, Shrike."

"I'm alive because of you." I offer him my hand. "I don't know how to thank you."

"Get your men to wear the armor I've been forging for the past year." He pulls me to the side as Darin and Musa converse. "The Empress Regent had it carted here at my request. But your soldiers say it's unnatural."

I have a vague memory of a glowing helmet. While Scholars attempt to find logical excuses for the supernatural, Martials are wary of it. It's why I hid my healing powers for so long. I had no wish to be killed for practicing witchery.

"Unnatural," I say. "Is it?"

"The Augurs taught me to make the armor. It will help our fighters blend in with the darkness. It will turn away arrows. It's resistant to fire. And it loses that glow as soon as it's put on."

I regard the smith thoughtfully. "I don't remember much about the journey out. But I do remember you saying you'd been waiting for me."

He turns to a scim awaiting polish. "The Augurs warned me you'd come," he says. "Told me much depended on me working in that damned cave, making armor until you showed up. I was starting to think they were crazy."

"Why you? And . . ." I glance at Darin. "Why him? You knew the risks in taking him on. In sharing our secrets. It's a miracle you weren't both executed."

"The secrets never should have been ours alone." Teluman's voice is harsh, and he glares down at the scim. "I had a sister," he says after a moment. "Isadora. When she was sixteen, she fell in love with a Scholar girl. They were discovered together by an Illustrian who had been courting Isa."

"Oh," I say. "Oh no."

"I tried to get her to Marinn, where she could love who she wished. I failed. The Empire used one of my blades to execute her. Or so they told me. They didn't let me see her, before the end."

His look of self-loathing is as familiar to me as my own face. "Do you know how many blades I made for them before Isa died, Shrike?" he says. "Do you know how many were used to kill innocents? But it wasn't until it affected my family that I finally did something. That fact will haunt me until I die."

"What happened to the Scholar girl?"

"I found her. Put her on a ship south. She lives in Ankana. Writes to me sometimes. Anyway, I met him a few months after." Spiro nods to Darin. "Curious, just like Isa. An artist like her. Full of questions like her. And he told me he had a little sister."

The smith gives me a level stare, snow dusting his many piercings. "I waited for you because the Augurs said you'd set things right. That you'd help to forge a new world. I will hold you to that, Shrike. I'm done siding with tyrants."

"Shrike." Darin interrupts us, a furrow between his brows. "Musa says one of his wights just returned from the Tribal desert. Aish has fallen to Keris. No one's seen Laia. She's been missing for days."

"Missing?" Worry gnaws at me, and I turn to Musa. "I thought you had eyes everywhere."

"I do," Musa says. "The wights can't find her."

"Which means I need to," Darin says. "I know we need weapons for the Scholars, but she's my sister, Shrike."

I cannot lose him now. We need his smithing skills—not to mention the fact that if he leaves and Keris gets to him, Laia will murder me. "Darin, give me until after we take Antium—"

"What if something's happened to her?"

"Your sister," I say, "is tough. Tougher than you. As tough as me. Wherever she is, she will be all right. I'll have my spies in the south keep an eye out for her."

As it happens, I already sent Laia a message, asking her to tell the Tribes that we'll offer support in their fight against Keris if they swear fealty to Zacharias. "When I get word of her—and I will get word of her—I promise, I'll let you know."

The Scholar is about to protest again, but if I have to argue further, I might lose my temper. "Musa." I grab the Beekeeper by the arm and walk him out of the forge. "Come with me."

"Now, Shrike." Musa follows me reluctantly. "While I *do* like my women tall and bossy, and while I know this face is difficult to resist, sadly, my heart belongs to another—"

"Oh, shut up." I stop when we're far from the courtyard. "You're not that pretty." He bats his eyelashes at me, and I wish he were just a bit uglier. "I need eyes in Antium, Scholar. Mine have all gone to ground."

"Hmm. Humans are sadly unreliable." Musa pulls an apple from his cloak and pares off a slice. Its sweet scent cuts through the damp, and he hands me the piece. "What do I get for helping you, Blood Shrike?"

"The thanks of the Emperor and his Blood Shrike," I say. At the distaste on his face, I sigh. "What do you want?"

"A favor," he says. "At a time and place of my choosing."

"I can't promise that. You could ask for anything."

He shrugs. "Good luck taking back your capital."

Of course. He wouldn't make things easy. Then again, if it were me in his shoes, I'd ask for the same. "Fine," I say. "But nothing . . . untoward."

"I wouldn't dare." Musa shakes my hand with only mildly exaggerated solemnity. "In fact, I'll offer you a little tidbit right now. Captain Avitas Harper is on his way here. He's in the northwest corridor, passing that very ugly statue of a yak, and moving rather quickly."

"How—" I know how he does it. Still, the specificity is uncanny.

"Ten seconds," Musa murmurs. "Eight—six—"

I stride swiftly away, wincing at the pain lancing up my leg. But I'm not fast enough.

"Blood Shrike," Harper calls in a voice that I cannot ignore. I curse Musa as he walks off, laughing quietly.

"Harper," I say. "You wouldn't happen to know where Quin is, would you?" I keep walking through the dark stone halls of the keep, fast enough that he has to jog to catch up. I am lightheaded—despite my swift healing, I'm not recovered from what happened in Antium. "I need to ask him if—"

Harper steps in front of me, grabs my hand, and pulls me into a side hallway with a force that surprises me.

"I know you're angry at me," he says. "Maybe I deserve it. But you're also angry at yourself. And you shouldn't be. Faris—"

"Faris knew what he was doing." I yank my hand back, and the fleeting hurt in Harper's expression makes me look down. "Faris was a soldier. Faris gave me a fighting chance."

"But you're still angry," Harper says softly.

"And why shouldn't I be," I snarl at him. "You know what they're doing to us in that city. The city I lost, Harper. The city I let Keris betray—"

"You didn't—"

"It was so quiet," I say. "All our people cowering because they are desperately afraid. Not of death or torture. They're too strong for that. No, they're afraid of being forgotten, Harper."

Harper sighs, and it feels like he can see right into me, into those moments I mourned Faris, those moments I spent staring into the eyes of a child's skull, thinking death had finally come.

He steps near enough that I can smell the cinnamon and cedar of his skin, the steel at his waist. Snow has melted in his black hair, cut so close that it looks like the feathers of a raven.

"That is a terrible thing, Shrike," he says. "But it's not why you're angry. Tell me why you're angry."

That hollowness that has gnawed at me since waking expands, and I cannot stop it. I feel every wound. Every scar.

"When I was in the tunnels," I say, "and I thought I was going to die, I thought about you."

Though people pass us, no one looks twice. All they see is the Blood Shrike standing with her second. A minute passes. Still, he waits.

"It might have been you with me," I finally whisper. "Instead of Faris. But it wasn't. And when he stayed back because there were too many Karkauns, I—" My eyes burn. Curse the Nightbringer for taking my mask. In this moment, I would have drawn strength from it.

"I've known him all my life, Harper. We survived Blackcliff together. Skies, he tried to kill me once or twice when we were Fivers. But when I was crawling through that tunnel, when I knew he was fighting and dying for me, all I could think was that I was so thankful it wasn't you up there. Because if it had been, we'd have died together."

I step back from him now, and tears threaten. "But it wasn't you," I go on. "So Faris died alone. Now I have Paters to appease, and an army to gather, and an invasion to plan. I have an Empire to reclaim. But I am afraid of everything I might lose. So yes, Harper. I am angry. Wouldn't you be?"

My eyes are full so I cannot see his expression. I think he reaches for me, but this time, when I walk away, he doesn't follow. Just as well. Far to the west, my people suffer under the violent rulership of Grímarr. I failed them. I let that bastard sack our capital. I do not have time to agonize over Harper, or to ponder how much it cost me to tell him the truth. I do not have time to feel.

I have a city to take.

CHAPTER TWENTY-NINE

The Nightbringer

For centuries, humans were enough. I welcomed those who came to the Forest of Dusk with love, as Mauth asked me to. It was no chore, for many were lost, and longing to be found, healed, and passed on to a kinder place.

But in time, a loneliness descended. No matter how rich and varied the lives of humans, they were falling stars in my world. They flared bright and brief, and then they burned out.

My powers were familiar terrain, and the Waiting Place itself no mystery. Even the nuances of the ghosts grew predictable. My domain was flooded with spirits as human civilization spread. But I could pass them with hardly a thought.

I grew restless. Emptiness gripped me, a vast chasm that nothing could fill. I wanted. I yearned. But I did not know what for.

Mauth must have sensed my agitation, for in time, I felt new sparks enter the Waiting Place. Fully formed and as bewildered as I was when I arrived.

Your own kind, *Mauth said, guiding me to them.* For those of clay and fire are not meant to walk alone. And the Beloved was meant to receive love as well as give it, else how could I have named you such?

I nurtured those young flames, until they were full grown and burning bright. Together, we discovered their names. Their magic.

214

Diriya learned to manipulate water in the flat heat of the summer, when we had forgotten the taste of rain. Pithar spoke to stone long before she realized it spoke back, and she raised up the Sher Jinnaat— our city. Supnar gave life to the walls, so we could imbue them with our stories. In time, the jinn began to pair and create their own little flames, each more beautiful than the last. We had a city, now. A civilization.

Still, I felt incomplete. Empty.

Little remains of Khuri. A few ashes that I gather close, untouched by the wind. Umber bunches to fly in pursuit of Laia and the Soul Catcher, but I stop her.

"They are unimportant," I say. "Protect Maro. Only the reaping matters."

Perhaps she will defy me. Her hands tighten on her glaive, and Faaz and Azul step forward, ready to quell her flame with stone and weather. Talis shudders, inconsolable at Khuri's loss.

"We will have our vengeance, bright one," I say to Umber. "But not if we think like mortals."

From the city, screams rise. Keris does her work well. And Umber is hungry to join in.

"Unleash your spite on the humans," I say. "I will return."

I gather what little I have of Khuri and ride the winds deep into the Forest of Dusk, to the place I hate the most. The jinn grove, or what is left of it.

As I enter, I sense a presence watching from the forest. A spirit. An ancient impulse to pass her on seizes me, so deeply ingrained that after a thousand years of ignoring the ghosts, I nearly go to her. But I crush that instinct.

Khuri's ashes fly away on a gentle wind, and I consider her life and all that she was: the deep burgundy of her flame; how she loved her siblings; how she took up a scim when they were lost, destroying an entire legion of Scholar invaders with her wrath.

When my pain is as sharp as the scythe on my back, I ram through Mauth's defenses and seek out a place that exists beyond the Forest of Dusk. A place of claws and teeth. A Sea of Suffering.

The suffering reaches out to me. *More*, it demands, and I sense its unending hunger. A maw that can never be filled. *More*.

"Soon," I whisper.

I consider, then, the problem of Laia. The girl knows now of the scythe. She realizes what it can do.

Yet I am no closer to understanding the unnatural magic that exists within her. Time to remedy that.

My son, do not do this.

Mauth has tried to speak to me before. Always, I have ignored that hated voice, so ancient, so wise, so monstrously unfeeling.

Thou art the Beloved, Mauth says.

"No, Father," I say after a long time. "I was the Beloved. Now I am something else."

CHAPTER THIRTY

Laia

After Elias departs, I sink onto the rock where we kissed, stunned as the depths of my failure sink in. For it is not just that Elias left again. After all, I told him to go.

It is that I did not get the scythe. I am alone in the middle of the Tribal desert with no food, no water, and no way of getting to either of those things quickly. All I have is my dagger and a freshly ravaged heart.

"Rehmat?" The creature does not respond, and I wince when I think of the dismay in its voice after I killed Khuri. Like I was a cruel child who broke the neck of a bird.

I drop my face into my hands and try to breathe, focusing on the desert scents of salt and earth and juniper. The wind yanks at my hair and clothes, its wail echoing in my head like the Nightbringer's keen. I wish for Nan and Pop. For my mother. I wish for Izzi. For Keenan. For everyone who is gone.

But there is one who *isn't* gone. Not yet.

I close my eyes, as I did weeks ago in the Forest of Dusk, and think about all that has bonded Darin and me. Then I call out softly, so as not to draw unwanted attention like last time.

"Darin?"

The minutes slide by. Perhaps I did not hear him before. Perhaps it was wishful thinking—

Laia?

"Darin!" I make myself speak his name quietly. "You can hear me?"

Yes. A heavy pause. So I did hear you before. I wondered if I'd imagined it.

217

Darin sounds as if he has not slept in an age. But it is his voice and I want to sob in relief.

How do I know this isn't a trick?

"When you were fifteen, you liked our neighbor Sendiya so much that you spent a month drawing a portrait of her even though I told you she was horribly vain. But she gave it back because she said you made her nose too small. You moped for weeks."

It wasn't weeks. Maybe three days.

"Three weeks," I insist, though I am grinning.

Thankfully my luck has improved.

"Ugh." I make a vomiting sound. "I don't want to know. You have terrible taste in girls, Darin."

Not this time! You know her, she says. *Nawal—she's a healer.*

I nod though of course he cannot see me. "I do know her. She's too good for you."

Probably. Are you all right? Where are you?

"I—I am fine."

The lie weighs heavy on my tongue. I have never been able to fool my brother. Not when I broke a jar of Nan's precious jam and tried to blame it on an alley cat; not when our parents and Lis died, and I told him I could fall asleep fine without him watching over me. In the end, he took the blame for the jam. And he watched over my sleep for months, though he was only seven at the time.

Laia, he says. *Tell me.*

His words are a boulder that breaks a dam. I tell him everything. My inability to break through to Elias and remind him of his humanity. My impotence when Khuri took control of my mind. The feeling of the scythe falling from my fingers. The only thing I do not mention is Khuri's death. It is too raw, yet.

"And now I am stuck." I am surprised that as I finish, a thin line of purple blooms on the eastern horizon, illuminating an undulating landscape of canyons and cliffs and massive fingers of rock jutting into the sky. "I have no idea what I am going to do."

Yes you do, Darin says. *You just can't see it yet. You feel defeated, Laia. And it's no wonder. It's so great a burden to bear alone. But I'm with you, even if I'm not beside you. You will sort through this, like you do everything that comes your way. And you will do it with strength. So stop. Think. Tell me, what are you going to do?*

I stare out at the desert, a speck of nothing against its vastness. These rocks, this dirt, it will abide for millennia, while I am but a moment in time that will be over all too soon. The thought is crushing, and I cannot breathe. I look up at the stars as if they will give me air. They have been the only constant in my life these past eighteen months.

Though that is not true. My own heart has been constant too. My will. That is not much. But it has gotten me this far.

"Water runs through a gully nearby," I say to Darin. "Rare enough in the desert that there's likely a settlement—or at least a road—nearby. I am going to find it. And I am going to find Mamie Rila and Afya."

Good. One step at a time, little sister. Just like always. Be safe.

Then he's gone and I am alone again. But not lonely anymore. By the time the sun rises, I have made my way to a settlement a mile or so from the gully. It is a small Tribal village where I am able to trade news of Aish for a pack, a canteen, and a bit of food.

The villagers tell me of a Martial outpost only a few miles away. In the dead of night, I sneak into the stables with my magic cloaking me and a small sack of pears. I find a likely looking mare, who stands still while I muffle her hooves with sackcloth and saddle her. When I go to put on her bridle, she nearly bites my fingers off. I have to bribe her with four pears before she will allow me to lead her out of the stable.

For the next two weeks, I make my way toward Aish in the hopes of finding the Tribes that escaped the city. Two weeks of gathering up scraps of news about the Nightbringer's location. Two weeks of rationing water, trading out stolen horses, and avoiding Martial patrols by the skin of my teeth.

Two weeks of plotting how in the hells I am going to get that scythe back.

And at the end of those two weeks, a storm that has been brewing on the horizon finally hits. Of course, it does not strike while I am at an inn or even in a barn. The skies open while I am scurrying through a narrow slot canyon. The wind whistles down the sheer rock on either side of me, and soon enough I am soaked through, my teeth chattering.

Whilst skulking about the last village, I learned that a large group of Aish's survivors was gathered near an abandoned guard tower a few hours south of the canyon. Hundreds of families, scores of wagons. The Saif caravan made it there, the villagers said, along with the Nur caravan.

If the rumors are true, Afya and Mamie will be with them. But if this storm doesn't let up, I will not reach them before they seek out shelter elsewhere.

Rain sluices down the canyon walls now, and I look up uneasily. Living in Serra, Pop warned us never to visit the canyons outside the city during the wet season. *You'll get swept away in a flash flood,* he had said. *They are quick as lightning and far more dangerous.*

I hasten my pace. Once I get to Mamie and Afya, I can plan. Keris is by no means done with the Tribal lands yet. But if we get the scythe, we could take out her allies. Stop her in her tracks.

The thought of killing a jinn again fills me with a bizarre mix of anticipation and nausea. Khuri's death flashes before my eyes for the hundredth time. The arc of her body as she fell. The Nightbringer's scream of loss.

Khuri would have killed me. She and all of her kin are my enemies now. Her death should not haunt me.

But it does.

"There is no shame in mourning the passage of so ancient a creature, Laia of Serra." Rehmat's glow is a soft light that reflects off the swiftly pooling water at my feet. "Especially when it passed by your hand."

"If your goal is to destroy the jinn"—I raise my voice so Rehmat can hear me over the rain—"why are you so sad about me killing one?"

"Life is sacred, Laia of Serra," Rehmat says, its voice deep as the thunder rumbling above me. "Even the life of a jinn. It is forgetting this fact that leads to war in the first place. Do you think that Khuri was not loved?"

The rain pours down heavier, and I do not know why I bother to wear a hood. My hair is soaked, and water streams into my eyes, blinding me no matter how much I wipe it away. In a few hours, it will be dark. I need to get out of this damn place and find a dry spot to spend the night. Or, at the very least, a boulder to hunker under.

"I did not mean to kill her," I say to Rehmat. "One second she was not there and then—"

"You did kill her. This is the nature of war. But you do not have to forget your enemy. Nor should you ignore the toll her slaying has taken on you."

"There will be a lot more dead jinn before this all ends," I say. "If I weep over every last one, I will go mad."

221

"Perhaps," Rehmat says. "But you'll remain human. Is that not worth a bit of madness?"

"Better if you help me get the weapon that could end this war," I say.

"The scythe cannot help you when you don't know how to wield it."

"I know I need his story," I say. "And I will seek it. But a story won't do much good without a weapon." The water is to my calves now and rising fast. I quicken my gait. "I do not fear him, Rehmat."

"What do you know of the Nightbringer, Laia?"

"He's careful," I say. "Angry. Capable of great love, but filled with hate too. He spent a thousand years trying to free his brethren."

"And his mind?"

"How the skies should I know what goes through his twisted brain, Rehmat?"

"You fell in love with him, yes? And he with you." There is a strange note in Rehmat's voice, but it's gone an instant later. "You must have learned something."

"He—he suffered," I say. "He lost family. People he loved. And—" Thunder booms overhead, closer than before. "He plays a long game. The moment he knew I had a piece of the Star, he began planning. When things did not go according to his plan, he shifted quickly."

"So do you think, Laia of Serra, that the Nightbringer, the King of No Name, will allow you to take the scythe now that he knows you want it?"

"Did you know him?" I am practically shouting, the rain is so loud. "Before he became what he is?"

"What I was before does not matter."

"I think it does," I say. "You want me to trust you. But how can I trust you when you will not tell me the truth about what you are?"

222

Wind howls down the canyon, and it sounds like a scream. Or a laugh. My blood goes cold and not from the rain. The last time I was in a storm this powerful, this angry, I was in the desert east of Serra, fighting to get a poisoned Elias to Raider's Roost. That storm was the handiwork of the Nightbringer. As was the sandstorm that nearly separated me from Elias just a few weeks later.

"Rehmat," I say. "This storm—"

"It is him." The creature realizes it as I do. "He knows you are out here, Laia of Serra. He seeks to harm you. Climb, child."

"Climb?" The path I am on is too narrow, the walls of the canyon too steep. Rehmat's light flares in alarm as the earth beneath me rumbles.

"The canyon is flooding, Laia! Climb!"

Rehmat flies a dozen yards ahead, where the canyon curves into a small ridge. I try to run, but can only lurch heavily through the water. A deafening groan splits the air. Something moves behind me, a shattered forest come to life, gobbling and chewing as it goes. A flash flood.

I slosh forward as the water around me rises to my knees, then my thighs.

"Faster, Laia!" Rehmat barks, and now I have reached the ridge, but it is too slick for me to hold on to. The roar of the flood is so loud I cannot hear myself think. The headwall approaches too quickly.

"Help me!" I scream at Rehmat.

"The only way is to join with your mind." Rehmat twists around me. "But we are too powerful together, Laia. And the Nightbringer is too close. If I lend you my magic, he would sense us!"

"Blast the Nightbringer!" I jump, clawing and scrabbling at the ridge. "Maybe that fiery bastard deserves to know I will not just lay down and die, Rehmat! He should know I'll fight. But I cannot fight if you do not help me!"

The water pummels me, dragging me from the ridge. "Help me or I die!" I scream. "Please, Rehmat!"

The creature lunges, and for a moment, I feel it within my mind.

But it is too late. The flood has me now, and before I can draw on Rehmat's magic, before I can even wrap my thoughts around the fact that it has joined with me, the water sweeps me away.

CHAPTER THIRTY-ONE

The Soul Catcher

At first glance, the City of the Jinn looks as it always does. The wind scatters leaves and dirt down empty streets. The clouds above surge and heave, promising a storm. A hush blankets the spare buildings, heavy as the doors of a mausoleum.

In the distance, the River Dusk gleams a dull silver, more sluggish than normal. No doubt because it is choked with debris. After leaving Laia, I returned to find more dead patches along its banks. In the two weeks since then, those dead bits have only expanded.

I did not wish to come here. For nearly a fortnight, I put it off. But Mauth does not speak to me. The ghosts remain absent from the Waiting Place. And it all ties back to the Nightbringer. Here, in his home, perhaps I can learn why.

As I enter the outskirts of the city, it feels different. Awake. I slide through the shadows and spot the drift of a curtain in the wind. When I look again, it's still. The edge of a cloak flits into view, followed by the low hum of voices in conversation. I follow the sound and find myself on a dead-end street. I think I smell cloves and coriander and apple on the air, but moments later the scent is gone.

I feel like I am chasing down memories, instead of reality.

The wind, which screamed through the trees of the Waiting Place just minutes ago, is muted here, and transformed into a melancholy music that echoes through pipes hidden among the buildings. The melodies are beautiful. They also mask the sound of my passage.

Mauth's magic does not extend to invisibility, so I must draw on all that

I learned at Blackcliff. I stick to the shadows and take my time, making my way to the center of the city. There, on a street lined with high buildings, I hear voices that do not fade. They come from a gate twice my height— or more specifically, from the courtyard beyond it. There is no way to approach directly—not without risking discovery. I glance up, but the rooftops of the city are sloped, and smooth as polished glass. I'll break my neck if I try to cross them.

Ten hells. Curse the jinn for not planting any bleeding shrubbery around their buildings. I edge toward a deep archway, hoping to the skies no jinn choose to walk past.

The murmur of conversation clarifies. Still, at first I cannot make sense of it. Then I realize why. The voices speak in Archaic Rei. The language of the jinn.

But Blackcliff's rhetoric Centurion made us study Archaic Rei. It's the parent language for Sadhese and Old Rei, the Scholar tongue. Thank the skies that old goat was so in love with ancient languages. After a few moments, I can translate:

"—cannot fight, you have yet to heal. There is no honor in death by idiocy—"

"—bring hot water and neem leaf, quickly—"

"—will be here soon. But he fights so we may forever be free of the Scholar scourge."

The voices fade. I catch enough to understand that I've stumbled upon some sort of hospital or infirmary. But for whom? Do jinn even catch illnesses? When I lived with Shaeva, she never so much as sneezed.

I inch closer, and at that moment, two shapes plummet out of the sky, thundering down to the street just yards away.

One is Umber in her shadow form, glaive clutched tight. The other is the dark-eyed, dark-skinned jinn who accompanied her before — Talis.

Umber collapses upon landing, her flame body dim and flaking to ash. I am surprised. She certainly did not seem so weak when she was trying to kill me.

"Surfraaz!" Talis calls out, and another jinn, pale with a jutting chin and dark hair, runs from the infirmary.

"I told you not to let her fight!" Surfraaz snaps. "Look at her — "

"You try telling Umber no." Talis struggles to stand, and Surfraaz grabs Umber's other side. Together, they carry her into the courtyard. "She faded too fast," Talis says. "This time, we need to keep her unconscious for a day or two, lest she — "

His words fade as he disappears from sight. Curiosity tempts me to follow, but I dare not risk being spotted. Instead, I sneak out of the archway and back the way I came. This city is vast. If there is one infirmary, there will be another, where I can figure out what is going on.

"Who are you?"

The speaker appears without warning, from a doorway I nearly walked past. It is a jinn woman regarding me with curiosity instead of rancor. She tilts her head, auburn hair falling in a waterfall down her back.

"You smell strange." She sniffs at the air but does not look directly into my eyes, which is when I realize that she is at least partially blind. "Very strange indeed — "

I take a step back. Her hand shoots out and closes on my wrist. She hisses.

"Human!" she screams. "Intruder!"

I wrench away and windwalk, streaking through the streets. But the jinn can ride the winds too, and in less than a minute, a half dozen trail me, their fingers clawing at my back and shoulders. "*Usurper!*" they scream, and their voices are layered, an echo that bounces between the walls until it seems as if the city itself is hunting me.

One of them grabs my wrist and unleashes its fire. Mauth's magic does not protect me in time. Pain bursts through my arm, and I stumble out of my windwalk, rolling to a stop at the border of the jinn city. The land flattens out into a large, empty plain before hitting a low escarpment. At the top: the jinn grove. It's a good quarter mile distant, but if I can make it there, the jinn may back off. They hate the grove.

When I scramble to my feet, though, the jinn trailing me are gone.

All but one.

Talis holds a Serric steel dagger loosely in one hand, his stance indicating both that the steel does not affect him and that he knows how to use the blade. He watches me with the curiosity one reserves for an unfamiliar if not particularly threatening dog.

I tug Mauth's magic into a shield, but it responds listlessly, like it can't decide if it wants to wake up or not. When the jinn approaches, I back away. I don't fear him. But I'm not an idiot either. I can still bleed. Still die. And Talis knows it.

"Our father's magic fades." Talis circles, taking my measure. "Mauth is locked in a battle with the Meherya, and I fear Mauth will lose."

"Mauth is Death. For the living, death is the only guarantee. It cannot be defeated."

"You are wrong," Talis says. "There are many things more powerful than death. Your kind wax eloquent about them in song and ballads and poetry."

"Love," I say. "Hope. Memory."

"Sorrow. Despair. Rage." Talis considers me, then casts his dagger aside. "Fear not, Soul Catcher. I used my magic on my brethren. The jinn who followed you are convinced you're on the other side of the city."

"What do you want?" I ask. "Unless you sent them chasing after a fake Soul Catcher out of the kindness of your heart?"

"To speak with you," the jinn says. "Without rancor or dissemblance."

At my hesitation, he throws up his hands. "If I'd wished to harm you, I'd have done it while you eavesdropped. Dozens of jinn lay steps away, all of whom would have loved to see you dead."

"Dozens of jinn who can barely muster their power, apparently."

Talis's back goes rigid. Interesting. "What are you doing in the Sher Jinnaat, Soul Catcher?" he asks.

Sher Jinnaat. The City of the Jinn.

"Is the Nightbringer stealing ghosts to restore the magic of the jinn?" I lob the question at him like a blade, in the hopes of catching him off guard. Confusion flashes on his face, and surprise. I might not be exactly on the mark, but I have hit close to the truth.

"You answer my questions," I say, "and I'll answer yours. An honest conversation, just like you wanted."

"Ah, a human bargain with a fey, like in the stories your *Kehannis* tell." Talis laughs. To my surprise, the sound is not menacing but warm, and a little sad. "Very well, Soul Catcher. One for one. You first. Why are you here?"

The Commandant's interrogation training kicks in. *If you must, offer the shortest answers you can while maintaining the illusion of cooperation.*

"Reconnaissance," I say.

"What did you learn, Banu al-Mauth?" he asks. "That we aren't as great a threat as you feared? That your precious humans are safe?"

229

"As for your second and third questions," I clarify, lest he think I've lost count, "I learned that you struggle with your powers, but that you are still a threat. Regarding the fourth, humans are not precious to me. Not anymore. Only the Waiting Place matters. Only the ghosts."

"Lies." The jinn motions me to walk with him toward the escarpment. "What of Laia of Serra?"

A fifth question. Yet none of my answers have given him any real information. This is too easy. Either he will go back on his word and refuse my questions, or there is something else afoot.

"Some names are etched into the stars," Talis goes on. "Melody and countermelody, a harmony that echoes in the blood. I hear such harmony in your names—Laia-Elias." He speaks them so they sound like one word, so they sound like a song. "You might seek to deny her, but you cannot. Fate will always lead you back to her, for good or for ill."

"I am not Elias anymore. And Laia is my past," I say. "The Waiting Place is my present and my future."

"No, Soul Catcher," Talis says. "War is your past. War is your present. War is your future. The Augurs knew it—they sensed it when you were but a child. Why else would they choose you for Blackcliff?"

My nightmare rears its head. The army behind me, the bloody scims in my hands. The maelstrom, churning and insatiable.

Talis slows, his gaze fixed on my face. "What did you see, just then?" There is a strange undercurrent of urgency in his tone. "The Augur's foretelling?"

I am surprised, but I hide it. Now I understand why he wasted his other questions. This was the one he wanted to ask from the beginning.

But Cain was desperate to keep the prophecy a secret from the jinn. *If the Nightbringer hears what I have to say, it will be the end of all things.* The Augur was cryptic and manipulative, but he never lied. Not outright. If he was afraid, perhaps there was a reason.

"You've asked enough questions for now. My turn," I say, and though Talis glowers, jaw tight with impatience, he nods.

"Why is the Nightbringer stealing the ghosts that should be going to the Waiting Place?"

Talis is silent for long enough that I wonder if he's going to answer the question.

"Revenge," he says.

I think of my own answer earlier. *Reconnaissance.* The more questions he gets out of me, the more likely it is that he can ask about the foretelling.

Think, Soul Catcher. Think. The Nightbringer isn't using ghosts to gather magic. He's using them for revenge. What flavor of revenge? My nightmarish visions come to mind, and I cast another guess.

"What does the Nightbringer's theft of the ghosts have to do with the maelstrom I've seen in my nightmares?"

Talis swings his head toward me, unable to mask his shock. "What nightmares?"

I do not answer, and he looks ahead, frustrated. "He seeks to create a gateway of sorts, between Mauth's dimension and your own. He wishes to return all the suffering that has been cleansed from the world back into it."

And though the Sea of Suffering churns, ever restless, verily does Mauth preside, a bulwark against its hunger. Aubarit spoke those words to me. And now it appears the Nightbringer seeks to pierce that bulwark. To what end, I don't yet know.

"Suffering is a state of mind, a feeling," I say. "It can't do anything."

Talis shrugs. "That sounds like a question."

Damn you. "How is the Nightbringer planning to weaponize this suffering?"

"Suffering is a monster, waiting to be released from a cage. You have only to look at your own mother to know the truth of that."

"What the bleeding hells is that supposed to mean?" The question is out of my mouth before I can stop myself.

"Keris Veturia's suffering runs deep, Soul Catcher. My brethren mistakenly believe that she is but a human stooge, a servant to carry out the Meherya's plan. But her suffering is why he sees himself in her. Why she sees herself in him. Suffering is the cup from which they both drink. It is the language they both speak. And it is the weapon they both wield."

The Mother watches over them all. So Keris is more essential to the Nightbringer's plan than I realized. The rest of the foretelling makes little sense, but that part, at least, must refer to her.

And though "watches over" sounds benevolent enough, when it comes to Keris, it isn't. Likely she's dispatched spies to surveil the Blood Shrike and Laia.

And me.

I regard Talis with new suspicion. This little game has gone on long enough. Time to end it.

"What is the Nightbringer's intent in releasing this suffering?"

"To cleanse the land of his enemy swiftly," Talis says softly, "that the fey might live in peace."

Bleeding, burning hells. He wants to kill all the Scholars at once. And he'll use this maelstrom to do it.

"Do you see now why war is your fate? I know well the Oath of the Soul

Catcher. *To light the way for the weak, the weary, the fallen, and the forgotten in the darkness that follows death.* There is no one to light the way for them now, Elias. No one to protect the spirits. Unless you take up the torch."

"I will not return to that life." I have waged enough war. Brought enough pain into existence. For all that I long for in the world of the living, war is one thing I will never miss. "Besides, if I fight for the Tribespeople or the Scholars, I will only end up killing Martials. Either way, the Nightbringer wins. I will not do it."

We have reached the escarpment, and here Talis stops. "And that is why it must be you," he says. "A commander who has tasted the bitter fruit of war is the only one worthy of waging it. For he understands the cost. Now—to my question."

"No more questions," I say. "For I have none for you. I will not tell you what the Augur said. Do not bother asking."

"Ah." Talis observes my face, and I feel like he's seeing more than I want him to. "That alone gives me the answer I seek. Will you fight, Soul Catcher?"

"I do not know," I say. "But since you asked a question, I find I have one more, after all. Why let me live? You got nothing out of this conversation."

Talis glances up at the escarpment, at the exposed, blackened roots of the jinn grove. "I love the Meherya," he says. "He is our king, our guide, our savior. Without him, I would still be locked away in that damnable grove, leeched on by the Augurs." He shudders. "But I fear for the Meherya. And I fear for my kin. I fear that which he calls forth from the Sea. Suffering cannot be tamed, Soul Catcher. It is a wild and hungry thing. Perhaps Mauth protects us against it for a reason."

The clouds above shift, and the sun peeks through for a moment. Talis lifts his face to the light. "We were creatures of the sun once," he says. "Long ago."

The hollows of his cheeks, the angle of his chin are strangely familiar. "I know you." I remember then, where I saw him. "I saw you with Shaeva, in the palace walls—in the images there. You were the other guard to the Nightbringer—to his family."

Talis inclines his head. "Shaeva was a friend for long years," he says. "I mourn her still. There must be some good in you if she saw fit to name you a Soul Catcher."

After he leaves, I go to the clearing outside my cabin. The soft grass is nothing but snow-dusted yellow scrub now. Shaeva's summer garden is a squarish lump beneath a fresh layer of powder. The cabin is dim, though as ever, I left a few embers burning in the hearth.

All is silent, and the silence is obscene, for this forest is the one place where ghosts are meant to find succor. And now they cannot. Because the Nightbringer is taking them all.

Inside the cabin, I do not light the lamp. Instead I stand before the two scims gathering dust above the fireplace. They gleam dully, their beauty an affront when one considers what they were created for.

I think of the Augur, that odious, cawing wretch. Not just of his fore-telling, which made no sense, but the last two words he spoke. Words that stirred my blood, that made the battle rage rise in me. My vow to Mauth rings in my mind, clear as a bell.

To rule the Waiting Place is to light the way for the weak, the weary, the fallen, and the forgotten in the darkness that follows death. You will be bound to me until another is worthy enough to release you. To leave is to forsake your duty—and I will punish you for it. Do you submit?

I submit.

No one has released me. I am still bound. And I do not know the fate of the ghosts the Nightbringer has already abducted. Whether I wish to fight his forces or not, I cannot let him steal away any more.

I reach for the scims gingerly, as if they will burn my palms when I touch them. Instead, they slip into my grasp like they have been waiting for me.

Then I leave the cabin and turn south to the Tribes, and the Nightbringer and war.

CHAPTER THIRTY-TWO

The Blood Shrike

From the knolls and ravines of the Argent Hills, Antium is cloaked from view, hidden by thick fingers of evening mist rolling down the Nevennes Range. Its towers and ramparts disappear and reappear, a city of ghosts.

No. A city of living, breathing Martials and Scholars, waiting for you to lead the charge.

I used to love nights like this in the capital. My work would be done, Marcus would retreat to his quarters, and I'd walk the city, sometimes stopping at the stall of a Tribeswoman who brewed sweet pink tea sprinkled with almonds and pistachios. Mariam Ara-Ahdieh left Antium long before the Karkauns came. I wonder where she is now.

"Good weather for a battle." Spiro Teluman hunkers down beside me, a scim hilt poking up over his shoulder. The smith's legendary skills and long disappearance give him an enigmatic aura. The men around me, including Pater Mettias, eye him with a wary sort of awe.

Despite my gloves, my hands are numb. In the snow-choked dell behind me, five hundred of my men hunch in their cloaks, their breath rising in white puffs.

"Sword-breaking weather, Teluman," I say. "I don't like it."

"The scims are Serric steel." Teluman's tattoos are hidden by the dark, form-fitting armor he forged. In the gloom he is nearly impossible to see. "They won't break. How's the armor?"

"Strange." It fits like a glove, makes me difficult to see, and is so light that I might as well be wearing fatigues. But it's strong—Harper and I tested it for hours before donning it.

Still, other than Mettias, the Martials refused to wear it. *Witchery*, they said. Teluman argued over it. But I wasn't willing to issue a command that wouldn't be followed.

"Shrike." Harper appears on my right. My heart thuds a bit faster, traitor that it is. This is the first time he has spoken directly to me in days. "Something is off," he says. "There aren't enough guards on the walls. The streets are empty—the squares are empty. This doesn't feel right."

It is the last thing I want to hear. The people of Antium await aid. They await the weapons and soldiers that will allow them to cast out the Karkauns.

"Where the bleeding hells is Musa?"

"Here." The tall Scholar, also clad in Teluman's armor, materializes from the darkness like a wraith. "The wights say the Karkauns have gathered near a big, bloody rock close to the main palace. They've turned it into an altar. They're shouting, screaming, murdering people—that sort of thing. And they're leading prisoners there. Mostly Martials. Some Scholars too."

He must speak of Cardium Rock. "Women?" My fist clenches on the scim at my waist. "Children?"

Musa shakes his head. "Men. Boys. Captured soldiers. Those who didn't fight or couldn't. There are thousands of them."

"Our spies said the men were killed—"

"Does Antium have an extensive system of dungeons?" Musa says, and at my silence, he nods. "They weren't killed, then," he says. "They were hidden. Saved for . . . whatever the hells this is."

"The Soul Catcher holds the ghosts," Teluman says. "The Karkauns cannot summon them again to strengthen their army."

"The Soul Catcher is hundreds of miles from the Waiting Place right now," Musa says.

"What the ten hells is he doing so far—"

"Skies know, Shrike," Musa says. "A wight brought me the information yesterday. I haven't had a chance to send her back for details." He levels a reproachful look at me. "Been a bit busy."

"We can still pull back," Harper says. "Get a message to Quin and Dex. Wait for a more opportune time to strike."

"Gather the men," I tell him, for there is no better time. I lost Antium. I let the Karkauns win. And Keris used my failure to steal the Empire from my nephew. I have to get it back for him. And I have to get it back for the people still suffering behind its walls.

When the men have gathered, I raise my hand for silence. They watch me with a flat sort of curiosity, even the Ankanese sappers, silent on the edges of the crowd.

"Tonight," I say, "the Karkauns believe they will defeat us."

The men hiss and spit, their rage as sharp as my own.

"They think they can turn our city into a butchering ground. They think their violence will frighten us. But we are Martials. And we fear nothing.

"Nearly every last one of you was in Antium. You saw what they did. You know what they've been doing since then. So I tell you now, no matter what happens behind those walls, no matter what horrors they have in store, there is no going back today. We will win, or we will die. We will take back our city for our people, or we will watch the Empire fall. Now. Tonight." I put my fist to my heart. "Loyal to the end."

They do not roar their support, for secrecy is our advantage this night. Instead, they thump their fists to their hearts once.

Then we are moving through the hills and down into the flats of the city, away from our mounts and the dozen men left to guard them. The cold drags at me, and my eyelashes frost over. But after a few minutes of running, I don't notice it anymore. By the time we take out the Karkaun sentries, my cheeks are flushed, my fingers tingling.

We make for the northern wall, shrouded by thick, old-growth forest. Within is a door, boarded over, collapsed and forgotten behind a ton of rubble.

There, an Ankanese sapper named G'rus begins rigging the door with charges. His four comrades disappear, each escorted by a Mask. Four more of the Ankanese travel with Quin Veturius. We will see if they prove their worth this night.

Harper appears out of the darkness, a grappling hook in hand. "Soldiers," he whispers. "Atop the wall, and headed this way."

Moments later, voices carry down. There weren't supposed to be soldiers near this side of the wall. According to my spies, it's thinly patrolled.

A scream from deep within the city pierces the night, high and chilling. My men shift uneasily, and I grab the grappling hook from Avitas and march down the wall, far enough from the Karkauns that they won't hear the hook land.

I cast it up, and when it takes, I'm moving up the wall, hand over hand, even as Harper hisses quiet protests beneath me.

Once at the top, I survey the two Karkauns. They are of medium height and build, like most of their people, with long, matted hair and skin as pale as mine. Their thick furs obscure both vision and sound, and before they notice me, I am upon them. The first manages a small yelp before I part his head from his body. The second draws his weapon—just in time for me to take it and stab him in the throat.

I drag the bodies to the side of the wall, throw them over in case any other Karkauns come searching for them, and rappel back down.

"That," says Harper, his jaw set, "was foolish."

"That was necessary," I said. "Are we nearly ready?"

G'rus gestures for everyone to take cover as he lights the fuse. Moments later, a deafening boom tears through the air. It is followed by another boom moments later, farther down the wall, and then two more. Decoy explosions. They are larger, and closer to the center of the city. By the time the Karkauns ensure there are no intruders at those spots, we'll be long gone.

"Shrike?" a soft voice calls through the dust and rubble, and a figure emerges out of the darkness. She is lean, with dark skin and curly hair. Neera, the woman who helped Faris and me escape the Karkauns.

I reach her in three strides, and before she can draw a weapon, I have a knife to her throat.

"Loyal." She speaks the code she was given without the slightest hesitation. "To the end."

"Well met, Neera." I clasp her hand, and her smile is a flash of hope in the darkness.

"Quickly, Shrike," she says. "Before the Karkauns come."

My men enter the city two by two. They drip with weaponry, and each carries a long, thin package weighing five stones. Twenty scims, light and strong. They are concealed, wrapped, and strapped tight against the backs of the men. Ten thousand scims for our people, everything we could scrounge up from Delphinium and the now-shuttered Kauf Prison. Everything we could manage to carry.

"Go!" I hiss to the men. "Faster!"

Musa finds me moments later. "The Karkauns are on the way," he says. "We have a few minutes, if that. And Quin is stuck in the tunnels. One of my wights says the passages you used are collapsed."

Those tunnels were fine only two weeks ago. And as Quin loves to say, only a jackass believes in coincidences.

"It was the Karkauns," I say. "Tell Quin his sappers must clear a path. The Karkauns are trying to herd him. They want to ambush him aboveground, no doubt, and stop his men from getting into the city. If he doesn't get through, he might as well turn back."

Harper takes me aside, voice low so that the soldiers still passing through the door don't hear us. "He should have been nearly through those tunnels by now. He won't make it on time."

"He's Quin Veturius," I say. "He'll make it."

"We need those men," Harper says. "We cannot take the capital with five hundred men and untrained citizens, no matter how many there are. Not with tens of thousands of Karkauns quartered here. It would be impos—"

"Don't say it." I put my finger against his lips, and he falls silent. "We know better. Keris trained that word out of us. Impossible doesn't exist. Not when the Empire is on the line."

The rest of the soldiers are through the doorway. Harper and I are the last. "I will take this city, Harper," I tell him. "With my bare hands, if I must. Come. I have an idea."

CHAPTER THIRTY-THREE

Laia

I walk along a river of death, but I am not alone.

"I have missed you, my love."

A shadow walks beside me. Pale hands pull down a hood, revealing fire-red hair and dark brown eyes that hid so much more than I ever imagined. Not my foe, but the first boy I ever loved.

"Keenan," I whisper.

My skin burns, and I feel like I cannot breathe. For the blink of an eye, I see seething, muddy water roiling around me.

Then Keenan speaks, and the image fades.

"You're in trouble, my love." He brushes a calloused thumb against my chin, and there is no lie when he calls me his love. "You're drowning."

"I do not feel like I'm drowning."

"You're strong." He takes my hand and we walk. Something calls out to me deep in my mind, a scream locked in a chest, locked in a closet, locked in a room that is too far away from this place to notice. "You always have been, because of the Star. But for other reasons too."

"The darkness," I say. "The one that lives within."

"Yes," he says. "Tell me of it. For I have darkness within me also, and I would know if we are two sides of the same coin."

"Two sides—" I look up at him, dazed. It hurts to breathe, and when I look down, my clothes are soaked, and my arms and hands bleed. I taste salt and put a hand to my head. My head bleeds too. A voice within calls out. *Laia.*

"I cannot tell you about it," I say. "I am not supposed to."

"Of course." He is so gentle. So kind. "Let's not wake it if we shouldn't."

"I have already woken it," I say. "I woke it when I defied you." I look down at my body again. I am so tired. "Keenan, I—I cannot breathe."

"You're drowning, my love," he says with such sweetness. "You're almost gone."

A flash across my vision. Darkness. The rain-heavy sky. Debris-choked water around me, dragging me along. High canyon walls rise on either side, streaked red and white and orange and yellow, like one of Darin's paintings.

Darin, my brother, who loves me, not like—

Fight him, Laia. A voice calls out. So far away. But insistent.

"I should not be here." I pull my hand from Keenan's, because if he does love me it is a twisted sort of love.

"No," he says. "You should not." Though his voice is soft, something behind it makes me draw away. Deep in his brown eyes, I see the flash of a feral creature, riven by a hunger that never ends. I feel surrounded by that hunger, suddenly, as if it's a pack of wolves, closing in.

"Get away from me," I say. "I will tell you *nothing*—"

His body changes, the way it did when I gave him the armlet. Except he is no shadow creature now, but something explosive and wild, an unchecked fire, malevolence emanating from every flicker of his body.

"You will tell me what lives within you and where it came from—"

"I'll die first!"

I open my eyes then to a nightmare world. A turbid river of rock and branches and debris tosses me to and fro like a rag doll, and though I try to stay afloat, I am yanked under again and again, until water fills my nose and I cannot breathe.

No, I think. *Not like this. Not like this.* I scream as I break through the surface of the water.

"Let me inside, girl!" Rehmat appears, reaching for me. "I can save you, but you have to let me in."

I barely hear it before the water pulls me down once more. I claw and kick and thrash, pain exploding along my hands and legs as the flood's undertow drags at me. When I surface again, Rehmat is somewhere between furious and frenzied.

"Stop fighting the flood!" it shouts. "Keep your feet up!"

I try to do as it asks, but the river is a starving giant clutching at my ankles, as hungry as the maelstrom I see in my nightmares.

"Let me in, Laia!"

As I break the surface, I imagine a door in my mind and fling it wide. Almost immediately, I go under again. My whole body is on fire. I swallow a lungful of water and this must be death.

Then, like that day weeks ago in Adisa, I am pushed to the back corner of my mind—this time with a shove instead of a nudge. My body shoots through the water, clothes ripping, my pack falling away. The wind bends beneath me, Rehmat manipulating it as easily as clay.

I wonder if this is real or if the flood has killed me.

It's real. When Rehmat speaks, it is from inside my own mind now. The creature's magic saturates my limbs and we are one, riding the wind as easily as I tread the ground. It carries me to the top of the canyon, and I collapse on my side, staring down at the flash flood in wonder and horror. *Rise, Laia. The Nightbringer is near—*

A soft thud beside me, and then there is a hand at my throat, lifting me, squeezing. The Nightbringer, cloaked and shadowed once more, fixes me with his hateful, sun-eyed stare.

"You—cannot kill me—Nightbringer—"

"But I am so much more than the Nightbringer now, Laia." His voice is that flood below, all-consuming and treacherous.

Once again, I am shoved to one side of my own mind. I stare down the Nightbringer in all of his wrath. But I feel no fear, because Rehmat feels no fear.

"You," the Nightbringer whispers, "have been hiding for a very long time. What are you? Speak!"

"I am your chains, Meherya. I am your end." But Rehmat does not sound triumphant. It sounds anguished. It sounds broken.

The Nightbringer releases me. He takes a step back, a slow shock rolling over him. I expect Rehmat to use the moment to spirit us away. But it does not. Nor does it attack the Nightbringer. Instead, we stare together at the king of the jinn, and an unexpected emotion unfurls within Rehmat. One that makes me recoil in disgust.

Longing.

The Nightbringer appears as paralyzed as I am. "I know you," he says. "I know you, but—"

Rehmat lifts my—our—hand, but we do not touch him. Not yet.

"I am your end," Rehmat says. "But I was there at the beginning too, my love. When you were king alone, solitary and ever apart from our people. You went wandering near the sea one day, and you found a queen."

I try to wrap my mind around what I am hearing, but it is too deep a betrayal for me to comprehend. This . . . thing living inside of me was a jinn? And not just any jinn, but their *queen*?

"Rehmat," the Nightbringer says, the name a prayer and a curse at once. "You died. In the Duskan Sea battle—"

What the bleeding skies is happening? I scream in my mind at Rehmat.

It—or she—ignores me. But when she speaks again, it is in the manner that I've become accustomed to, as if she has finally remembered why she is here.

"I did not die," she says. "I saw what was to come and I called on an old magic, blood magic. Lay down your scythe, Meherya. Stop this madness—"

But the Nightbringer flinches. "I was alone," he whispers. "For a thousand years, I thought I was—" He shakes his head, and it is such a human gesture that I actually feel sorry for him. For in this moment, we have both been betrayed.

Damn you, Rehmat, I shout at her in my head. *Get out of my mind.*

Laia—

Get out! Her magic fades first, then her presence, and I am alone.

"I'm sorry," I whisper to the Nightbringer, "I—I didn't know—" Why am I telling him this? He will only use it against me. He might have loved me, but he hated himself as he did so, because his hatred for my people is the air he breathes.

An aroma of cedar and lemon fills my senses, and I return to a cellar miles to the north, where a red-haired boy I loved made me feel less alone. I have spent so long hating the Nightbringer that I never mourned who he used to be. Keenan, my first love, my friend, a boy who understood my loss so deeply because he had endured his own.

"We are doomed, you and I," the Nightbringer whispers, and when he touches my face with his hands, their fire cooled, I do not quail. "To offer more love than we will ever be given."

He is not violence then, or vengeance. All his hate has drained away, replaced by despair, and I put my hands on his face. I am glad Rehmat has fled, for this strange impulse is mine alone.

Salt flows over his fingers as fire trickles down mine. Would that we all knew the cracked terrain of each other's broken hearts. Perhaps then, we would not be so cruel to those who walk this lonely world with us.

Our moment is over too quickly. As if realizing what he is doing, he wrenches his hands from my skin, and I stumble back, toward the canyon's edge. He snatches me from peril, but that act of mercy seems to rekindle his fury. A fey wind howls out of the somber sky, and he spins away.

Just like that, we are at war again.

I watch him until he is gone and then look down at my hands. They are unmarked by his fire, appearing whole, as if I'd touched a human and not a creature of flame.

Still, they burn.

CHAPTER THIRTY-FOUR

The Blood Shrike

As we enter the city, a horn wails. A Karkaun warning call, rousing them from sleep and drink and less savory entertainments. In minutes, the sound echoes across the city.

"Teluman." At my summons, the smith looms out of the night, a group of twenty men behind him.

"After you secure the drum towers," I tell him, "get to the southeast barracks, in the Mercator Quarter. A good part of their army is there. Burn it down."

"Consider it done, Shrike." Teluman moves off, and I turn to Mettias.

I'm heartened to see that though the thud of Karkaun boots closes in on us, the young Pater is unfazed. He'd have made a good Mask.

"Make sure those weapons get to every Martial and Scholar willing to fight," I say. "Get the word out to hold the attack until Teluman sounds the drums. Musa, send a wight to Quin. When he gets through, he needs to bring his forces to Cardium Rock."

"Shrike," Harper protests, for this is not part of the plan. "Grímarr is too well-protected. He'll have the bulk of his men up there. He's luring you to him."

"You are a man of few words, Harper." I signal to my men, and we move away from the walls. "So don't waste the ones you *do* utter on things I already know. He needs to die. And I'm the one who is going to kill him."

Harper looks taken aback, and then laughs. "Sorry, Shrike."

Musa, Harper, and my last thirty men are behind me as we weave through streets we know better than any Karkaun. We leave weapons throughout the city, passing through a prearranged system of alleys and courtyards and homes. Everywhere, the Martials and Scholars of Antium thump their fists to their hearts in salute.

Eleventh bell tolls. We approach the Hall of Records, a building as massive as Blackcliff's amphitheater. The hall's roof, carved with sculptures of Taius's victories, is held up by stone columns as wide around as trees in the Waiting Place.

We enter, making our way across a thick layer of ash from the fire that burned here when the hall was hit by a Karkaun projectile. A stone statue of Taius lies on its side, the head broken off and half-buried beneath scattered scrolls and shattered masonry.

The Hall of Records takes up one entire side of Cartus Square. Palace outbuildings line another side, and shops and businesses the third. The last side is taken up by a jumble of rock that leads to a vast bone pit. A scarred granite cliff stretches above the pit and at its top—Cardium Rock, where a dozen massive bonfires light up the sky.

As I send men out into the square to kill off any guards, Musa comes to squat beside me.

"Spiro ran into trouble. He's battling a Karkaun force at one of the drum towers." Musa pauses. "Three hundred men."

Bleeding, burning hells. At that moment, Harper, who slipped ahead to scout, returns.

"The palace entrance to the Rock is blocked by thousands of Karkauns," he says. "They're bringing prisoners out from the dungeons and—" Disgust ripples across Harper's silver face. I move forward to get a better view of the Rock, only to see prisoners being shoved off the top and into the bone pit a hundred feet below.

"How fast can you get our men changed into the stinking furs the barbarians wear?" I ask Harper.

"Before you get up that cliff, Shrike."

"Get to the top of the Rock, hide among the Karkauns, and wait for my signal. When the time is right, raise the hells. And—"

He meets my eyes, his own burning with battle rage. I want to tell him to be careful. To take no foolish risks. To survive. But such sentiment has no place in war.

"Don't fail me," I tell him, and turn away.

It is the work of a few moments to flit across the square. Once I reach the pit, I mutter a curse. I thought I could swing a grappling hook up from the furthermost edge of it, but it is too broad.

Which means I must cross it. I must make my way over the skulls and bones and bodies of the dead.

You are all that holds back the darkness. My father spoke so to me, more than a year ago now. I do not think any longer. I simply move, dropping down into the pit.

Bones crunch as I land, and soft flesh bursts. I retch from the stench, and the darkness is something out of a nightmare.

It lasts so long. The pit is a hundred yards wide, but it might as well be a continent. For as I make my way over the dead, I hear things.

Moans.

Ghosts! my mind screams. But it is not ghosts. It is something far worse. It is those men who survived the fall. I want to find them. To grant them mercy in this hellish place. But there are too many and I have no time. Teluman has not yet sounded the drums. For all I know, he and his men could be dead, our attack over before it even started.

Defeat in your mind is defeat on the battlefield!

A lifetime passes as I walk across the pit, over the rotting flesh of the dead. I know I will never speak of these moments to anyone. For they have changed something inside irrevocably. If I do not kill Grímarr at the end of this, this will be where I die too, and I will deserve it, because I did not avenge the injustice done to all those whom I tread upon now.

Finally, I reach the cliff. It is rugged and will be difficult to traverse. My eyes adjust to the darkness as much as they can, and I can just make out crags and pits in the rock face that I can use to pull myself up.

I unsheathe my knives, dig them into the rock, and climb. The world below falls away. I still bear the scar of Grímarr's bite. A half-moon-shaped reminder that he sunk his jaws into my city, my people, and sucked them dry. I quench the idea of death and think of how it will feel to hold that bastard's neck in my hands. Of how it will feel to break it.

Foot by agonizing foot, I climb. By the time I approach the top, I am covered in sweat and panting, every muscle screaming. I drag myself the final few inches, taking in deep draughts of air as I peer over the edge.

Cardium Rock is shaped like a wedge with a flat tip. The narrowest point, where I am, is thirty feet wide, and the broadest is a hundred. At its far edge are three terraced levels for viewers to watch the executions that usually take place here.

Right now, the terraces are filled with Karkauns. Grímarr, meanwhile, is just steps away.

He is naked but for a loincloth, his pale body drenched in blood. He gibbers maniacally—*Ik tachk mort fid iniqant fi!*—as the air around him quivers. The skin where I severed his left arm is pink and scarred, as if he's had months to heal instead of a fortnight.

Which means that even if he hasn't been able to raise ghosts, he has other magic at his disposal.

A bonfire burns behind him, ringed with guards. As I calculate whether there are enough to be a real threat, the drums thunder out with such force that I nearly lose my grip on the knives holding me in place.

North tower for the rightful emperor. Attack.

East tower for the rightful emperor. Attack.

West tower for the rightful emperor. Attack.

A cry rises up, one voice joined by a dozen, then a hundred, then thousands. It is not a cry of sadness or defeat, but of fury and vengeance. Across Antium, the women and children and wounded and elderly who have been at the mercy of the Karkauns take up arms. It is a blood-stirring sound. The sound of impending victory.

I close my eyes and remember Antium falling. Remember my men, possessed by ghosts, killing their own people. I think of Madam Heera, and the weeping from the brothels.

Loyal to the end.

I vault upward and tear off my hood.

"*Grímarr!*" I bellow his name, flinging three throwing knives at him. But he moves with unnatural swiftness to evade them. Without turning to face me, he laughs, an uncanny cackle.

"Blood Shrike," he says. "At last."

His men approach, but I spit at his feet, cut my hand, and let the blood drip to the stones of Cardium Rock.

"I challenge thee, Grímarr." My voice carries over the bonfires and up the terraces. "To battle with no steel and no stone, no blades and no bows. Until one of us lies dead."

I cast my scim to the ground, along with the knife belt at my waist.

"To the death." Grímarr turns, grinning, his eyes the pure white of a man possessed. *Ten hells.* Somehow, the Karkaun warlock has managed to harness a ghost.

"Come then, girl." His voice sounds like one overlaid against another, an eerie echo. "Come to your doom, for with your soul I shall open a door into the hells."

The Karkauns holler in excitement. Grímarr's guards keep their hands on their weapons but step back. The challenge has been accepted.

I ignore the warlock's blathering and focus on how I'm going to beat him. Ghosts lend humans impossible strength. If Grímarr gets his hands on me, I'm dead.

He drops into a sort of half crouch, preparing to leap. He is taller than me—wider and heavier too. But the ghost possessing him makes him pre-ternaturally quick. I dart forward, landing two hard jabs on his chest and a kick to his windpipe.

A normal man would stagger. He shrugs off the blows and snatches at my leg when it's still flying through the air. I whip it out of the way with only inches to spare.

I dart around the bonfire, and he dives for me, hitting me in the stom-ach so hard that I nearly retch. I elbow him in the eyeball, grimacing as it squelches. When he howls in pain, I escape his grasp yet again. This time, I edge toward the cliff, watching it carefully, allowing myself to get closer to it. Grímarr narrows his eyes and backs away, understanding my intent.

It appears as if he is retreating from me. Beyond the bonfire, his men jeer at him. An angry snarl forms on his milk-white face. He speeds forward, impossibly fast. I have only a moment to crouch and barrel into his legs as fast as I can in the hopes that he'll roll over me and into the pit.

He simply leaps over me. In seconds, he will tackle me and break my neck or spine or both. I spin out of my crouch and swipe up my knife belt, still lying near the bonfire. When I turn, he is there, foam flecking his mouth, eyes that uncanny white.

He is too strong. I will never beat him in hand-to-hand combat. And as a Martial, I don't bleeding care. War has rules—this monster followed none of them. Saving the people of Antium means I must choose between honor and victory. Without hesitation, I choose victory.

He sees the blade too late. I plunge it into his heart, rip it out, and plunge it in again, and again and again.

He should not be able to speak. But the ghost in him rages. "Karkaun— challenge—" he rasps. "No—steel—"

"I'm not a Karkaun." I kick up my scim from where it rests near my feet and swing it at his neck. He blocks the attack, the ghost in him lending him strength when he should be bleeding out, and I dance away from him.

"You think—you will win," he whispers, and now he weaves, having lost too much blood.

"This is my city. And as long as I have breath left in my body, I will fight for it."

"Cities." He drops to his knees. "Cities are nothing. I am nothing. You are nothing. *Ik tachk mort fid iniqant fi.*"

His shoulders sag, and when I whip my scim across to take off his head, he cannot stop me. Blood geysers over me as I kick his twitching body off the cliff, dig my fingers into his hair, and hold up his severed head.

"This is your leader?" I turn to his men. "This is the man you called king?"

For a seemingly unending moment, the Karkauns are silent. The city is filled with the sounds of battle, and in the distance, the lockstep thud of boots echoes. *Quin!*

Come on, Harper, I think. *If ever there was a clearer signal than this . . .*

A cry of victory goes up from the Martial prisoners still being marched through the Karkaun crowd, and all the hells break loose. It begins at the back of the Karkaun throng, but my men move quickly. Fights break out, and the Karkauns shout, grasping for their weapons, realizing that the enemy is among them.

I tear another knife from my belt and plunge into the fray. All of my hate, all of my frustration, every sleepless night during which I raged against my own inaction pours out of me.

When the Martial prisoners realize what is happening, they fight too, chains and all. Without Grímarr to lead them and without the ghosts to lend them strength, the Karkauns panic, stabbing and slashing indiscriminately. As they die at the edge of my blades, I hear the phrase Grímarr uttered. *Ik tachk mort fid iniqant fi.*

Within the crowd of Karkauns, a squad of my men fight their way toward me, Musa among them. I try to join them, but the Karkauns surround us. Musa disappears, his scims flying, and I remind myself to ask him who the hells trained him before I am inundated by the enemy again.

Soon enough, the sheer number of Karkauns grows overwhelming. Even with the prisoners fighting, we are heavily outnumbered.

I spot raven-black hair and brown skin. Harper appears beside me, blood-spattered and snarling, tearing into the Karkauns with a savagery that matches my own. Kill by kill, we press the barbarians back.

Until a knot of them comes between us. One of Harper's scims goes flying. I hear the crunch of fist against bone. A Karkaun dagger flashes high and blood geysers in the air.

One second, Harper is there. The next he is not. As I fight, I wait to see him, wait for him to stand up. But he doesn't.

My mind goes horribly blank. I scream and battle through the Karkauns closest to me, heart thundering in terror. It wasn't his blood. He'd have blocked that attack easily. No. No. No. I should have ordered him to stay in Delphinium. I should have had him accompany Quin. I shouldn't have tried to take back Antium, not if this was the cost.

And now—now—

Dead. This cannot be. Harper cannot be dead. For I did not say any of what I should have. I did not touch him or kiss him or tell him that without him, I never would have survived this long. *Dead like Father and Mother and Hannah and Faris and all those who you love—*

Suddenly, he is charging through the Karkauns and beside me once more, limping but alive. I grab his arm, ensuring that he's real, and he glances up in surprise.

"You—" Bleeding hells, I think I am crying. No. It's sweat. It must be. "You're—"

His eyes shift to whatever is behind me. He shoves me aside and impales a Karkaun on the end of his scim. From the south, the drums thunder again.

Enemy retreat, southern quadrant. The news gives my fighters and the prisoners new heart. A group of Karkauns, those closest to the palace, breaks away, running for their lives.

Harper grins and turns to me as more and more flee from Cardium Rock. "They're running!"

I nod, but I can hardly muster a smile back. My chest is still tight from seeing him go under, from the fear that grabbed hold of me like a mailed fist, when I thought he was gone.

The rhythmic march of Martial soldiers grows louder, and even as we follow the fleeing Karkauns, I spot white hair and the sigil of Gens Veturia. I move toward Quin quickly—anything to get away from the thoughts in my head.

"Ten hells, old man." I clap him on the back. "It took you long enough."

He surveys the Karkauns. "Seems like you have it well in hand. Shall we send them crawling back to their holes?"

The night is bloody, but the Karkauns are nothing without their alpha. Those who fight are quickly destroyed. The rest simply run, escaping the city like rats from a ship on fire.

"Get a message to the southern Paters," I tell Harper. "Tell them those loyal to Emperor Zacharias liberated Antium this day."

Dawn brightens the eastern horizon, and my men gather on a staircase in Cartus Square. Quin hoists Zacharias's hawk-and-hammer flag atop the palace.

As he does, Antium's survivors emerge into the streets. Emaciated Martial and Scholar men, chained but unbroken. Women clutching weapons in one hand and children in the other. Fighters all.

The square fills up, and then the streets. I spot Neera in the crowd, and a chant starts up, one that is spoken and whispered at first. Then shouted by all of those who fought for Antium, by all who survived.

"Imperator Invictus! Imperator Invictus!"

My blood surges when I hear it. First in pride. Then in dawning unease.

For they are not chanting for Zacharias.

They are chanting for me.

"They should be chanting the Emperor's name," I hiss at Quin, who has descended and stands beside me on the stairs. "Not—this."

"The Emperor is a child, Shrike. A symbol. You are the general who fought for them. You understood the strength of their spirit. And you were fearless. Let them call you whatever they please."

My mind snags on one word: *Fearless*. For I am not fearless. To be fearless means to have a heart of steel. But my heart betrayed itself. It is soft and hopeful.

And I know now that it belongs entirely to Avitas Harper. No matter how I wish to deny it, my reaction when I thought him dead tells me I am fully, foolishly in love with him. He is the weak spot in my armor, the flaw in my defense.

Damn my traitorous heart to the hells.

PART THREE
THE JINN QUEEN

CHAPTER THIRTY-FIVE

The Nightbringer

One evening on my way home from visiting the Ankanese, I stopped to rest and eat south of the Waiting Place, along the shores of the Duskan Sea. As I let the stars and waves lull me to sleep, a flicker caught my eye. A fire burning bright and solitary, the lamp of a wanderer on a great, dark plain.

It drew closer, and I flowed into my flame form, for this jinn carried weapons in either hand, and though I did not enjoy battle, I was more than prepared for it.

"Hail, kindred." She brought with her the scent of citrus and juniper, her voice husky and accented strangely. "Will you share your meal? For I have traveled long, with nary a bite. For your kindness, I will offer you a tale. This, I vow."

I confess my bewilderment, for I knew all of the jinn in the Waiting Place, and yet I had never met her.

"I am called Rehmat and am a creature of flame, like you, my king," she said. "But born elsewhere, that I might live among the humans for a time and understand them. I have bled with them and battled with them, but Mauth bid me join you, for my destiny lies now with our people."

Rehmat. A strange name. One with a meaning that unsettled me.

She told her tale, as she promised, and then traveled to the Sher Jinnaat with me. But ever after, she was never content to remain in the wood. A strange mood would overcome her, she would strap her blades across her back and wander, a warrior-poet who found a home wherever she laid her head.

The first time she disappeared from the Waiting Place, I searched and searched until I found her draped in the branches of a Gandifur tree in the far west, trading poetry with the Jadna tribe—the forebears of the Jaduna.

She drifted thousands of miles south, to the Ankanese, and taught them the language of the stars. Then she sang stories with the first Kehannis of the Tribes, teaching them to draw magic from words. She found those Tribespeople who saw the dead and instructed them on the Mysteries they would later use to pass ghosts.

"Why," I asked her, exasperated, "do you always wander so far? Why can you not remain in the Sher Jinnaat?"

Her smile pulled at my heart, for there was a deep sadness to it. "You have found your purpose, my king. You have much magic in you. I still seek mine. When I find my power, I will return. This, I vow."

It had not occurred to me that she lacked magic, for to me, she burned with life and wit, humor and beauty.

One day, weeks after she'd disappeared again, I woke from sleep. Her anguished voice called to me across hundreds of miles. I made for an island empty of human life, but teeming with every other kind. The ocean was peaceful, a brilliant azure, the winds sweet as summer cherries.

I found Rehmat along the northern coast of the island. She wore her human form, brown-skinned and brown-eyed, with black hair woven into a plait. She rocked back and forth, her arms clasped tight about her legs.

"Rehmat?" I cradled her to me, and she dropped her head against my heart.

"This is an island of death, Meherya," she whispered. "Many ghosts will pass from here. It will not be you who passes them, but another who has not yet come. And you will call her traitor, though she meant no harm."

She screamed, her dark eyes burning into mine. "The Ember will walk these sands, and here the seeds of his defiance will flower, but for naught, for the forest will call him and suffering will sunder him."

Thus did we learn Rehmat's power, one far more treacherous than anything we had yet encountered. She foresaw the future. My own ability to scry was limited to impressions, brief images. Rehmat saw possibility after possibility.

She returned to the Sher Jinnaat, as she promised. But the price was high. She locked herself away in her home and spoke to no one but me. I begged Mauth to free her from the torment of her magic. But he spoke less and less. We were created to pass the ghosts. Our powers had their uses—and though we might not like it, hers had a purpose too.

"If only I could master it," she whispered to me once after a particularly difficult episode. "I would teach others. This, I vow."

I cared for her during those difficult months, and something kindled between us, a soul-deep fire that others had found but that had, until then, eluded me. My heart was hers, and I knew that if she did not wish to become my queen, I would never have one.

In time, she learned to understand and control her magic. As she promised, when other flames kindled and discovered they were haunted by the curse of foresight, it was Rehmat who taught them to see it as a gift.

After she made peace with her visions, she found her poetry again. But now she shared it with me alone, whispering it into the deepest chambers of my heart.

When she consented to be my queen, the Sher Jinnaat celebrated for a month. And when we brought our own little flames to the world, the entire city turned out to sing the song of welcome. All was well.

Until the Scholars came.

After they murdered our children, Rehmat donned her blades once more. She spoke strength into the jinn who yet lived. She used centuries of experience to outwit the Scholars in battle.

But it was not enough. Even as Cain's accursed coven plotted to chain the jinn, Rehmat fell in combat near the Duskan Sea, where I first beheld her. I pulled her to me as her flame flickered into darkness, and she fixed her liquid-fire eyes on my face.

"You are strong," I said. "You will survive this."

"Remember your name." There was such urgency to her whisper. "You are the Beloved. Remember, or you will be lost."

"Do not leave this world," I begged her. "Do not leave me alone, my love."

"I will see you again." She squeezed my hands. "This, I vow."

Then her flame faded. But I left her ashen body, for far to the north, a great evil was unfolding. The imprisoning of my kind.

I tried to stop it. But just like with Rehmat, I was too late.

"I forsake thee." I forced my way to Mauth's domain, to that vast, wretched sea into which I had cast so much human suffering. "I forsake thee, and I am thy creature no longer."

"Thou wilt always be mine. For thou art the Meherya."

"No," I said to him. "Never again."

I returned to a desolate world. For my Rehmat was gone. My kin were gone, all but Shaeva.

She died slowly—I made sure of it before bringing her back to be Soul Catcher, before chaining her to the Waiting Place to pass ghosts.

And I wept over Rehmat's final words to me, for she took such pride in keeping her vows, and this was one she had broken.

What a fool I was. All those years I knew her, she never once broke an oath. Not even the smallest, simplest promise.

Why would her last and greatest vow be any different?

CHAPTER THIRTY-SIX

Laia

It takes me an hour to find my fallen pack, and three more to discover a path that will take me to Afya and Mamie. My clothes have finally dried, though they are stiff with mud and scrape painfully against the bruises and cuts from the flash flood. I feel as if every bone in my body has been broken.

The storm has fled with the Nightbringer, leaving the brilliant blue spill of the galaxy in its wake. The light makes it easy to see, but the rain-churned desert floor is sludge now, perilous and sticky. My pace is maddeningly slow. My body shakes, and not just from the cold.

Despair takes hold. At this pace, I will not reach the guard tower before I collapse from pain. I think of calling out to Darin, but I will only worry him. And I do not want to draw the attention of any fey creatures right now. If I am attacked, I cannot fight.

"Laia."

Rehmat's luminous form casts a glow across the starlit desert, sending night creatures scurrying into their burrows. Beside it—her—I am but a smudge in the darkness.

I have a thousand questions. But now that she is here, it takes me long minutes to find any words that do not drip with rancor.

"You're his wife," I finally say. "His *queen*."

"I *was* his wife. No longer. I have not been his wife for a millennium." Only days ago, I wondered if Rehmat was male because of how irritatingly stubborn she was. But now there is a shift in her voice, her form. She no longer hides who she is.

"I did not tell you," she says, "because I thought the truth would anger you. I worried you would not trust me if you knew I was a jinn —"

"*Are* a jinn!"

"Was a jinn." She greets my outburst with infuriating aplomb. "The Jaduna's blood magic did not allow me to keep my corporeal body, my fire. But jinn souls are linked to our magic. If the magic lives, so do our souls."

"So they . . . extracted you?" I ask. "*He* did not know you had died. Did you trick him too?"

"It was necessary."

"Necessary." I laugh. "And the deaths of tens of thousands of my people? Was that necessary too?"

"My gift as a jinn was foretelling." Rehmat keeps pace with me easily, lighting the way, though I wish she wouldn't. Darkness is what I want right now. Darkness in which to nurse my pain.

"I saw one path forward, Laia. Before our war with the Scholars, I befriended the Jaduna. We shared much lore over the centuries. When I learned that the Meherya would turn, I went to them, hoping their magic could help me stop it."

She opens her hands and looks down at her form. "All they could offer was this. They said that upon my death, they would draw out my soul and nest me within their own people. A hundred men and women volunteered. It was a testament to our years of friendship that they would do such a thing, not knowing the effect it would have on their progeny. They found my broken body after the battle and took me to their home, far to the west."

"So you lived in them," I say. "Like a disease."

"Like gold eyes." She is as quiet as a breeze. "Or brown skin. They traveled to Martial lands and Scholar lands and Tribal lands. The blood-lines spread. And with each generation, I grew more removed from wake-fulness and watchfulness. Until all that was left was the spark of magic. In some, like you and the Blood Shrike and Musa of Adisa, the magic was awoken under duress. And in others, like Tas of the North, or Darin or Avitas Harper, the magic sleeps. But all of you have *kedim jadu* in you."

"Ancient magic," I mutter. "All that time you were lurking? Did you try to influence us?"

"Never," she swears. "Blood magic has conditions. For my rebirth, I had to agree to three sacrifices. The first: that my life as a jinn remain in the past—I may never speak of my time with the Nightbringer, my deeds as queen, or even—even my children."

The misery in her voice at the last is clear. I think of Mother, who strug-gled to speak of my father or Lis, so deep were her wounds.

"The second," Rehmat continues, "that I remain dormant until one of the *kedim jadu* directly defied the Nightbringer. And the third: that I have no corporeal body, unless one of the *kedim jadu* allowed me to use them as a conduit."

Skies know, I'll never make that mistake again. "Why did you want to stay away from the jinn? Can they hurt you?"

"Not exactly—"

"You still feel for them." I cast the accusation too swiftly for her to refute it. "That's why you disappeared in the Waiting Place and when I was with Khuri. You're not afraid of them. You're afraid of yourself around them."

"That's not—"

"Please don't lie," I say. "The jinn were your family. You loved them. I felt that within you. That sense of—of yearning. Is that why you do not want me to get the scythe? Why you always say *defeat* instead of *kill*? Because you love him and don't want him dead?"

"Laia—his losses, what he has suffered—it is incalculable."

"I do not love my family any less than he loved his." I turn on her, and if she had a body, it would currently sport a black eye.

"I lost my mother," I say. "My father. My sister. My friends. My grand-mother. My grandfather. I was betrayed by the Resistance. Betrayed by the first boy I ever loved. Abandoned by Elias. You think I don't want to sink a dagger into the Commandant's heart? You think I don't want to see the Martials suffer for what they have done to my people? I understand loss. But you do not fix loss with mass murder."

"Your love is powerful," Rehmat says. "It is your love that woke me—your love of your people. Your desire to save them. But the Nightbringer is not human, Laia. Can you compare the rage of a storm to the rage of man? When Mauth created the Meherya, he created a creature that could pass on ghosts for millennia, despite all of their pain, all of their sadness. Do you know what *Meherya* means?"

"No," I say. "And I don't care. I *do* wonder what your name means. *Traitor*, perhaps?"

"*Meherya* means *Beloved*." She ignores my barb. "Not just because we loved him, but because of the love he offered. To his kin. To the ghosts. To the humans he encountered. For thousands of years."

I think of all those the Nightbringer loved in order to get back the Star that would set his people free. I remember how he loved me, as Keenan. Something occurs to me then, and my face heats.

"Did you—you know that he and I—that we—"

"I know," Rehmat says after a pause. "And I understand."

"*Beloved*," I whisper. The word makes me desperately sad. Because even if that's who he was once, that is not who he is anymore.

"Love and hate, Laia," Rehmat says. "They are two sides of the same coin. The Nightbringer's hate burns as brightly as his love. Mauth does not love or hate. So he was not prepared when his son turned against him. But we can imprison the Meherya," she says. "Bind him. My magic is the only force on this earth strong enough to contain him—"

"No," I say. "The Nightbringer must die."

"His death will usher in only more despair. You must trust me, child."

"Why?" I say. "You deceived me. And now you will not tell me his weaknesses. You won't tell me anything about him. Instead I go to the Tribes to beg for scraps of his story, which may or may not exist."

"I cannot speak of my time with him. If I could, I would tell you all. What I can say is that he was the Beloved. His strength is in his name. And his weakness. His past and his present. You must understand both to defeat him."

"To defeat him," I say, "I need that scythe. And if you want me to trust you again, you'll help me get it. You know how he thinks. You know him so well you spent a thousand years hiding just for the chance to defeat him."

"I do not know him anymore."

"Then I suppose we are finished," I say. "And I'm doing this alone."

I walk swiftly away from her, the soft sand dragging at my feet. A gust of wind blows the smell of roasting meat and horse to me. When I get to the top of the hill, I spot dim lights far ahead—the Tribal encampment.

"What if your theft of the scythe is part of his plan?" Rehmat comes around in front of me, so that I cannot walk forward without going through her. "A trap, a way to outwit you."

"Then you will help me outwit him first."

She considers me, drifting like a dandelion in the wind. Finally, she nods.

"I will help you get the scythe," she says. "This, I vow. And—and kill him if that is what you wish."

"Good." I nod. I am glad then that she is not in my head anymore. For if she was, she would know that for all of her persuasive words, I no longer trust a single thing she says.

CHAPTER THIRTY-SEVEN

The Soul Catcher

The Tribes who escaped Aish left many of their wagons and fled into the labyrinthine desert canyons north of the city. It requires not inconsiderable skill to track them.

Still, after a couple of days, I manage it. Which means their enemies could follow them too.

I find Aubarit on the edge of the camp, sitting atop her wagon seat. She picks at a bowl of stew, listless despite the fact that it smells of cumin and garlic and coriander, and sets my stomach to growling. The walls on either side of the camp are high and the nearby stream rages, heavy from the rains.

"You need to hide your trail," I tell her, and she glances up in surprise as I step out of the dark. "The only reason the Martials haven't found you is that they're too busy burying bodies."

The *Fakira* does not smile, and her shoulders are stiff. "I thought matters of the human world were not yours to worry over, Banu al-Mauth."

"They aren't," I say. "But matters of the Waiting Place are. And right now, the two are one and the same."

The *Fakira* calls over one of her Tribesmen and speaks to him in Sadhese. He glances at me curiously before leaving.

"Junaid will see to our tracks," she says. "You have not asked about Mamie Rila, Banu al-Mauth, or Tribe Nur or your own Tribe."

"I have no Tribe, Aubarit," I remind her. "However, I do have a problem. One that only the Tribes can help me with." Admitting it is frustrating. But it is the truth and cannot be avoided. "Who escaped Aish?"

"Tribe Nasur. Tribe Nur. Tribe Saif. Tribe Rahim. A few others. They are scattered through the canyons, wherever the water is. In the immediate vicinity, there are perhaps three thousand."

"Call the *Kehannis* and the *Zaldars*." I refer to the Tribal leaders. "Call the *Fakirs* and *Fakiras*. Tell them the Banu al-Mauth has need of them."

"Many are still in mourning." Aubarit cannot hide her shock at my callousness, but I shake my head.

"There is no time to mourn," I say. "Not if they wish to survive and not if they wish their dead to pass on in peace instead of torment. Harness their anger, *Fakira*. Call them to me."

Within the hour, the area around her wagon is crowded with people. Some are vaguely familiar, like a tiny woman with black-and-red braids and a beautiful face. Her arms are crossed over a mirrored dress of gold and green, and she stands with a young man who looks like the taller version of her. *Afya*. I remember her from my memories of Laia. *And her brother, Gibran.*

I find I am relieved to see him. A memory ricochets through my mind—him attacking me, possessed by a ghost. Trying desperately to stop him, and the fear that in doing so, I'd damaged him irrevocably.

Mamie Rila arrives with a cauldron of tea and passes cups around to ward off the chill wind blowing in from the north. She nods silently to me, but keeps her distance. A tall man steps out from beside her. His curly hair is half-hidden beneath a scarf, and his skin is lighter than mine. He closes the distance between us in two steps, arms wide for a hug.

"Ilyaas—brother—"

I extricate myself from him carefully.

"Ilyaas," he says. "It's me—Shan—"

I know the name now. He is my foster brother. Mamie's other adopted child. I nod at him stiffly. He wears the tattoos of a *Zaldar*, freshly inked. Behind him are other faces I recognize. Mamie's cousins and brothers, her nephews and nieces. My old family.

They eye me with awe and a touch of wariness. Only Shan looks at me like I am one of them.

Mamie Rila touches his arm gently, whispering something into his ear, and his smile fades. After a few moments, he steps back. "Forgive me, Banu al-Mauth," he says. "If I overstepped."

You didn't, the trapped voice inside me calls out. I crush it.

"*Fakira* Ara-Nasur." I find Aubarit speaking to Gibran. "Is everyone here?"

At her nod, I look out at the crowd. Conversations hush, and the only sound is the sand susurrating restlessly against the canyon walls.

"The Nightbringer steals spirits," I say. "He keeps them from crossing over."

Gasps arise and Aubarit looks sick. Afya Ara-Nur's hand goes to the blade at her waist. "Those in Aish—" she says. "All of our dead?"

I nod. "All have been taken, and—" I stop before mentioning the maelstrom, my old Blackcliff training kicking in. *Share only what is necessary.* Telling them what the Nightbringer is using those spirits for will frighten them. And frightened people make poor foot soldiers.

"Why?" Mamie Rila says softly, her tea forgotten in her hands. "Why do such a horrible thing?"

"The jinns' strength is more limited than it appears." I let them draw their own conclusions. "They are powerful, yes, but in short bursts only. When their power is spent, they heal slowly. A side effect of their imprisonment, perhaps."

"So—they are feeding off the spirits?" Shan says.

"In a manner of speaking," I say. "The Nightbringer seems to want ghosts who have suffered. Those who would have come to the Waiting Place. That is why it is empty. He is taking them."

"But what does he do with them?" A young *Fakir* I don't recognize speaks up from the back of the crowd. I can barely see him—the torchlight near Aubarit's wagon does not extend so far.

"I do not yet know," I say, because Talis did not explain the mechanics of the Nightbringer's plan. "But the jinn *need* the ghosts, which means they need dead humans. The jinn terrify a city, make a populace panic and capitulate. Keris Veturia sends her army in to butcher at will. The Nightbringer gets his suffering, and Keris claims another city."

"What can we do against the jinn?" Gibran says, and his sister answers.

"It's not the jinn we're after." She glances at me. "You want the Martials. If the jinn don't have their foot soldiers, there would be less butchering. Less suffering. Fewer ghosts for the Nightbringer to steal."

Beyond the ring of *Zaldars* and *Fakirs* and *Kehannis*, the crowd expands. Their fear spreads like an insidious fog.

"If we battle the Martials," Mamie Rila says, "will that not simply make more ghosts?"

"Soldiers rarely enter the Waiting Place," I tell her. "Especially Martial soldiers. Perhaps because they go to battle prepared for death. In any case, it is suffering the Nightbringer wants. Agony. We won't give it to him."

"What do you propose?" Shan asks.

"We fight." My hands fist and my battle rage stirs, restless in my blood. "We attack in small groups, insurgency style. We aim for their food stores, their livestock, and supplies. We empty out the villages in their path. If Keris's men are going to walk lands that do not belong to them, we can make that walk as difficult as possible. And we can do it without creating a glut of new ghosts for the Nightbringer to thieve."

"Why not empty our cities?" Afya says. "Scatter into the desert and the Serran Range? The Nightbringer wants death, no? We could simply deny him that by hiding."

"How long will you hide for?" Mamie says. "Keris Veturia will not give up. It might take longer, but she will hunt us down. And not just to kill us."

Now Shan speaks up. "Her Empire has need of slaves. She killed too many during the Scholar purges."

"We have a treaty with them—" a voice calls out, but Mamie snorts.

"Keris sold her own city to the Karkauns," she says. "Do you think treaties mean anything to her?"

"We should fight," Gibran says. "If the cost of staying in the Tribal lands is too high for the Martials, they'll leave. Keris has another enemy to the north. The Blood Shrike and her nephew."

"Yes, but if Keris defeats her," Afya says, "she'll send her armies back for us. Then what? Do we keep fighting? Living in canyons and gulches? When will it end?"

The crowd shifts, small conversations and arguments breaking out and echoing off the canyon walls. I am losing them.

Then a dark-haired, gold-eyed figure steps from the crowd into the firelight. She wears an embroidered Tribal tunic that brushes her knees, and her hair is freshly braided.

Fate will always lead you back to her, for good or for ill.

"Laia." Mamie Rila is by her side instantly. "You should be resting—" But Laia shakes her head, a new sadness rounding her shoulders.

"All this sorrow. This suffering." Her gold eyes fix on me. "All of it is because of the Nightbringer. Afya asks when will it end. It will end when the king of the jinn is dead."

The Tribes nod and mutter in agreement.

"Killing him is not simple," she says. "It will require the theft of a weapon he carries, and powerful magic. Until we can get that weapon, we must find other ways to hinder him. Stripping him of his allies is one such way. Keris is his strongest ally. To that end, Elias's plan is sound. And he knows the Martials. He knows how they think. With him, we have a chance at victory."

The Tribespeople glance at each other when she uses my old name, though I spot Mamie hiding a smile. I consider correcting Laia, but she has them mesmerized, so I keep silent.

"The Martials crushed my people," she says. "Keris would do the same to you. And her master, the Nightbringer, would inflict that indignity upon your dead. So do we stand with the Banu al-Mauth and fight them? Or do we roll over like cowed dogs and let them do what they want with us?"

"Tribe Saif will fight." My foster brother stands, but he doesn't look at me. "For our land and our dead."

"Tribe Nur will fight," Afya says after a nudge from her brother. "If the other Tribes join," she adds.

"Tribe Nasur will fight." A silver-haired *Zaldar* steps forward. "And if the Banu al-Mauth's plan works, we will continue fighting. If not . . ." He shrugs.

The sentiment spreads, and one by one, the Tribes agree to my plan. Laia turns to me, tilting her head as if to say, *What next?*

"We'll meet in the morning," I say. "To discuss the first attack."

As the group breaks up, Laia approaches. She looks exhausted, covered in scratches and cuts, with a large bruise on the side of her face. I get an odd prickly feeling in my chest.

She puts her hand to it when she sees me looking. "It was a river," she says. "So unless you strangle a force of nature, you cannot do much. Besides, you're the one who left me stranded in the desert. If you want to be angry at someone, go find a mirror."

"I am sorry. But—"

"No." She puts a finger to my lips. "*I am sorry* was the perfect place to stop."

She stands close enough for me to see the myriad tiny scratches all over her face. I brush my fingers against one lightly.

"The river that did this to you," I say. "I don't like it."

Her smile is a lightning flash in the dark. "Are you going to find the bad river, Elias? Make it pay?"

"It's Soul Catcher. And yes." My thoughts toward this river turn baleful. "Maybe I can divert it down a canyon, or—"

The fire turns her gold eyes molten, and she throws back her head and laughs. Watching her is like watching a waterfall thundering down a gorge. Like watching the Northern Dancers illuminate the sky. I cannot describe it. I only know that a tightness in my chest loosens, and I am different— lighter—for witnessing it.

"That's good," she says. "That's a start."

"It will be a hard fight." I force my thoughts toward the challenge that lies ahead. "Keris is a wily enemy."

Laia holds up a scroll. "I've had a message from the Shrike. She is offering aid. She wants fealty in return, but it might give the Tribes a chance to renegotiate their treaty with the Empire."

She examines me. "You could help with that if you chose," she says. "Negotiate well, and they might be more willing to fight for you." She nods after the retreating Tribespeople. "You weren't doing so well there."

"Thank you for talking to them," I say. At her shrug, dismissive and embarrassed at once, I find myself thinking of when I first became Soul Catcher.

Darin was still recovering from Kauf, and Laia and I were walking along the border of the Forest of Dusk, speaking of the Empire.

Nothing ever changes, she had said. *Nothing ever will.*

Maybe we're the ones who change it, I'd told her. *If there was one thing you could do right now to change the Empire, what would it be?*

I'd get rid of the ghost wagons. Set free the Scholars locked up inside. Light those skies-forsaken death boxes on fire.

You can disappear. I'd taken her hand then, even knowing that Mauth would punish me for it. *I can windwalk. What's stopping us?*

She offered that same smile. That same shrug. And then she started planning. Afya helped smuggle the Scholars we freed south, and Darin aided in the fighting. But Laia was the heart of it.

"You're good at bringing people together," I tell her now. "You always have been."

"And you're good at leading them." She holds my arm and walks with me, and I'm so astonished I let her pull me along. "If you want your ghosts back, you'll have to channel that skill."

"Isn't that what I'm doing?"

She shakes her head. "Elias, you need the Tribes to fight for you. You need to save the ghosts from whatever hellish torment the Nightbringer is subjecting them to. But"—she cuts me a look—"you cannot lead them if you do not understand them. No one wants to draw blades beside someone who views them as lesser. You are too distant. Too cold. If you want the Tribes' loyalty, then appeal to their hearts. You might want to start by finding your own."

CHAPTER THIRTY-EIGHT

The Blood Shrike

"Lord Kinnius! We are pleased to grant you an audience."

Livia rises from her simple black onyx throne and smiles at the dour-faced Illustrian staring her down. My sister arrived in Antium this morning, a week after we took the city, and barely had enough time to change.

But she appears serene and composed, as if she's been settled here for ages. Rain drums on the roof, washing away the Karkauns' filth. The muted light filtering through the throne room's high windows illuminates her face just so. She looks every inch the Empress Regent.

I stand behind her, flanked by Rallius and Harper. When the latter fidgets, I almost look at him. Since we took Antium, I've been finding excuses to. And I don't like it. Avitas Harper is a distraction.

He was a distraction as I oversaw the cleansing of the palace, which the Karkauns degraded into a nightmare pigsty. He was a distraction as I sent troops into the city to help the citizens rebuild.

And he is a distraction today in the throne room, as Livia welcomes our first potential ally from the south.

I fix my attention on the advisory council—including Teluman, Musa, and Darin—all of whom are gathered in front of the throne. Lord Kinnius's gaze falls on the Scholars—standing equal to the Martials and armed with Serric steel blades. He scowls.

My sister offers him a brilliant smile in return. "Welcome to the capital."

"Or what's left of it." Kinnius glances around the throne room, pointedly not using Livia's title, and I stiffen at his insolence.

Harper quells me with a look. *We need allies*, he seems to be saying.

Winning over Gens Kinnia, with its grain stores and barges and gold, is more important than pride or titles.

Livia's smile does not shift, but her blue eyes are cold.

"The city stands, Lord Kinnius," Livia says. "As do its people, despite the traitorousness of Keris Veturia."

"You mean despite the failure of the Blood Shrike."

"I did not expect a man of your intellectual caliber to be taken in by the usurper's honeyed words," Livia chides him, and I stifle a laugh. *Intellectual caliber* indeed.

"There are thousands in Antium who witnessed Keris's betrayal," my sister says. "You may speak to them if you wish."

Kinnius snorts. "Plebeians. Scholars." He looks Darin up and down before turning to Quin. "If I'd known you were so desperate for men, Veturius, I might have sent a platoon or two."

Thank the skies Livia is Empress Regent, because if I were, Kinnius would be attempting to reattach his head right now.

"But you didn't send a platoon, did you?" Livia's smile vanishes, and I am reminded that she survived the murder of our family. She survived Marcus. She survived giving birth in the midst of a war.

"Instead," she says, "we won Antium with the aid of the Scholars, who conducted themselves with far more bravery than you. Do not mistake me, Kinnius. We are not so desperate for allies that we will tolerate the insults of a man too weak to fight for his people. If you wish to discuss your support for Zacharias, the rightful emperor, then remain. If your fear of Keris is so great that you'd rather spout horse dung, my Blood Shrike will escort you to the city gates."

And you can crawl back to your bitch of an empress, I don't add.

"I hear, Shrike, that the people hailed you as Imperator Invictus." Kinnius turns to me. "Could it be that you wish to take your nephew's throne for yourse—"

I have a knife to Kinnius's throat in two seconds. "Go on." I draw a bit of blood. "Finish that sentence, you cowardly pissant."

"Shrike," Livia says sweetly. "I'm certain Lord Kinnius regrets his hasty tongue. Don't you, Kinnius?"

Kinnius opens his mouth and closes it, nodding frantically. I step back, and Livia levels her smile at him again. I see it hit him like a punch in the face. She steps down from the throne and takes his arm.

"Walk with me, Kinnius," she says. "See the city. Speak with the people. Once you learn the truth of what happened here, I believe you'll have a different opinion."

My hands shake, even as Livia guides Kinnius to the door. Quin gives me a long look, and he is not the only one. I remember what the jinn said to me weeks ago.

You do not love the child. He is your blood, but you'll see him dead and yourself upon the throne.

But I'd die before I let anything happen to my nephew. That is a truth I know in my marrow, and nothing will change it.

Harper remains in the palace, and I follow Livia and her guards out, trailing them through the city.

Despite the rain, the bazaars are full, and children run past with barbecued kebab skewers and bread slathered with honey and ice plum jam. Dozens of merchants who have returned to the city call out their wares. Scores of people greet Livia and me with flowers and smiles, while glaring

at Kinnius with hard suspicion. He has the decency to at least look cha-
grined.

When I'm certain Livia has the man well in hand, I return to my
quarters in the palace. They are small and east-facing, unlike Livia and
Zacharias's expansive rooms, which, though only a few minutes away, face
the Nevennes. The drop from their windows is a sheer fifty feet, while I'm
on the ground floor. But my doors are unguarded, while Livia has four
Masks outside hers.

"Why," Dex says when he finds me a few minutes after I arrive, "do you
not have guards at your door?"

"We need city patrols," I say. "And the Empress Regent requires a full
complement. I can handle myself. What news?"

"Our spy has returned from Adisa," Dex says. "He's outside, waiting to
deliver a report. And this arrived from the Tribes." He hands me an enve-
lope. "Also, Darin of Serra has requested a private audience."

"Send him in," I say. "And find Musa. I promised him if I heard from
Adisa, he'd be the first to know."

Darin enters after I've heard from our spy and read the message from the
Tribal lands.

"Laia contacted me," he says. "She needs aid, Shrike. And I'm going
to her."

I briefly consider protesting—we still require more weapons. Armor. But
the glint in Darin's eyes tells me that he will not be swayed.

"I requested that you wait until we had taken Antium," I say. "You
waited. I won't stop you. But I will ask that you go with the troops I'm
sending." I hold up the missive I've just received. "I heard from Laia too.

The Tribes have agreed to support Emperor Zacharias in exchange for a renegotiation of their tithes and our military support. Five hundred men and two Ankanese sappers."

"That's quite an escort, Shrike."

"If anything happens to you, it's my throat your sister will tear out."

Darin laughs. "She will indeed." I wish suddenly that we had met when we were younger. That he could have been a brother to me too. He is, I think, a good brother.

"Give her my best," I tell him. "And tell her I hope she's practicing her bow."

After he leaves, I congratulate myself on resolving the issue so neatly. But then Musa of Adisa arrives. He's followed by Corporal Tibor, the spy we sent to the Mariner capital who has already given me his report.

"I could not get through to Marinn," Tibor says. "And I couldn't reach our people inside. No one can get in. I took the northern route, past Delphinium and out through Nerual Lake. As soon as I got to the Mariner coast, the weather was so bad I had to turn back."

"Was it bad up until that point?" Musa's chiseled face is as tense as I've ever seen it, and Tibor shakes his head.

"Gray skies, a bit of snow. Typical for late winter. But the seas raged near Adisa. I tried to get through. But I ran into a dozen others who said their ships couldn't so much as approach the coastline. I thought it was more important to tell you than to keep trying and failing."

When Tibor has left, I turn to the Scholar. His arms are crossed to hide his clenched fists.

"Does Marinn usually have storms so bad that the kingdom is completely cut off?"

284

"Never. And I've tried to spy on the Commandant, to see if this is the Nightbringer's handiwork. But there are jinn all over the south, and the wights refuse to go near them."

"My spies are more afraid of me than they are of jinn." I rise, because if I'm going to rally five hundred troops to travel south, I must tell the Empress. Musa follows me out the door and into the busy hallway.

A window stands open and I breathe in Antium's scents. Rain and mountain pine, roasting meat and clay-oven flatbread drizzled with butter and cinnamon. I glance out at the gardens, where a dozen Masks patrol. Amid the drizzle, Dex walks with Silvius, their shoulders touching as they pass a cup of some steaming drink back and forth. The wind carries the sound of Dex's laugh, rich and joyful.

What would it be like to walk with Harper that way? To share a mug of cider. To touch him without feeling like I will come apart?

"Shrike?"

I snap back to Musa. "I'll send my own spies south to infiltrate Keris's network," I say. "We'll get news soon. I promise. I *hate* unsolved puzzles. I have too many as it is."

"More?" Musa says. "Do tell."

"Just the blather the Karkauns were spewing. *Ik tachk mort fid iniqant fi.* Haven't been able to get a translation of it, but—"

"'Death wakes the great sea,'" Musa translates, nodding a greeting to a group of Scholars as they pass. "Or—no, wait. 'Death *feeds* the great sea.'"

I stop in the middle of the hall, ignoring the irritated grunt of a Mask who nearly runs into me. "Why didn't you tell me you spoke Karkaun?"

"You didn't ask." Musa keeps walking, and now I am trying to keep pace with him. "The Mariners used to trade with the barbarians, before

Grímarr became their high muckety-muck. The crown felt that Nikla's prince consort should speak the languages of her trading partners."

"Is that how you learned to fight too?" I ask. "Because Quin Veturius gives out compliments once a decade or so. *If* he's feeling generous."

"Perhaps that's why I like him." Musa stares off thoughtfully. "My grand-father taught me to fight. He was a palace guard. Saved old King Irmand's life when he was a boy. Got a beekeeping estate for his trouble. My father became a healer, but I spent more time with the bees. I think they both thought training would toughen me up."

"Did it?"

"I'm still alive, aren't I?" He grins suddenly, and I turn to see Harper coming down the hallway. His sleeves are rolled up, and there's rain in his hair and glistening along his cheekbones. *No distractions, Shrike. Do not stare at his forearms—or his face—*

"Shrike, Musa." He doesn't slow, or even meet my eyes, and then he's past. After he turns the corner I realize two things: First, that my heart is thudding so loud, I'm stunned people aren't turning to stare at me. And second, that Musa *is* staring at me.

"You know—" he begins, but I wave him off.

"Do not," I say, "give me some sad story about love and loss and your broken heart."

Musa doesn't laugh as I expect him to. "I saw your face," he says. "During the attack on Cardium Rock. When Harper went down. I saw."

"Stop talking," I say. "I don't need advice from a—"

"Go on, insult me," Musa says. "But you and I are more alike than you know, and that's not a compliment. You're in a position of great power,

Shrike. It's a lonely place to be. Most leaders spend their lives using others. Being used. Love isn't just a luxury for you. It's a rarity. It's a gift. Don't throw it away."

"I'm not throwing it away." I stop walking and pull the Scholar around to face me. "I'm afraid, Musa." I don't mean to blurt the words out—especially to a man whose arrogance has vexed me from the moment I met him. But to my relief, he does not mock me.

"How many in Antium lost those beloved to them when the Karkauns attacked?" he asks. "How many like Dex, who hide who they love because the Empire would kill them for it?" Musa runs a hand through his black hair, and it sticks up like a bird's nest. "How many like Laia, betrayed and then left to claw her way through her pain? How many like me, Shrike, pining for someone who no longer exists?"

"There is more than love of another," I say. "There is love of country— love of one's people—"

"But that's not what we're talking about," Musa says. "You are lucky enough to love someone who loves you back. He is alive and breathing and in the same vicinity as you. By the skies, do something about it. For however long you have. For whatever time you get. Because if you don't, I swear that you'll regret it. You'll regret it for all your years."

CHAPTER THIRTY-NINE

Laia

The Martial army is smaller than I expected. After Aish fell, I imagined tens of thousands of soldiers. But Keris has managed to take much of the Tribal lands with a mere ten thousand men.

"Three hundred of whom are Masks," Elias says to the Tribespeople he's appointed as platoon leaders for our first mission. We've gathered atop a small butte in the rugged lands between Taib and Aish. The Martial army is sprawled a half mile away, their outermost sentries moonlit glimmers beneath a cloudless night sky.

"It's the Masks who walk the perimeter of Keris's army," Elias says. "I'll take care of them. At my signal—"

He goes through each leader's duties, and they buzz with adrenaline and anticipation. But I feel numb with anxiety for everyone here: Afya standing beside her little brother, Gibran; Mamie Rila's younger son, Shan, and his group of Saif Tribesmen; Sahib, Aubarit's uncle and the taciturn *Zaldar* of her tribe.

The rest of Aish's survivors, including Mamie Rila and Aubarit, have decamped to a labyrinthine cave system a few miles to the north. We cannot fail them tonight. We cannot fail those in Taib and Nur, who will suffer Keris's violence if we do not slow her and her army down.

Out in the darkness south of us, the Martials' fires light up the horizon. *Ten thousand is not so many*, I tell myself.

But one hundred—the size of our force—is even less.

Focus, Laia. Elias assigned me a duty for this raid, but I have my own mission to carry out. The Nightbringer will likely be with the army. Which means the scythe will be there too.

A gold glow at the corner of my vision stiffens my spine. Though I am at the back of the crowd, I slip deeper into the shadows.

"Well?" I ask.

"The Nightbringer is in the camp with Keris," Rehmat says. "I wish you would not seek him out, Laia. There are *Kehannis* in these lands. Seek stories instead."

But all of the *Kehannis* who escaped Aish walked away the moment they heard what I wanted. Only Mamie Rila was brave enough to speak with me.

We draw our stories from the deep places, Laia. I sat in the lamplit warmth of her wagon, but the air grew cold as she spoke. *They are not just words. They are magic. Some are potent as poison, and strike you dead upon speaking them. The woman you met in Marinn—the* Kehanni *of Tribe Sulud—she knew this. It is why she could not tell the Nightbringer's story right away. It is the reason the wraiths killed her. I fear the words you seek, Laia,* Mamie whispered. *I love life too much to utter them.*

"If the story kills the *Kehannis*," I tell Rehmat, "then it isn't worth it."

"The weapon alone will not defeat him."

"Laia. *Laia!*" Afya pokes my side. The entire group stares at me. Elias, arms crossed and head tilted, meets my gaze, bemused. I flush under his regard.

I realize we're reviewing the plan of attack. "I'm to poison the food stores. Without being seen."

Everyone turns back to Elias, perhaps waiting for encouragement. But despite my warning to him that he is too cold, he only nods. "Midnight, then," he says, and cuts through the crowd toward me.

"A word?" When we stand apart, he looks down, brow furrowed. "The jinn may be among the soldiers," he says. "And when I first suggested the mission, you seemed reluctant to use your magic. Will you be able to hold your invisibility?"

I have been reluctant. Ever since I found out who Rehmat really is, my magic has felt unknowable. Like it belongs to someone else.

"I'll be fine."

"No detours."

"You sound almost worried about me, Elias."

"Soul Catcher," he corrects me, sounding so much like a Blackcliff Centurion that I want to kick him. "Your skills are important for the success of other raids, Laia. Get in, get the job done, and get out without getting distracted."

Afya strolls to me as he walks away. "What a charmer," she says, and at my glower, she shoves me. "I told you not to fall in love with a ghost-talker," she says. "But did you listen? Forget about him for a moment. Your armor is no good." She glances critically at the hodgepodge bits of protection I've collected over the past few months and steers me toward the horses. "Let's fix it before we have to leave."

Two hours later, I follow Shan through the desert with ten other fighters from Tribe Saif. All my concentration is fixed on cloaking us with my magic—not easy when there are so many and we are spread out. Finally, Elias calls a halt in a shallow depression within spitting distance of the sentry line. I sigh in relief when he signals for me to drop the invisibility. His gaze fixed on the sentries, he windwalks away.

"I cannot get used to that," Shan says to me. "No matter how many times Mamie tells me he is gone, I still see my brother."

I know so little about Shan. But I remember Elias speaking of him when we traveled to Kauf Prison. They spent the early years of their lives together. Perhaps Elias must be reminded of that.

"You should tell him," I say. "He needs to hear it."

Shan glances at me in surprise, but before he can speak, a hoot drifts through the night. The sentries—patrolling only seconds ago, are nowhere to be seen. The Tribesman rises.

"That was quick," he mutters. "Skies speed your way, Laia of Serra."

I close my eyes and reach for my invisibility. It comes reluctantly, but once it is on, penetrating the camp is simple enough. The fires are low, for which I am thankful. The shadows will aid us this night.

A large tent looms in the very center of the camp and a black flag flies atop it, a *K* at its center. My scar itches. Would that I could choke Keris Veturia with her own banner.

Poisoning her army will have to do. I weave past slumbering men and guards sweeping dirt out of a tent, past a soldier cursing the loss of a bet and a few others playing dice and cards. I spy the food stores in the southeast corner of the camp. A livestock pen sits in the way, lightly patrolled.

As I move around it, I hear whispers. Cries. Red eyes flash—ghuls? Why would ghuls be lurking among the livestock?

I draw closer. The shadows in the pen resolve into faces and bodies. People. Almost all are Scholars, chained at the wrists and packed tightly, lash marks suppurating on their visible skin.

No detours, Elias said, but he did not know of the slaves. I cannot let them remain here.

There are only two soldiers guarding the pen's gate, likely because the rest of the army is within shouting distance. The whips at their belts turn my vision red. I ready my bow. Mother could nock two arrows so quickly that they hit their targets at almost the same time. But I am not so skilled. I will have to be quick.

I nock, aim, and fire. Nock, aim, fire. The first Martial goes down quietly, clutching his throat. But my second shot flies into the darkness. As the remaining guard draws his scim and shouts for aid, drums thunder an alarm from across the camp. Our fighters have been spotted.

The quiet is shattered. The guard I shot at bellows at the top of his lungs. *"Attack! Slave pens! Attack!"* A bell peals, the drums bellow, horses gallop past, soldiers stumble from their tents half-armed. I put an arrow in the shouting Martial, wincing at the squelch it makes when it hits his chest. He topples back and I break the lock on the pen with two strikes of my dagger.

The Scholars within stare out, bewildered. Of course. They cannot see me.

I dare not risk dropping my invisibility. I do not trust my ability to raise it again if I see the Nightbringer.

"Run!" I say. "Into the desert!"

They stumble out, some of them chained, others too wounded to do more than limp. Martials appear almost immediately and cut them down. I realize then how stupid I have been. Even if the Scholars could run, they have nowhere to go. If they clear the camp, they cannot navigate the desert.

Always us. Always my people.

*"Oof—"*An emaciated Scholar runs into me. I jump quickly out of the way, for I must get to the food stores. Time runs short. But the camp is chaos, the path to the supply wagons blocked.

The boy I ran into bolts past me. One moment he is cutting between two tents. The next, he stiffens, a scim driven through his chest.

The Martial who killed him tears his blade out and moves on. The boy falls.

I run for him and find him on his side, gaze glassy. I pull his head into my lap and stroke his hair. And then, though I know it is foolish to do so, I drop my invisibility. I do not want him to die alone.

"I'm sorry," I whisper to him. "I'm so sorry."

I want to ask his name. How old he is. But I know his name. It is Mirra. Jahan. Lis. Nan. Pop. Izzi. I know how old he is. He is the three-year-old child thrown into an inky ghost wagon before he can understand why. He is the eighty-year-old grandfather slain in his home for daring to look at a Martial soldier wrong.

He is me. So I stay with him until his last breath leaves him. This, at least, I can do.

I have a moment to close his eyes, but nothing more. Bootsteps thunder behind me, and I turn with barely enough time to parry the blade of an aux soldier. He bowls me over, and I scream, claw for a handful of dirt, and fling it in his face. When he rears back, I shove my blade into his stomach, then push him off. I try to draw my invisibility again, but it does not come.

In the distance, I see Elias atop a massive horse he's stolen. He is clad in all black, his face half-hidden by a kerchief. With his gray eyes flashing as cold as the scims in his hands, it is impossible not to see him as the creature of war he was bred to be. His scims gleam with blood, and he destroys the men trying to kill him, moving with dizzying speed. The Martials around me stream toward him, determined to take him down.

I break away from the heart of the chaos and run for the supply wagons.

Goats and pigs careen past me, and I barely avoid a goring. Gibran must have succeeded in opening the livestock pens.

The supply wagons are in sight when something at the edge of my vision makes me turn. Amid the stampeding animals and shouting soldiers and burning wagons, I see a flicker of black. A flash of sun eyes.

The Nightbringer.

"Rehmat?" I whisper to the dark. "Are you ready?"

"He waits for you, Laia," Rehmat says. "I implore you—do not do this."

"You promised to help," I say through gritted teeth. "You swore."

"I am helping you. We will get the scythe. But this is not the way."

My heart quails in warning, perhaps. Or weakness. The latter, I think. I make my way toward where I saw the jinn. I reach for my invisibility. *Disappear, Laia!* For a moment, the magic eludes me. But then I have it in my grasp and draw it over me quickly.

"You need to distract him, Rehmat," I say. "Just long enough that I—"

"Laia." A warm hand closes around mine, and I jump.

"No detours." Elias looks into my eyes, his own magic piercing mine easily. "You didn't get to the wagons."

"How—"

"I saw you. With the boy who died." Sorrow flashes across his face, and his hands shake. I think back to the night in Blackcliff's barracks after the Third Trial. He looked just like this. Like his heart had been razed. "Come. We need to get out of here."

"The Nightbringer has to die, Elias," I say. "That scythe he wears is the only way to kill him. And it's here. He's here."

"He expects you to take it." Elias does not release me, though I tug at him. "Don't do what he expects, Laia."

I glance toward where I saw the Nightbringer, and the scythe flashes again. It is *so* close.

Too close, I realize. Too obvious. Rehmat and Elias are right. The Nightbringer is trying to lure me in.

I turn from the weapon, clenching my fists so I'm not tempted to break free from Elias. The Soul Catcher wraps his arms around me, and we step into the wind. As we leave, half the camp is on fire and the rest is in an uproar. Even though I didn't get to the supply wagons, our attack worked. The Martials—and the Nightbringer—have suffered a blow tonight.

Still, as Elias and I race through the desert, I think of the Scholars killed after escaping the pen. I think of the boy who died in my arms. I think of the scythe, out of my reach yet again. And it doesn't feel like a victory at all.

«« «

The Tribes hide deep in the Bhuth badlands, a maze of canyons and hoodoos, ravines and caves that are impossible to navigate unless you have traveled them before. The thousands of Tribespeople who escaped Aish are scattered through the caves, finding water, making camp, and keeping a close eye out for Martial outriders.

Afya, Gibran, Shan, and the others arrive back at the hideout a little while after I do. Mamie, Aubarit—everyone, it seems—are waiting and euphoric at the victory. They wish to know every detail.

Elias extricates himself quickly and disappears into the camp. It takes me longer, but after an hour or so, I leave the celebrations for Afya's wagon. There, I strip off my armor and rinse away the blood in freezing-cold stream water. The Tribeswoman lends me a soft black shift that is small on me, but cleaner than anything I have. Then, perhaps sensing my disquiet, she throws me a sack of mangoes she filched from the Martials and leaves me alone.

But I am restless. I cannot forget the face of the boy who died, or the screams of the Scholars. I cannot stop thinking of the Martials who I put arrows into.

"You mourn the enemy, Laia." Rehmat materializes beside me. "There is no shame in that."

"Isn't there?"

She fades, and I stand up. There is one person in this entire camp who might understand how I feel. One person as lost as I am. I grab the mangoes, pull on a long cloak, and wind my way through the caves until I find him.

He has not made himself easy to find. His tent is pitch-black and tucked into the shadows beyond two supply wagons, in the lee of a cave wall.

I understand why he hides. No one will look for him here. No one will congratulate him or clap him on the back, ask him to share how he took down so many sentries.

"Elias," I call softly from outside the flaps, in case he is sleeping. For a long minute, there is no answer. Then:

"Come in."

He sits cross-legged with a green mirrored pillow at his back, no doubt burgled from Mamie Rila's wagon. A lone lamp burns low, and he tucks something away in his pocket, a small knife covered in wood shavings still in his hand.

There is no sign of his blood-spattered armor, or his scims. He's changed into his usual black fatigues, and as ever at night, he appears to have misplaced his shirt. I hide a smile, thinking of the way the Blood Shrike would roll her eyes.

Then I let myself take him in, the hard lines of his biceps and jaw, the sharply carved ridges of his stomach, the black hair curling at his neck and falling into his face as he leans forward to light another lamp.

"Do the fighters sleep, Laia of Serra?" His baritone is soft, its deep timbre eliciting a lurch low in my body. But he does not look at me. He has no idea what he does to me. I hate him a little for his ignorance.

My hands tremble, and I tangle them in the hem of my cloak. "They sleep," I answer. "But I couldn't."

"I understand," he says. "I can never sleep after a battle." He sits back, and if I didn't know him so well, I would think he was relaxed. "The Scholar boy," he says. "Did you know him?"

"Not really," I say. "But no one should die alone."

"His ghost did not enter the Waiting Place," Elias says, and I realize that in the time it took me to change and bathe, he's been to his home and back. "It crossed to the other side. I felt it. Most of them did."

"The Nightbringer didn't take them?"

Elias shakes his head. "We killed clean. Quick. He wants suffering."

I do not know what to say to that, so I lift the bag of mangoes. "I brought you something."

"You can leave one there." He unties the neat knots of his bedroll, turning his back on me. "Thank you."

He still will not look at me, so I shift over to sit next to him. I let the cloak fall from my shoulders and take out a mango.

"Mangoes shouldn't be eaten alone." I roll the golden fruit along my thigh, softening it up, the way I used to in the midst of a Serran summer.

The Soul Catcher's gaze flicks to the movement, and suddenly, I am glad for the way Afya's shift sits on my skin. Elias follows the path of the mango up and down my bare thigh before looking away.

It is so dismissive that I almost leave. But his hands are clenched into fists, the veins on his arms standing out, and though the sweep of his hair hides his face, his jaw is tight.

A hot thrill of victory shoots through me. I do not know what he's feeling. Maybe it is anger. But some feeling is better than none at all. I tear off the top of the mango with my teeth, setting it beside me. Then I squeeze it, drawing the sweet pulp out with my lips, letting the juice trail down my wrists, my neck. I imagine him watching me the way I want him to. Him kissing the sweetness from my throat. His arms around me, driving the chill night air away.

"How is it?" he asks, voice pitched low.

"It's fine," I say. "But mangoes are not as sweet if you are not sharing them with someone you love."

Silence, and then the whisper of his body shifting. His fingers are on mine, and my breath catches when I look up at him. Somewhere deep within those gray eyes, I see the Elias I knew. I feel the heat of the man who has blazed with life from the first moment I met him.

I let him take my hands, every inch of me tingling as he licks the juice from my wrists. He runs a finger up my neck and puts it in his mouth. Then he puts the mango to his lips and closes his eyes. His long lashes cast shadows on his cheekbones, and he makes a small moan of satisfaction at the taste of the fruit. At the sound, my desire spikes. Every part of me aches toward him.

"Laia." He reaches out, his hand closing on my waist. My breath grows shallow. The tent is warm suddenly, and a flush rises in my cheeks as he moves closer. His gaze is on my lips, his own just a hairsbreadth away.

Kiss me, I want to tell him. *Touch me. Rip this stupid shift off.*

He lifts the mango. "And now," he whispers, "is it sweeter?"

His finger brushes my lips, and I rake my teeth across it ever so briefly. He jerks and pulls away, and I wonder if his heart stutters like mine does.

"Not as sweet as it could be." I make him meet my eyes. For a moment, it is Elias I see. My Elias, just like in Aish.

Then he's gone, windwalking from the tent so fast that I startle and drop the mango. It thuds to the earth, ruined now, its sweetness curdled by dust.

CHAPTER FORTY

The Soul Catcher

For ten days, we attack the Commandant's army in small, surgical strikes. As Keris tightens her defenses, our attacks grow more complex—and take a higher toll. In the fourth raid, we lose five fighters.

When we return to the camp that night, the Tribespeople are silent. Most do not meet my eyes. My instinct is to sit with them. Mourn with them. Listen to their stories. But doing so only reminds me of the death I have meted out. Of the death I have yet to deliver. So I stay away.

When we are two days from Taib, we abandon the raids and ride for the city. Keris is a day behind us—and we need to help with the evacuation. Everything is going to plan.

But something is not right.

"What's bothering you, Elias?" a voice says from behind me.

Laia. I've avoided her since the first raid. That night, I wished to comfort her. For like me, she was tormented by the killing. I wished to listen to her and hold her and pass the hours with her in my arms.

But as Mauth said, *wishes only cause pain.*

I mumble an excuse and make to ride off, but Laia angles her horse in front of mine.

"Stop, Elias," she says. "I'm not here to seduce you. Just because I'm in love with you does not mean I lack in pride—"

"You—" Her words wrap around me like a breeze on a hot day. *Mauth, damn you, this is when I need your magic to wipe away what I feel.* But with every day that passes, the magic grows more unresponsive. Today is no different.

"You shouldn't say that," I manage.

"Why?" she asks blithely, but her knuckles are stiff against the reins. Her hair is caught in a braid and she no longer tries to hide the layers of emotion in her dark eyes. "It's true. In any case, I'm not here to talk about us. Something eats at you. Is it the raids?"

Even with our losses, our raids have been successful. We have no shortage of volunteers, for our band of refugee fighters has grown from a little more than three thousand riders and half a hundred wagons to nearly double that. Survivors fleeing Sadh and Aish have joined us, as well as Tribespeople escaping smaller villages scattered across the vast desert.

"It's the Commandant," I tell Laia. "I feel like I'm missing something. Keris doesn't make the same mistake twice. And we've hit her four times now."

"She's tightened her defenses."

Know your enemy. In Blackcliff, it was the first rule the Commandant taught us about war.

"If our strikes were hurting her," I say, "she would have done more than tighten her defenses."

"We've decimated her supplies and livestock, Elias," Laia says. "Slowed them down by days. Our attacks *are* hurting her. She'll arrive in Taib with a far weaker army than she expected."

But why should she care about Taib? It hits me then, and I feel like a fool for not seeing it before. Keris is herding us. Distracting us.

"She split her forces." I say. "She doesn't give two figs about Taib, Laia. She wants Nur."

Capturing the crown jewel of the Tribal desert will net the Nightbringer three times as many souls as Taib. I slow my horse and dismount, throwing my canteen and some provisions into a pack. "I have to go. I have to see if it's true. I'll return."

"Send out scouts," Laia says. "Or at least tell the fighters you're going. Even if you don't . . . care about them—"

"Mohsin An-Saif. Sule An-Nasur. Omair An-Saif. Isha Ara-Nur. Kasib An-Rahim." I tighten my scim straps and swing my pack on. "Those are the five fighters who died last night. They leave behind four mothers, three fathers, eight siblings, and two children."

Horses move around us, and some of the fighters stare at me surreptitiously. While a few call out greetings to Laia, most look away from me.

"I do not speak to them because I'm not their savior, Laia," I say. "I can't tell them everything will be all right. Or that I can make them safe. Instead, I tell them they can flee their enemies or fight, knowing that they will fight. Knowing that as a result, many will die. And I'm doing all of it so the ghosts find peace in the Waiting Place. I do it to save the dead, not the living."

"Fine," she says. "But no one wants to fight for nothing, Elias. You need to give them a reason. Let them know and understand you. Let them care for you. Otherwise you might return and find you have no army left."

"The fate of their dead is their reason," I say. "And it will have to be enough." I hand her the reins of my mount. "I shouldn't be gone more than a few hours."

"Elias—"

"Soul Catcher," I tell her, before windwalking out into the desert, scouring for any sign of Keris's army. I consider what Laia said as I travel. *No one wants to fight for nothing.* My grandfather, Quin Veturius, is a legendary leader of men. His soldiers follow him because they trust his battle acumen. They trust that he cares about them and their families and their lives.

Keris leads through fear. Through threats that are reinforced by a fierce and uncanny understanding of human weakness.

Tribe Saif followed Uncle Akbi because they loved him. The same reason Tribe Nur follows Afya. The Tribal fighters do not entirely trust me. Nor do they fear me. They certainly do not love me. Because I am their Banu al-Mauth, they respect me. I have no right to ask for more.

Windwalking lends me speed, but it does not make it easy to find Keris's army. I check every canyon, every depression in which they might be lurking, zigzagging over the Tribal lands. But I find nothing.

That night, I take shelter in a ravine. As I build up a fire, I step back into the memories Cain gave me of Blackcliff, of training, of *her*.

The Commandant taught me that to defeat your enemy, you had to know her better than you knew yourself. Her wants. Her weaknesses. Her allies. Her strengths.

The next day, I do not make for ravines or canyons. Because I know now that I will not find her army there. Instead, I head for the open desert and put my hand to the chill, cracked ground.

Keris has jinn who can magic away the sights and sounds of the army. She cannot, however, erase their passage from the earth itself. Midway through the day, I feel a distant rumble. Thousands of boots marching. Horses. Wagons. War machines.

I make for that thunderous drone until suddenly, I'm among the army. I windwalk amid the neat rows of infantrymen, their heads bent against the sharp desert wind.

A scream cracks the air. "Breach!" an unearthly voice shouts. "Breach! Find the intruder!"

It's Umber who cries the warning, and she streaks through the skies toward me, kneading the wind to lend her speed. Though I bolt away before the soldiers notice my presence, fiery hands swipe at my back. She's caught my scent.

"Ah, the humans' savior!" Umber pursues me in full flame, glaive in hand. She swings it down through my armor and into the flesh of my back. "How does it feel to fail?"

Mauth's magic surges weakly. But it is not enough to block Umber's next attack, or to keep me from spinning out of my windwalk like a wounded bird.

The ground rises up at me far too swiftly, and I fall with a bone-numbing crash. Pain rolls through me in relentless waves, and blood pours from the wound in my back, but Umber is not done. As I lurch away from her, frantic to escape, she swings the blade across my stomach, slicing into my side.

"I will find you, little Soul Catcher," she grinds out. "You cannot run from me."

But I can bleeding try. I just need to get away long enough that she can't track me. Her fire does not burn as bright as it did in Aish. She is still recovering. If I'm clever, I can outwit her. *Come on, Soul Catcher,* I snarl at myself. *You've dealt with worse.*

I force the pain into one corner of my mind and windwalk, spinning sharply around Umber, striking at her with my scims. They dig deep into her hip, and she screams—perhaps from the wound, perhaps from the salt coating I applied to the blade. She tumbles to the earth in an explosion of dust and fire, and I am away.

Though not for long. After only seconds, she is behind me again. My head aches, and my vision doubles. Soul Catcher or not, I'm in danger. My scims feel like anvils in my hands—it is all I can do to hold on to them.

"Where is Mauth now?" Umber follows me turn for turn, hacking at me with her glaive, crowing as it tears through my shoulder. "Where is the magic, little Soul Catcher?"

The sun-blasted earth blurs beneath my feet as I turn and turn and turn again. Anything to shake her loose, slow her down.

Magic surges around me—not mine, but not Umber's either. She disappears, her vitriol abruptly silenced. I don't know what happened to her and I don't care. I keep running, until finally, I can go no farther. Slowing down could mean death; skies know what else is out here. But I must. My heart pumps too frantically. I've lost too much blood.

The moment I stop, I retch, and if Umber appeared now, I'd be a dead man. Mauth's magic slows the damage, but I can't stand.

My canteen is still in my pack—thank the skies Umber didn't tear it from me—and I drink the entire contents down as I try to comprehend what I just saw. Keris's army was vast. Twice the size of the army we've been bedeviling. It will crush Nur like a Mask crushing a flea.

Nur must be warned. Laia, Afya, Shan—all the Tribespeople who fought with me—still have time to protect the city. But I have to get to them.

As I mull, my neck prickles.

I am on my feet, if unsteady, but there is no one here. *Hallucinations. Excellent.* The last time I hallucinated in a desert, I nearly died of poisoning.

Not today. The wind rises, nudging me northwest, so I follow it. Instinct is instinct. Sometimes it's a shout in your head, and sometimes it's your mind telling you the wind wants you to move in a particular direction.

Whenever I stop—which is often—I get that same feeling, as if I'm being watched. But it is not hostile. Nor is it kindly. It feels wary. One animal observing another.

By sunset, I spot the lights of the Tribal caravan. It has stopped for the night, and though all I want is to find a quiet corner of the camp to nurse my wounds alone, the wind appears to shove me to the center of it. I teeter to a stop beside Mamie Rila's wagon.

"Elias!" Laia drops the bowl in her hands and runs toward me. "Where have you—you're bleeding!"

"S-Soul Catcher," I correct her, and she shoots me a glare, wedging herself under my arm. My legs give out the moment she does.

"I'm sorry," I mumble. "Too—too heavy—"

"I dragged you on and off a horse for a week when you were poisoned," she says. "In armor heavier than this. Shan!"

My foster brother appears with two other Saif Tribesmen. A few minutes later, we are in Mamie's wagon, Afya, Mamie, and Shan bent over me.

Laia disappears, returning a moment later with a black rucksack. She shoos everyone else away and snips off my leathers, wincing at the sight of my wounds.

A joke teeters on the tip of my tongue. Something about her trying to get my shirt off. I bite it back, my body jerking as she applies bloodroot to Umber's slashes.

"Who did this?" Her jaw is clenched, and if Umber were to fight Laia right now, I'd bet my marks on the latter. "And why didn't Mauth's magic protect you?"

"I don't know." Skies, my head is spinning. Laia's face blurs. "The magic's weaker—"

"Because of you?" She glances at me. "Because you're remembering who you were?"

I shake my head. "He's weakening. Mauth. I need to talk to the *Zaldars*—Afya—"

"You need to stay still. These are deep, Elias. I'll have to sew them up."

I don't bother to correct the name. My strength wanes, and there are more important things to say. "We can't go to Taib," I tell her. "Keris is sending an army to Nur."

"Afya and the other *Zaldars* already gave the order to evacuate Taib," Laia says. "We'll send Gibran ahead to warn Nur. How far out is the army?"

"Far enough that we can make it. But we need to break camp now. L-leave the wagons." My tongue feels heavy in my mouth. "Anything and anyone unessential. Just—sew me up so I can give the order."

"Someone else can give the order. It doesn't always have to be you! It was stupid of you to go off alone."

"Had to," I mutter. "No one else. Nur cannot fall, Laia." I grab her arm, but I do not know what I'm saying anymore. "If it falls, he'll open the door to the Sea—"

The wagon creaks, and Shan appears. "Sorry." He winces as he takes in my injuries. "But there's someone here to see him—"

"*Look* at him." Laia puts a hand on her hip and stands. Shan backs up, alarmed. "He's not talking to *anyone*."

"Let me up," I grumble, and Laia shoves me back to the bed, something that is both irritating and intriguing at once.

"Shut it, you," she growls at me, eyes flashing. She turns back to Shan, but he has stepped away, and a strange, shifting figure stands in his place. Rowan Goldgale.

"You," I say. "How did you find me?"

"Find you?" The efrit laughs, and it's the deep hum of a dune shifting. "It was I who brought you here, Banu al-Mauth. Did you not feel the wind?"

And here I thought my instinct led me back. "Why would you help?"

"Because you need the efrits, Banu al-Mauth," he says. Behind Rowan, outside the wagon, other figures take shape. One of water who I vaguely recognize as Siladh, lord of the sea efrits. Another that undulates like wind in a bottle. "And we need you," Rowan says. "The time for our alliance has come, whether you wish it or not."

CHAPTER FORTY-ONE

The Blood Shrike

I do not muster up the courage to seek out Harper until evening, and by then, he has disappeared. An hour into my search, one of the Black Guards tells me he is in the baths, in the lower levels of the palace.

I make my way through a dozen hallways and down three staircases to arrive at a plain wood door that looks, at first glance, like an entrance to a broom closet. The bricks here are ancient, likely dating back to the Scholar Empire. It is one of the few places unspoiled by the Karkauns—probably because they didn't much like bathing.

The hallway outside the bath is abandoned, the blue-fire torches burning low. Through a window at the end of the corridor, evening deepens to night.

It's just a door, Shrike. Go through it. He's probably not even there. You'll clean up and leave.

But I can't bring myself to go in. Instead I pace back and forth, wishing Laia wasn't off with the bleeding Tribes, because she'd have useful advice. I wish Faris was here. He'd have been so thrilled for me that he'd have built me up like I was going into battle.

I wish I'd had more lovers. My first was a Mercator boy I met at a masquerade in Navium while on leave. He was handsome and seductive and far more experienced than I. I'd worn an ornate mask over my own—and I never took it off. My next was Demetrius—an ill-fated and dissatisfying tryst when we were in our second-to-last year at Blackcliff. It left us both uneasy. He wanted peace. I wanted Elias. Instead, we ended up with each other, week after week, until I finally ended it.

But I didn't care about either of them. Not the way I care about Harper.

Admit it, you coward, I say to myself. *The way you* love *Harper*.

How I have feared that word. Feared it more than Karkauns or Keris or jinn. But to think it now is strangely freeing. A knot inside me releases, as if some part of me is finally unfettered.

Go on, Shrike.

I open the door to the bath and find Harper with a towel about his waist, another one raised to his dark hair. The brown skin of his body gleams, and I follow a droplet of water as it drips onto his wide shoulders, down his chest, to the rigid muscles of his stomach.

I realize I'm staring and jerk my gaze up, stepping past him into the room, scanning for anyone else, a hand on my scim.

"Shrike?" He peers past me into the hall, assuming there must be a threat. "Are you—is the Emperor—"

"No. Nothing like that." My voice is hoarse. The baths are empty but for Harper. The pool is massive, tiled in green and blue, with water piped in from the bottom. Steam disappears into two large vents to keep the room cool. I eye them warily.

"Already clear, Shrike," Harper says. "I'm alone."

My armor creaks as I shift from foot to foot, still staring, which is when I realize that I have not thought this through at all. Because no one in her right mind would wear armor to seduce the person she's been pining after for months.

Silence descends, and I meet his pale green eyes with a plea in my own, begging him to understand, to not make me any more embarrassed than I already am.

"Shrike—" he begins, and at the same time, I speak.

"I—ah—" Bleeding hells. "Did you—get the orders about the half legion that's to head south?" I say. "Because they shouldn't be delayed, but I wasn't certain if the armory was up to outfitting them—"

"Why are you here, Blood Shrike?" he says.

"I—I'm—"

Bleeding Musa and his bleeding advice. I can't just come out and say why I'm here. I've been horrible to Harper. Avoiding him, ignoring him, barking orders at him, never offering him a word of kindness or gratitude. What if he doesn't feel anything for me anymore? What if he has moved on? There are plenty of—

"Shrike—why are you here?"

"How's the water?" I squeak, and begin removing my armor. Almost immediately, one of the buckles on my chest plate gets stuck. Usually I'd have Livia or one of the guards help me with it, but here, in front of Harper, I tug at it stupidly, my face growing redder with every second that passes. How I wish for my mask.

His hand closes over mine.

"Let me," he murmurs, and a moment later, the buckle is loose. He loosens the others with quick fingers. Then he kneels to pull off the leather greaves from my shins. Moments later, I am in nothing but my shift, and he stands, closer than he was before.

"Could you—" I cannot meet his gaze, and he turns around, dropping the towel. *Oh hells.* I close my eyes immediately though I do not want to, and wait until I'm certain he's in the water.

When his back is turned toward me, I kick off my boots, throw my shift and drawers into a corner. For a long moment, my hand hovers above my hair. I have worn it in this braid since I was a girl, since I got to Blackcliff. The Centurions tried to cut it, but Cain told them that if they touched my hair, he would take off their arms.

I rarely wear my hair loose. The last time I remember doing so was the night of graduation, and only at my mother's insistence.

But I pull it free now. It cascades down my back, and I submerge myself in the water, letting the heat of the pool sink into my muscles. When I come up for air, Harper has turned toward me.

I cross my arms in front of me awkwardly, well aware that I am all muscle, that I have none of Laia's lush curves or Livia's softness.

Harper moves toward me, takes me in slowly. His mouth quirks in the closest thing to a smile I've ever seen from him. Skies, how long have I been staring at his face without realizing it, memorizing his most minute expressions.

For some reason, I keep my attention on the water. I am afraid of rejection. Or mockery. Or realizing that his feelings are shallower than the well of desire within my own heart.

"Look at me," he whispers. But I cannot. "Helene," he says, and the sound of my name on his lips is marvelous. My eyes are hot, and his hand comes up beneath my chin. "Look at me."

I drag my gaze to his, and my breath catches at the look in his eyes. Desire to match my own, just as dark, just as heady. He holds nothing back with this look. He hides nothing.

"Tell me why you're here."

"You know why." I try to turn away, but he will not let me.

"But I need you to say it. Please."

"I'm here because it's been months since you kissed me, but I think about that moment so often it feels like it happened yesterday," I say. "And because when I saw you go down in the battle, I thought I'd—I'd tear apart the world if anything happened to you. And because I—"

His hands are at my hips, and he pulls me closer. My legs rise easily in the water, wrapping around his waist, and his fingers dig into my skin. He mutters something and kisses my throat, slow and careful as he follows the column of my neck to my jaw and settles finally on my mouth, where, suddenly, he is careful no longer.

But I don't care, because I don't want to be careful either. I bite his lip, savage, hungry, and he makes a sound low in his throat. I do not know we have reached the edge of the pool until the cold stone digs into my back and he is lifting me up, trailing kisses up my thighs, higher. In his hands, I am beautiful, sacred, beloved. Beneath his lips, I am undone.

I close my eyes and run my hands over his taut arms, his shoulders, his neck, marveling at his perfection, that impression of coiled strength. My breath quickens, and my legs, my arms, corded with muscle from years of training, quiver beneath his touch. When I slide back into the pool, trembling and impatient, he smiles, a smile that belongs to me alone.

"Helene," he whispers against my ear.

I sigh. "Say it again."

"Helene." He tilts my face toward him, and as our bodies come together, as I cry out his name, my fingers digging into his back at the ache of him inside me, he says it again, and again. Until I am the Blood Shrike no longer, but simply Helene. His Helene.

CHAPTER FORTY-TWO

Laia

Mamie Rila finds me not long after we enter Nur. The city is vastly changed from the last time I was here. The sand-colored buildings are stripped of the Tribal flags that once draped them. The only sound in the streets is the whisper of wind and the occasional bleat of a forgotten goat.

In some ways, I prefer this Nur, for the oppressive presence of the Martials is gone. They left months ago, Afya told me, after Tribe Nur attacked their barracks.

Now we have set up a base of operations not far from where I first met the *Zaldara*, in a courtyard hidden by trellises choked with winter-dead vines. From above, we are invisible.

As I sharpen my blades, Mamie approaches, a thick robe pulled tightly around her and a fur hood framing her face. Unlike most of the *Kehannis*, she has not avoided me, despite my endless pestering about the Night-bringer's story.

"How is he?" she calls out, and I do not ask for clarification.

"He's trying to clear out as many people as he can," I say of Elias. "Says Keris will be here by nightfall."

"I did not ask what he is doing, my love." Mamie tilts her head, dark eyes seeing too much. "I asked *how* he is."

"Physically, he's recovered." For most people, those injuries would have taken months to get over. But not Elias. "Mentally, he's troubled. The magic should have healed him within minutes—hours at the most. The fact that it took a week is eating at him. He's worried about Mauth."

"If the magic is loosening its hold on his body, do you think . . ."

"It might let go of his mind?" I consider. "I do not know, Mamie. Elias's inhumanity is his own choice. Mauth simply makes it easier for him by numbing his emotions. Mauth took away the memories of those Elias killed. Those he hurt. But now he's being forced to do it again and he hates it. Maybe forgetting would be a blessing. He—he would be gone forever, but at least he would not feel such pain."

"We'll bring him back, Laia." Mamie guides me to a nearby bench and bids me sit. "First, you must survive. And that means—"

"I have to kill the Nightbringer."

"It means"—Mamie raises an eyebrow at my interruption—"that I owe you a story."

I go still. She had been so adamant that she would not help me. As if sensing the direction of my thoughts, she shrugs.

"I have learned to love you these past few weeks, Laia." She says it casually, as if it is not extraordinary to gift someone with love. "I find it hard to deny anything to those I love. Already, I have begun to seek out the tale. Though it is not easy. Many of our revered elderly do not wish to speak of the jinn. Yet I need a source to draw from. A person. A scroll. Even a fireside myth." She draws herself up. "But I have hunted stories before and speared them. This one will be no different."

"You say it like it's a living thing, Mamie."

"It's *Kehanni* magic, child. A *Kehanni* can sense a story. Feel out its contours, its breath. I do not just speak a story, I sing it, I become it. That is what it means to be a *Kehanni*. All of us trained to tell stories have a bit of magic in our bones."

The idea of *Kehanni* magic sparks a hundred questions in my mind.

But Mamie kisses me on the cheek and leaves, clearly preoccupied with her new task.

Free for the first time in hours, I find a quiet spot on the side of the courtyard, close my eyes, and reach out to my brother.

Laia. He sounds startled. *Where have you been?*

"I'm in Nur," I say. "About to try to get the scythe. I have much to do, but I need to—I need to ask you something."

The scythe? Is the Nightbringer there?

"He's coming," I say. "Darin, if I fail, promise me you'll defy him. You'll find the scythe. You'll fight him."

Of course, I promise. In fact, Laia, the Blood Shrike is sending troops.

"Finally! We've been waiting. Where are they?"

But I do not hear Darin's response, for Elias rides into the courtyard with a clatter and my concentration is broken. *After*, I think to myself. *I will speak with him after.*

Elias swings down from his horse and makes his way toward me. Though he still wears his black fatigues, something about him speaking Sadhese among the dun buildings of Nur makes me smile and remember the Moon Festival. He dressed as a Tribesman and danced with me, graceful as a cloud.

"Laia," he says. "You should rest. It will be a long night."

"Do you remember the Moon Festival?" I blurt out, and for a moment, he looks confused.

"In Serra," I say. "It was the first time I saw you without your mask. You asked me to dance—"

"Stop." He takes a wary step back. "I'm not asking on my own behalf. I'm asking because I will only hurt you, Laia. I've proven it over and over. I don't want to hurt anyone anymore."

"You still think you can decide things for everyone." My hands curl into fists. "But you cannot. And you cannot make me stop loving you, Elias Veturius. Not when I know that somewhere in there, you feel the same."

I grab his cloak, rise up on my tiptoes, and kiss him. Hard. Angry and bruising. His nose is cold from the wind, but his lips are soft and deliciously warm. *Kiss me back, you dolt*, I think, and he does, but far too carefully, his desire caged. It drives me mad.

When I break away, he stares at me, dazed.

"Uh—Um—"

I leave him there, stammering. It is a small victory. But even those are hard to come by these days.

«««

Night falls reluctantly, as if she does not wish to witness the horrors it will bring. When the stars finally rule the sky, the horizon brightens, glowing orange, then white.

The jinn approach.

"We'll need more than magic to survive that, Laia." Afya enters the courtyard. Her gaze is trained on the eerie glow of the sky, visible even through the trellises. "Are you ready?"

"Doesn't matter if I'm ready." As I dip the last of my arrows in salt, I remember the words I said to my mother long ago, just before I broke Elias out of Blackcliff. "It's time."

"Be careful." Afya glances over her shoulder at Elias, who sends the last of the Tribespeople into the desert. "I don't trust him to defend you."

"I do not need defending, Afya."

Afya nods at the flames drawing nearer. "With that on our tails, we all need defending." She clasps my hands and leaves, heading to the edge of the courtyard, where Aubarit and Gibran hitch up the last wagon leaving the city. The air flickers around them—wind efrits who will speed them through the desert. The young Tribesman says something to the *Fakira* that makes her cheeks rosy. They have spent many hours together, those two, and it makes me smile.

"Not much time, Laia." Elias speaks from beside me, though I did not see him approach. "Shall we?"

"Do not windwalk." Rehmat's gentle glow flares between us. "He will sense you."

I nod, but say nothing else. My anger toward her has cooled, but she has made herself scarce these past few weeks. Whenever she has appeared, there has been a fractured aura about her, as if her focus is fixed elsewhere.

It seems to take ages to wind through the city to the abandoned Martial garrison in its center. By the time we reach the building, the jinn have reached Nur, and the screaming has begun.

I smile at the sound. For if one were to listen carefully to those screams, one might notice that there is something off about them.

"*The barbarous keen yokes us to the low beasts, to the unutterable violence of the earth,*" Elias mutters, and when I look at him askance, he shrugs. "Something the Warden of Kauf Prison said. For once, that evil old bastard was right."

Indeed, a human scream is unique because of its rawness. A fey cry, however, is round and clean, without edges. A stone instead of a saw.

It is the fey who scream now, the sand efrits who are immune to fire, and who agreed to provide a distraction to cover the evacuation of the Tribespeople.

We make our way to the rooftop of the garrison. It is a broad space, scattered with patchy armor, sandbags, and a few piles of pale brick—whatever the Martials failed to take when the Tribes drove them out.

"Does this remind you of anything?"

Elias looks around, nonplussed. "Should it?"

"Last year," I say. "When we were breaking out Scholars from Martial ghost wagons. Only difference is that now I can do this—" I raise my hand to his dark hair, pushing it back. "And Mauth won't give you a splitting headache."

He catches my hand, gripping it for a moment before the Soul Catcher takes hold again and he releases me.

"I wish you luck, Laia," he says. "But I have my own mission. If you're in trouble, I can't help."

"I am not expecting you to," I say. "But if something happens to me—"

"Defeat in the mind is defeat on the—"

"You Blackcliff types and all your sayings." I kick his boot. "Listen, for skies' sake. If something happens, be a brother to Darin for me. Swear you will."

"I don't—" He takes in my scowl and nods. "I promise," he says.

"Thank you, Soul Catcher."

"Elias," he says after a moment, the slightest bit of warmth entering those cold gray eyes. "From you I prefer Elias."

Now it is my turn to be stunned. If we were not about to confront the Nightbringer, I would kiss him. Instead, all I can do is stare as he disappears over the side of the building.

Mission, Laia. Focus on the mission.

As I scurry across the rooftop, wind howls out of the south, a spine-chilling preface to the approach of the jinn and their human army.

I look up to find the entire southern horizon obscured by a towering wall of sand. The storm is ten times larger than the one the Nightbringer conjured up in this very same desert the first time Elias and I came through. And it moves fast—too fast.

When I am only halfway across the roof, it hits, propelling me backward with its force. Though I bend my head against it, the sand is so thick and the wind so strong that I can barely see. I am forced back—finding shelter between a pile of sandbags and the wall—which is no shelter at all. I crouch, coughing the sand out of my lungs, frantically pulling a kerchief over my eyes so I do not go sand blind.

My plan was to hide in a weapons shed on the other side of the wall. But I cannot possibly make it now. Not before the Nightbringer arrives.

"I can help." Rehmat's glow flickers as thick clouds of sand float through her. "If you let me in."

"Will he not sense you?"

She hesitates. "Yes. But I am ready for him. And this storm, it is hurting you." Her form shifts, as if she's fidgeting, and her voice is so soft I almost can't hear it. "I would not see you harmed, Laia. Whether you believe it or not, I am bonded to you, the way a fine blade is bonded to its maker."

Like with Mamie, I feel a sudden flush of warmth at her words. But it is tempered with wariness. Rehmat is so fey. So unknowable. How can I trust her again?

"I'm not ready for you to join with me," I say, and she recoils in frustration. I do not wish to hurt her. But I will not be betrayed again. She has not met the Nightbringer since the flood. This is an opportunity to see if she truly is my ally instead of his. "Let's stick to the plan."

Something thuds atop the tower. A voice speaks, and I clench the hilt of my dagger, fighting back the urge to disappear, and trying desperately not to give myself away by coughing.

"Whip up the winds to spread the fire." The Nightbringer's thunderstorm voice rolls across the roof. "And take the storm north. Slow the rats who flee until the Martials can slaughter them."

"Yes, Meherya," a voice responds. From what Elias told us, it must be Azul, the jinn who can control the weather.

Azul leaves, and the sandstorm howls past, the thick grit billowing toward where the Tribes evacuate the city. Behind me, the screaming intensifies as the Nightbringer's kin set houses alight. The sand efrits, it turns out, are excellent actors.

I tense, hoping to the skies that the Nightbringer does not pay close attention to those screams. But he hardly seems to notice them.

Instead, he stares out at Nur. In Aish, Sadh, and most of the villages in Marinn, he always found the tallest building in the city from which to witness the carnage. As despicable as it is, at least it's predictable. He bows his head, and something flickers behind him.

Maro, Rehmat told me when Elias and I first conjured up this plan. *The jinn who steals the souls for him. The two of them will be distracted by the exertion required to perpetrate such a vile theft. And confused when the souls do not appear. When they are deep in their work, I will tell you.*

That is all she is supposed to do. Elias will neutralize Maro. And I will take the scythe.

The screams from the city rise in pitch, but the Nightbringer remains immobile. I try not to fidget, waiting for Rehmat to appear. But she does not. Soon, he will realize that we have tricked him. That the screams are not human. What in the skies is taking her so long?

Suddenly, his back goes stiff. He turns toward the sandbags. Toward me. *Oh skies.*

"Laia!" Rehmat whispers in my ear. "Let me in—"

I ignore her and stand, dagger high. The last time I saw him, he was not exactly reasonable, but not murderous either. "Hail, Meherya," I say. "You have something I want."

Distantly, a building crumbles, and the jinn fire roars closer. Smoke curls through the air, stinging my eyes, my throat.

"Come to watch a city burn, Laia?" he says. "I did not think you had such a taste for blood. Or punishment."

Though his presence has always twisted the air around him, the Nightbringer's shadow seems to drag with some new weight. The hatred in his flame eyes is bottomless. He unsheathes the scythe with a flick of his smoky hand and holds it to my throat.

Rehmat manifests beside him.

"Meherya," she says. "Stop this. This is not who you are—"

"You." He turns his wrath upon her, but the malice drains out of him, and there is only pain. "Traitor to your own—"

"No—never—"

322

"Do you remember nothing?" he cries. "Who we were, what we lost, what we suffered—"

Laia. She speaks in my mind. *Let me in. Please. He is lost. He will kill you.*

But he does not kill me. Instead he lowers the scythe, and I back away, astonished. Waiting for some new cruelty. But he ignores me completely.

"Come back to me," he says to Rehmat, sheathing the weapon. "Help me remake this world for our kin. You were a warrior, Rehmat. You fought and burned and died for our people. For our—our children—"

"You dare invoke our children?" Rehmat's voice is raw and terrible. As she speaks, I shift toward the scythe, readying my dagger. "When you murder other children at will? I will never join you, Meherya. I am not who I was. As you are not who you were."

"Do you not understand why?" he pleads with her. "I do this because I love. Because I—"

I lunge for his back, slicing through the straps of the scythe. As he turns, as his fiery hands rise up to snatch it back, I call out, but not to Rehmat.

"Elias!"

Almost instantly, a voice screams out from behind the Nightbringer.

It is Maro, a Serric steel blade coated in salt at his neck. Behind him, hood pulled low, stands Elias.

The Soul Catcher's gaze shifts to me briefly. *I can't help,* he'd said. And yet when I called, he was there. As if he catches my thought, he shrugs and jerks his head toward the stairwell. *Get out of here.*

Scythe in hand, I go.

CHAPTER FORTY-THREE

The Soul Catcher

Maro does not put up much of a fight. His skill is limited to soul stealing. The Nightbringer would not keep him so close, otherwise. The touch of my salted dagger elicits a cringe.

To my relief, Laia is gone. When she screamed my name, I had not a whisper of hesitation. It doesn't matter that I said I wouldn't help. It doesn't matter that I need to interrogate Maro to figure out what the hells he's doing with the ghosts. When she called out, all that mattered was her.

But now she's gone, and the Nightbringer turns toward me. I drag Maro back a few steps. The soul-stealing jinn wears his shadow form, and he is narrow-shouldered and slender, almost emaciated. When he opens his mouth, I dig in my blade, and he gasps, huffing in pain.

"You've been stealing ghosts, Maro." I fix my gaze on the Nightbringer. "Tell me how to get them back."

"You cannot get them back," the Nightbringer says. "They are gone."

"What have you done with them?"

"They feed the maelstrom." Maro's fear makes him talk. "It must be fed if we are to breach the wall between worlds."

"Silence, Maro!" the Nightbringer hisses, but all his wrath is for me. "Release him, human." His magic lashes out like a whip, and it burns the skin of my arms so badly that I nearly release Maro. But Blackcliff has trained me well. I hold on to the jinn and reach for Mauth's magic. I need a shield — something to protect me so that I can spirit Maro away and question him without the Nightbringer's interference.

But the magic is too far away, just like when Umber chased me. The power fills me slowly, like droplets in an empty bucket.

"Give me back my ghosts," I tell the king of the jinn, "and I'll let him go."

The Nightbringer's flame eyes narrow, his attention drifting to the city, to the screams of the efrits, louder than before as the fire draws closer. Understanding lights his gaze, and it is terrible to behold.

"Ah, I see now, little Soul Catcher, the game you have played," he says. "So clever to empty out the city. To use the efrits. But it changes nothing. Your kind is a plague on this world. There are *always* more humans, and so there will always be more to reap. If not here, then another city."

"Not if you don't have your soul thief." I dig my blade into Maro again, and this time, fire leaks out.

"Stop." The Nightbringer's fists clench. "Or I will find her, I swear to the skies. And I will tear her soul from her tortured body myself."

"Spending time with my mother, I see." The Nightbringer is usually completely in control. But now his anger is reassuring. He is vulnerable.

And I can take advantage of it. I need to understand him. If he were a human, I would reach out with the tendrils of my magic, a touch too light to be felt. But the Nightbringer will sense any scrutiny—and he will not welcome it. If I want into his head, I will have to force my way in. So I scrape up every last drop of Mauth's magic and launch my consciousness at him.

The moment I do, I hit a wall, miles high, miles thick, and I drift through it like a ghost. I know instantly that I am not in the Nightbringer's mind. I am somewhere else. Somewhere real, even if it is a place where I have no corporeal form. The wall is magic, and that magic speaks to my own, for the source is the same. This wall is Mauth's creation. I am in Mauth's dimension.

Behind the wall is an aching Sea of Suffering that is too powerful to understand, too vast for any earthly being, fey or human, to control. I have seen it before, I realize, every time I have visited Mauth in his realm.

The Sea surges against Mauth's wall, even as the Nightbringer pours the suffering of the ghosts he has thieved into it, giving the Sea more power than it should have. With every ghost, that raging ocean grows stronger. With every bit of suffering fed to it, it wears away at Mauth's wall a little more. In time, it will destroy the wall altogether.

How much time, I wonder? How much more suffering does the Nightbringer need?

"Where are you?"

The Nightbringer's question is heavy with contempt. For the blink of an eye, I think I see him, a thread of fire in the darkness, blazing with hate. Between us, an enormous whirlpool of wailing souls cries out, spinning down endlessly into the Sea. I reach for them, trying to pull them with me, trying to escape this place with them.

Then I am flung away from the Sea, the wall, the ghosts, and back into my body. I still have an arm around Maro, but he wrenches away from me and runs toward the Nightbringer.

Bleeding, burning hells. The king of the jinn pushes Maro behind him and strides toward me, murder thrumming in every sinew of his body.

Then an arrow flies out of the night from the staircase, sinking into Maro with a strange, hollow thump.

She didn't run. Of course she didn't.

Maro collapses, and the Nightbringer howls as he did in Aish. I am already past him, down the stairs, grabbing Laia and leaping out a window, harnessing the wind so we do not break our necks. Still, I hit the flagstones too hard and spin into a roll. Her head hits the ground with a sickening crack, knocking her out cold. I sweep her over my shoulder and tear through the city away from the jinn, not stopping until I reach the desert beyond the northern gate, empty now that the Tribes have evacuated.

"Soul Catcher!" Afya appears from over a hill, my brother Shan riding beside her.

"What the hells happened?" Her face drains of color as she looks at Laia. "Did you fall?"

"She hit her head on the flagstones."

Blood trickles from the corner of Laia's mouth. As I lay her down on the earth, it feels as if a giant fist is trying to squeeze all the blood out of my heart. *Please, please.* I don't know what I'm asking for. Or who I'm asking. I only know that when I feel her pulse at her throat, strong and steady, I can breathe again.

I glance over my shoulder, but the Nightbringer has not pursued us. I find I am shaking, not in cold or exhaustion, but in dread. I thought the Nightbringer's intent was to destroy the Scholars. But if he pours enough pain into the Sea of Suffering, he will unleash it. And it will destroy all human life.

The horror of it is too great, and even through the Mauth-inspired fog in my brain, I can't bring myself to stand up. Why? Why is he doing this?

He is lost, Soul Catcher. His grief has taken him.

The voice of Death is so soft, I nearly miss it. "Mauth?" I whisper.

Afya and Shan exchange a glance and step away from me.

You have been away too long, Banu al-Mauth, Mauth says, and I feel the pull I have not felt in months, to return to the Waiting Place.

I turn to Afya and Shan. "I'll come back," I swear to them. "Tell her."

The words are barely out of my mouth when I feel myself dragged, inexorably, back to the Forest of Dusk. Mauth speaks again, and this time his words resound in my very core.

It is time to come home.

CHAPTER FORTY-FOUR

The Blood Shrike

Perhaps the shrieking wind from the north is a portent. Spring is not far, six weeks away at most. And yet the storm out of the Nevennes puts a foot of snow on the ground and howls down the palace chimneys until it sounds as if the place is possessed by ghosts.

"It's not a bleeding portent," I tell myself as I lurk near the kitchens. "It was one night. It never has to happen again."

"Pardon me, Blood Shrike?" A passing Martial servant glances at me, alarmed, but I wave him off. I've been here for nearly a half hour, contemplating how to ask for the herbs I need without engendering gossip. If there's one thing I know, it's that I do not want children. Ever. Watching Livia give birth taught me that much.

"I was looking for you." Harper's voice makes me jump and my cheeks burn.

"It's going to be difficult to act like nothing's happened if you blush every time you see me, Shrike." He holds a cup in his hand, and the smell is familiar. Mamie Rila taught me to brew it when I needed to slow my moon cycle at Blackcliff. Training while suffering cramps was a special sort of hell. The brew also prevents pregnancy.

"This might be what you're looking for."

"How did you—"

"You've mentioned you don't want children," he says. "Once. Or ten times. And I've brewed this concoction before."

I nod and keep my expression bland. He's had lovers—of course he has. Many, I imagine. Though imagining isn't the wisest idea.

"The last Blood Shrike didn't want unexpected heirs," Avitas says, and the fact that he offers this information with a straight face despite my obvious jealousy makes me want to kiss him.

Instead, I nod emphatically. "Right. Thank you." I take the cup from him and make a face, remembering how awful it tastes.

Harper's eyes drift over my shoulder. "If you'll excuse me, Shrike." He disappears quickly, and a moment later I understand why.

"Good morning, sister." Livia comes down the hallway, her guards behind her. And there's nowhere to throw the damned tea. The only thing to do is drink it as fast as possible, but of course, it's bleeding hot, and I nearly scald my face trying to get it down.

"Careful there," she says. "You'll burn—"

She takes a deep sniff. Her eyes follow Harper leaving.

"You—" she says, a slow smile spreading on her face.

"It doesn't mean anything." Two servers emerge from the kitchen holding trays, a Scholar and a Martial. They giggle together, going silent when they see us, curtsying to Livia before hurrying away. I drag Livia away from her guards. "Shut it—"

"Your eyes are glowing," She hooks my arm in hers and starts marching breakneck toward her apartments. "Your *skin* is glowing. Tell me *everything*."

"There's nothing to tell!"

"Lies!" my sister hisses. "You dare deceive the Empress Regent? Tell me, *tell me*, I need some joy in my life, sister—"

"We just won back the capital. For your son!"

"Not joy then, romance." She digs her fingers into my arm, and I yelp as we step out into the storm. I scald my throat as I drink down the rest of the tea, lest someone else smell it. Not that it's anyone's bleeding business. But Paters are more judgmental than a luncheon full of Illustrian grandmothers.

"Fine," I say. "I'll tell you a little, but get your claws out of my arm, this is untoward behavior for a—"

"Blood Shrike," Pater Mettias calls out from across the snowy courtyard. "Empress Regent." His gaze lingers on my sister. "Captain Dex bid me find you. Another food shipment just arrived from Pater Lenidas's northern estate, along with a messenger. And there are emissaries from Gens Candela and Gens Visselia. They await you in the throne room."

"Thank you, Pater Mettias." Livia glances at me, one eyebrow arched. *We'll talk later.*

As she departs, I notice how Mettias's eyes follow her. His normally grim face is softer. He shakes himself and looks back at me quickly.

Interesting.

Gens Mettia is powerful. Having its Pater on our side has been invaluable. But having him bonded to us more tightly would give Gens Aquilla unquestionable legitimacy with all of the northern Gens.

"—another messenger." I realize too late that Pater Mettias has been speaking for a few seconds. "She's in your quarters, under guard."

"Under guard?"

"The Mariner, Shrike." Pater Mettias gives me an odd look, likely because he's already said this. "She said her message is urgent."

As I leave him and return to my quarters inside the palace, I am unsurprised to see Musa approaching. Dex follows him, looking irritated.

"You didn't need to lock her up," the tall Scholar says to me without preamble. "I know her. She's not dangerous."

"It's just protocol," I tell him. "We caught another assassin at the gates three days ago. I have to question her. Alone. Don't go far. If I need you, I'll call you in."

Dex and I enter my quarters, where two legionnaires wait with a third person. She is taller than me and wears the blue-and-silver cloak of the Mariner army. Her dark skin is dirt-smudged, and she has a dozen wounds that are fresh-dressed and seeping blood. Her hair is straight and clipped short against her head. After a moment of staring, I recognize her.

"Eleiba," I say. "Guard to Nikla. Did your queen send you?"

"Blood Shrike." She bows her head in brief acknowledgment. "Thank you for meeting with me. I am formerly of Princess Nikla's guard, but have since been disgraced in her eyes. I was released from service for arguing against an alliance with Empress Keris Veturia."

To my surprise, the woman drops to one knee. "I come to you now not as a formal ambassador or emissary, but as a Mariner who fears for the survival of our kingdom. We are in desperate need of your aid, Blood Shrike."

My stomach sinks, and I think of our spies, gone silent in Marinn, and the storms that have kept the kingdom isolated.

"Sit down." I pull out a seat for her. "And tell me everything."

«««

Though Livia's quarters are close to my own, I take my time getting there. For I know what she will say when she hears Eleiba's request. And I do not yet know how I will answer her.

Her eyes are shadowed when she opens the door, and she pulls me into the room with a finger over her lips.

"The baby just fell asleep," she whispers. "My ears are still ringing. Poor Tas rocked him for an hour."

The door between Livia's chamber and Zak's is slightly ajar, and Tas emerges.

"I'll be back soon," he whispers. "Just going to get dinner."

"Go get some rest after, Tas," Livia says. "I'll call Coralia—"

Tas shakes his head. "She doesn't know the songs he likes," he says. "Don't fret about me, Empress Regent. I'll be back soon, in case he wakes up."

After he leaves, I sit down with my sister, searching for the words to explain what Eleiba told me. But when Livia launches into a long description of her day—a nightmare, from the sound of it—I decide that I will say nothing tonight. Tomorrow will be full of difficult decisions and more difficult conversations. Let tonight be easy.

"It is all so exhausting," Livia says. "Is it wrong that I just want it to be over? This is no way to live—"

"Don't speak it." I know what she is going to say. But the more she talks of leaving, the more real the idea will become. "Your son is ruler, sister. And you are his regent."

"Ruler of what?" Livia says. "A broken Empire. Some won't accept him because of his father. Others because they fear Keris. We wish for him to live in the world, but it is such an ugly world."

"We are making progress," I say. "We have a dozen more Gens backing us than we did a week ago—"

Livia rises and walks to the mirror our father brought me years ago from the south. It is one of the few things we salvaged from the Karkauns' destruction. As she runs her finger along the gilt edge, I rise and stand beside her. She drops her head against my shoulder.

Once, I stared into this mirror as Mother tended my wounds. Elias had just escaped his execution and Harper had given me a vicious drubbing on the Commandant's orders. Hannah was there that morning with Mother and Livia. The four of us reflected in the mirror.

Now it is just Livia and me, and the space feels too vast. Too empty.

"I miss them." The words escape me, and once I say them, more come that I cannot stop. "Sometimes I think I failed them, Livvy—"

"You did not fail them." Livia takes my shoulders, and though she is smaller than me, I see my father in the steadiness of her gaze, the strength of her hands. "You held fast against the tide, Blood Shrike," she says. "None could have stood as you did. Without you, we would all be dead."

I dash my hands against my eyes. "Bleeding Avitas has turned me soft," I mutter, and Livia bursts into laughter.

"Thank the skies someone has," she says. "And don't you go getting mean on him now. Tell him how you feel, sister."

I shove her and go back to my tea, putting my feet up on her table because I know it will irritate her. "With candles and oud player?" I say. "Shall I make him a flower crown too? Skies, Livia, next you'll want me to propose."

"That's not the worst idea you've ever had."

I nearly spew out my tea. "Harper and I are just—this doesn't mean anything—"

Livia rolls her eyes. "And I'm a three-headed Karka vulture."

"Well, you are one in the morning."

"*You* try being cheery when you're being woken up every three hours and yelled at for food."

I snort, and my sister smiles, taking years off her face.

"Ah, Helly," she says with such sweetness that I cannot even get angry at her for calling me by that old name. "It's so good to hear you laugh. You don't laugh enough. Too bad Avitas is as serious as you are."

I grin at her. "He has other skills."

She giggles, a high-pitched wheeze that sounds like a goat being choked. When I say so, she giggles harder, until we are both laughing far too loudly to not wake a sleeping child.

In the next room, Zak shrieks.

"Oh, now you've done it." Livia shoves me and grabs one of the lamps off the table. "You're rocking him to sleep this time! Poor Tas needs a break, and I need dreams."

"I have plans this evening," I call after her. "I need to make a flower crown, remember—"

My sister snorts and enters my nephew's room, her tone softening. "Zakky, my love, Mama is *tired*, and fed you twice this eve—"

Her voice chokes off. Instantly I am on my feet, across the room, scims out, screaming for the guards. No one could have gotten in without us seeing. There are no passageways into that bleeding room. The windows are fifty feet off the ground. The gardens below are guarded, day and night.

I burst through the door. Zacharias's chamber is small, only a dozen feet across, but right now, it might as well be as wide as the space between stars. For Keris Veturia stands by the window, mask gleaming, a wickedly curved dagger in hand. And Livia is frozen before her, not fighting, not screaming. Just standing there, arms loose at her side, voice low and pleading.

Don't stand there, Livia! I want to scream. *Move! Run!*

Instead my sister's begging chokes off as the Commandant steps forward and slides her blade across Livia's throat. The sound is like cloth tearing, and at first, I cannot believe what I hear. What I see.

The scream building inside me never emerges, for as my sister drops, as her life pours out of her, all I can think of is getting to Keris.

But the Commandant holds a squirming Zacharias in her arms—and I understand now why Livia was frozen in fear. When I leap toward the Bitch of Blackcliff, she throws Zacharias at me. My nephew howls as he flies through the air and I drop my scim to catch him, stumbling.

It is a delay of only seconds. But it's enough for the Commandant to escape out the window. I am at the sill in three steps, in time to see a swirl of cloak and the glare of two sun eyes.

Then the Nightbringer and his minion are gone, disappearing on the back of a screaming wind.

Livvy moans, and I am at her side, her son wailing in my arms as she bleeds out. The guards, including Rallius, burst into the room, going silent when they see the Empress Regent fallen.

I hold up a hand so they don't speak. I do not have much time. The desire to heal overwhelms me. I close my eyes and search for her song. It comes to my lips immediately, but as I hum, Livia scrabbles at me with her hand. It is slick with blood, but I hold it tight.

I keep singing, but Livvy's face is bone-white. The need to heal fades as it never has before. Zacharias reaches out to her, crying, no doubt wondering why Auntie Shrike holds him so tight.

"Don't leave us," I whisper to her, because I understand now that she's too far gone. That I cannot heal this. "Livia, please don't leave us alone."

Her blue eyes drop from mine to her son's. She smiles at him and touches his small fingers with her own. His cries fade into whimpers.

Then her hand goes slack, and my baby sister, my Livvy, closes her eyes and does not open them again.

CHAPTER FORTY-FIVE

Laia

I drift in and out of consciousness for days after stealing the scythe. By the time the Tribes take shelter in a canyon a hundred miles north of Nur, I am able to stay awake for longer stretches. But my recovery is slow. I am like a cat with no whiskers, unable to walk ten yards without lurching.

All I want is to remain in Mamie Rila's wagon, nursing my aching head. Unfortunately for me, Rehmat is not one for brooding. A week after I face off with the Nightbringer, when Mamie leaves the wagon to prepare dinner, the jinn queen appears.

"You think you can simply cut the Nightbringer's throat." Rehmat hovers on the opposite end of the wagon, keeping her distance from the scythe—which has not left my side. "But he will be ready for that. You must surprise him. Outwit him. And for that, you need his story."

"I believe you." I curl into the knit blanket Mamie gave me. "I'm the one who wanted his story in the first place. But we have to fight a war, Rehmat. Can you at least tell me how his story will help us win?"

"War is like the sun. It burns away all the softness and leaves only the cracks. The Nightbringer has been at war for a long time. Learning his story will teach us his weaknesses. It will help us exploit the cracks."

I hoped for something more specific. "You know his weaknesses," I say, frustration taking hold. "But you won't tell me what they are."

"The magic will not allow—"

"But have you tried?" I ask. "Tell me something small about your life with him. Anything."

"He and I—we—" Rehmat's gold form flickers. "We were—" Her voice

337

chokes off and she screams—a bloodcurdling sound. Her color fades so rapidly that I think she will disappear entirely.

"Stop!" I stand. "Forget it—"

The jinn queen is a pale shadow now, her vitality leached away by the magic that binds her. "I told you," she whispers. "The blood magic will not allow me to speak of my life with him. You must ask the *Kehanni*."

A few minutes later, Mamie Rila spots me emerging from her wagon. She glares at me from where she is stirring a pot of squash stew and brandishes her spoon.

"Get back into bed, child. You're still recovering—"

The fire makes her shadow massive on the canyon wall behind her. Shan looks up from the stone where he's rolling out flatbread and grins.

"Says the woman who was driving our wagon the day after leaving a Martial interrogation."

I wince as I sit on the earth beside Mamie, head throbbing, body shivering from the sound of Rehmat's scream. The scythe is slung in a sheath across my back, unwieldy, but too precious to leave unattended.

All along the canyon, fires have sprung up. Their glow is cleverly hidden beneath overhangs and vented tarps. The scent of roasting leeks and buttered flatbread has my mouth watering.

"I thought you might want company," I tell Mamie. "And I'm—a bit lonely."

The *Kehanni*'s face softens, and she hands me the spoon so I can stir the stew as she sprinkles a pinch of cinnamon into it, followed by a handful of dried cilantro. The omnipresent desert wind whistles down the canyon, muting the quiet talk of thousands of people, and the fires spark and dance.

Efrits walk beside Tribespeople. High above on the canyon's rim, guards patrol.

"Mamie," I begin. "I was wondering—"

Horses' hooves sound behind me, and I turn to see Afya and her little brother, Gibran, dismounting near their own caravan.

"Anything?" I call out to the *Zaldara*, but she shakes her head.

"Not so much as a forgotten shoe," she says. "Rowan was with us for most of the trip." She nods to the sand efrit, drifting to a group of his kin who have gathered on one side of the canyon. "He sensed no magic. They're gone."

Mamie ladles out a bowl of squash stew for me and another for Afya. When the latter protests, the *Kehanni* gives her a dark look, and she sits.

Gibran drops beside his sister, lured by the scent of stew as well as the fluffy stack of flatbread Shan has produced. "They might be headed for Taib," he says. "Though by now, they should know it's empty."

"At least we have time to recover," I say. "And to plan our next move."

"A bit hard to do that when our general is missing," Afya mutters. Mamie gives her a sharp look, but I do not blame the *Zaldara* for her irritation. Elias's disappearance sent ripples of unease through the Tribes, even when Afya told them of his assurances that he'd return.

"He'll be back," I say. "Nur was a small victory in a greater war, and he has a stake in it. Mamie"—I turn to her now—"how goes the story-hunting?"

"It is slow," the *Kehanni* says between bites of stew. "Our stories have two qualities. *Sechei* and *Diladhardha*."

"Truth . . . and—" My Sadhese is limited, and I shake my head.

"*Diladhardha* means 'to know the heart of pain,'" Mamie says. "We seek truth, Laia. And when we find it, we must approach it with empathy.

We must understand the creatures, fey or human, who populate our tales. Respect them. Love them, despite the villainous things they do. We must see them. Else how will our stories echo in the hearts of those who hear them? How will the stories survive beyond one telling?"

The *Zaldara* and Gibran listen, rapt, and even Shan, who has lived with the *Kehanni* his whole life, stares at her with his spoon frozen halfway to his mouth.

"*Sechei* and *Diladhardha* are the first steps to hunting a story. When you have attained them, then a story might be coaxed from the shadows. I have heard many tales of the Nightbringer. But none that will allow me to understand him or love him or respect him. I know him only as a creature of great evil. I fear loving him. I fear respecting him. I fear if I do, I will lose myself."

"Such stories are dragons drawn from a deep well in a dark place," I murmur.

"Where did you hear that?" Mamie asks.

"The *Kehanni* of Tribe Sulud," I say. "She knew the Nightbringer's story. But wraiths killed her before she could tell me."

Mamie's food is forgotten, and she looks at me intently. "Do you remember anything else of what she told you? Any hint at all as to what the story could be about?"

"She didn't really—" I stop then and consider. "She spoke of his name. She said the story she told would be about his name. About how—how important it is."

"His name," Mamie considers. "The Meherya, you said. And it means . . ."

"Beloved." Even thinking the word makes me sad. But Mamie shakes her head.

"It is not enough," she says.

"You couldn't help, could you?" I mutter to Rehmat. But she doesn't respond.

A sharp call sounds from the northern end of the canyon, followed by the chilling rasp of dozens of scims being drawn at once.

Mamie is already kicking sand over the fire and shooing me toward her wagon. Afya sprints for her horse, Gibran following. Then Afya calls out.

"Laia," she says. "Wait, look!"

She peers down the canyon, and I can see the glimmer of Martial armor now, and what appear to be about two dozen soldiers.

But it is not the soldiers who have my attention. It is the brown-skinned, lanky figure who rides with them, sandy hair blowing in the desert wind.

"Darin?"

I'm too far away for him to see, but I limp through the camp toward him now, until I can make out his face. He spots me and dismounts, a giant smile on his face.

"Laia!"

"Lower your weapons," I call out to the Tribesmen, many of whom have never met him. "Skies, he's the one who made them!"

My brother weaves through them and envelops me in a bear hug. I do not let him go, even when he tries to put me down. *My brother. My blood.* The only blood I have left in this world. I find that I am sobbing, and when I finally break away, his face is wet too.

"Thank the skies you're all right," he says. "I tried to tell you I was coming, but you didn't let me get a word in edgewise when we spoke. The Shrike sent half a legion with me, to help the Tribes fight Keris. Most of them are a few miles away. The last we heard, Aish had fallen."

"So much has happened since then." I do not know where to begin. "What matters is that I have the scythe. I can kill him, Darin. But we cannot find him or his bleeding army. We think they're here in the Tribal lands. Probably using fey magic to hide. We just need to get to them."

Darin glances at the Martial commander with him—Jans, the Blood Shrike's uncle. Something passes between them.

"That will be harder than you think, Laia," Darin finally says. "Keris sent a massive force east. Three hundred ships. They left Navium when the rest of her forces were marching on Nur."

"I don't understand," I say. "Keris was here—I saw her—"

"Not anymore. She and the Nightbringer are laying siege to Marinn. Laia—they're a thousand miles away."

CHAPTER FORTY-SIX

The Soul Catcher

For long days and nights, I am at peace as I haven't been since I first merged with Mauth. Spring eludes the Waiting Place, but the vicious bite of winter has finally eased, and I spend my time passing the ghosts.

It is not easy. For the rot near the river has spread, and the ghosts do not wish to pass. But when I worry, the gentle sweep of Mauth's magic eases it away. There is a rightness to this work. A clarity.

But that changes one night when I enter my cabin and knock something off a small table by the door. It hits the ground hard and bounces toward the fireplace. I stare at it, perplexed. It is a half-carved armlet—but where is it from? I should remember—I *need* to remember.

Laia.

Her name bursts in my head like a firework. The memories that Cain returned to me come back all at once—along with everything that happened since then. Laia was injured in Nur. Is she all right now? Afya and Mamie would have taken care of her, but—

A slow tide of magic sweeps through my mind. My worry fades. My memories fade.

No! a voice screams in my head. *Remember!*

I stumble back out the door of the cabin, the armlet clutched in my hand. From the trees, a ghost watches me.

"You're back," Karinna whispers. "You were gone a long time, little one."

"I'm sorry," I tell her. "I was . . ." *Remember*, the voice in me screams. But what does it want me to remember?

"You've seen what's coming," Karinna says. "The maelstrom. I smell

343

the knowledge on you. And yet you do nothing. What if it hurts my lovey? You told me she was out there, still alive. What if the maelstrom destroys her?"

Maelstrom. Hunger. Darkness. Suffering.

The Nightbringer. I drag the name out of the molasses that Mauth has made of my brain. The Nightbringer is waking something up. Something he cannot control. He is using ghosts to strengthen it so it can break through Mauth's protections and destroy the human world.

"What you see cannot come to pass," Karinna says. "It will hurt my lovey. I can feel it. You must stop it."

"How?" That tide of forgetting is upon me, Mauth manipulating my mind, but this time, I resist it.

"Yes." Karinna nods. "Fight him. Fight for my lovey. Fight for those who live."

"Mauth!" I call out. He ignores me, yet again.

Or perhaps, I realize with a sudden flash of intuition, he cannot hear me. I keep expecting Mauth to respond to my call. But he battles the Nightbringer endlessly. In the midst of a fight, I might not hear my own name called from beside me, let alone from another dimension.

I drop to my haunches beside my cabin. For long minutes, I keep my eyes closed and do not move. Instead, I feel out the magic, imagining it as Cain showed it to me, thick gold ropes that bind this place together. The image falls apart in my mind over and over. Each time, I rebuild it, rope by rope, until I feel as if I have the whole of the Waiting Place in my mind.

Then, like I did with the Nightbringer, I throw myself at it. At first, the image shudders and flickers, as if about to come apart. *No, damn you—*

Then the oddest sensation grips me, like some enormous hand has dragged me into the bowels of the earth itself. I see my body, kneeling in the world of the living.

But my consciousness is not there. Instead I am pulled down through the web of magic, and I emerge onto a rocky promontory beneath a pale yellow sky. The promontory stretches behind me, lost in fog. A savage ocean tosses below, the waves so massive that they defy understanding. I have a body—or a semblance of one, but it is more a suggestion than anything solid.

When I attacked the Nightbringer's mind, I was seeing this very place, this dimension, from his perspective. The jinn lord sees Mauth as the wall between himself and vengeance. Now I see Mauth's dimension from my own perspective.

Along the horizon, a familiar, man-like form approaches.

Soul Catcher, Mauth says. *You do not belong here. Return.*

"There's something wrong with the Waiting Place," I tell him. "I've tried to tell you—"

I fight wars you have no concept of, child. Return.

"The Nightbringer siphons souls from the living."

I know the sins of my son. They are no concern of yours. I have given you enough of my magic to uphold the wall. To aid the ghosts. Go then, and pass them on. You have spent too much time away.

I must break through to him. But how? I speak to Death itself. I am an ant, waving my feelers, attempting to get the attention of the universe.

"There are no ghosts," I say. "The Nightbringer has taken them all. Only a few remain, and those will not pass, for they sense only a great evil awaiting them on the other side."

A long silence.

Speak.

I tell him of the rot along the River Dusk and the ghosts' fear. I tell him of the Nightbringer's war, how he has used Maro to steal souls. I tell Mauth what I saw when I entered the Nightbringer's mind.

"How can you not know this?" I say. "How—how can you not see?"

I am not of fire or clay, Banu al-Mauth, he says. *The minutiae of your human lives is beneath me. It must be, else I would be mired in it.*

A sigh gusts out of him, and his magic weakens.

To my folly. The Nightbringer's wrath is unending. I did not know. As you see my dimension in one way, I see yours in another.

A universe, I realize, trying to understand the world of the ant.

I believed the jinn needed to be freed and returned to their duty. That is the purpose for which I created them. I did not understand the depth of their pain. Nor did I understand the Nightbringer's fury. Thus I battle him, and I fear I am losing.

"How can you lose against him?" I ask. "You are Death."

If you underestimate the spider, Banu al-Mauth, it can bite. And if its bite is poison, it can kill. So it is with the Nightbringer. He knows where to bite. And he is riven with poison.

"Why can you not take the magic from him as you took it from me?" I say.

The magic you use to pass the ghosts and hold the wall is an extension of my own. You borrow it. Nothing more. Your windwalking, however, was a gift. I cannot take it away. When I created the Meherya, I gifted him all of my magic. What I have given I cannot take back. Even Death has rules.

"He wants to release the Sea of Suffering. Destroy all life," I say. "I could stop him. And I think I can remind the jinn of their duty. Bring them back into the fold. But I have to be able to leave the Waiting Place. I cannot be trapped there."

Mauth appears to stare down at the roiling ocean. *Tell me your vow.*

"To light the way for the weak, the weary, the fallen, and the forgotten in the darkness that follows death."

Then that is what you must do. The balance must be restored. If this means leaving the Waiting Place, so be it. But hold to your duty, Banu al-Mauth. Memory will make you weak. And emotion will not serve you well.

Even as he says it, numbness steals over me. But this time, something in me bucks wildly against it.

"If Cain hadn't put memories of Laia and Helene and Keris back inside me," I say, "I never would have left the Waiting Place. I never would have realized what the Nightbringer is doing. I need my memories. I need my emotion." I think of Laia and what she's been trying to tell me for weeks. "I cannot inspire humans to fight if I'm not one myself."

The Sea slams itself against the promontory, and enormous, repugnant shapes move beneath the water. Teeth flash. *More*, the Sea growls at me.

I will not interfere, Mauth says. *But do not forget your vow, lest you be destroyed by the magic I used to bind you. You are sworn to me until another human—not jinn—is seen fit to replace you. Your duty is not to the living. Your duty is not to yourself. Your duty is to the dead, even to the breaking of the world.*

His words are as final as the first fistful of dirt in the grave.

"The jinn have escaped," I say. "The ghosts are imprisoned. The Nightbringer has leveled entire cities and stolen countless souls. The world is broken, Mauth."

No, Soul Catcher, Mauth says softly. *The power of the Sea of Suffering cannot be controlled. Not even by the king of the jinn. If he unleashes it, it will not just destroy humanity. The Sea will destroy everything. All life. Even the jinn themselves. I fear, Banu al-Mauth, that the world has yet to break.*

«««

The bulk of the Tribal fighting force has hunkered down in the Bhuth badlands north of Nur. Near the center of the camp, a large knot of elders and *Zaldars*, *Fakirs* and *Fakiras*, and *Kehannis* have gathered around a fire half the size of a wagon. I slow as I approach, for an argument rages.

"—we are not going to bleeding Marinn—" The *Zaldar* of Tribe Nasur speaks, shouting down a dozen other voices. "If you wish to help the Mariners, that is your choice—"

"If we do not all go, the Nightbringer will win." Laia's voice is low, and she struggles to temper her frustration. "He will have his vengeance on the Scholars, and Keris will hunt you down like she hunted down my people. You'll be enslaved. Destroyed. Just like we were."

"You have the scythe," another voice calls out. "You go fight him. Was it not your people whose violence led to the Nightbringer's ire?"

"That was a thousand years ago—" Darin speaks, which is when I notice Martials sprinkled through the crowd. The Blood Shrike's men.

"There's no point in staying if we're just going to be hunted," Afya says forcefully. "We go. We fight. Laia takes down the Nightbringer. Maybe we win."

"That will take weeks—"

"Months," Gibran calls out. "Maybe years. But at least we fight instead of hiding like rats."

I think of Mauth's warning, and Khuri's prophecy. *In flowerfall, the orphan will bow to the scythe.*

We do not have months or years. We have weeks, if that. Spring is close.

It is Laia who sees me first. Laia whose eyes go wide as I step out of the dark.

Whispers of *Banu al-Mauth* streak through the crowd gathered around the fire. They could shout at me. Ask me why I left. Instead they shift back, giving me space to pass. Watchful. Defiant.

"The Nightbringer's maleficence runs deeper than we thought," I tell them. "For he is not stealing your ghosts to empower his people. He is stealing them so that he can destroy all life. And if we wish for a future—any future—we have no choice but to stop him."

CHAPTER FORTY-SEVEN

The Blood Shrike

We bury the Empress Regent two days after her murder, as the sun goes to rest in the west. Thousands line Antium's streets, littering it with winter rose petals as six Masks carry her to the Aquilla Mausoleum on the north end of the city. There, under a rainy, slate-colored sky, she is movingly eulogized by a handful of highborn Paters and Maters who barely knew her.

Or so I am told, after. I do not attend. I do not leave the palace for days following. Instead, I plot how I will destroy Keris.

Two weeks after the funeral, I am holed up in a meeting chamber with Livia's advisory council, listening to a group of recently arrived generals arguing over why their war plan is the only one that will allow us to take back Silas—and eventually Serra and Navium—from Keris.

"We should wait," says old General Pontilius, fresh from Tiborum. He paces around the long table where I sit with Mettias, Quin Veturius, Musa, Cassius, and six others.

"No. We strike now," Quin says. "While she's trying to take the Free Lands. Secure Silas, and move south from there."

"And what if it's a trap?" Pontilius asks. "She could have an army lying in wait for us. Reports put her forces in Marinn at nearly forty thousand men. She has another thirty thousand in reserve. That leaves fifty thousand men unaccounted for."

"They're scattered throughout the south—" Musa offers, and Pontilius recoils as if slapped.

"How would you know, Scholar?"

Once, Musa might have laughed off such insolence. Now he frowns. Eleiba's tidings from Marinn have sobered him. All I could send was a token force. Two Masks. Two hundred soldiers. They will not have even reached Marinn yet. *They won't get through in time*, Musa had fretted. *We have to draw Keris off. We have to take back the Empire so she has no choice but to return.*

He could have gone back with Eleiba. He'd wanted to, even. But his people are here, so he stayed.

"Do you know where Musa of Adisa was in the fight to take Antium, Pontilius?" I say now. "At my side, bleeding for an Empire he'd never set foot in until a few months ago. Fighting for the Scholars. Tell me, *General*, where were you during the fighting?"

Pontilius pales. "You've been taken in by a handsome face—"

My blade is at his throat before he finishes. "Do not make the mistake," I say, "of thinking I won't slit your throat for discourteousness, old man. Everyone at this table knows I won't hesitate."

Pontilius swallows and, in what he no doubt thinks of as a more reasonable tone, says, "He is a *Scholar*—"

My punch lands with a *crack* across his jaw, and he topples backward, stunned. I am embarrassed for him. He's younger than Quin. At the very least he should be able to handle a punch on his feet.

"You—" he sputters. "How dare you—"

"She could have killed you." Pater Mettias, wan and quiet until now, speaks up. "Count yourself lucky."

"You should remember, Pontilius"—Quin spits out the Pater's name—"Empress Regent Livia freed the Scholars. The advisory council supported her."

"The Empress Regent is dead." Pontilius moves as far away from me as he can. "And now this—this woman—"

"As the people have named her Imperator Invictus, and as she is the Mater of Gens Aquilla, I move for the Blood Shrike to serve as regent," Quin says. He'd warned me this morning that he'd make such a motion. But I did not expect it to come so soon—and I wish he had not invoked the title of Imperator.

"Until we have dealt with Keris," the old man goes on. "Yea or nay?"

It's not really a question, and the *yea* that rumbles through the room is unequivocal.

"She cannot be both Shrike *and* regent." Cassius speaks up, the cretin. He and Pontilius don't look at each other, but my sources tell me they've been plotting. It's a shame I need their men. "There's no precedent."

"There is no precedent for a Blackcliff commandant to betray her own people to barbarian invaders, leave her capital to burn, and declare herself Empress," I say. "There is no precedent for her to then enjoy the support of hundreds of Illustrian Paters, including yourself, despite such crimes. There's no precedent for her to murder the rightful regent with the help of an ancient supernatural evil." I open my hands. "But here we are. Help us or leave, Paters. It makes no difference to me. I will secure the Empire for my nephew with or without your aid, and with or without your men."

After the meeting is over, Dex finds me. My old friend has shadows beneath his eyes. He looks like he slept about as much as I did. But he does not offer me kind words or understanding. He knows I do not want either.

"The new wet nurse is ready to meet you, Shrike," he says, and I follow him toward the Black Guard barracks, which we've moved to the palace grounds. "Her name is Mariana Farrar," Dex says. "She was recommended by Coralia Farrar. They're cousins."

"So she's related to the Emperor too," I say. "How has he been with her?"

"Much better than the last wet nurse," Dex says. "I asked Silvius to observe too, since he's worked with mothers and children. He had no concerns."

"Family?"

"Husband's a tanner. They escaped Antium with us after the siege. They're well-known. Well-liked. They have a sixteen-month-old son. He'll be weaned soon."

When I enter Dex's quarters, Mariana stands. Her Farrar blood is instantly visible—she has Marcus and Zacharias's yellow eyes. A young man holding a child stands beside her—her husband, I presume. I can tell they want to curtsy or bow. But my armor is throwing them off.

"I am the Blood Shrike and Regent of the Emperor." My title feels strange on my tongue, and I call on the Mask in me that I might deliver the words with no inflection. "My duty is to protect the Empire and the Emperor at all costs. You are a necessary part of a machine designed to protect him. If you harm the Emperor, what do you think I will do?"

Mariana lifts her chin, but her voice is a whisper, and she has to force herself to meet my gaze. "Kill me. As you should."

I nod to the child and the man who holds him. "I will kill your boy, there, first. I will kill your husband. I will find everyone you love or have ever loved and I will kill them too. I will insist you watch before I throw you in prison forever, that you might live with the horror of your actions. Do you understand?"

Mariana nods frantically but I hold her gaze. "Tell me in your own words."

"I—I understand."

Dex and I escort her and her family out, and once they are down the hallway, I turn to him. "Four guards when she nurses, not two." I say. "Her husband and son remain in the palace and under watch. If she so much as looks at the Emperor wrong, you let me know."

I make for Zacharias's room, which now connects to mine on the second level of the palace. It faces the palace garden, though he cannot see it. His window is boarded up, and despite a number of colorful lamps hanging from the ceiling, it feels less like a nursery and more like a prison cell. Likely because of Silvio Rallius and Deci Veturius, each hulking in a corner. Would that I had stationed them in Zacharias's room before this.

In addition to the Masks, Coralia sits in a rocking chair in deepest black, her eyes puffy as she watches Tas and Zacharias playing. She rises when I enter, but I wave her back to her seat.

Tas is on the floor with my nephew, making a small wooden horse dance along his arm. I watch for a moment before the boy notices me. He stands, but I give him space and bid him sit. I know his history. Harper told me of him and Bee and the other children of Kauf.

"Shrike," he says after a few moments, and I can tell he has worked himself up to this. "I—I owe you an apology. If I hadn't left Zakky that night, if I'd stayed with him—"

I go to Tas and kneel down. In a corner, Coralia sniffs quietly, attempting to muffle her sobs.

"Then you'd be dead too," I say. "Don't you take the blame, Tas. That belongs to me, and me alone. I do have a request for you, though."

I've been considering this for days—since before Livia was assassinated.

"The Emperor needs a companion. Not a regent like me, or guards like

Rallius." I nod to the big man, who observes Tas soberly. "But a friend. A brother. Someone to laugh with him and play with him and read to him, but who will also guide him and keep him safe. Someone he trusts. Someone who understands him. But that person, Tas, must be trained in battle and combat. He must be educated. Will you undertake this task?"

Tas shifts uncomfortably. "I—I cannot read, Blood Shrike."

"You're a smart lad—you'll pick it up quick. If you want it, of course—" I realize suddenly that the child might be afraid to say no. "Think on it," I tell him. "When we see Laia again, maybe you can ask her. She's wise about these sorts of things."

Zacharias takes the horse from Tas and throws it a few feet away. He rolls onto his stomach, rocking toward the horse, perplexed that he does not appear to be getting closer to it.

I cannot help but smile. My first since Keris murdered Livvy. "He's never done that before."

Zacharias loses interest, rolls onto his back, and puts a foot in his mouth.

"He'll be running before long," Tas says. "For now, feet. Quite tasty, apparently."

"Very tasty." I pick up my nephew and tickle his toes. He flashes two teeth at me and giggles.

"Ah, little one." I narrowly evade his fist as he lunges for my braid. "Determined to ruin Auntie Shrike's hair, I see. Tas, why don't you go get lunch and some air. You shouldn't be cooped up in here all day, little one."

The boy leaves and I walk Zacharias into my quarters, dismissing the Masks within. My nephew flops toward the window, toward the light. But I keep him well away and in the darkness, where it is safer. Where no errant assassin's blade can touch him.

This is no way to live, Livia said. But it is all we have. I hear footsteps behind me, a familiar gait. I do not turn.

"Soon you'll walk in the light again, nephew," I tell Zacharias. "Auntie Shrike will make you safe. You'll ride and run away from your tutors and have great adventures with good friends. Auntie Shrike will destroy all of your foes. I pro—"

The words die on my lips. Because I promised my sister I would keep her safe. I promised myself I would not let anything happen to her, not after what happened to my parents and Hannah.

"Make that promise, Shrike."

Harper stands beside me, greeting the Emperor with a rare quirk of the lips and a kiss to his head. Zacharias offers him a tentative smile.

"Look your nephew in the eyes," Harper says, "and make a vow."

I shake my head. "What if I can't keep it?" I whisper because the alternative is to scream, and if I kept silent as my sister died, then I can keep silent now.

"You will keep it," Harper says.

I shake my head and call out to Coralia, who takes Zacharias from me. Harper follows me as I leave. It has been easy enough to avoid him this past fortnight—I've had months of practice. Before he says something that makes me come apart, I speak.

"Bring Quin Veturius to the small chambers off the throne room," I say. "I want his thoughts on what to do about Pontilius—what are you—"

Harper takes my hand and brushes a finger across my lips—*sh*. He pulls me in the opposite direction of the throne room and down a set of stone stairs. Near the bottom, beside a pile of rubble and just before an enormous, recently restored tapestry, he touches part of the wall and the stone moves away.

I know this passageway, and it leads to a dead end, with a few storage closets in between. Rallius has the palace guard check it twice a day.

But of course, Harper would know that. I understand why he's brought me here, and I am so grateful I want to grab him and kiss him right here with the hallway door hanging open.

Oblivion is what I need right now. A way to escape this feeling in my chest, like if I say Livia's name aloud, my heart will wither and die. Harper is a distraction. One I am desperate for.

He releases my hand once we're in the hallway and lights a torch. When it flares, we are moving again, past a storage room filled with rubble and wood and into another, which is larger than I realized. It is big enough for a rope pallet and a small table with a lamp. In one corner sits a club and a pile of large stones.

"Is this where you sleep?" I ask him, eyeing the cot, but he shakes his head.

"Only ghosts down here, Shrike."

The room is cold, though I hardly feel it. I unhook my cloak, but Harper shakes his head and hands me the club.

"Ah." I glance down at it uneasily. "What am I doing with this?"

"I found this place when we first came to Antium, after you told me how my father died." He looks me level in the eye.

"I don't understand."

"I came here to shout into the darkness," he says. "To scream and break things."

"But you're always so calm."

"Always, Shrike?" He arches a silver brow, and a flush creeps up my face. He is not always calm—that was clear enough in the baths.

"I don't need to—to shout or cry or . . . break stones." I drop the club. "I need to—I need—"

"To scream," he says quietly, and hands me the club again. "And break things."

It is as if his words have breathed life into something twisted and aching that has lived within, unacknowledged, for too long. Lurking ever since I watched Marcus slit my father's throat. Since I heard Hannah cry out, *Helly!* Since I watched Antium burn. Since Cook and Faris and Livvy all died.

I only know I hit the floor when my knees slam into it. The scream breaks out of me like a prisoner who hasn't seen light in a century. My body feels alive, but in the worst way, a betrayal of all those who are gone. All those who I didn't save. I scream over and over. And the scream dissolves into something primal, so I howl then, and weep. I snatch the club from Harper and break every stone in the room.

When there are no stones left, I drop the club and curl into a ball on the cot. Choked sobs leak out of me, and I have not wailed like this since I was a child safe in the arms of my parents. Then even the sobs fade away.

"I am unmade." I whisper to Harper the words the Augur uttered to me so long ago. "I am b-broken."

Harper kneels and wipes my tears away with his thumbs. Then he lifts my face to his, his own eyes wet, his gaze fierce in a way I've rarely seen.

"You are broken. But it is the broken things that are the sharpest. The deadliest. It is the broken things that are the most unexpected, and the most underestimated."

I sniff and wipe my face. "Thank you," I say. "For—" *For being here. For telling me to scream. For loving me. For knowing me.*

I say none of it. I am glad now that we did not make love here, in this place. I am glad I pushed him away for so long, for it will make doing it again easier.

I return the club to its corner and stand. Then I walk away. He says nothing. But I hope he understands.

I have seen what happens to those I love.

« « «

At dawn the next morning, I leave my room and go next door, to Zacharias. He sleeps, Tas on the cot beside him and Rallius standing near the door.

"Shrike," Rallius murmurs, before stepping outside to give me a private moment.

I stand over my nephew's crib and stare down at him. His brown curls are fuzzy and soft beneath my hand, just like Livia's used to be when she was a child.

"I promise I will keep you safe." I fight back the tears that threaten. I have done my screaming, my weeping. No more. "Whatever the price. I will protect you as I didn't protect them. This I vow, by blood and by bone."

And with that I leave, and go to secure my nephew's empire.

CHAPTER FORTY-EIGHT

Laia

The moon is high and fat when Elias finds Darin and me sitting atop a boulder on the rim of the canyon. I sense the Soul Catcher before I see him, the way you feel the air quiver when a falcon stoops for prey.

"What is it?" As I jerk my head up, Darin draws his scim, for we are on guard duty. "What do you see?"

My heart thuds against my chest like a penned bull as Elias approaches. Darin spots him and groans.

"Can I kick him?" my brother asks. "I'm going to kick him."

"He saved your life, Darin."

"A small kick," he argues. "It wouldn't even hurt him. Look at him, skies. It would probably break *my* foot."

"No."

"Fine." Darin grabs his pack, ignoring the Soul Catcher's nod of greeting. "I can tell when I'm not wanted." Once past Elias, my brother turns around and mimes a kick, grinning.

Skies. Brothers.

"Any progress with the Tribes?" I ask Elias, for when I came up here, the *Zaldars* were still arguing over whether to leave for Adisa or try to fight for Aish.

Elias shakes his head. "Most wish to fight for Aish," he says. "Few wish to go to Marinn."

My fingers tighten around the staff of the scythe. The blade is folded into a slot in the wood, and it appears for all the world like nothing more than a fine walking stick. Which is essentially what it will be if I cannot get to the Nightbringer. And if Mamie cannot find his story.

None of us have slept for the past few nights, knowing now what the jinn king intends to do with all his soul thieving. I shiver, dread crawling over me like a carpet of spiders.

Elias clears his throat and nods to the rock. "Do you mind?"

I shift over quickly, surprised. He always seems like he struggles to even be near me. But I do not ask questions, instead letting myself enjoy the warmth of his body so close to mine.

"It's a two-month journey to Adisa from here." He stretches his long legs in front of him. "If we can get ships to take us across the Duskan Sea. If we survive the Commandant's blockade. And if the weather holds."

"You could order the Tribespeople to follow you," I say. "The Banu al-Mauth's word carries great weight. And they have trusted you thus far."

"Only to see their cities destroyed —"

"Only to survive," I say. "If you had not mobilized them, Nur and its people would be ash."

"You said something to me a few weeks ago," Elias says. His hands are upturned and he runs a thumb across a callous, worrying at it. "*You cannot lead them if you do not understand them.* Now I understand the Tribes. I understand their fear. They do not wish to die. And if we go to Adisa to fight, we take them to their deaths. Besides which, I wonder if we won't be playing right into the Nightbringer's hands by going to Marinn."

"You think he's trying to lure us there?"

"I think we shouldn't be reactionary," Elias says. "We need to consider."

"We can't consider for much longer," I say. "Spring is only a few weeks away. *In flowerfall, the orphan will bow to the scythe.* I think—" I shudder. "I think that prophecy speaks of me—"

I cannot finish the thought. Are there people in the world who still experience happiness? Enjoy it, I want to tell those people. *Enjoy it, because soon it might all be gone.*

Elias shifts closer, and his arm comes around me. He might as well have transformed into a talking rabbit, I am so surprised.

"You did say to be more human—" He quickly lets go. "You looked sad, so . . ."

"No." I return his wrist to my shoulder. "It's fine. Though if you're going to comfort me, your embrace should be less like a tree branch and more like a—a shawl."

"A shawl?"

Of course, I had to pick a singularly unromantic word. "Like this." I let my own arm rest naturally about his waist. "We're not drunken schoolfellows singing chanties about wanton fishwives. We are—you and I—we—"

I do not know what we are. I search his face, wondering if I'll ever see the answer there. But he tilts it up to the glittering sweep of the sky, so that I cannot see his expression.

Still, after a half dozen too-swift thuds of my heart, his arm relaxes, muscle by muscle, until it is draped comfortably across my back. His big hand encircles my hip, and when he pulls me closer, it feels as though all the heat in my body has pooled beneath his fingers.

For all that he is the Banu al-Mauth, he still smells of spice and rain. I forget the cold and breathe him in. It is not all that I wanted. But it is not nothing either.

I wait for him to pull away, but he does not. Slowly, the tension eases out of me. With him beside me, I feel more myself. Strong. And less alone.

"Do you think the jinn know?" I ask him. "What will happen if the Nightbringer releases the Sea?"

"They must at least suspect." The rumble of Elias's baritone hums through my body. "They are not fools."

"Then why support him?" I say. "To be imprisoned for a thousand years and then released only to wreak havoc and die—it seems like a terrible waste."

"Perhaps imprisonment drove them mad."

But that doesn't feel right. "It's not madness that grips the Nightbringer," I say. "It is intent. He *wants* to destroy everything. I think he's hiding that fact from his kin." I shiver. "Yet he claims to love them. He *does* love them."

Footsteps crunch behind us, and we jump away from each other.

"Banu al-Mauth!" Gibran and Aubarit approach, and the latter bows her head in respect and then smacks Gibran, who quickly does the same.

"Dinner's ready, Laia," Gibran says. "Afya sent us up to take over."

When Elias and I reach the canyon floor, he disappears, his eyes far away in that manner that tells me he's working through a problem. Most of the Tribespeople have bedded down for the night. Those few remaining sit around the fire quietly, any arguing drowned out by the lonely wind wailing down the canyon, trying its best to put out our flames.

"Bleeding cold." Afya's teeth chatter around her spoon. "And there's little enough wood. We won't be able to stay here much longer."

"Did you change any minds?"

"My Tribe will stay, as will Mamie's and Aubarit's," Afya says. "The rest plan to leave at first light. They hope to take back Aish."

"Aish won't matter," Darin says from where he hunches by the fire, "if the Nightbringer sets that maelstrom free and kills everyone."

I leave Afya and Darin and turn to Mamie, just a few yards away. Though it is cold enough that the stream has iced over, she sits on the earth of the canyon, staring up at the stars.

"Can't sleep?" I ask her.

"Not when I know that the story is out there, waiting for me." Mamie turns to me, her dark gaze piercing. "I feel it on you, Laia. Near you. Part of you, almost. Think again on all you know. There must be something you've forgotten. Some bit of the story locked away in your mind. When the Augur died—what did he tell Elias again?"

"He said to go *back to the beginning—*"

"What about the book?" Darin comes to sit beside us. "Don't suppose there's anything in there?"

I look at him askance. "What book?"

"The book I gave you." He looks offended. "Back in the Empire. Just before you headed south."

At my blank stare, he shoves my shoulder. "Well, hells, Laia, it's nice to know my sister appreciates my thoughtfulness. When we parted ways, I gave you a gift, remember? I found it in Adisa."

I run for my rucksack in Mamie's wagon and bring back an oilcloth-wrapped package. The string is stiff from the floodwaters when I lost my pack, and I have to cut it open. Wrapped tight within is a worn book bound in soft leather.

Gather in the Dark, it says.

"Why does this look familiar?"

"You were reading it," Darin says. "Before the raid. Before the Mask came—before Nan and Pop—" He stops and clears his throat. "Anyway. You were reading it."

I think of the Augur's prophecy, and despite the fire and my cloak, I am suddenly shivering. *"Go back to the beginning."* I turn to Mamie. "Could this—"

She has already taken the book from me. "Yes," she breathes. "This is what I needed. What I've been waiting for."

I open my hand, hoping she'll return it. She ignores me and stands, her frustration replaced by single-minded determination.

"Shouldn't I read it—" I call after her. But she waves me off, the book tucked under her arm as she seeks a story in a place I cannot follow.

CHAPTER FORTY-NINE

The Soul Catcher

Love. I consider the world without sentiment after I leave Laia and retire to my tent, squeezed between two supply wagons on the far side of the Saif encampment. Without thought, I take out Laia's armlet and begin to carve.

Love cannot live here. Shaeva told me that, when I became Soul Catcher. Yet it was love that began all this in the first place — the love the Nightbringer had for his people is what drove him to murder and madness and retribution.

And it is love that drives him still.

The way he fought for centuries to save the jinn. The way he howled when Khuri died. The way he raged when Laia shot Maro. Bleeding hells, his very name. *Beloved.* Love is at the heart of what the Nightbringer was. It is his greatest weapon.

But I can use it as a weapon too.

«««

The *Zaldars* do not take kindly to being woken up in the middle of the night. Especially when most were planning on leaving at dawn.

So I make them an enormous pot of hot, sweetened tea, as Mamie Rila used to do in the deep winter.

"More honey," Laia whispers after tasting it, surreptitiously raiding Mamie's rapidly shrinking stash.

When the tea has been passed around, and the *Zaldars* — along with

Fakirs and *Kehannis*—are settled around a large fire, I make my case.

"We must fight the Nightbringer, for the survival of the world depends on us defeating him." A low grumble starts up, and I speak over it. "But we cannot go to Adisa. It is a two-month journey, at least, over Martial-infested lands and treacherous seas. And we do not know if the Mariners will still be fighting by then, or if Keris and the jinn will have defeated them."

"Get to the point." The *Zaldar* of Tribe Shezaad speaks so insolently that his *Fakira*, a woman Mamie's age and dressed in black, slaps him on the back of the head. He ducks, gaze as surly as an alley cat's.

"We take a shorter journey, to the Sher Jinnaat, the City of the Jinn, deep within the Waiting Place." I consider my words carefully, for I'll have this one chance to convince them. "Everything the Nightbringer has ever done has been for his people. He will not allow them to be killed. We can draw him and his army away from Marinn and to a place where we have an advantage."

"How do we have an advantage if it's their city?" another *Zaldar* asks. "They will tear through our army with their fire."

"Most of the jinn in the city are still weak." Laia speaks up. "They have not recovered from their imprisonment."

"An army of four thousand Tribespeople and a thousand efrits is no small thing," Afya says. "The Nightbringer will know we are coming."

"Not if Elias and I are hidden," Laia cuts in. "Darin too. We can disguise our fighters and supplies. From a distance, the army will just look like a band of refugees."

"We like this not, Soul Catcher." Rowan Goldgale sweeps forward, his fellow efrit lords following. "We will not stand for a massacre. We have witnessed too many."

"The goal is not to kill the jinn," I say. "It's to draw the Nightbringer away from the Free Lands so that he no longer reaps souls. So the Mariner armies can regroup. The Mariners are our allies. They offered sanctuary to the Scholars when the Tribes could not. It is wrong to abandon them when our foe is the same."

"You say *our*," the Nasur *Kehanni* points out. "But you are a Martial."

"He is the Banu al-Mauth, *Kehanni*." Aubarit's voice is ice, and she is no longer the scared girl I met one winter ago. "The Chosen of Death. Have a care in how you speak to him, lest I leave your soul to wander."

The *Kehanni* bites back whatever retort she had prepared. "The Mariners did not aid us," she points out. "Sadh and Aish and Nur burned, and we heard nothing from them."

An old emotion rises in me. One of the first I felt, when Cain awoke my memories. Anger—at the stubbornness of nearly everyone here, at their cussed refusal to see.

But I catch myself. The *Zaldars* fear they'll lead those they love to a swift death. They are afraid we'll fail. The *Kehanni* of Tribe Nasur fears the same.

"It is a risk," I say. "But this way, we force the Nightbringer to act. To come to us. We prepare for his attack, and when he comes, we hold off the army as long as possible so—"

I look to Laia, standing in the shadows, hand gripped tight around her scythe.

"So that I can kill him," she says.

I say nothing of my plan to speak to the jinn in the Sher Jinnaat, to try to persuade them to serve as Soul Catchers once more. Doing so will only complicate matters.

"What other choice do we have?" Afya speaks out. "We arrive in Marinn in time to be massacred? We wait here, until either this maelstrom destroys us or the Commandant does? Our suffering begins and ends with the Nightbringer. Let us finish him."

"*If* she can finish him," the *Zaldar* of Tribe Shezaad says. "Give the scythe to someone who can wield it. Why not you, Soul Catcher?"

My ire rises, and I find my fists are clenched, but I keep silent, for Laia steps forward, dark eyes reflecting the flames as she regards the *Zaldar*.

"How many times have you faced the Nightbringer and survived, *Zaldar*?"

The man fidgets from foot to foot.

"I have defied him and survived him again and again. He has tried to hurt me. But I will not allow myself to be hurt. He has tried to break me. But I will not allow myself to be broken. And I will not be dictated to by a man so afraid to fight the jinn that he must criticize a woman to make himself feel bigger."

"If we bring the fight to the Sher Jinnaat," I say, "we choose our own destiny, instead of letting the jinn and Keris Veturia choose for us."

"I want vengeance on those *herrisada* for what they did to our cities," Afya says. "To our people. Tribe Nur is with you, Banu al-Mauth." Her fighters are arrayed behind her, and as one, they raise their fists and shout one word.

"*NUR!*"

"You are our Banu al-Mauth." Shan, sitting beside Mamie Rila, looks back at the Saif fighters. "But you are also our brother." He takes Mamie's hand. "Tribe Saif is with you."

This time, Tribe Saif's fighters call out. "*SAIF!*"

"The Martials are with you." Jans Aquillus, leader of the Martial legion, steps forward. Seconds later, Rowan Goldgale joins him.

Tribe Nasur and Tribe Rahim call out their support, then Tribe Ahdieh, Tribe Malikh—even the few fighters of Tribe Zia who survived Sadh's destruction. The leader of Tribe Shezaad declares himself last, prodded by his fighters and his *Fakira*.

I turn finally to Laia. She's the first person I told my plan to. Still, I want to ask.

"I am with you too." She folds her arms and fixes me with her dark stare. "But you have a bad habit of doing everything yourself. Carrying every burden. Fighting every battle alone. Not this time, Soul Catcher. This time, we do it my way."

CHAPTER FIFTY

The Blood Shrike

The palace hallways feel strangely empty without Livia. Before, her ladies-in-waiting were out and about, running errands for her, and she was only ever in her room to sleep.

Now soldiers are everywhere, auxes and legionnaires in their dark fatigues. Masks in their bloody red capes. I pass Quin Veturius near the training yard, Pater Mettias at his side. They salute, breath clouding in the frigid air, but both have a question in their eyes.

Why are we still here, Blood Shrike?

Antium's army is outfitted, armed, and ready to move south. A hundred barges wait along the River Rei to bear my men to Silas. And onward to Serra, Navium, and victory.

The scouts have already sent back their reports: the way is clear. The Paters of the advisory council, Quin and Mettias included, grow impatient with me. We finally have the forces to seize Keris's territory. And though she's left thousands of soldiers to guard her cities, she herself is away, fighting the Nightbringer's war in Marinn.

I should order my troops south. I should take back the Empire for my nephew. But I don't give the command.

Because it's too easy.

Keris's plans are always more layered than they first appear. The Commandant wouldn't just leave the south open to me. She's up to something.

As I walk through the freezing palace, I search for a flash of color amid the drear. Musa can always be counted on to wear at least one loud item of clothing—and I need his information now.

Something flickers near my ear. "Thank the skies," I say. "Tell your master to stop spying on me and to come see me." I turn toward my quarters. "I need his—ow!" I hiss at the sight of a welt blooming on my hand. "Did you *bite* me?"

It bites me again, but this time flickers into view, iridescent wings fluttering. Its body is vaguely human, but green and covered in soft yellow down.

But it is the wight's face that catches my eye before it disappears again. Frantic. Sad.

"What's happening?" I reach for my scim. "Is Musa all right?"

The wight flickers ahead of me, and I hurry after it as it guides me to Musa's quarters. But once there, no one answers at my knock.

"Musa," I call out. "Are you in there?" The wight buzzes around me frantically, and I curse, looking left and right. Of course, the moment I need soldiers, there are none around.

"Scholar!" I shout. "I'm coming in."

I take a few steps back and then kick the door in, scims out, expecting . . . I don't know. The Commandant again. A jinn.

Musa's sitting room is empty, and it's not until I enter the bedroom that I see his crumpled form slumped against the bedframe.

"Musa—" I'm at his side in two steps. His eyes are red, his face wet and haggard. "What the hells happened? Poison? What did you ea—"

Then I see a parchment in his hands. I take it from him gently. The missive is from Eleiba, and it is not long.

> Ayo has fallen. Adisa has fallen. Thousands dead. Princess Nikla
> killed defending King Irmand. Both murdered by Keris Veturia.
> Request immediate aid.

"Oh bleeding hells." I sit down next to him. "Skies, Musa. I'm sorry. I'm so sorry."

The paper falls. He sinks his face into his knees and weeps. I have no idea what to say. His grief is raw and unabashed and so very different from my own. After a moment, I take his hand, because it seems like something Laia might do. He grips it tight as he sobs, and my eyes grow hot as I watch him grapple with the horror of losing the love of his life as well as his king.

"Shrike?" a voice calls from the door. Harper scans the room, scims in hand. "The wights called me."

"It's clear," I say. He sheathes his blades as I hand him the note. Our eyes meet over Musa's head, and I know he is thinking what I am: Keris Veturia needs to bleeding die.

After a moment, Harper kneels down, and I scramble back, thankful that someone else has come. Someone who will know how to deal with Musa's pain. But the Scholar does not release my hand.

"I shouldn't mourn her." He wipes his face, and I almost don't hear him. "She jailed my father. Took my lands. My title. The Scholars suffered under her rule."

"She sounds . . ." *Horrible*, I think. "Complicated." I wince as soon as I say it. But Musa chuckles unexpectedly.

"We got married a decade ago. I was eighteen. She was nineteen. Her brother was crown prince, but he died of an illness and the palace healer— my father—couldn't save him. She—" He shakes his head. "Grief took her. The ghuls found ripe prey with her, and they nibbled at her mind for years. And when I spoke of them to her, she called me insane. King Irmand was so grief-stricken after his son's death that he did not see what was happening to his daughter."

"My father died in prison. My mother soon after. And yet—" He looks between Harper and me. "I still loved her. I shouldn't have, but I did." His hands curl into fists. "Keris slaughtered Nikla's guards. Stabbed her through the—the chest and pinioned her to the walls of her palace. Then—killed her father in front of her. The ghuls finished her off."

Skies above. The details unsettle me because they are so barbarous. So vile.

But also because of the timing. First Livia. Now Nikla. These murders are targeted. Keris knows how essential Musa and his wights are. She is trying to weaken us.

"I have to go to Marinn," Musa says. "Find Keris. Kill her. Nikla's heir is a first cousin. Skies know if he's still alive, but he's young. He'll need help."

I look at Harper helplessly. How do I tell Musa the Commandant is manipulating him when his heart is broken? I wish Laia were here. Or Livia.

But it must be me. And in that moment, it hits me that with Livia gone, and until Zacharias comes of age, it will always be me. For a thousand things I don't wish to do.

Damn you, Keris.

"Musa, this is a great blow," I venture, and as he searches my face, I am thankful for the first time that I do not have my mask. "I have been a victim of Keris's cruelty also. And it is never without intent."

"You want me to stay," he says. "But the Mariners were my people first. They need me. And you owe me a favor, Shrike."

"I know that," I say. "If you still want to go tomorrow, then I will offer you my best horse, and an escort. All I ask is that before you leave, consider all you know of Keris Veturia. She is manipulative. Ruthless. She kills who she must to weaken her foes."

Musa is silent. But at least he's listening.

"She wants you angry. Alone. On your way to the Free Lands instead of working against her. Your people are here, Musa. Thousands of Scholars that Nikla drove out. They look to you too."

"I will wait until tomorrow," Musa says. "But if I wish to leave, you cannot keep me here."

"I won't. I swear it."

We leave him then, and though I wish to put guards outside his door to protect him, I do not want him to think I'm locking him in. His wights, I hope, will keep him safe.

All the way to Avitas's quarters, where we can speak without interruption, I think of Musa's cries. The way he sounded as if his soul had been dug out of his body.

"We cannot let him go," Avitas says as soon as we enter his room. "He is too important. What if we —"

"*Emifal Firdaant*," I interrupt Harper. *May death claim me first.*

"What does that mean?"

I do not answer, instead drawing him toward me with the strap of his scim. I kiss him, trying to put all that I cannot say into that kiss. His hands land on my hips, pulling me closer, and then he is unbuckling my armor.

Now is not the time for this, I know. I should speak to our spies again and try to figure out what Keris is up to. I should find Quin and ask him if he really thinks we should head south.

I should break away. Because every time I touch Harper, I fall deeper into a place I know I will not be able to emerge from, should I lose him.

My soul aches with all that I should do. It weighs on me like a mountain, and I cannot bear it.

So I lead him to his bed, to do what I wish, not what I should. And hope that I will not pay for it.

« « «

Avitas is asleep when I wake. The sky outside his window is littered with stars. I let myself appreciate their beauty. I pretend that I do not have to decide the fate of thousands of people. I am just a normal woman, in bed with my lover. Am I a soldier? No. Something completely different. I am a baker. I am safe. The world is safe. I will rise, put on my clothes, and go bake bread.

And that is why you must rise. To protect all the lovers and bakers, the mothers and fathers, the sons and daughters.

I have a decision to make. This far north, winter's grip is still tight, and if the army is to go, then we must leave today. I feel a cold snap coming, and would not have the river freeze and delay us.

But I still do not know what to do. So I leave my armor and slip out to walk the city, as I always did when I was troubled.

The streets outside the palace are dark and empty, but when I am nearly to the gates, a step sounds behind me. Harper—staying close, for he is my second, and that is his duty. A moment later, wings flutter near my face— Musa's way of reminding me that I have a promise to keep.

Think, Shrike. What does the Commandant want? To rule. Not just over the Empire, but over the Tribes, Marinn, even the Southern Lands. Why then would she leave her Empire vulnerable to me? Why would she want me to sail south?

Because she'd know exactly where I am. She'd be keeping me occupied, so that she could—what? Claim Antium or Delphinium? No—we've already confirmed that there are no armies lurking, waiting to attack.

The sky brightens, the sun still tucked behind thick clouds, and a heavy snow falls. The orchards I pass through are bare, but this is winter's last vicious assault before bowing to spring. Soon, the trees will bud. Within a month, they will bloom, and winter's chill will be a memory.

The bells toll seven. The snow falls thicker. I must return. Hear what Musa has to say. Give the order to move out before the river freezes.

But I keep walking. Because I do not yet have my answer. The orchards are long past and I move now into the open land beyond the capital, some instinct drawing me farther from the city.

"Shrike," Harper says. "We should—

"I'm missing something," I say. "And I'm not going back until I know what it is. I will not let her fool me, Harper. Never again."

Now I move urgently, and an old feeling steals over me—the desire to heal. To help.

"Harper." I unsheathe my blades. "Someone's out here."

Against the unending stretch of white, something moves. No. Many things—and at speed.

"What in the ten burning hells?" Harper says.

"Wraiths," I say. "A half dozen. Chasing down—"

But I cannot make sense of the shimmer they are chasing. I only know that if it's running from the wraiths, then we share a common enemy.

"You have to behead them," I tell Harper, but he's already charged forward, his scim flashing as he slices through one of the wraiths. It screams, and the sound is followed by another.

Then they are upon me, their spectral hands reaching out. One closes its fingers on my throat, and cold lances into me.

"Not today," I snarl at it before wrenching away and slicing off its head. The last two rush me, but they are sloppy—panicked. Their screams still linger in my ears when I turn to the shimmer in the air, which is not a shimmer at all, but a cloud of glittering sand, roughly man-shaped and clearly in distress.

"Peace, Blood Shrike," the efrit whispers, and though I feel as though I *must* heal it, I realize that I cannot sing for it. Sand efrits hate songs.

"I bring a message," it says. "From Laia of Serra. A message Keris did not wish you to hear."

"How do I know I can trust you?"

"Laia said you should ask this question of me: What were Marcus Farrar's last words?"

Laia is the only person with whom I shared that detail, one night a few months ago, when neither of us could sleep.

"Very well," I say. "What were Marcus Farrar's last words?"

"'Please, Shrike.' Satisfied?" At my nod, the efrit goes on. "The Nightbringer sought to draw the Soul Catcher's army to Marinn. Instead, the Soul Catcher moves his forces toward the City of the Jinn, in the Waiting Place. There, they hope to lure the Nightbringer and finish him for good. But—but—" The efrit's breathing grows labored. It has seconds, if that. "They cannot do it alone."

"I can't possibly march an army—"

"Laia of Serra said something else." The efrit's sand grows dull, its light fading. *"Strive even unto your own end, else all is lost—"*

The efrit's words trail off. Between one breath and the next, he is gone, his sand form disappearing in the wind.

Thank the skies Harper tends toward silence, because it gives me a moment to piece it all together. The Commandant left the south open because she wanted me to attack. Because if I'm focused on Silas, I cannot help the one person who can destroy her master.

"Shrike," Harper finally says. "We need to leave. It's getting colder. The river will freeze, and we won't be able to sail south."

"Let it freeze," I tell him. "Today, we do not sail. Today, we march."

PART FOUR
THE SHER JINNAAT

CHAPTER FIFTY-ONE

The Nightbringer

§ઠ

For years, I raged. Villages burned. Caravans disappeared. Families murdered. But in the end, there were too many humans. I annihilated thousands, yet when I turned, I would find hundreds more.

Vengeance would take years. Centuries. And I could not do it alone. I needed to prey on humanity's worst traits. Tribalism. Prejudice. Greed. And while I pitted them against each other, I needed to reconstitute the Star, a far more difficult task. For it had shattered, its pieces scattered to the winds. Each piece had to be hunted down. Each returned to me in love.

The first human I ever loved was a Scholar. Husani of Nava— what would later become Navium. She wore the shard of the Star as a necklace, fashioned by her late husband. Her child died of a fever when she had only just learned to speak. So I came to her as an orphan, red-haired and brown-eyed, grappling with my own pain. She called me her son and named me Roshan.

Light.

My presence filled a hole within her. She loved me instantly.

It took me longer to love her. Though I lived in the body of a human child, my mind was my own, and I could not forget what her kind had done to mine. But she soothed my nightmares and tended my wounds. She attacked my face with kisses, and hugged me so much that I began to crave the comfort of her arms.

Soon after coming to her, I learned to respect her. And in time, I loved her.

She gave me the necklace after I told her I was leaving home to seek my fortune. All my love goes with you, beloved son. *Those were her words when she set the necklace around my neck, tears in her eyes.*

In that moment, I wanted to transform. To scream at her that I was beloved, once, but that all who loved me were gone. That her kind had not just stolen my people, but my name.

The only parent I had ever had was Mauth, and his love for me was rooted in the duty he laid upon my shoulders. Husani offered me the love of a mother: fierce where Mauth was sober, pure where Mauth was calculated.

And how did I, the one she loved the best, repay her? How did I thank the human who gave me everything, who taught me more of love in a few short years than I had learned in all my millennia?

I abandoned her. After taking her necklace, I left. I did not return.

When she died a few years later, she died nirbara—forsaken. She left this earth with her adopted son's name on her lips, not knowing where he had gone, or whether he lived, or what she had done to deserve his silence.

I mourned her then. I mourn her still.

Like the Tribes, the Mariners have their own rites for the dead. Like the Tribes, they begin to understand that against me, those rites mean nothing.

The palace of the Mariner royal family is rubble around me—as is much of Adisa. The city that gave haven to my enemies has been laid low by Keris Veturia. Thousands of souls flow from her killing fields and into my hands.

Maro still recovers from the wound Laia dealt him. But I catch nearly as many spirits as him. The souls of men are fickle and thin. They come to me easily. Almost willingly.

"The city is ours." Keris walks gingerly through the ruins of the palace, her gaze snagging on the shattered glass dome that used to sit above Irmand's driftwood throne. There is a proprietary air about her. This is her city. Her palace. An extension of her Empire. Just as I promised.

She is splattered with the blood of Marinn's brave soldiers, none of them a match for her savagery. "Before I killed her, Nikla raised the white flag—"

I give her a withering look, and she bows her head, barely cowed. "My lord," she adds.

"Adisa is a fallen city," I tell her. "But the Mariners are not a broken people. Many in the city fled. How many dead?"

"More than twelve thousand, my lord."

More, the Sea whispers in my mind. *More.*

I shift my gaze to my lieutenant. "What troubles you, Keris?"

"I should have killed the child." She shifts from foot to foot, her boots crunching the multicolored glass of the dome. "Zacharias."

"You had your opportunity. Why did you not strike?"

"I needed him," she says. "To lure the Blood Shrike. But as I was holding him, I was reminded of Ilyaas."

"There is no weakness in having remembered your child," I tell her. "The weakness lies in denying it. What did you feel?"

Keris is silent for a long time, and though she is a grown woman, she looks, for a moment, like the child she was long ago. I suppose to me, they are all children.

She grasps at the hilt of her bloody scim.

"It does not matter—"

But I do not let her turn away, for the weakness must out, so that it does not fester within her.

"When you see your son again, will you be able to do what must be done?"

"I did see him again," she says. "In Aish. He was—different. But the same. A Veturius." She offers the name unemotionally. For a long time, we do not speak.

"I do not know," she finally says, "if I will be able to do what must be done."

It is one of the talents of humans to surprise, even after millennia of knowing their kind. She meets my flame eyes, for of all creatures who walk this earth, only Keris Veturia has never flinched from my gaze. Her darkest moments are long behind her.

"There are some things that do not die. No matter how many blades we put into them," she says.

"Indeed, Keris." I know it better than any.

We stare out at the burning city. A white flag hangs limp in the still air. The Sea stirs, hungry. *More.*

Thousands are dead. So much suffering.

But not enough.

CHAPTER FIFTY-TWO

Laia

We trek out of the Tribal desert and into the grasslands of the southern Empire. It is sparsely populated, so it is easy enough to stay far from villages and garrisons. About three weeks after we set out, the mottled horizon thickens into a mass of tangled green branches.

"The Waiting Place. Not long to go, Laia." Darin speaks from beside me. I have cloaked him so it appears his horse is riderless—something the horse protested with vigorous head-tossing and angry whinnies. Elias, riding ahead of us, is also invisible, though I can hear the steady hum of conversation between him and Jans Aquillus.

All around, weapons and armor are stowed away. A great many of the fighters travel inside wagons, while their mounts bear supplies instead of riders. The sand efrits settle the dust of the caravan so it's unnoticeable from afar, and the wind efrits lure clouds over us to mask us further. A jinn would have to get close to tell that this is an army, and according to the efrits none have.

"Once we're in," Darin says, "the Soul Catcher said there won't be a need for the invisibility."

"Because we won't be able to hide from him," I say. Rehmat wished to strengthen my magic by joining with me. But exhausted as I am from hiding so many of us for so long, I cannot bear having her inside my mind again. It feels too invasive.

"Don't worry about hiding from him," Darin says. "We've gotten this far, haven't we? No sign of those fiery bastards."

All I can offer is a weak smile. Fear flares in my bones. It is an old enemy, my companion since childhood. Fear of what is to come. Fear of what awaits among those trees. Fear that all the Tribes and the Scholars have suffered was only a precursor to something worse.

"I am with you Laia." Rehmat has given me space, sensing my distrust. Her sunlight figure floats alongside me, steady despite the wind. "When he comes, I will not leave your side."

I nod, but I do not trust her yet. For I must kill the Nightbringer, and once, she loved the Nightbringer.

Love. Always, I return to that word. Darin went to prison because of love. Elias gave up his future because of love. The Nightbringer seeks vengeance because of love.

But, I shake myself out of my doldrums, love is why I still live. Why, when I look at Elias, I do not see the Mask or the Soul Catcher, no matter how he wishes me to. Love is why the Blood Shrike agreed to march her army hundreds of miles to support us, instead of stealing the Commandant's Empire out from under her.

Though love will not help me if I do not have the Nightbringer's story. With the Waiting Place only a day away, we are out of time. I pull my horse aside to wait for Mamie Rila's wagon. Shan drives it, and she sits beside him, eyes closed, muttering.

"Not yet, child," she says when I draw up beside her, somehow sensing my presence.

"We do not have much time."

When she opens her eyes, the whites are reddened, as if she has not slept in days. A depthless well of night beckons from her gaze, and I am dizzy suddenly, grasping the pommel of my mount so I do not fall. It is not until she looks away that I return to myself.

"Not yet."

"It must be soon," I tell her. "The moment we enter that forest, he will know. And he will come for us."

Mamie observes the trees ahead, as if she has just noticed them.

"Come to me in the darkest hour of night," she says. "When the stars sleep. Come and hear the Tale." She emphasizes the last word as if it a singular entity, and closes her eyes again. "Though I do not know what good it will do you."

«««

Rehmat wakes me from a deep sleep just after midnight. A fat half-moon tints the dead grass blue, and lights my way to Mamie's wagon. Despite the fact that I can see the path clearly, my steps are heavy. I have begged Mamie for the story. But now that it is time to hear it, I do not know if I wish to.

On my way, I see Elias on watch, walking the perimeter of the camp. His whole body shifts as I approach, but not with that tension he had when I walked through the Waiting Place with him. This is different. He is not a wounded thing, avoiding my touch. Instead his tautness is that of an oud string, aching to be played.

"The Blood Shrike will be here by dawn." He keeps his attention fixed on the rolling hills of the Empire. "It won't take more than four days to get to the jinn grove."

The woods appear gnarled and impassable, but Elias senses my skepticism. "The forest will open for us," he says. "And the jinn grove will hold us."

I shudder when I think of that place. Rehmat hates it the way I hated Kauf, for it is where her kin suffered. But I hate it because of what I learned there. What I saw and what I heard: my mother killing my father and sister to spare them torment at Keris's hands. Mother's song, and the sound of her crime. The soft crack of lives sundered, of her heart destroyed.

I still hear that sound in my nightmares. Often enough that I never forget. Often enough that it lurks at the back of my mind.

"Come back," Elias says, and I emerge from my recollections and look down in surprise, for his hand is twined with mine.

"I'm with you, Laia," he says. He spoke those words to me as we fled Blackcliff, what feels like eons ago.

"Are you?" I whisper, for though I wanted this, I am scared to trust it. Scared he will pull away again.

He tucks a curl back from my face. A simple gesture that sets me aflame. "I'm trying."

The space between us is too great, so I step nearer. "Why?"

"Because—" His voice is low and we are close to—something. Skies know what, but I just want to get there. "Because you are—you are my—"

His head jerks up then, and he steps back, a rueful half smile on his face. "Ah—someone is waiting for you."

I glance around and spot Mamie vanishing behind a nearby wagon. Internally, I curse.

"One day," I tell Elias, "we won't be interrupted. And I expect you to finish that sentence."

When I reach Mamie's wagon, I put thoughts of Elias aside. For it is not familiar, loving Mamie Rila waiting for me, but the *Kehanni* of Tribe Saif. She wears eggplant-purple robes with bell sleeves and a severe neck. They are hand-embroidered in a dozen shades of green and silver, and edged in tiny mirrors. Her thick hair is unbound and curls magnificently about her shoulders, a midnight halo.

Without a word, she gestures for me to follow her. I look back at the camp, worried it will be visible from above, but the wind efrits have enticed a thick fog to hide it.

"Go," Rehmat whispers. "They are safe."

Mamie Rila and I make our way past the sentries and up a hill shrouded in mist. When we reach the top she bids me sit on the damp grass, and settles herself across from me. I cannot see the camp from here. I cannot see anything but Mamie.

"The Tale lives in me now, Laia of Serra," she says. "It is unlike any that I have told. I am changed. But do not fear. For I will return."

Her eyes fade to white, and she grasps my hands. Her voice deepens, transforming from a gentle lilt to a growl from the very heart of the earth.

"I awoke in the glow of a young world," she says, and I am gripped. "When man knew of hunting but not tilling, of stone but not steel. It smelled of rain and earth and life. It smelled of hope.

"Arise, beloved."

For the next few hours, I do not sit with Mamie, but with the Nightbringer. I am not in the Empire, but deep in the Waiting Place, and then in lands far beyond. I am not enthralled by the story of a creature I'm only just beginning to understand. I *am* him.

I learn of his creation, his education, his loneliness. His relationship to humans and his marrow-deep love of his people. I discover Rehmat as she was in life, a fierce wandering poet. When Cain is mentioned—when Mamie speaks of what he and the Scholars did—I burn with hatred. And when I hear of the Nightbringer's vengeance, of his love for Husani, my heart breaks.

"—I mourned her then. I mourn her still."

As suddenly as it begun, the Tale is over. Mamie's eyes darken to their familiar brown, and when she speaks, it is with her own voice.

"It is done," she says.

"No." I stop her from rising. "It cannot be done. There must be something else. Something about—about the scythe, or when he is at his weakest. Something more about him."

Mamie bows her head. "That is all the darkness gave me, my love," she says. "It will have to be enough."

But it is not. I already know that it is not.

CHAPTER FIFTY-THREE

The Soul Catcher

The Blood Shrike and her army approach from the north, on the plains that sweep out from the Waiting Place. When the rumble of hooves is deafening and the smell of horse and men overwhelming, the Shrike lifts her fist and slows her forces to a halt.

Wind howls along the plains, and the two armies stare each other down. Scholars stand with the Blood Shrike's troops, true. But there are far more Martials, and the Tribes have seen their people destroyed by the Martials.

The Shrike swings off her horse and approaches. My magic, scant as it is, rises, and I sense what is in her. Love. Joy. Sadness. And as she looks at Mamie, a deep well of self-hate.

Mauth's warning rings through my mind. *Your duty is not to the living. Your duty is not to yourself. Your duty is to the dead, even to the breaking of the world.*

But when I look at the Blood Shrike's bare, scarred face, the past overwhelms me. She is not just the Shrike. She is Helene Aquilla. Friend. Warrior. Comrade-in-arms. We did violence together. We survived together. We saved each other from death and madness and loneliness in those long years at Blackcliff.

Not seeing her made it easy to ignore the memories Cain gave me. Now that she stands before me, those recollections hit like one of her scim attacks—swift and painful.

"Hail, Shrike."

"Hail, Banu al-Mauth." We regard each other, wary as two eagles meeting over a dead antelope.

Then she quirks an eyebrow at me. "Didn't want to start without me?" she asks.

"Didn't want to listen to you whining about it, more like."

A collective exhale from both sides, and then everyone is dismounting and greeting each other. Laia steps past me and pulls the Shrike into a hug.

"Where's my favorite tyrant?" Laia asks, but gently, for the wights brought news of Livia's death. A shadow passes over the Shrike's face.

"Zacharias is at a safe house," she says, "with Tas and Uncle Dex and a full complement of Masks. Thought it was wiser than bringing him here." Pink shadows nest beneath her eyes. "Another war. Will it ever end, Soul Catcher? Or will this be the legacy I leave my nephew?"

I have no answer for her, and she turns to greet Darin. Laia seeks out Musa, putting her hand against the tall Scholar's face, speaking quietly with that sweet smile of hers. Though I had nothing against the man a moment ago, I suddenly find his face vexing. Laia spots me and grins.

"By the skies, Soul Catcher," she says as Musa moves away. "Is that jealousy?"

"Do you want it to be?" *Stop it*, I tell myself. *You idiot*. But the old me, who appears to be cheekier by the day, shoves that voice into a bin.

"Still flirting at inappropriate times, I see." Strong hands pull me around. My grandfather, Quin Veturius, regards the rows of Tribespeople behind me. If haughtiness could wither, both armies would collapse into dust. "At least you're leading an army. Good at it too, I'd wager. Runs in the blood."

As I meet his gray eyes, a mirror of my own, I consider walking away. We're about to fight a battle, and even if we win, I'll have to return to the ghosts and forget all of these faces once more. Even if I can persuade the jinn to return as Soul Catchers, Mauth made it clear that doing so would not mean my freedom.

But Grandfather pulls me into a bear hug, nearly breaking my ribs.

"I missed you, my boy," he says, and my arms rise, for there is comfort in hugging one of the few people I know who is bigger than me. Stronger than me.

"I missed you too, Grandfather."

"Right." The Blood Shrike steps away from Mamie. Her face is stricken from whatever Mamie said to her, but she pulls herself together. "How do you plan to get nearly ten thousand troops, and their horses, wagons, and supplies, through that?" She nods to the gnarled forest.

"Getting through it isn't the problem," I say. "It's what happens once we're inside." I look past her toward her massive supply train. "Did you bring the salt?"

"Wasn't bleeding easy," she says. "But we have a dozen carts' worth."

"Set extra sentries around it," I tell her. "We'll need every last bit."

We reach the Waiting Place an hour later. Wary conversation dwindles to silence as we close in on the wall of trees. Low brush chokes the space between the trunks. I urge my skittish mount forward and bid the trees to open a path. The forest is reluctant, so I push harder. *Mauth. This army is essential to my cause.*

A shimmer in the wood and then, ever so slowly, it shifts. Where there was naught but a deer trail, there is now an earthen road, wide enough for ten wagons. When I attune myself to the map of the Waiting Place, all is as it usually is, just compressed, as if to make room for us.

For most of the day, we pass through the forest swiftly. I do not need to warn the army to be silent. The trees loom oppressively over the road, vines shifting and twisting just out of sight, as if considering whether they should make a meal of a passing human.

The place has never felt emptier. I fear for Karinna for a time, worried the Nightbringer has taken her too, until I spot her flitting near a stream. She flees when she sees the approaching army. Laia, riding beside me, sees her too.

"Who was that?"

"No one," I say quickly. But the Blood Shrike, on my other side, snorts in disbelief.

"It's the ghost of my grandmother," I relent. "Quin's wife. He doesn't know she's here, and it needs to stay that way. Knowing would only cause him pain. Stay away from her, in any case. She's very shy and she's been through enough."

The Shrike seems taken aback by my vehemence and draws Laia into conversation as Avitas Harper comes up on my right.

"Banu al-Mauth," he says. "The supply train sergeant has requested that we slow down. Says the horses need a rest."

I nod and give the order, and as the Mask snaps his reins to move past me, I think of all the questions I quelled when I first met him months ago. The questions Mauth washed from my mind. I call out.

"Do you—" I probably should have thought this through. "I don't know anything about our father. And I thought if you did—of course, if you don't wish to—"

"He looked like you," Avitas says. "I was only four when he died. But I remember his face. Had green eyes, though. Like me. Skin much darker than the both of us. Closer to Musa's. He had big hands and a laugh that carried through a village. He was good." Avitas cocks his head and looks me dead in the eye. "Like you."

Avitas's words fill a part of me I didn't know was empty. For years, I did not care to reflect upon my father. Quite suddenly, I want to know everything.

"Do you know why he came to Blackcliff to teach? Usually Centurions are older."

"According to my mother, it was that or be discharged. He was bad at following orders apparently."

I smile at that, and the conversation comes easy, after. We talk until evening approaches and the Shrike rides up to us.

"Are we going to stop and camp?" she asks. "Or do you two plan on gossiping all night?"

Later, as everyone beds down on the road, I reflect on the day. On how it felt to see the Shrike and Grandfather, and to talk to my brother. On how it felt to learn about my father.

I have deadened my emotions for so long that it is jarring to feel so much in so short a time. *Emotion will not serve you well*, Mauth said. But there are no ghosts to pass now. And I am tired—so tired of telling myself not to feel.

So the next day, instead of holding myself aloof or immersing myself in battle preparations, I find Shan. We laugh over the tricks he pulled to avoid getting married. Later I wheedle a story out of Mamie and talk with Grandfather. I seek out the Shrike, and we speak of Faris and Livia, of the Empire, the jinn, and the coming battle. For the first time in ages, the angry voice within is at peace.

And then there's Laia. There are fewer words between us, yet our conversation never ends. She touches my arms or shoulders as she passes, and smiles when she watches me with my family. If she catches me gazing at her, she stares back, a promise and a question in her dark eyes. At night, she wanders through my dreams, and I wake from them aching with need.

Years ago, when I was a Fiver at Blackcliff, I was sent into the Nevennes on a spying mission. It was deep winter, and one morning, I woke to find the fire I'd kindled the night before had gone out. I had no more flint, so I hunched over a lone ember. The deep red glow at its core promised warmth, if I was willing to give it time and air. If I was patient enough to wait until it was ready to burn.

Laia is far more patient with me than I was with that ember. But I struggle to open up to her. Because if we survive all of what is to come, I will return to the Waiting Place. I will forget her.

Or perhaps I won't. Perhaps the memory of her will haunt me worse than any ghost, even as she returns to the world of the living and builds a life on her own, or with someone else. The thought brings me perilously close to despair.

All I can do is quell it. For three days, as we march through the forest, I focus instead on memorizing the music of her laugh, the poetry of her body. I savor every touch and every look.

Until, on the third night, I'm compelled to seek her out. I must at least try, for a few moments, to set the Soul Catcher aside and let Elias Veturius speak.

When the moon is high, I slip out of my tent and make my way toward Tribe Saif, where Laia usually sleeps. The fires burn low, and other than Mamie Rila, the Tribe is at rest. The *Kehanni* spots me. She smiles faintly, then nods at her wagon.

A lantern glows within and Laia's silhouette moves past a window. My heart thuds faster. What will I say to her? *I miss you. I'm sorry. I wish—*

I do not complete the thought. For suddenly, the hair on the back of my neck rises.

Almost before I register the feeling, I've drawn my scims and turned to the forest, where something moves sinuously amid the trees. *Ghosts?* No—a fog, low and noisome, creeping slowly toward the army.

Above, the wind efrits shriek out a warning, their sudden cries sending a tremor through the slumbering camp.

"*Jinn!*" they scream. "*The jinn have come!*"

Instantly, I am shouting orders as Mamie rouses the Tribes, and the Blood Shrike calls for extra guards to protect our precious salt supply. The sentries already have salted arrows nocked, and the army forms up along the perimeter of the camp quickly, weapons at the ready.

But the jinn do not approach with fire. Nor do they descend from the sky. Their weapon of choice appears to be the fog. Exclamations of fear echo through the ranks as the soldiers attempt to bat away the mist. It curls around them, concealing something vicious and cunning.

Laia emerges from the wagon, scythe in hand. "Elias?" she says. "What's happening?"

"Wraiths," I say to her, before calling out the warning. "Wraiths! Draw scims. Take off their heads!"

"Finally, something to kill." Grandfather strides out from the center of the encampment. "I was getting bored. Elias, my boy—"

But I don't hear the rest. The mist closes in, muffling sound, blurring vision. My heart clenches. Mamie Rila is near, and Shan. The Shrike and Avitas. Afya, Gibran, and so many others. All these people I care for, death lapping at their heels.

Maybe I should rage at myself for allowing emotion to rule me. But there's no point. I do not regret the time I spent with my family, my friends.

The wraiths attack, and shouts ring out, warped by the mist. I raise my blades. The map in my head tells me where the wraiths are, and I let the battle rage take me, tearing through them. A tornado of sound shrieks around me as I take off their heads, making sure that none gets close to Laia or Grandfather, the Shrike or Avitas, Mamie or Shan.

Then the fog roils and shifts, taking on a flickering orange hue. Fire streaks overhead. I back away from the mist, until I can see and hear more clearly.

"Protect the supply wagons!" I shout, for if we don't have food, it doesn't matter if we reach the jinn grove by tomorrow. We'll starve there.

The Blood Shrike appears beside me. "Soul Catcher. We can't see the bleeding enemy. How are we supposed to—"

"We can stop them." I sense a group of jinn moving just beyond the line of wraiths. "Come."

She follows me into the mist-choked trees south of the encampment, her scims singing through the air when wraiths approach. She sends their heads flying with little enough effort, and I glance back at her, remembering how we fought during the Second Trial.

"You've improved."

"You've lost your touch." Her smile is a welcome flash of mirth in the murk. "Give me a moment. If the jinn are nearby, I should salt the blades."

Of course. She wants to kill the jinn, or at least hurt them. I'd planned to scare them off—and get them to take their wraiths with them. I cannot allow the Shrike to harm the jinn. Not when I promised Mauth I'd find a way to restore them as Soul Catchers.

"Wait here," I say. "I'm just going to—"

"No chance." She puts away her salt. "I didn't march an army all the way out here only to be the idiot who stands by as its commander is killed." She goes still. "Listen."

It takes a few moments to separate out the distant shouts and scim-clashes of battle from the heavy silence around us. The Blood Shrike meets my gaze.

Then she leaps to the left, barely in time to avoid a group of fire-formed jinn streaking out of the mist. The Shrike roars, her scims lashing the air, and one flaming figure goes down, only for another to take its place. But she is more skilled than the jinn with her blades—and her weapons are coated with salt. That alone cannot kill them—but it will wound them.

She darts behind a tree as one of the jinn attacks her with a wave of heat, then steps out and whips her scim at the creature's neck. As it skitters away, I shove into the Shrike, knocking her back.

"What are you doing, Soul Catcher?" She wheels, baffled, but before I can explain, a jinn I recognize—Talis—strikes out with a spear and knocks the Shrike down. Her head hits the ground hard, and she goes still.

Talis tackles me, but I shove him off. "Wait," I say. "Please, wait. I'm not here to harm you."

The jinn rolls to his feet, his spear at my throat. "Do you know what happened the last time an army of men came to the forest?" he asks.

"I just want to talk." I stand, raising my hands and thinking quickly. "You were right. Suffering isn't meant to be controlled. And the—the Meherya cannot control what he seeks to release. Mauth himself told me. Once free, the Sea of Suffering will destroy all life. Even you. He will break the world—"

Another jinn steps forward, still in her fire form. "Perhaps the world needs to be broken."

"There are millions of people who have nothing to do with this," I say. "Who live thousands of miles away and have no idea what is coming—"

"And yet you are here with your army, your steel, your salt, repeating history." Talis's rage is potent, fueled by a sense of betrayal. He trusted me. And I repaid that trust by bringing an army to his home.

"Only to draw the Meherya away from Marinn." I speak quickly, for the Blood Shrike stirs. "Talis—please persuade him to lay down arms. To stop this endless killing."

"What would you have me do?" Talis steps so close that though he wears his human form, my skin burns. "Turn against my own?"

"Come back to Mauth," I say. "Take up your duties as—as Soul Catchers—" Even as I say it, it sounds so deeply unjust. Why should the jinn pass on human ghosts, if it was humans who imprisoned them?

"We cannot come back." Talis's gaze is bleak. "There is no return from what was done to us. From what we have done in retaliation. We are tainted now."

He speaks with such finality that hopelessness envelops me. I know what it is to do terrible things. To never forgive yourself for them. Mauth wants me to restore the balance, but how can I? Too much violence lives between humans and jinn.

"Talis!" Another jinn appears from the trees. "We must retreat—there are too many—"

Talis gives me a last, considering look and then whirls away, the other jinn following. The mist disappears with them. Cries and shouts resound from behind us, where the bulk of the army still fights the remaining wraiths.

Something cold pokes at my throat. I turn to find the Blood Shrike back on her feet, scim in hand and digging into my skin.

"Why in the bleeding hells," she hisses, "did you just let the enemy walk away?"

CHAPTER FIFTY-FOUR

The Blood Shrike

The Soul Catcher puts a hand to my blade, but I growl at him, and he raises his arms.

"You're in league with them," I say. He was talking to the bleeding jinn. Pleading with them. He let them go free. "You don't even want to fight them."

"What good is war, Blood Shrike?" The sadness etched into his face feels ancient, the sorrow of a Soul Catcher instead of the friend I've known since childhood. "How many have died because of a king's greed or a commander's pride? How much pain exists in the world because we cannot get past what has been done to us, because we insist on inflicting pain right back?"

"This war isn't out of greed or pride. It's because a mad jinn is attempting to destroy the world, and we need to save it. Skies, Soul Catcher, do you even remember his crimes? Laia's family. Navium. Antium. My sister—"

"What did we do to the jinn first?"

"That was the bleeding Scholars!" I poke him in the chest, then wince, because it's like poking a stone. "The Martials—"

"Have oppressed Scholars for half a millennium," the Soul Catcher says. "Crushed them, enslaved them, and murdered them en masse—"

"That was Marcus and the Commandant—"

"You're right," he says. "You were too busy trying to catch me. A great threat to the Empire, no? A man alone, running for his life, trying to help a friend."

I open my mouth. Then close it.

"There's always a reason that something isn't our fault." He pushes my blade away now, and I do not stop him. "I understand why you don't want

403

to accept responsibility for the Martials' crimes. Neither do I. It hurts too much. Skies, the things I've done." He looks down at his hands. "I do not think I will ever make my peace with it. But I can be better."

"How?" I ask. "I talked to Mamie, you know. I—" I did not wish to. I was ashamed. But I made myself go to her. Made myself ask for forgiveness for imprisoning her and her Tribe when I was hunting Elias. And I made myself walk away when she refused to grant it. "How does one move past such huge sins?"

In a strange way, I realize I am asking him a question I've been asking myself since that moment in the tunnel that I found myself staring at a dead child.

"Skies if I know," he says. "I'm as lost as you, Shrike. The Empire trained us. It made us what we are. But at some point, you accepted it. Not everyone does. Do you—do you remember Tavi?"

I jerk my head up. It is an old memory and one that I don't like. A memory of a friend lost when we were Fivers. Tavi sacrificed himself for Elias and me—and for a group of Scholars who would have died if not for his courage.

"Tavi was the first person I knew to reject the idea that we had to be what the Empire wanted us to be," the Soul Catcher says. "I didn't understand it fully until the Fourth Trial. Sometimes, it is better to die than to live as a monster."

He takes my hand and I start. I expected his skin to be cold, but he rubs warmth into my fingers.

"We have to fight," he says. "We have to give Laia a chance to kill the Nightbringer. But we don't have to be monsters. We don't have to make the mistakes of those who have gone before. I showed the jinn mercy. Perhaps they, too, might show mercy. Perhaps when they see what the Nightbringer intends, they will remember this moment."

I think about his words all the way back to camp. The wraiths have withdrawn, and though the troops are in some disarray, order is restored swiftly.

"At least two hundred dead from the Martial forces." Harper finds me as I return. "Another three hundred from the Tribes. Afya's cut up, and Laia too."

Bleeding hells. Five hundred dead out of ten thousand is not a small number. Not when we'll be facing an army three times our size.

We bury the dead quickly. Laia triages the injured, and after a few hours, we're on our way again. The Soul Catcher sets a punishing pace, but I glare at my soldiers, daring them to complain. They don't. No one wants to be caught on the road again.

"We'll reach the jinn grove by midday," the Soul Catcher says to me and Quin as we lead the column through the darkness before dawn. "The jinn hate it there. They will not approach. At least, not right away"

"Banu al-Mauth." A wind efrit appears, and I strain to catch her words. "The Nightbringer's army is just east of us, across the river. They will reach the grove by dawn tomorrow."

"Not possible," Quin growls. "They could not move so quickly."

"They can with his magic," the Soul Catcher says. "It's how they got to Marinn after leaving the Tribal lands. We'll only have a day to prepare. How quick can the sappers get the trebuchets up, Shrike?"

"A few hours, according to the Ankanese," I say. "Though"—I raise my eyebrows at him—"I'm surprised you want to use them."

"We'll use the war machines to deter." His words are iron. "Not to kill."

I bite my lip, trying to mask my frustration. Deterring the jinn won't be enough. And if that's the mentality we take into battle, we will lose.

"He's no fool, Shrike." Harper, riding on the other side of me, glances at his half brother. "Trust him."

"It's the Commandant I don't bleeding trust," I say. "That hag will find a way to use this against us. We need something on her. I was thinking"—I turn back to the Soul Catcher—"about how you said we don't have to repeat the mistakes of those who have gone before."

He glances at me askance. "And?"

"And the Martials who follow Keris do not do so because they love their empress." My mouth twists around the word. "They follow her because they fear her. And because she wins."

"You want to assassinate her."

"She'll see it coming," I say. "Cook knew the Commandant better than anyone. She told Laia to learn Keris's story. Said if we learned her story, we'd also learn how to stop her. She even told Laia to ask Musa about it— but he didn't know much. No one knows Keris's full story. No one living, anyway."

The Soul Catcher catches my meaning and pulls in his horse, waiting for Quin to move out of earshot. "I'm not summoning Karinna for you to interrogate," he says. "My duty is to pass the ghosts on. Not torment them."

"I just want to talk to her," I say. "And if she doesn't talk to me, fine."

The Soul Catcher shifts atop his mount, agitated. "I will not call her for you," he says. "But—" He glances out at the trees, their tops visible now as dawn approaches. "She is curious about you. I've seen her watching you. I think you remind her of her daughter."

I recoil at the thought of reminding anyone of Keris bleeding Veturia, but the Soul Catcher goes on.

"Her curiosity might be a boon, Shrike. Karinna has not looked at a single other living being here. Not even her own husband, who, presumably, she loved. You'll need to be gentle. Patient. No quick movement. Let her talk. But offer her something to talk about. Find running water. She likes it. And wait until night. Ghosts prefer the dark. Last—"

He turns his gray eyes on me, and they are icy and stern, the glare of a Soul Catcher offering a warning. "She calls Keris *lovey*. Remembers her as a child. Knowing what Keris has become would distress her."

For hours, I ponder what to say to the ghost. By the time I have figured it out, the sun is high and the troops grumble in exhaustion. The road curves upward through a thick patch of trees before flattening out into a broad, scarred plain.

"The jinn grove," the Soul Catcher informs us.

It stretches for acres, flat as the Great Wastes, with only the occasional burned-out tree breaking the empty sweep. In the center, a great dead yew reaches its charred limbs to the sky, a chain hanging from the lowest branch.

"It feels haunted." Laia shivers as we urge our reluctant horses out onto the field.

"It is haunted," the Soul Catcher says. "But it's big enough for the army. And"—he nods to a valley visible beyond the rim of the grove—"there lies Sher Jinnaat. The City of the Jinn. This is the best, most defensible place from which we can launch an attack."

I dismount and walk toward the rim. It slopes sharply down a dozen feet.

"We can position our pikemen here." The Soul Catcher comes up beside me, and we look over the valley. It is massive, hemmed in by the river to the east and south, and forest to the west. "Then archers and catapults."

"It's unlike Keris to attack from below," I say. Despite the sun shining above me, the valley is cloaked in thick mist, similar to what seeped into our camp last night. "It's unlike her to give us any advantage. Even if her forces outnumber ours."

"She has jinn," the Soul Catcher says. "They will bring fire to take out the pikemen and the trebuchets. It will be an ugly battle, Shrike. All we're doing is buying time for Laia."

"In all our years at Blackcliff," I say, "I never imagined this was how you and I would draw swords. Fending off our old teacher while a Scholar hunted a jinn."

"There is no one I'd rather have at my back, Blood Shrike," he says, and there is a fierceness to his voice that makes my heart ache, that reminds me of all we have survived. "No one."

Tents are erected, horses picketed, fires lit, and latrines dug. When it's clear that everything is well in hand, I disentangle myself from the war preparations and make my way into the trees.

I head north, away from the Sher Jinnaat and the jinn grove. Spring has come to the wood, and the green of unending pines is broken by the pink-wreathed branches of the occasional Tala tree. An hour from the encampment, I reach a small stream. I sit. And then I sing.

It is a quiet song, for I do not want to draw the attention of creatures that will harm me. The song is one of healing. Of mothers and daughters. Of my own mother and her quiet love, which bathed me like the rays of the sun for as long as she lived.

A shiver of air against my neck. I am no longer alone.

Ever so slowly, I turn, and catch my breath. There she is, a wisp of a thing, just like the Soul Catcher said. She watches me and I do not speak.

"My lovey is close," she whispers. "But I cannot reach her. Do you know how I can reach her?"

Elias's warning echoes in my mind. "I do know your lovey," I say. "But—she's a bit—a bit different."

"There is only one lovey." Karinna sounds angry. "My lovey. My little one."

"Tell me of her," I say. "Tell me about your lovey."

Karinna turns away from me, as if to leave, and I think of what the Soul Catcher said. To be patient. To offer her something to talk about.

"I just want to help you get to her," I say. "My—my mother is gone." My heart clenches in sorrow, an emotion that has chased me for far too long. An emotion I hate letting myself feel. "My sisters too," I say. "My father. I know loss. I know pain."

"Yes." Karinna turns back, tilting her spectral head. "I feel it in you like I feel it in the other."

"The other?" I reach for my scim, and the movement startles Karinna. She rears back, and I lift my hands, keeping my voice low. "What—what other? Who else have you been talking to?"

"A spirit." Karinna flutters past me, and I think I feel her hands along my hair. "Haunted like you."

She shifts behind me now, and I'm afraid to move, worried that when I look, she will be gone. But she returns, drifting in front of my face.

"Come, little broken bird," she whispers. "Walk with me. I will take you to the other ghost. I will tell you of my lovey."

CHAPTER FIFTY-FIVE

Laia

·"Have you eaten yet?"

Darin finds me among the Tribespeople, where I am tending those still struggling with injuries from the wraith attack. Aubarit just joined me, her intrinsic understanding of the body making her an excellent partner. I look at my brother, dazed. I have not had time to eat. I have not had time for anything besides trying to help the wounded.

"She hasn't. Nor have I." Musa, his long hair pulled into a knot on top of his head, carries my supplies—*mostly to irritate the pretty Martial*, he'd chuckled to himself.

"Go on, both of you." Aubarit takes my bag from Musa. "You've been at this for hours. Gibran can help me." She glances from under her eyelashes at the handsome young Tribesman trailing Darin.

"Ah, young love," Musa says, and I glance at him, wondering if I will see bitterness in his regard. But his smile takes years off his face, which has been drawn and desolate of late.

Darin leads Musa and me to the Blood Shrike's tent. It is the largest in the camp, and doubles as a command center. Within, the Shrike, Avitas, and Elias gather around a central table with Spiro, Quin, and a few Martial Paters. Afya stands across from them, moving stones around on a large map.

Darin heads immediately to the far corner of the tent, where someone has laid out dried fruit, flatbread, and lentil stew. My stomach twinges hopefully. I do not remember when I last ate.

The Soul Catcher glances up at me when I enter, and briefly over to Musa, before he turns back to the Shrike.

410

"—catapults won't be done until the morning," she is saying. "And since that's when the enemy army will arrive, it doesn't give us much time to break down the city."

"We're not trying to break them down," Elias responds. "We just want the jinn in the Sher Jinnaat to keep their distance until Laia can get to the Nightbringer. If we put archers here"—he points to a map—"along the river—"

"He's jealous," Musa murmurs in my ear. "Mark me."

"He's not jealous." I thought before that he might have been. But while Elias has been more himself these past few days, he has still kept his distance. "He's the Soul Catcher, and he is here in service to the dead."

"Rubbish." Musa nudges me. "Look at him."

"He's ignoring me."

"Ah, but you're thick, *aapan*." Musa gives me an exasperated look as we make our way to the food. "To ignore you, he first has to be aware of you. And he is. He's aware of every move you make. If you tripped right now—"

At that, Musa deviously sticks out his foot. I stumble and nearly fall on my face, catching myself just in time. Almost before I've righted myself, the Soul Catcher shoots out a hand, as if to catch me from across the room. The Blood Shrike and Avitas Harper exchange a glance. Musa, meanwhile, has caught my arm, and watches the tableau with a smug grin.

"See," he says. "I told—ow!" He winces when I dig my fingers into his arm with more force than strictly needed.

"He has a battle to plan, Musa," I say. "He doesn't have time for me right now. Nor I for him."

"Love can be more powerful in a battle than planning or strategy. Love keeps us fighting. Love drives us to survive."

"Skies, stop meddling—"

"I meddle because I hope, *aapan*." The humor bleeds from his voice, and I'm certain he's remembering his beloved, doomed Nikla. "Life is too short not to hope."

Musa excuses himself, moving to Darin, but by the time my brother's made a plate for me, I can only pick at it. After a few minutes, I step out into the night. A drop of rain lands on my nose. Within seconds, a spring drizzle falls, promising a muddy morning.

I do not wish to go to Mamie's wagon, where I have been sleeping. Instead, I wind through the camp, my hood low so that no one calls out to me. A gold form appears and Rehmat speaks.

"What troubles you?"

That I don't trust you, I think. *That I might die in the morning. That I've never felt more alone in my life.*

"Tomorrow I will fight with you," I tell her. "I will allow you to join with me so that we might defeat the Nightbringer. But right now, I just want to be alone."

She bows her head in assent. "I have another I must seek out. I will return when it is time, young warrior, and not before." Her glow fades, leaving me in the dark once more.

I pass by a group of soldiers struggling to keep their lamps lit as they work on the catapults. What will tomorrow be like? I know what the Blood Shrike's troops are supposed to do, and where the efrits are meant to be. I know how the Tribes will be divided, and where we expect Keris's forces to attack.

But facing the Nightbringer—I cannot wrap my mind around it. Rehmat says defeating him will not be as simple as killing him with the scythe strapped across my back.

Yet Mamie's story gave me such little knowledge.

Love can be more powerful in a battle than planning or strategy.

So Musa said. But my love is a stream of water poured into a desert. Down a crevasse where it will never see the light. Never bloom into anything greater.

Rubbish, Laia. A calmer voice prevails—a wiser voice. If there is anything I have learned since the day that wretched Mask killed my grandparents and arrested Darin, it is that you must love while you can. For tomorrow, all that you love might be ash.

I pass by Tribe Saif and Mamie Rila's wagon, my thoughts on Elias. On what it felt like the first time I met him. That fire blazing in his eyes, that need for freedom, so like my own. The slow, careful way he built my trust after we escaped Blackcliff, and how he believed in me before I did.

And I think of the way he held me after I learned, in these very woods, that my mother was a murderer and that she still lived.

Afterward, he spoke words that I haven't wanted to remember. Because I feared I would never again see the man who said them, no matter how much I called him by his name.

If I seem different, remember that I love you. No matter what happens to me. Say you'll remember, please.

"I remember," I whisper, and make my way across the jinn grove. "I remember."

«« «

Elias's tent sits at the northern end of the camp, closer to the trees than to the rest of the soldiers. But I know just by looking at it, and by listening to some voice inside me that connects me to him, that he is not there. I follow that voice south, to the edge of the jinn grove, where he stands alone, soaked to the skin, looking over the Sher Jinnaat.

I step toward him, only to hear the hiss of a blade. Cold steel meets my throat. He makes out my face and drops his scim instantly.

"Sorry." He turns back to the city. "Jumpy."

"Me too." I ask him, "Is it always like this before a battle?"

"You've fought in a fair few yourself now," he says.

"Not one where everything depends on me."

"You're not alone. You have Darin. Afya, Mamie, and the Tribes." Elias's gaze flashes to me. "The Blood Shrike and the Martials. Musa and the Scholars. Those who love you. Those—those who you love."

"You forgot yourself, then," I say. "You most of all."

He shakes his head. "I'm here because I must be," he says. "It is my duty. My burden to make up for my wrongs. I do not deserve your love, Laia—"

"Haven't you learned?" I say. "You don't get to decide if you deserve my love or not. I decide that. You are worthy of my love. You are worthy of the love Mamie has for you, and the love the Blood Shrike feels. You've done terrible things? So have I. We were born into war, Elias. It is all we've known. Your mistakes only define the rest of your life if you let them. Don't let them."

He regards me thoughtfully and reaches for my hand. A spark jumps between us and he hesitates, but then laces his fingers through mine.

"There's a question I have been meaning to ask you," I blurt out, for if I do not ask now, I never will. "But it is from before you took your vow to Mauth. I don't know if you will remember—"

"When it comes to you, I remember everything," he says, and my pulse quickens.

"After we escaped Nur with Afya, you left," I say. "You said something to me before you did. I was sleeping, but—"

"How do you know I said something to you?" He turns to me, but his face is in shadow.

"What did you say?"

"I said—" But he stops short. The drizzle thickens and threatens to transform into a downpour.

"Never mind." He raises his voice as the rain intensifies. "We should get back to camp, Laia. You need dry clothes—"

But camp is full of people and weapons and reminders that tomorrow is coming. I shake my head, and when he tugs me, I dig my heels in.

"Take me somewhere else," I say. "You can windwalk. There must be a place we could go."

He steps toward me slowly, deliberately. His eyes burn, sweeping across my skin with as much heat as a caress. We could windwalk with just our hands connected, but he wraps his arms around my waist, and I bury my face in the hard expanse of his chest as we fly through the dark.

I do not dwell on tomorrow or on the war or the Nightbringer. I immerse myself in the feeling of Elias's touch. I breathe him in, that spice and rain scent that weaves itself through my dreams.

We stop abruptly, stumbling forward a few steps before he steadies us.

"This is the only other place in the forest the jinn won't go," he says. His cabin.

The door is not locked—for no human would come so far into the Waiting Place. Once we are inside, Elias scrapes tinder against flint, and the barest glow bursts from the fireplace. When the flame is higher, he lights four or five lamps before turning to me.

415

"You need dry clothes." He opens a chest near his bed and rifles through it until he finds a soft black shirt.

I set my scythe down beside Elias's weapons and change in the washroom, stripping my sodden clothing and toweling off. I am thankful there is no looking glass. His shirt is far too big on me, and my hair is a disaster, the dozens of pins I used to tame it this morning tangled in one big mass. It will take me ages to pull them out. I sigh, reach for Elias's lone wooden comb, and step out.

The Soul Catcher has changed into dry fatigues and kicked off his shoes. He sits on a deerskin rug before the fire, warming his hands.

"You can sleep there." He nods to his bed. "I'll take the floor. At least you'll get a good night of rest before tomorrow."

Sleep isn't what I had in mind, but I shrug and sit near him cross-legged. Ever so carefully, I begin to pull out my pins. The first few make me wince, so tangled that I'm worried I'll pull out half my hair with them.

Elias looks over at me and I catch my breath. The fire tinges his brown skin a deep, beguiling gold, and his hair, dark and unruly, falls into his eyes. The cabin is chilly, but beneath his gaze, I am not. His regard does not feel like the regard of the Soul Catcher.

He shifts his attention to the pin in my hand and my ineffectual efforts to remove it.

"Let me." He comes around and sits behind me atop a fat cushion, long legs stretched on either side.

I feel his hands in my hair, removing the pin with deft gentleness. I shiver, and he shifts closer, his chest against my back now. The scrape of his stubble on my neck is maddening, and I find myself knotting my shirt in my hands, then unknotting it. I am suddenly without words, my thoughts a jumble of desire and confusion and anger. *Why are you so cruel? I want to shout at him. Why offer warmth and gentleness and your touch if you are so determined to be the Soul Catcher instead of the man I love?*

But I banish those thoughts. I will not feel anger tonight. Nor fear. Only hope.

My body melts against his, and I tip my head back so it's easier for him to reach the pins. He pulls out a particularly stubborn one, and I marvel that hands so big, hands calloused from holding scims and daggers, could so cleverly work the pins from my hair.

"Does that magic of yours extend to hair knots?" I murmur.

His deep, quiet laugh echoes through my chest. "Apparently. They seem very agreeable."

"They must like you."

He shifts back again, and though I want to protest the fact that I cannot feel him anymore, his legs press against mine in a way that leaves no doubt that I am not the only one whose heart now beats faster.

"That night in the desert, when I was leaving," he says, his lips so close to my ear that I tremble, a thrill running down my body. "I did say something to you."

He removes another pin. My shirt slides off one shoulder, and the hard muscles of his arm brush against it slowly.

"I said: You are my temple." His voice is low and hoarse. I lean my body into his, unable to stop, desiring him with a soul-deep wanting that aches. His scent intoxicates me, and I inhale so that I might remember it always. Even as he carefully removes another pin, his hard thighs tighten against my hips. I feel him, all of him, enough to know that Soul Catcher or not, he wants me as badly as I want him.

"You are my priest," he says. His lips brush my neck, and I'm not dreaming it. He pulls out the last pin. He threads his fingers through my hair, loose now, with great care. His touch on my waist is less patient—he pulls my body around until my legs are slung to the side, my chest pressed against his.

My hands fall to his hips, and I gasp and dig my fingers into them as he tilts my head back, as he skims his lips along the hollow of my throat. I want him. Skies above, I want him. More so because I can feel him holding himself back, feel his entire body thrumming with need.

"You are my prayer," he says, and now his eyes meet mine, and I see the war in him. See him teetering between the Soul Catcher and Elias. Between duty and hope. Between the task thrust upon him and the freedom he so craves. I know what he is going to say next. I have heard him whisper his mantra many times, though never like this. But as he teeters between who he's become and who he wants to be, I say nothing. *You're in there*, I think. *Come back to me.*

"You are my release," he whispers.

A breath then, a slice of time that will mark the before and the after of this moment. A heartbeat during which I do not know who will win the battle inside him or if our love is enough.

Then his eyes clear, and he is Elias Veturius, warm and beautiful and mine. I pull him to me, reveling in the feel of his lush mouth as I steal the words from his lips. I run my hands over the hard planes of his shoulders, his arms—it isn't enough. I want more of him, all of him.

He yanks me closer, as hungry as I am, kissing me with the same dark heat, as if he knows that this night, our last night, our only night, will never come again.

CHAPTER FIFTY-SIX

The Soul Catcher

If Mauth objects to Laia and me being together, I don't hear it. And if the duty-obsessed Soul Catcher whispers at me that I am a fool, I don't hear him either. I lose myself in the feel of her lips against mine, her scent filling my senses. She pulls her fingers through my hair, trailing kisses from my jaw to the ridges of my shoulders.

Her nails dig into my back, and she bites me, gentle and forceful at the same time. I curse at the frisson of heat that grips me and push her away.

We have a battle to fight tomorrow. I have a duty to fulfill. This won't end well.

"Laia—"

But she shakes her head, gold eyes fiery, and puts a finger against my lips. "You love me," she says. "And I love you. And that is all that matters this night."

She runs her hands down my chest, straddles me, and with one smooth pull, tears open the buttons of my shirt, defiance suffusing every move. *Stop me*, she dares. But I wouldn't. Not for the world, and in seconds, I'm pulling off hers.

I marvel at the perfection of every curve, every muscle, every scar, every last inch of her, but I don't have words for it, and she looks away, embarrassed, her arms rising to cover herself.

"Don't you dare," I say fervently. "You're perfect." She smiles then, the smile I dream about.

"That," she says, "is the most gratifying look I have ever seen on your face."

I pull her to me, grazing my teeth across her lips, and then down her neck, across the hard perfection of her collarbone and to the silk below.

Clothes—accursed clothes—we remove what is left, laughing as we do, and then, still atop me, she takes my hand, moving it to the sweetest part of her body, dropping her head back, her breath going shallow when I do as she wishes. I smile, inordinately pleased at watching her eyes flutter closed as she rocks above me, as she loses herself to her pleasure.

Her body shudders, and I nearly lose my control at the feel of Laia losing hers. When she is still again, she looks at me, ducking her head in sudden shyness, but I lift her chin. The light of the fire deepens her gold eyes, and they burn like embers.

I kiss her slow then, the way I've wanted to for so long. I take my time, savoring the fullness of her mouth, tracing circles on the smooth swell of her hips. When I move my lips down her body, I watch her face, the delicate shifts in her expression, the way her pulse flutters at her throat, rapid as my own.

But she moans impatiently, and the sound undoes me. I flip her onto her back, settling only a little of my weight on her. Her fingers lace through mine, and when I lift them over her head, she curves into me.

"Yes—"

"Laia." I want her so badly that making myself slow down is torment. But I do not want to hurt her. I am Elias now, but tomorrow, and every day after, I must be the Soul Catcher again. "Are you sure?"

She answers by hooking her leg up around my hips and pulling me toward her until it is not her moving, nor me, but us. And though I want nothing more than to disappear into this moment, she breathes my name.

"Elias," she says between her gasps, and I know she wants me to look at her. I hesitate, for if I do so, my heart will be bare. But love rolls off her in gentle waves, enveloping me, and finally I meet her gaze.

Laia's steady stare captures me, and I am lost, hypnotized by the dark passion that blooms there as she loses herself to the movement of our bodies, to that ancient alchemy melding the agony of desire with the ecstasy of its fulfillment.

I do not look away as she cries my name, as her fingers tighten on my fists, as her body arches into me, as we move toward the same place, that ineffable crossroads of pain and pleasure, together as one at last.

«««

Hours later, as we lie on our backs, both drawing in draughts of air like water, she rises up on her elbows and looks at me sternly. "We have to win," she says.

"Why?"

"Because this cannot be the only night we spend together." Her fingers are light as she traces lines on my skin, but her voice is fierce. "I want a life with you. Adventures. Meals. Late nights in front of fires. A thousand rainy walks. You talking me out of my clothing in inappropriate places. I want ch—" She stops, sadness in her eyes, though she hides it quickly. But I know what she was going to say. Because I want children too, perhaps not now, but one day. "I want more," she says.

I smile, but it fades quickly when I remember that she wishes to destroy the jinn. That I do not. And that if, by some miracle, the Nightbringer is defeated and the jinn are restored to their place as Soul Catchers, there is still no future for us. *You are sworn to me until another human—not jinn—is seen fit to replace you.*

"What is it?" She folds her arms across my chest and rests her chin there, so I can only see her eyes. "What is eating at you?"

We can never have a life, she and I. No adventures. No meals. No late nights. No rainy walks. No talking her out of her clothing in inappropriate places.

No children.

This night is all we get. As soon as Mauth is restored to his full power, he will pull me back. And Laia will fade away once more.

Even as I search for the words to answer her question, the light changes. The night flees as the cabin, warm and gold-brown only moments ago, now fades to blue.

Far to the south of us, the army will be waking, the soldiers readying themselves. Beyond, near the river, the Nightbringer prepares to unleash an apocalypse upon us all.

I pull Laia to me and kiss her once more, putting all of my love and hope and desire into that kiss. Everything I wanted to give her in a lifetime together.

She senses what I'm doing, and I taste salt on my lips.

"Elias—" she whispers. "Don't—"

But I shake my head. "Soul Catcher," I say. "It's Soul Catcher."

She nods and straightens her shoulders. "Of course," she says. "We should go."

We find our clothing, dry now from a night beside the fire, and don it silently, sliding on boots and weapons and armor. When Laia pulls on the scythe, she sighs, as if weighed down. She walks out the door first, waiting for me in the clearing, her back turned.

I close the cabin door firmly, taking a breath as I am hit with a premonition as strong as any Augur's, that she and I will never return here together again.

CHAPTER FIFTY-SEVEN

The Blood Shrike

As I emerge from the forest, forever altered, I do not think of the words I heard. I do not think of what I saw. I cannot risk a jinn—any jinn—picking the thoughts from my mind.

Instead, I think of Avitas Harper. His calm, his warmth, the way he looks at me like I am the only thing in the world that matters.

It is deep night when I return, and the army camp is quiet. I find him pacing outside my tent, brow furrowing when he sees me.

"I know," I say, for I have his *You cannot wander off, you are the Blood Shrike* speech memorized. "But I had to attend to something alone."

"Tell me—"

"I cannot." I dismiss the guards near the front of my tent. "All things depend on my silence."

"Blood Shrike—"

"Helene," I whisper to him. "Tonight, call me Helene."

He observes me for a moment before flashing that half smile that drives me mad. Then he pulls me into the tent, his hands in my hair, his lips on mine before the flap has even closed. I drag him toward my cot, and we topple onto it silently, frantic for each other, not even bothering to fully undress until after we've sated our desire.

Later, in the wee hours of the night, I wake, a chill running through my body.

"What's wrong?" he asks, arm flung over my hips, still half-asleep.

"Nothing," I say. "Go back to sleep."

"You should too."

"I will." I kiss him and let myself look at his dark lashes, his scim-sharp cheekbones, the way his skin ripples as he sits up.

"Harper," I say hesitantly. "Avitas . . ."

"Mmm?"

I love you. Such simple words. But they are not enough. They don't convey what I mean.

"*Emifal Firdaant,*" I say to him.

"You've said that before." He runs his fingers through my hair. "What does it mean?"

I cannot quite look at him when I say it. "May death claim me first."

"Ah, no, my love." He gathers me close. "You cannot go first. I could not make sense of the world if you did."

With that, he closes his eyes, but I cannot sleep. I stare up at the peak of the tent and listen to the rain drum down on the canvas. *Emifal Firdaant,* I beg the skies. *Emifal Firdaant.*

CHAPTER FIFTY-EIGHT

Laia

The moment Elias and I arrive back at the camp, the Blood Shrike pounces.

"There's an issue with the catapults, Soul Catcher." She wears Spiro's battle armor, her hair tight against her head in its impeccable braid. "Where the hells have you—"

She looks between us, and her pale eyebrows arch up, then furrow as she takes in the devastation in my eyes, the cold detachment in his.

Musa appears at my elbow. Though he must know I disappeared in the night, he says nothing. His wights shift around him, an antsy cloud.

"I told them to leave," he says, noticing me watching them. "They fear the jinn. But they refused." He nods to the center of the camp. "Darin is looking for you, *aapan*. He and Spiro are near Mamie Rila's wagon."

I give the Scholar a grateful nod and hurry away to find my brother and the smith, the former of whom holds a sack and the latter a scim.

"A gift for you, Laia." Darin holds up the bag. "To go with that scythe of yours. Can't have my little sister and the savior of us all running around in mismatched armor."

"As if there wasn't enough pressure," I say, only half-joking.

The armor is light and flexible, but there's another feeling to it too, one that I cannot name.

"It's shadow-forged," Spiro says. "I learned it from the Augurs. It will help you blend into your surroundings, make you harder to spot. And it will protect you from jinn fire."

He buckles a belt around my waist, a short scim and dagger attached.

Darin hooks my bow to my back, over my scythe, and they both smile as they take me in, like two proud big brothers.

A Tribal horn sounds a warning. The enemy is near. I take a deep, bracing breath as a group of Martials in formation jogs past, toward the edge of the escarpment. A cart filled with giant blocks of salt rumbles by. Elias's voice echoes across the camp, cool and calm, ordering troops into position.

Everyone around me moves, but I am rooted to the dead earth. What if I fail? This is not a fair fight. The Commandant has more than thirty thousand men. We have less than a third of that. She has wraiths and jinn and a horde of Masks. We have a few dozen Masks and efrits that can be weakened with song or steel or fire.

Keris has the Nightbringer.

We have me.

Darin's hand closes on my shoulder. He knows the racket in my head—of course he does.

"Listen to me." He gazes at me with our mother's eyes, the eyes of someone who believes in you so deeply that you have no choice but to believe in yourself. "You are the strongest person here. The strongest in the camp. Stronger than me, Spiro, the Blood Shrike, the Soul Catcher, Afya. You are the daughter of the Lioness. The granddaughter of Nan and Pop. You are Lis's sister and mine."

His eyes fill, but he does not stop. "Tell me what you've done. Tell me."

"I—I've survived the Commandant," I say. "And Blackcliff. Our family's deaths. I've survived the Nightbringer. I've defied him. I saved you. I've fought. I've fought for our people."

"And you will keep fighting." Darin grabs both shoulders now. "And you will win. There is not a single person alive who I trust more than you to do what must be done today, Laia. Not a single one."

From the Shrike or Elias, these words would be encouraging. From my big brother, they are life-giving. Something about him, of all people, believing in me makes me grip my scim and set my jaw and stand taller. I will win today.

"I can come with you," he says. "I want to come with you. Why should you fight him alone when you *aren't* alone?"

But I shake my head, thinking of the snap of my father's neck, of Lis's neck. Of the way the Commandant used family to manipulate my mother.

"The Nightbringer has always used my love against me, Darin," I say. "I do not want him to do it again. I cannot be worried about you. Stick to the plan."

"Laia—" He appears uncertain, then grabs me in a hug. "I love you. Fight. Win. I'll see you when it's all over."

"Laia!" Elias calls out as Darin disappears into the camp. Afya and Gibran are beside him, and a platoon of Tribespeople and Scholars armed with longbows waits nearby. "It's time. We're the last."

"Rehmat?" I say quietly, jogging toward Elias. But the creature does not appear.

We wind through the trees, the last of a thousand soldiers Elias has already dispatched. The path we follow takes us east, angling upward before ending at a sheer cliff that drops sixty feet to the river. To our left and right, hundreds of Tribespeople and Scholars wait, bows at the ready.

Skies know how the Nightbringer cleared the way for Keris's army. Perhaps he manipulated the forest, like Elias. Perhaps he had his jinn clear a path. Whatever the case, the enemy Martials approach a narrow strip of shallows along the river, the only place they can cross without boats.

And just close enough to the cliffs to leave them exposed to our arrows.

"Do not shoot," Afya breathes from my left. "Only the longbows have the range."

Though my aim has improved, I heed her advice. In any case, I am here to watch for the Nightbringer. To spy on him when hopefully, he cannot do the same.

Though the sky above is clear, the forest from which the Martials will emerge is cloaked in mist. And before our eyes, the mist thickens.

"What in the bleeding skies is that?" Afya points to a thick bank of cloud, rolling up along the river from the south. There is a sulfuric fetor to it, and it is completely at odds with the wind, which blows in from the north, favoring our arrows.

"The Nightbringer," Elias says. "He knows we're here. Runner!"

A young Scholar appears immediately at Elias's side. "Call the wind efrits," he says. "Tell them they're to scatter the fog."

The boy disappears, and now the fog has enshrouded the river below. We hear splashes in the water, but looking down is like looking into a bucket of milk.

"They're crossing," Afya hisses. "We have to do something."

"Not yet," Elias says. "We wait for the efrits."

Trails of stinking mist approach the ridge where we've taken cover, and we hear shouts now, orders given as Keris's army makes its way across the shallows. From there, they will travel along a cleared area that runs in a strip between this ridge and the jinn city. And then, up the short escarpment to battle our troops.

I fidget as the minutes drag on. "Elias—"

"Not yet." His pale eyes are trained on the mist. The soldiers shift uneasily, and he calls down the line, "Steady."

Then a whoosh over our heads, and the shrieks of the wind efrits as they arrow through the mist, swirling and ripping and tearing, scattering it as a child scatters fall leaves.

Elias lifts his hand and signals for the archers along the ridgeline to nock and aim. The cloud thins enough that we see men below, crossing the river in large groups.

Elias swings down his arm, and the thrum of a thousand arrows launching at once sings through the air. One of Keris's men shouts a warning, but waterlogged as the soldiers are, they cannot raise their shields in time. They drop in waves. Elias lifts and drops his arm again, before signaling to fire at will. Another wave of soldiers goes down, and then another.

We could stop them right here. Perhaps a thousand Tribal longbows are enough to finish the Martials. To make Keris crawl back to Navium, licking her wounds. To make the Nightbringer think twice.

Then a knife, its hilt still glowing as if fresh from the forge, whistles out of the sky and lodges itself into the chest of the person standing beside me. Afya.

She grunts and steps back, staring down at the blade in surprise before crumpling into my arms. *No, oh skies, no.*

"Afya!" Gibran screams and gets his arm around her in an instant. *"Zaldara, no."*

"Get her to triage," I say. "Quickly. It didn't hit her heart. Go, Gibran!"

But the clouds above burn orange and then a deep angry red as jinn streak out of the sky. Umber, with her fiery glaive, is among them. She thuds to the earth not thirty feet away, flattening the trees around her. Afya and

Gibran both go flying as her glaive sweeps out, setting fire to two dozen of our soldiers at once.

"Retreat!" Elias calls, and we expected this. I know we did. But I am still unprepared for the swift deaths the jinn mete out. The way they tear through our troops like wind through paper. A score of our men go down. Two score. Five score.

"Run, Laia!"

"Afya—Gibran—"

"*Run!*"

Elias pulls me away, rage in his voice. Instantly I know his anger is born of fear, for here I stand, unmoving as death inches closer.

But though Umber is before me, though she could strike me down with her glaive, she only snarls and turns away. Elias windwalks me through the trees and back to the jinn grove, even as the soldiers we have left behind trickle from the woods.

Our camp is an organized sort of chaos, and Elias is instantly barking orders. The catapults are loaded, the sea efrits hovering above them to defend them from the jinn. The war machines are aimed not at the approaching army, but at the Sher Jinnaat. We will hurl not fire or stones, but massive blocks of salt, to keep the jinn in the city from joining their brethren and deciding the battle before we've had a chance to fight it.

"How many down?" the Shrike calls to Elias.

"Nearly two hundred on our side," he says. "Perhaps a thousand on theirs."

"We sent the messenger as you requested," the Shrike says. "Keris sent the head back. Body tied to the horse."

"Soul Catcher!" Rowan Goldgale materializes before us. "The Martials are here. The Nightbringer—"

Elias grabs the Blood Shrike, already drawing her scim for battle.

"Don't give Keris an inch, Blood Shrike. She'll have something up her sleeve. She always does."

The Shrike smiles grimly. "And who is to say I don't, Soul Catcher?"

He grins at her, that old Elias smile, and with that she is gone. The sky is alight, the jinn among us, raining down hell on the army, trying their best to destroy us before we can fight back.

Elias turns to me, but I shove him away. "Go," I say. "Hold them off."

"Laia—"

I leave him, because if I say goodbye, I am already giving in. I will see him again. I will.

The camp is madness now, but I am not afraid. For Umber could have taken me down, and she did not. The Nightbringer wants me for himself.

An old calm consumes me. The same calm I felt before I rescued Elias from execution, and before I broke into Kauf. The calm of delivering Livia's child in the middle of a battle. A calm born of the knowledge that I am as ready as I can be.

I plunge into the trees west of the jinn grove and make my way up to a small plateau of rock that looks out over the Sher Jinnaat. The rock is impossible to miss. Especially for a jinn watching the battle from above.

When I reach the plateau, Rehmat's gold glow appears before me.

"I am here, Laia."

"Thank the skies for that," I say to Rehmat. She comes around to stand in front of me, and there is something almost formal about how her hands are clasped before her. She tilts her head, a question offered without words.

I nod, and she flows into me, joining my consciousness so completely that it takes my breath away. I am her and she is me. And though I know this is the way it must be, though she limits herself to but a corner of my mind, I chafe against her presence. I hate having someone else in my head.

We move to the edge of the promontory and peer down. Keris's army has reached the escarpment and hurtles up it. The first wave of soldiers is impaled on the pikes there, but the army is not held back for long.

Umber swoops into a dive, incinerating the pikes, and Keris's Martials are through, throwing themselves at Elias's forces.

My eyes sting as I watch. So many dead. Who they fight for does not matter, because we are all the same to the Nightbringer. He has manipulated us into hating each other. Into seeing the other side as he sees us. Not as humans, but as vermin, worthy only of slaughter.

But where is that creature? Nowhere to be seen, though his jinn wreak havoc.

Enough of this. Every second that passes means more people dead, which is exactly what he wants.

The scythe is heavy on my back. Too heavy. I unsheathe it. Wan light glints upon the black diamond blade before the sun disappears behind a cloud. Rain threatens, and I stare at the approaching storm. If only it would break upon us, for the jinn hate the wet. But the sky does not open.

"Come on then, you monster," I hiss, hoping the wind will carry my words to him. "Come for me."

"As it pleases you, Laia of Serra."

That deep growling voice. The voice of my nightmares. The voice that has taken so much.

I turn and face the Nightbringer.

CHAPTER FIFTY-NINE

The Soul Catcher

The troops from Antium do not wish to fight. I see it in their eyes, feel in it their spirits as they lock shields to face Keris's cavalry, roaring up the escarpment.

If I have my way, they won't fight for long. But I must get to Umber. She is the Nightbringer's second, commanding the other jinn in his absence. If I could get her to listen to me, we could end this madness.

The air grows heavy and strange. As if some unseen hand presses up from the earth, seeking to tear through it. The maelstrom, I fear, is close.

Umber streaks across the front of the escarpment, laughing as she incinerates the stakes we've laid to deter Keris's troops. Our soldiers cry out first in anger, and then in fear as the ground rumbles and shakes beneath them—Faaz using his powers to throw them off balance.

"Rowan!"

The sand efrit and his kin are already streaking toward the jinn, and my army stands fast.

Protected by their armor and wielding spears of their own, our infantry hold the line, supported by volley after volley of arrows from a thousand Scholar bowmen behind them. I shudder at the death—brutal and unending. The screams of the wounded fill the air.

The catapults creak as the Blood Shrike unleashes her unusual missiles: giant blocks of salt. One of the jinn screams as a block gets too close, and plummets. A cheer rises up from our soldiers, but Umber wreaks havoc in revenge. She slips through the dozens of bowmen we have guarding one of the catapults, ignoring the salt-coated arrows that penetrate her flame form, and slices through the ropes to render the war machine inert.

As I windwalk to the front line, an old rage rises up in me, the battle wolf howling, baying for blood. My scims sing as I whip them from their scabbards, and I weave through the fighters as easily as if I am born of smoke. I could kill dozens if I wished. Hundreds.

But it is not the humans I want. And it is not killing that will help. I must reach Umber.

I find her on the far western side of the line, tearing into a tightly packed phalanx, swiping their shields aside. She shrugs off the arrows sticking out of her, and Spiro Teluman appears, sliding under her guard, his scim whipping toward her neck.

But it only glances across her fiery body before she twists her glaive and disarms him. She moves in for the kill, but I meet her this time, and the wood of her glaive glances off my scims.

"Usurper," she hisses. "You have no place here. No place fighting beside them."

"And you have no place murdering people who had nothing to do with your imprisonment." I dart around her, drawing her toward the forest, where there are fewer soldiers. But even with my speed, she smashes her glaive into my arm. It would be a bone-shattering blow if not for Spiro's armor. Umber roars and strikes out again, but I parry, catching her blade between my scims.

"Your kind are a pestilence." She tries to yank her glaive away, but I do not let her. "One that must be eradicated."

"It's not just us that will be eradicated," I tell her. "If the Nightbringer brings the Sea of Suffering into this world, everyone—everything—will die. Including you. The world will fall—"

"Then let it fall," she screams. "We will have peace, finally—"

"The peace of the dead," I say. Why does she not understand? "Can't you feel it, Umber? The air isn't right. Has the Nightbringer told you what he is doing? Has he shared his plan with you?"

"The Meherya need share nothing with us. He is our *king*. He freed us. And he will rid us of you and your kind, that we may live quietly in the Sher Jinnaat—"

"He is waking the Sea of Suffering," I shout at her, because reason doesn't appear to be working. "He seeks to gather every bit of pain and horror and loneliness we took from the dead and return it to the world. Do you think that when it wakes, it will have mercy on you because you are a jinn?"

"You know nothing of what we have suffered!"

I wrench her glaive from her and cast it to one side. "I will not kill you," I say. "But your Meherya will. Look at me and know that I do not lie. If you let your king continue to reap souls, what he awakens will destroy us all."

I step back and lower my blades, even as the battle edges closer. "Please," I say. "Stop him. He might not realize what he is doing, what he is unleashing."

"I would not go against my Meherya." Umber shakes her head, a shudder rippling through her flames. "He understands what you do not, Soul Catcher. We are too broken. We can never go back to what we were before."

"You are needed," I say desperately. "Essential to the balance—"

"The balance!" Umber cries. "Who benefits the most from the balance, Soul Catcher? Mauth, who let our children die, but expects us to do his bidding? Your kind, who kill and maim and give us all of your pain to clean up? We held the balance for millennia, and look what it got us. If it is so important to you, then tell Mauth to find more humans to pass the ghosts."

She streaks away, and the battle closes around me, too swift for me to escape. I cut through a knot of legionnaires. Not far from me, Darin, Spiro, and a group of Saif Tribespeople fight off a platoon of Keris's soldiers.

I move to help them, but another battle surges in front of me, and I catch a flash of blonde streaking past, a silver mask and pale gray eyes lit with unholy fury.

My mother impales a Tribeswoman and an aux soldier with two slashes of one scim while taking the head off a Scholar with her other, moving so swiftly that one might think she was windwalking. Her skill is otherworldly and yet grounded in savagery that is deeply, uniquely human. Though I have seen her fight hundreds of times, I have never seen her like this.

At first, I'm certain she doesn't spot me—that she is too deep in the battle.

Then she stops, and though all around us, men and women strive and die, we are trapped in a pocket of quiet. All my memories of her flood my mind at once, sharp words and whippings and her watching—always watching, more than I ever knew.

"Stay far from the Nightbringer, Ilyaas," she cautions me, and I disappear back into a moment years ago, in a desert far to the west of here. *Go back to the caravan, Ilyaas. Dark creatures walk the desert at night.*

Before I can make sense of her warning—of her—she is gone, her scim crashing into that of a man a foot and a half taller than her and decades older. Her father. My grandfather.

"Go, boy," Grandfather says. "She's been waiting to fight me for years. I'll not disappoint her. Not in this."

Grandfather evades Keris's first attack easily, though she moves twice as fast, and seems to anticipate her every stroke. His mouth is a grim slash, his body taut, but the shrewd self-assurance I'm used to seeing in his gaze is gone. Instead, he looks like a man haunted, a man wishing to be anywhere but where he is. Strength and the wiles of more than seventy years as a fighter might be enough to keep him alive against Keris.

Or they might not.

A scream turns my head, and I barely avoid a spear aimed at my heart. Shan knocks the attacker unconscious, and then he is swallowed up in the battle, and though I try to make my way toward him, the sheer mass of bodies is impossible to get through, even windwalking.

"Soul Catcher!"

Darin appears, panting and blood-streaked, Spiro at his back. "Where is Laia?"

"I don't know," I say. "She was on her way to the plateau—"

Darin glances over his shoulder toward the rocky promontory, but we cannot see anything from here.

"I know she doesn't want us there." He is frantic. "I promised I wouldn't interfere. But everything feels wrong. There's something coming—and she's the only family I have left, Soul Catcher. I can't just leave her alone."

Laia feared he would do what older siblings do and put himself in danger to help her. I grab his shoulder, sensing his anguish—and his intent. "If you go after her, it might distract her. It's the last thing she needs or wants, Darin. Please—"

My words are drowned out by the shriek of rock—Faaz hurling a giant boulder down upon the farthest reaches of our army. Keris's forces roar in triumph as it digs a grave-deep runnel into the earth, taking out dozens of our soldiers with it.

The Martials and Scholars around Darin howl at the abrupt death of so many comrades, and attack Keris's men with newfound strength, driving them back toward the edge of the escarpment. My battle rage rises, screaming at me to fight, to kill. *War is your past. War is your present. War is your future.* So Talis, the jinn, told me. And so it is. I give in to my wrath, my scims whipping through the men around me.

"Darin!" I call out, but he does not respond. Spiro Teluman is next to me, scanning the faces around him for his apprentice. But Darin has disappeared. Distantly, the Blood Shrike bellows orders, and Keris shouts in horrific triumph. The earth groans, a jinn-spawned temblor, and huge fissures open and swallow dozens of my troops. One of the catapults explodes as Faaz slings a boulder into it. Two more erupt in a roar of flame.

The air, already weighted with the cacophony of war, thickens, as if a thunderstorm is about to break.

Banu al-Mauth.

Mauth's voice is so quiet, but it rings in my head like a bell.

Forgive me, Banu al-Mauth, he says. *I have not the strength to stop him.*

Oh bleeding, burning hells. A vision flashes in my head—Mauth's foresight. A terrifying, hungry maw, spearing through Mauth's barrier, erupting into the world.

"Mauth," I whisper. "No."

CHAPTER SIXTY

The Blood Shrike

When I see Elias streaking for the woods where Laia disappeared, I know something is wrong.

I cannot go to him. I cannot even call out to him. Keris's forces have killed half our bowmen, and Umber lights up our catapults with that damnable glaive of hers. All our attempts to stop the jinn have been met by their fey superiority. The Soul Catcher said the creatures have their limitations. He said they would grow weak as they poured their life forces into destroying us.

But if there is weakness, I do not see it. I only see our forces being annihilated, with no sign of Laia, no indication that she even still lives. The efrits fight valiantly—and fail, for they are no match for the jinn, fading sparks against screaming suns.

Wraiths pour from the Commandant's ranks, and while her men shy back, ours do not. Scholars stand shoulder to shoulder with Martials and Tribespeople. A wave of wraiths is upon us, their infernal cold sending man after man to his knees. But I scream and swing my scims, lopping off their heads as if they are stalks of corn.

"Imperator Invictus!" My troops rally around me. "Imperator Invictus!"

But it's not enough. There are too many wraiths, too many jinn, too many soldiers fighting for Keris.

Panic envelops me, the same terror I felt in Antium. The hopelessness of defeat, and the knowledge that nothing can be done to stop it.

You are all that holds back the darkness. Today, I will not be defeated. Today, I take vengeance for Antium. For Livia.

"Shrike!" Harper appears beside me, gasping, bleeding from too many wounds to count. I feel the urge to heal him. It is so powerful that his song is already on my lips. But I transform it into a demand.

"Where is she, Harper? This cannot end until she is destroyed."

"Her standard is there—" Ahead of me, well past the catapults and near the escarpment, Keris's banner snaps in the jinn-spawned wind. Near it, a man stands inches above those around him, white hair flying as he fights his daughter.

"She's battling Quin," I say. This is my best chance. I turn to Harper, catching his gaze. "You stay away," I say. "She'll use you against me. Do you understand? Stay away."

I do not let him protest, instead shoving forward, breaking a path. As I close in on Keris's standard, Quin drops out of view. Has she killed him? *Her own father, bleeding hells.*

The fighters coming toward me fall beneath the edge of my blade. I scream, snarl, and pitch fighters twice as wide as me out of the way, wrath consuming my mind, until Keris's spike-crown standard is nigh and she is before me.

This demon. This tiny slip of muscled, deadly madness. This murderess, eviscerating one of my legionnaires, then turning to face me with a sneer.

My men surge around me, fighting hers back, leaving the Bitch of Blackcliff and the Blood Shrike to each other.

Don't give Keris an inch, Blood Shrike. She'll have something up her sleeve. She always does.

And who is to say I don't, Soul Catcher?

I force away the memory, for with it comes the words Karinna spoke, what she showed me deep in the Waiting Place. The Nightbringer or his minions could pick such thoughts from my mind. They are a weakness, and today, I can have no weakness. Today, I must be a thousand times smarter and faster and better than I have ever been.

Keris unleashes her fury like she's been saving it just for me. *I will pay you back for every escape, every defiance.* She screams the words with the violence of her body, the ferocity of her scims. *I will punish you for all of them.*

Her savagery is so startling that I stumble, on the defensive. She is not a normal foe, nor a fair one. This is the woman who taught me every-thing I know about war, survival, combat. The woman who honed killing machines—none more effective than herself.

Though she knows my skill, she does not know my heart. Keris did not witness her parents and sister's throats slit in front of her. Keris did not watch her last living sibling stare into her child's eyes as she died, all her hopes dead in the flash of a blade.

Keris is fueled by anger. But mine burns hotter because of grief. And I unleash it.

The Commandant's weapons of choice are dual scims. She is smaller, so she has to risk getting in close. I keep her at a distance, dodging her thrusts, matching her parry for parry, until I get a hit on her shoulder, and another on the side of her neck.

But she moves too quickly for me to slice at her legs or throat—her weakest spots.

A sting across my face—and the warm rush of blood pouring down my cheek. I jerk my head back as Keris's blade comes within inches of my throat. At the same time, she whips her other scim across my left side so viciously that even Spiro's armor cannot stop the blow. If I was wearing my ceremonials, I'd be dead.

The battle still swirls around us, and I catch sight of Harper shoving his scim into the throat of an attacker—barely avoiding the swing of a club at his legs. My men are beating the Commandant's forces back, outnumbered as they are, and the sight gives me heart.

I move as if blood does not pour down my side, feinting with the scim in my right hand before pivoting around her. My blade is inches from her hamstrings, and I whip it across.

But instead of the satisfying give of metal cutting through flesh, I feel a deep burn in my left wrist. She tricked me. Left her back open so I'd go behind her and leave my left side, my weak side, exposed. *Shrike, you fool.*

My scim falls uselessly from my hand, and her blade rips through my armor into my hip. I stagger back before she tears me in half, my vision doubling. *Get up, Shrike! Get up!*

I lift my remaining scim in time to parry a blow that would have taken my head from my body. The force with which our scims meet knocks mine loose, but she slips on a stray bit of mud, giving me a chance to fall back.

Though it does little good. I am weaponless, my scims too far away to reach.

"Shrike!" Harper, ever watchful, breaks free from the battle on Keris's left side and throws a dagger to me. *No. No. Stay away. Stay away, you fool!* Keris catches the dagger, but Harper has already thrown another.

Even as he hurls the second blade at me, as I pluck it from the air, I see his chest plate is askew, knocked loose in battle.

"Harper!" I scream, but Keris has turned, the blade she caught hurtling through the air at him. Death with wings.

It sinks into his chest.

A flesh wound, I think. I crawl through the mud toward him. *I can fix it. I can sing him back*. But another flash of steel cuts through the air. This blade lodges in his heart. He falls.

"No!" I reach him, my knees sinking into the mud. His green eyes glaze as the life leaves him, as blood oozes from his chest.

"Harper, no—" I whisper. "No—please—"

"Helene—" He says my name, but I cannot hear it. The battle is too fierce, my heart thunders too loudly. *No—no*. I do not want victory if this is the cost.

"*Em-emifal F-F-Firdaant*—" he whispers, and his hand, gripping mine only a moment before, drops to the mud.

I will sing him back to me. I will. But I do not, for something tears again into my left side. I cannot help the scream that explodes from my throat. It feels unending, the sum of all my pain, all my defeat and sorrow.

Keris watches me. Dagger in hand, she approaches, relishing my suffering, basking in it.

I try to rise. I cannot. *Loyal. Loyal to the end.*

But the end is here. And I am not ready.

CHAPTER SIXTY-ONE

Laia

Beware, Laia. Rehmat's voice is sharp in my mind. *Something isn't right.*

I do not speak as the Nightbringer thuds onto the plateau. Fear will not claim my mind. I will defeat him. I will destroy him.

"Can you feel it, my love?" the Nightbringer says, and I do not know if he speaks to me or Rehmat. When he steps toward me, Rehmat pushes me back, even as I hold my ground. I stumble.

Stay with me, I say to her in my head. *I know this is difficult. I know you loved him. But we cannot win if we do not move as one.*

"We will stop you." Rehmat and I speak together, and though my voice trembles, I steel myself. "You will not crack open this world to the Sea of Suffering. I will not allow it."

"Won't you?" he says, and as he closes in, he lifts his hands to my face.

Stay with me, I say again to Rehmat. This time, we hold steady even as within my mind, she flinches at his touch.

"It does not have to be this way," we say. "You are the Meherya. Meant to love." I gesture to the battlefield below. "This is not your way."

"All that I do is driven by love," he says, and his flame eyes meet mine. My heart—or Rehmat's—lurches. "Love of all that was taken from us. Love of what is left."

He's so close that if my scythe was in hand, I could kill him. Ever so slowly, I edge my arm back. But Rehmat holds me fast. My limbs do not cooperate.

We have to kill him, I remind her. *You promised you would not take over. You swore it.*

Something is not right, she whispers.

444

"This is not the way forward." Rehmat speaks now, though I try to stop her. "You do not honor our love by letting vengeance consume you. You do not honor our people. Or our—children—" The last word is choked off, for the blood magic will not allow her to speak of her life with him. "Show remorse," she urges him. "Repentance. Dedicate your life to the task Mauth gave you. Restore the balance."

What are you doing? Now I am furious, for this was not the plan. *There is no forgiveness for what he has done.*

Rehmat does not bend. *Stay your anger, Laia,* she says. *For something is wrong, and I must draw it out of him.*

She does not sound weak, or unlike herself. She seems as stern and alert as ever. And yet she will not move. She will not let me reach for the scythe. I grit my teeth and fight her, scrabbling at it. The Nightbringer grabs my wrist.

"You would kill me, my love?" he says. "Your own Meherya?"

Laia, you must escape here. Rehmat's voice rises in pitch, frantic. *I do not know what he has planned, but you must escape quickly.*

I try to back away from him, to reach for the scythe. But I cannot. My body is frozen.

Let me go, Rehmat.

It's not me! Rehmat shouts. *Fight him, Laia! Break free!*

But the Nightbringer holds me still, and though I strive against him, I cannot even blink. Through Rehmat's increasingly frantic exhortations, I hear a voice that has gotten me through so much.

"Laia! I'm here—"

Darin.

He bursts from the woods, but my heart drops, for he hurtles toward the

Nightbringer too swiftly. He is yards away, then just a few feet. His scim sparkles with salt, and he raises it high, hoping, no doubt, that an attack will give me a few moments to escape the Nightbringer's grasp.

"Darin!" I shriek. "Stop!"

The Nightbringer does not even turn his head. He simply releases me, reaches back without looking, and breaks Darin's neck.

The sound.

It has stalked my nightmares for months. This is how my father died. How Lis died. How my mother's hope died.

Darin slumps to the ground, dark blue eyes open, but defiant no longer. He is—

My brother is—

He will never forge another scim or draw whole worlds with a few strokes of charcoal.

No.

He will never laugh until he snorts, or hunt down rare books I read, or shoot Elias dirty looks, or tell me that I am strong.

No.

I will never hold his children. He will never hold mine. He will never offer advice or eat moon cakes or tell stories of Mother and Father and Lis with me.

Because he is dead.

My brother is dead.

Laia, Rehmat cries out in my mind. *Do not kill the Nightbringer. It is what he wants. What he needs. It is the last—*

Her voice fades, for all I can hear is that hellish crack. As I look down at Darin's broken body, I see my mother and my father. I see my sister, Nan,

Pop, Izzi. I see the endless Scholar dead, all of us brutalized children of war who have had everything torn from us. Homes. Names. Families. Freedom. Power. Pride. Hope.

Laia, Rehmat whispers. *Heed me. Please. Listen.*

But I am done listening.

CHAPTER SIXTY-TWO

The Nightbringer

Laia's face contorts with a horror I know well. She trembles, consumed by her suffering. A sound halfway between a snarl and a keen shreds her throat, and seconds later, she flings Rehmat out of her mind. My queen's glowing form sprawls onto the ground behind me.

Laia's hands tighten on the scythe. Rehmat scrambles toward her. Whether her foresight has told her what is to come or she simply knows me best, I do not know. It does not matter.

"Please, Laia," she pleads with the girl. "It's what he wants."

Laia ignores my queen, as do I. Rehmat does not exist. Nor does the battle below. This moment is between me and the girl I loved. The girl who helped to save my people without realizing it. The girl I betrayed and spurned.

For a moment, as she raises the scythe and surges toward me, I am moved by pity. I want to hold her. To tell her that soon, all of our pain will disappear. The world will be consumed by suffering incarnate, and there will be no survivors, not even my own kin.

All will be well, for all will be darkness, I wish to say.

For I did love her, this brave, wild-haired, gold-eyed girl, terrified yet defiant, hesitant yet determined. I loved her for all that she was and all that she would become.

The scythe whistles through the air and slices into my throat. Once. Twice. Three times.

Laia is not careful. The training the Blood Shrike gave her has been forgotten, robbing the grace from this murder. She does not kill me. She kills all of her suffering. All that has been done to her, her family, her people.

But as Keris said, there are some things that do not die.

Pain lances through me, ice penetrating the fire that burns at my core. My legs give way, and I am on my knees, staring up at her, weeping in gratefulness.

Tears streak down her face as she comprehends what she has done. For Laia's soul is intrinsically good. She drops the scythe, her body shuddering. But she does not understand fully. Not yet.

Though it takes great effort, I shift from flame to flesh, to the human form she knew, red-haired and brown-eyed, bleeding, fading away at the edges. Perhaps this, at the end, will bring her some comfort.

"Laia. Laia, my sweet love." Though she will not believe I loved her, it is the truest thing I have ever said.

For though Rehmat lived within her, it is Laia of Serra who walked beside me on the last leg of this long journey. Laia of Serra who defied me and ensured the doom of her people and her world when she swore to defeat me.

The Sea will come for me now. It will punch a hole into this world. It will consume me. After months of hunting and killing and hoarding suffering, I realized that the despair of humans would never equal mine. That the only way to release the maelstrom, to bore a hole between this world and Mauth's, was to pour a thousand years of my own pain into the Sea of Suffering.

"Do not weep, love," I whisper to her. "This world was a cage. Thank you for setting me free."

My body goes rigid, and the Sea is within me now, bursting out from Mauth's dimension and through me into this accursed one. For a moment that feels like an eternity, I stare up at the sky, pale blue, with wisps of cloud ambling across it.

My memory takes me to the River Dusk. Rehmat sits beside me, warm skin pressed to mine, her dark hair piled high on her head. Our children are but babies, and they dance between flame and shadow, tumbling over me, giggling as Rehmat and I point out stories in the clouds.

Such a beautiful day.

And then all that I am, all that I was ruptures and splits. The Sea pours through me, compressing into something minuscule and impossibly heavy. Not darkness but emptiness, the whitest white, the absence of hope and the fullness of suffering—trenchant, tentacled suffering.

On the battleground below and in the Sher Jinnaat, my kind stop and pivot toward me. They feel it, the breach between worlds. They streak up, perhaps hoping to stop it. The Soul Catcher erupts out of the forest, moving beyond the strength of any human, grabbing a stunned Laia, tearing her away from the monstrous *thing* taking form within me.

My corporeal body disintegrates, but I still exist. The Sea wraps itself around me, consumes me. Every last scrap of my essence is suffering. Not the Meherya anymore, nor the King of No Name, nor the Nightbringer.

But something else entirely.

PART FIVE
THE MOTHERS

CHAPTER SIXTY-THREE

The Soul Catcher

I do not know what makes Laia scream so, not until I am nearly to the plateau and see Darin slumped on the ground, his neck broken. Her cry is endless, sorrow upon sorrow, as if it is not just her screaming but a thousand sisters and daughters and mothers who have lost their loved ones to the madness of war.

She whips her scythe across the Nightbringer's throat, hacking at him again and again. But something is wrong, for though his body jerks, his arms are relaxed. He uses no magic to stop her.

Because he has been waiting for this moment. Because if he wants enough suffering to release the Sea, then he is the only creature alive who can provide lifetimes and lifetimes of it, all at once.

His body shifts into his old human form. The air, already leaden, goes still. Far away, in a place beyond the ken of any human, a barrier tears open. Mauth's power, deeply drained, fades entirely as the Sea of Suffering bursts through his wall.

I windwalk to Laia, snatching her away from the Nightbringer as he dissolves, transforming into a viscous gray smoke. A figure kneels within the pall, head tilted back, staring up at the sky. The Nightbringer's spirit, flame eyes dim, seemingly at peace.

Then the Sea of Suffering breaks through him, and he explodes into a vast, spinning cyclone. Darin's body disappears into the maelstrom, then two of the jinn who flitted too close, trees, rocks—

"Rehmat!" My feet slip, and though I windwalk, the pull of the storm is too powerful. A glowing figure appears and, without my having to explain,

453

she merges with Laia. With all my strength, I shove them at the woods, at the trees that bend toward the maelstrom but have not yet broken.

The maelstrom drags my body back, away from Laia. I fight the pull, trying desperately to dig my heels into the ground, but the plateau is smooth, gray rock, and I find no grip. The Sea of Suffering rumbles. Hungry. So hungry.

My will is not weak. I will not die now, not like this. The maelstrom will not steal my life from me. It will not consume me. For I am the Banu al-Mauth, Chosen of Death. I am the Soul Catcher, the Guardian at the Gates.

But all my willpower is nothing against the force of the Sea of Suffering. It wants me and it will have me, for I am mere bones, blood, and pain, held together by skin and sinew. *Laia. Laia, run.* I see her, battling Rehmat as she tries to get back to me, as the jinn queen forces her away.

Our eyes meet for one frantic moment. Then the Sea of Suffering drags me into darkness and claims me, body and soul.

CHAPTER SIXTY-FOUR

Laia

Darin's body disappears into the cyclone. But I have no time to mourn the loss, because I am suddenly aware that Elias is far too close to the storm. I reach for him, screaming when Rehmat holds me back.

You cannot save him, Laia. Her voice is anguished, for she, of all creatures, understands what this means to me. *He gave his life for yours. Do not let it be for nothing.*

I shout his name. Gray eyes meet gold.

He disappears between one moment and the next, as if he never existed. I lose the feeling in my body, and it is only Rehmat, infusing me with strength and forcing me to hold on to a tree branch, who keeps me from being pulled in after Elias.

"Let me go," I cry, for the Nightbringer has won. Our battle is over. *What have I done? What have I unleashed into this world?*

My voice is lost—I can only reel at the knowledge that the Nightbringer is not dead, but transformed into the very suffering he sought to release into the world.

A collective scream from below as the maelstrom sweeps down from the plateau, a ravening gray funnel. Within minutes, it tears through Keris's army, sucking up hundreds, then thousands of soldiers. With each life it claims, it grows larger, feeding off the suffering. A deep, eerie roar sounds from within it, the rage and pain of eons.

We cannot stop it. It will consume all because of me. Because I killed the Nightbringer and gave him what he wanted.

I thought I knew what it was to be alone. All those nights as a child in the great quiet of the Scholar's Quarter, wishing for my parents and my sister. The silence of Blackcliff, when I thought I'd never see Darin again.

But this loneliness is different. Devouring. The loneliness of a girl responsible for the breaking of the world.

The world must be broken before it can be remade, or else the balance will never be restored.

Elias spoke so to me, months ago, outside this very forest. *The world must be broken before it can be remade.*

Before it can be remade.

"Rehmat," I say. "You said you were his chains."

It is what I saw, long ago in my visions. But he is gone now, Laia. Lost in the Sea of Suffering. I failed you. Forgive me, but I failed you. I did not see his intent until it was too late.

"I should have trusted you, Rehmat." I walk to the edge of the plateau. "Because you've been with me my whole life. Because you're a part of me. I trust you now. But you must trust me as well. It was a jinn and a human who began this madness a thousand years ago. A jinn and a human must stop it. I must go to him."

Let me go with you.

"When I am ready," I tell her as she steps out of me, "I will call you. Will you come, Rehmat of the Sher Jinnaat?"

"I will, Laia of Serra."

I turn toward the raging cyclone and summon it with a word.

"Meherya."

It shifts toward me, enraged and hungry, lured by my pain. I wait until it has reached the promontory, until it is close enough to touch.

Then I cast myself into the dark.

CHAPTER SIXTY-FIVE

The Soul Catcher

The Martial man who walks beside me through Blackcliff's halls is familiar, though I've never met him. He has deep brown skin and black hair that falls in waves down his shoulders. It is held back by a dozen thin braids, wrapped in the way of the northern Gens.

His eyes are the color of spring's first shoots, and despite his height, which nears my own, and the imposing breadth of his shoulders, there is a kindness in his face that makes me feel immediately at ease. Though in life he was a Mask, he does not wear one now.

"Hail, my son," he says softly. "It is good to see your face." His eyes travel over me. "You're tall like your grandfather. You have his cheekbones too. My hair, though. My face. A bit of my skin. And . . ." He meets my gaze.

"Her eyes," I say. "You're Arius Harper." *My father*, I do not add.

He inclines his head.

I'm wary of him. All I know about my father is what Avitas told me: Arius Harper loved the snow and never got used to the warm Serran summers. His smile made you feel like the sun had just come out after a long, cold winter. His hands were big and gentle when teaching a young boy to hold a slingshot.

Yet months ago in a dungeon beneath Blackcliff, Keris Veturia spoke one line that has stayed with me.

I wasn't about to let the son kill me after the father had failed.

"You were married when you met my mother."

He nods, and we pass from one of Blackcliff's dim halls into another. "Renatia and I married young," he says. "Too young, like most Martials.

The marriage was arranged, as is common with the northern Gens. We . . . understood each other. When she fell in love with another, I told her to follow her heart. And she did the same for me."

"But you and Keris—did you—" Bleeding hells. How do you ask your father if he forced himself on your mother?

"Keris was not always as she is now," my father says. "She was a Skull when I met her. Nineteen. I was a combat Centurion here." He glances at the oppressive brick walls around us. "She fell in love with me. And I with her."

"The Commandant—" *Is not capable of love*, I want to say. But clearly, that was not always true.

"The Illustrians who killed me made her watch." My father says the words as if he speaks of someone else. "They told her that as a Plebeian, I was not worthy of her. She tried to stop them, but there were too many. It destroyed her. She gave in to her pain."

My father and I leave the dimly lit halls of Blackcliff and step out into the belltower courtyard. I suppress a shudder. My blood irrigated these stones. Mine, and so many others.

"Mauth demanded I give up my emotions before he let me use his magic," I say. "After I did, he helped me suppress them. Washed them away. And I wanted that. Because it let me forget all of the terrible things I've done."

"You cannot forget," my father says. "You must not forget. Mauth erred when he took love from you. When he took anger and joy and regret and sadness and passion."

"He did it because Cain's greed and the Meherya's love led to ruin," I tell my father. "But now Mauth wants the balance restored. He wants the jinn returned. And they will not listen to me."

"Why would they? You cannot convince them unless you first open yourself to all of the joy—" My father touches my shoulder. I see Mamie sing a story, feel Laia's lips on mine, hear the Blood Shrike's joyful laugh.

"And all the suffering," my father adds, and now I see Cain wrench me from Tribe Saif. I scream at the pain of my first whipping, weep as I stab a young man—my first kill.

I want the death to end. It does not. Demetrius and Leander die by my hand. Laia and I escape Serra and I execute soldier after soldier. Kauf burns, and prisoners die in the ensuing havoc. The ghosts escape the Waiting Place and kill thousands.

Murderer! The cave efrit in the Serran catacombs points and screams. *Killer! Death himself! Reaper walking!*

I feel sick. For though I know my sins, I have not faced them. Every time they came to the forefront of my mind, Mauth eased them away.

"How do I go on?" I ask my father. "When I've wrought such devastation? When all I have to give is death?"

I wish for Mauth then, for that quiet rush of calm and distance that his presence gives me. But it is not there. Nothing exists between me and the memories of what I've done but naked horror.

"Steady now, my son," my father says. "What did your grandfather tell you just after the Second Trial?"

"He—he said I'd be trailing ghosts."

"You trail suffering now too," my father says. "Like the Nightbringer. Like your mother."

"Suffering is the cup from which they both drink." I quote Talis as I meet my father's gaze. "It is the language they both speak. And it is the weapon they both wield."

"Yes," he says. "But you do not have to be like them. You have suffered. You have created suffering. You have killed. But you have also paid. With your life, twice over now, and with your heart, with your mind. You have guided thousands of lost souls. You have saved thousands of lives. You have done good in this world. Which will define you? The good? Or the suffering?"

He places a hand on my chest, and I witness what it would have been like to have had him as a father. It is a life so different from my experience that it could only exist in the after. Keris—my mother—holds me, her sweet smile a revelation. My father takes me from her and swings me onto his shoulders. Avitas runs past us, green eyes sparkling as he pulls me down, and I chase him. My parents speak, and though I cannot hear their words, their language is that of love.

Seeing it is a scim to my soul, for I want so much for it to be real. For this to be a memory and not a wish. I want for suffering to have never touched any of us.

"Ah, my boy." My father takes me in his arms. "It was not to be."

He holds me to him for long minutes, and I close my eyes and let myself grieve.

"What if I don't go back." I pull away. "I could stay here. With you. Though—" I glance around, for a mist has rolled in, thick and cool, and Blackcliff's stark walls fade. "Where is *here*? And how are you here? You died years ago."

"I live in your blood, my son. I live in your soul."

"So I'm dead too."

"No," he says. "When the Sea of Suffering broke through the barrier, it took you, but before it could consume you, Mauth snatched you away. You are in between. Walking a scim's edge, as you have for so much of your life. You could fall into the Sea of Suffering and lose yourself in your pain. Or you could return to the world, for you are Soul Catcher still, and you have a duty. The balance must be restored."

"The jinn." *Your duty is to the dead, even to the breaking of the world.* "But the world is—" *Broken*, I was about to say, before I remember my words to Laia months ago. *The world must be broken before it can be remade.*

"Will you help remake the world, my son?" my father asks me.

"I—I begged the jinn already," I say. "I told them the balance couldn't be restored without them. They didn't listen."

"Because it was the Soul Catcher who asked them." My father takes me by the shoulders, and his strength flows into me. "But that is not all of you. Tell me, who are you?"

"I am the Banu al-Mauth." I do not understand him. "I pass the ghosts—"

"Who are you, son of mine?"

"I—" I had a name. What was my name? Laia said it. Over and over she said it. But I cannot recall it anymore.

"Who are you?"

"I am—I—" *Who am I?* "I am born of Keris Veturia," I say. "Son to the *Kehanni* who told the Tale. Beloved to Laia of Serra. Friend to the Blood Shrike. I am brother to Avitas Harper and Shan An-Saif. Grandson to Quin Veturius. I am—"

Two words echo in my head, the last words Cain spoke to me before dying. Words that stir my blood, words that my grandfather taught me when

I was a boy of six and he gave me my name. Words that were burned into me at Blackcliff.

"Always victorious."

Some door bursts open inside me, and Blackcliff fades. The great maelstrom drags at me, as if the conversation with my father had never happened, as if there were only seconds between when the Sea of Suffering took me and now.

I fight my way out, toward a light coruscating distantly. The Sea is so close that I feel it dragging at my feet, but I battle my way up to the world of the living, screaming those two words over and over.

Always victorious.

Always victorious.

Always victorious.

CHAPTER SIXTY-SIX

Keris Veturia

The Blood Shrike will die as her sisters died. As her parents died. Throat slit, a slow enough death that she will walk into the hereafter knowing I defeated her.

Part of me rages against how easily she fell. All she had to do was not love. If she hadn't loved, she'd have been a worthy foe. I'd never have been able to hurt her, no matter who I killed.

Far away, a deep, earth-shuddering growl resounds. I ignore it.

The Shrike clutches her side as I approach, and she is a small, broken thing. A version of myself, if I had allowed defeat to enter my veins like a poison. Me, if I'd let myself love or care.

Give me a foe who challenges me, I shout in my mind. *A foe who makes my body scream, who forces me to think faster, to fight harder.*

"You sad creature," I say. "Look at you. On your knees in the mud. Your army dies around you, and not one of them is brave enough to come to your aid. You weak, broken bird, mourning a man who was dead the moment he called out your name. You are a fool, Helene Aquilla. I thought I trained you better."

She gazes up at me with fading blue eyes, her crown braid dark with blood and mud.

"Lovey."

The word is a whisper, a breath from the Shrike's mouth. My fingers go numb, and my belly twists as if crawling with snakes. I do not recognize the feeling. Not fear, certainly.

How did she learn that name?

"That's what she called you." The Shrike clutches her side ineffectually. If I do not kill her now, she will simply bleed to death.

Suddenly, I do not want her dead. Not yet.

I close the distance between us and crouch to grab her throat.

"Who told you that name?" I hiss. "A Scholar? A Martial—"

"No one living," the Shrike whispers. "A ghost told me. Karinna Veturia. She waits here in the Forest of Dusk, Keris. She has waited for more than thirty years."

As I stare down at the Shrike, the battle still raging beyond us, memories rise, a dark miasma I put to rest a lifetime ago. Blonde hair and eyes as blue as a Serran summer sky. A barge traveling along the River Rei, north, toward Serra. Long hours with her inside a cabin brightly lit with multifaceted Tribal lamps and strewn with pillows of a thousand colors. The comforting *thunk-thunk-thunk* of my father's men keeping guard on the decks.

A green string that danced in her hands, transforming into a broom and cat's whiskers, a pointed hat, a ladder, a man with oysters on his back.

How do you do it? I remember asking.

Magic, little lovey, she said.

Show me, Mama.

Then strange sounds above us. The ominous steps of heavy boots. Shouts and smoke. Fire and unfamiliar faces pouring through the door, grabbing me. Grabbing my mother.

"You were a child." The Blood Shrike brings me back to the killing field. To the battle. "It's not your fault the Resistance took your mother. It's not your fault they hurt her."

I release the Shrike and stagger back. Yes, I was a child. A child who did nothing but watch as Scholar rebels killed off our guards and the barge captain. A child who was struck dumb even as my mother and I were kidnapped and taken to a grimy mountain lair. A child who wept and wailed as, in the room next to mine, those rebels tortured my mother.

A child who did nothing as her mother screamed.

And screamed.

And screamed.

The rebels wanted to get at my father. They wanted to strike a blow at one of the great Martial houses. But by the time he came, she was already dead.

"Your mother tried to be brave, Keris," the Blood Shrike says, and I am so startled she's still talking that I don't bother to silence her. The Shrike should be dead. Why isn't she dead yet?

"Your mother tried to be silent, but the rebels hurt her. The screams scared you at first. She could hear you begging them to stop hurting her."

My own mother. My first love. I cried and then I begged and then I shouted at her to stop screaming because her cries drove me mad. She was weak. So weak. But I was weak too. I could have been silent. I could have been strong for her and I wasn't—

"You were a child, Keris," the Blood Shrike says, though I did not speak my thoughts out loud. Did I?

"What the Scholar rebels did to you and your mother was unforgivable. But what you did—crying out for her to stop screaming—skies, she forgave you for that the moment it happened. She only wants to see you again."

The earth trembles, and a great groan splits the air. But I hardly notice, unable to look away from the Shrike. She staggers to her feet, not defeated as I expected, but grimly determined.

"She waits for you, Keris."

Distantly, I sense the shadow that spins out of the battle seething around us. It slides a blade across the back of my legs, hamstringing me, and I drop — not understanding what has happened. The shadow knocks my scim free and whirls in front of me.

Then it throws its hood back and I am face-to-face with my own handi-work, a ghost out of the past, and my mind goes blank. For the first time in a long time, I am surprised.

"You die by my hand, Keris Veturia," whispers Mirra of Serra, very much alive and still wretchedly scarred, her blue eyes burning with murderous fervor. Her blade is at my throat. "I wanted you to know."

I could stop her. The Blood Shrike sees and screams a warning at Mirra, for instinct had me drawing a blade the moment she stepped out of the fray.

But I think of my mother. *She waits for you, Keris.*

And Mirra's blade finds its mark.

Pain burns through my neck as the Lioness shoves the dagger into my throat, as she drags it across. She does not know my strength, that even bleeding out like this, I can stab her thigh, tear a hole into her that will leave her dead in moments. Even dying, I can destroy her.

But quite suddenly, I am not on the battlefield anymore. I rise above it, above my body, which is nothing but a shell now. Weak and useless and growing cold in the mud.

A great, violent maelstrom swirls down toward my army, tearing through it, annihilating it before my eyes.

"Lovey?"

"Mama." I turn. And it is *her*, my mother, who I have mourned in the forgotten corners of my soul. Her smile is radiant, hitting me with the force of a sunrise. I reach out my hand to her.

She does not take it. A gasp escapes her, shock rippling through her vitreous form as she backs away.

"K-Keris?" She peers at me, bewildered. "You are not her."

"Mama," I whisper. "It's me. Keris. Your lovey."

She drifts farther from me, those familiar blue eyes enormous and stricken.

"No," she says. "You are not my lovey. My lovey is dead."

I reach for her, and a strange, strangled sound comes from my throat. But something else approaches. That great, earth-shattering roar, as if a thousand hounds have been unleashed on my heels. I turn to find myself facing the maelstrom. It consumes the horizon, swirling and ravenous.

I have never seen its like before. And yet, I know it.

"Nightbringer?"

Keris. He utters my name, though he doesn't sound like himself.

"Nightbringer. Bring me back," I say. "I am not finished. The battle yet wages. Nightbringer!"

He does not hear me—or he no longer cares.

"I fought for you," I say. "I would never have forded that river or fought a foe on higher ground if not for you. I *trusted* you—"

The storm rolls on, and I know then that I am dead. That there will be no return.

Fury consumes me—and terror. This betrayal at the last from the only creature I ever trusted—this cannot be borne. This cannot be my death. There is more—there must be more.

"Mama—" I call out, searching for her.

But she is gone, and there is only the hunger and the storm and a suffering that, for me, does not end.

CHAPTER SIXTY-SEVEN

Laia

The maelstrom has teeth, and they sink into my mind, injecting me with memory. My father, my sister, my mother—everyone who has ever been taken from me.

The memories fade, replaced by others I do not recognize. First a few, then hundreds, then thousands swirling around me. Story upon story. Sorrow upon sorrow.

Though the bodies of the dead have disappeared, I am still corporeal, and I let myself fade into the nothingness. This is a jinn-made madness and I have had a jinn living within me for a long time.

But she is in you no more, the maelstrom hisses. *You are alone. I will consume you, Laia of Serra. For all is suffering and suffering is all.*

Flickers alight near my vision. Sweet laughter, and small figures of flame—Rehmat's children, I realize. The Nightbringer's children. Though I want to look away, I make myself watch their family, their joy. I make myself witness their light go out.

This maelstrom—it is all him. He has subsumed the suffering of generations, combined it with his own. He was right. For him, the world was a cage. Now he is everywhere. Living in all of these memories, all of this suffering. Lost in it.

But even a maelstrom has a center. A heart. I must find it.

Each step takes an eon as memories shriek past me. *Laia.* I whip my head around, for it is Darin's voice howling out of the darkness. He says something, and I cannot understand it. I know if I reach out to him, we will be reunited. Death will have claimed us all—Darin and Father and Mother and Lis and Nan and Pop. When was the last time the seven of us were together and happy?

When was the last time we were not running, or hiding, or whispering so the Empire would not catch us? I do not remember. All I remember is fear. Mother and Father leaving and the ache of their loss. The knowledge, that day when Nan howled for her daughter, that I would never see my parents again.

But Mother came back. She came back and she fought for me, and I hold on to her words. *I love you, Laia.* I immerse myself in her love. For, tortured as it was, it was still love, in the only way she could give it to me.

All is suffering, the maelstrom says. *And suffering is all.*

How many more has this cyclone swallowed? Is anyone left? I force myself to think practically. There must be. And as long as even one person remains, they are worth fighting for.

One step in front of the other, I battle my way through the swirling wind. If I stop fighting, for even one second, I am lost.

But then, the Nightbringer is also lost. Perhaps if I accept it, we will end up in the same place.

I let go.

I expect the storm to tear at me, but instead I float up and drift, a leaf in the wind. The Nightbringer's memories flow through me. All the years and loves I did not see. All that he has endured. My heart shudders at the loneliness. Once before, I saw a glimpse of this, when I gave him the armlet. Now the abyss of his pain yawns before me, and there is no place to hide.

I realize I am circling something—the center of the maelstrom. Once, twice, each revolution shorter, until the mist settles and I can make out a scrap of bright white—a tear between worlds, through which sorrow after sorrow explodes. Each one breathes, and they claw at each other in a frenzy of cannibalistic hunger.

At the heart of the rent, a thin scrap of soul writhes in torment, vaguely human-shaped, a thousand bruised colors.

The Nightbringer. Or whatever it is that he has become.

"All the world will fall," I whisper to him. If I cannot get him to close the tear between worlds, we are lost. "And I know you do not want that. You must stop."

"What would a child know of such things?" the Nightbringer says. "You are dew on a blade of grass fresh born. I am the earth itself."

The maelstrom buffets me, and I move closer to the Nightbringer. I call his name. But he ignores me, enmeshed in his pain. Rehmat's words come back to me.

His strength is in his name. And his weakness. His past and his present.

Nightbringer was the name humans gave him. Along with *the King of No Name*. But before that, he had another name.

"Meherya," I say. "Beloved."

He howls then, an echoing cry that breaks something inside me. But still, he hides away, for he is not the Beloved anymore either. He has turned his back on his duty and humanity. On Mauth.

But in truth, humanity turned against him first. And Mauth, who should have loved the Meherya best, did nothing when his son and all that he cherished were destroyed. The Nightbringer gave Mauth everything—and Mauth repaid him with a thousand years of torment.

And how did I, the one she loved the best, repay her? How did I thank the human who gave me everything?

Mamie's words, as she became the Nightbringer and told me his tale. As she told me of the woman Husani. The first—and perhaps only—mother the Nightbringer ever knew.

"Nirbara," I whisper. "Forsaken."

He turns.

"Forsaken by humans and by Mauth," I say, and the maelstrom grows more violent with each word. "Forsaken by the Scholars, who you sought only to help and who stole all that you loved. Forsaken by Rehmat, who left you alone with all of your pain. What a terrible thing love is, when this is the cost. But it does not have to be this way. There are millions who might yet live, who might yet love, if only you returned this suffering to Mauth."

"It is done," the Forsaken says. "You do not know pain like mine, child. All is suffering and suffering is all. Let it destroy the world."

"I know suffering," I say, and he raises his head, a hiss on his lips. But I hold open my hands. "You think because you were a jinn, you felt more deeply? Because you were the Beloved, your grief is greater than my own? It is not, Nirbara. For I—I was beloved too."

I struggle to speak, to put all the darkness in my life, all the things I have never understood, into words. "I was beloved to my mother and my father. I was beloved to my sister and my brother and my grandparents. I was beloved to Elias. I was beloved to you."

I wish I could touch him. I wish he could feel what I feel.

"Perhaps you and I are doomed." My voice is raw, aching. "Doomed to always hurt. But what we do with that hurt is our choice. I cannot hate. Not forever. Are you not tired of it, Nirbara? Do you not seek rest?"

He looks at me and shudders, so alone. So I reach out and pull together the shreds that remain of him. The scraps solidify into the shape of a child, a young boy with brown eyes, and when I pull him into my arms, he collapses. Together we weep over all we have done and all that has been done to us. Though I do not speak, I pour what love I have into this, the truest manifestation of a broken creature.

How long since anyone offered him comfort? How different would his life be if the greed of man had not led to his madness, and the hurt of millions?

We kneel, locked in that embrace as the suffering of years swirls around us. Until he pulls away, and he is a child no longer, but a man. He is a shadow I recognize, who pulses with the gravity of thousands of years and thousands of souls. I see all that he has done and I choose not to hate him.

The maelstrom around us slows.

"You didn't deserve this," I whisper to him. "None of it. But those you hurt, they didn't deserve it either. End this madness. Release your pain. Stop fighting Mauth."

Rage sparks in his eyes at the mention of his father. "Mauth would have us forget," the Forsaken says. "He would take the pain of the world and lock it away—"

"So that we might be free of it," I say. "But I will not forget."

Rehmat. I call to her with all the force of my mind. Her light is a beacon through the swirling silver mist, and in a moment, she is beside me.

But she does not speak to me or even look to me. She has eyes only for her Meherya.

"My beloved," she murmurs. "Come to me now, for I have waited long years for this, our last union. Come now, and give me your pain. I must bind you, that you may never release this agony upon the world again. You must submit to me."

"Finally, Rehmat," the Meherya says, "I understand the meaning of your name." He turns to me. "Do not forget the story, Laia of Serra," he says. "Vow it."

Sabaa Tahir

"I swear I will not forget," I say. "Nor will my children. Nor theirs. As long as one of my line draws breath, Meherya, the Tale will be told."

The very air shudders with the force of the vow, and a deep crack echoes beneath me, as if the axis of the earth has shifted. I wonder what I have bequeathed to my own blood.

The Meherya lifts his hand to my face, and I feel his sorrow and his love, extant still, despite all that has happened.

Then he turns to Rehmat, who opens her arms, drawing him to her. Her gold body shudders and splits, exploding into hundreds of burning ropes, inexorable as they wrap around him tighter and tighter. He does not resist. He is lost within the binding as it drains him of his pain, his suffering, his power—and releases it back to Mauth.

The maelstrom slows, dissolving first at the edges as it drains back through the rift the Meherya opened. It thins, disappearing faster and faster, swirling blue, then gray, then white, until finally there is nothing left.

I stand upon the promontory, though it is riven down the middle as if struck by a giant hammer. The rift is only a few feet away from me, closing before my eyes.

Rehmat is nowhere to be seen. I find that I regret her loss. I regret not being able to say goodbye and not thanking her. And I regret that she never told me the meaning of her name.

A voice whispers in my ear. "*Mercy*," she says. "My name means *mercy*."

Then the Queen of the Jinn is gone, dragging her prisoner with her to some unknown plane where I cannot follow. In that moment, the wind ceases. All falls silent. All goes still.

For the Beloved who woke with the dawning of the world is no more. And for a single, anguished moment, the earth itself mourns him.

473

CHAPTER SIXTY-EIGHT

The Soul Catcher

The plateau splits down the middle as I emerge from the maelstrom. The earth shudders with the force of it, a tremor rippling through the Waiting Place, eliciting great arboreal groans from the woods.

The shaking drops me to my knees, and I slide back toward the tree line. A figure emerges from the cyclone, and, as suddenly as the storm entered this dimension, it drains away, as if through a crack in the air. All is silent. Even the trees do not move.

Then the figure at the edge of the plateau collapses, and the world breathes again. I scramble to my feet, and at the sound, she turns.

"Are—are you real?" She half lifts her hand, and in five steps, I have reached her and pulled her to me, shaking in relief because she is impossibly, miraculously alive. The rock of the plateau groans, and in moments I have windwalked us away from it, down the tree line to the edge of the jinn grove.

"He's gone," Laia whispers when we stop. "Rehmat chained him. At the end he was destroyed, Elias." She looks down at her hands, and her eyes fill, voice cracking. "He killed my brother. Darin is d-dead."

What can I say to her that will comfort her? She defeated a creature that defies description—more than a king, more than a jinn, more than a foe. And in the process, she lost the only family she had left in this world.

A wind stirs the trees behind us, and the first of the Tala tree blossoms detach and swirl through the air.

"*In flowerfall, the orphan will bow to the scythe,*" she says. "*In flowerfall, the daughter will pay a blood tithe.*" Her dark eyes are red and dull. "Skies-forsaken foretellings."

"The same foretelling said I would die." I remember the jinn's prophecy as clearly as if she spoke it yesterday. *The son of shadow and heir of death will fight and fail with his final breath.*

"But it didn't say I'd find my way back." I pull Laia close. "And it didn't say that you'd win."

"Have we won?" Laia says as we stare out at the jinn grove. Soldiers on both sides of the escarpment stumble to their feet, still shaken from the maelstrom. Musa has an arm under the Blood Shrike's shoulders, and together they stagger away from the front line, anguish emanating from both. Spiro and Gibran carry an injured Afya toward the infirmary tents.

Laia and I walk to the edge of the escarpment, and she gasps, for Keris's army appears to have taken the brunt of the maelstrom's wrath. A deep gash in the earth and a few pockets of stunned-looking soldiers are all that remain of the Commandant's one-massive host.

As for Keris herself, her standard flaps in the wind near the edge of the escarpment. Beside it, she lies faceup, blonde hair streaked with mud, her throat bloody, gray eyes fixed on the sky.

Dead.

Laia releases me, her hand on her mouth. I kneel beside the body of my mother, whose heart and mind will now forever be a cipher. Despite her violence, her implacable hatred, I grieve her loss. Her skin is cold and soft beneath my hands as I close her eyes. My eyes.

Stay far from the Nightbringer, Ilyaas. Such a strange and unexpected warning. Why did she caution me, when she spent so many years trying to kill me?

Perhaps she was never trying to kill me. Perhaps she was trying to kill some part of herself. But I will never know. Not truly.

Just a few feet away, Avitas Harper lies dead too. Now I understand the Blood Shrike's devastation. We had one meaningful conversation, Avitas and I. It was not enough.

Even as my heart aches for my brother and my mother, Mauth's magic swells, a wave of forgetting that he will unleash to wash away the mess in my mind.

"No," I whisper, knowing that he can hear me. "My duty is not yet done. I must restore the balance."

You will speak to the jinn. Mauth has returned to full power, and his voice thunders in my bones. *But you must be clear of mind and heart, Soul Catcher. Not distracted by love and regret and hope.*

"That is *exactly* what I must be distracted by," I tell him. "Love and regret and hope are all I can offer."

A long silence as he mulls it over. Laia watches me knowingly—the one person on this earth who understands the bone-deep intrusion of having a supernatural voice in your head that is not your own.

Do not fail me, Banu al-Mauth.

Behind me, the air hisses as hundreds of scims leave their scabbards.

"Look at that, bleeding hells—"

"Must be scores of them living in that city—"

Down in the Sher Jinnaat, across the gash in the earth, figures emerge. Most are in human form, though some wear their shadows, and others swirl in full flame.

"Soul Catcher." The Blood Shrike limps toward me. Behind her, our ranks of Tribesmen, Scholars, and Martials are already forming up again into neat lines. Her gaze is fixed on the jinn watching us from the Sher Jinnaat.

"The catapults. There are two still working." She raises her voice. "Load the salt—"

But I turn on her, Mauth's power filling me, and my voice booms out across the jinn grove.

"You will not touch them."

The Blood Shrike looks at me in surprise. As the rest of our men realize what I am saying, an angry mutter rises.

"We cannot let what they've done stand, Soul Catcher," the Blood Shrike says. "Their leader is dead. Their human minions are dead or scattered. This is our chance."

"They are not the Nightbringer," I say. "The Augurs imprisoned them for a thousand years for doing nothing more than defending their borders. Unless you wish to punish yourself for defending Antium against invaders?"

"You saw what they can do at full strength. Such a threat—"

"We can treat with them," I say. "This is what the Augurs worked toward, Blood Shrike. The foretellings, the raising of Blackcliff, the Trials. All their machinations were to bring us to this moment. They knew there was going to be a war years ago. Ever since they stole the jinn's magic, they've been trying to make up for the evil they did. But they are not here to see it through." I look at Laia and the Shrike in turn. "That falls to us."

As I regard them, I wonder at the strange twists of fate that have led us here. The impossibility of this outcome, of the three of us alive, together, and standing before a host of the creatures desperately needed to restore balance to our world.

"Right." Laia takes my hand in her left, and the Blood Shrike's in her right. "Let's get on with this."

Hand in hand, we make our way down the escarpment and to the waiting jinn. We stop at a far enough distance that they don't feel threatened.

"Where is he?" Umber steps forward, recognizable only by her wrathful voice and the glaive in her hand. Even her eyes have dimmed, her fire a bare flicker of what it was in the battle.

"He is gone." Laia steps forward. "Bound by Rehmat, who gave her life so yours might be spared. For he would have destroyed this world, and there is yet much good in it."

"No." Umber crumples, weeping, not in rage as I expected, but in desolation. "No—he loved us—"

But the other jinn are silent, for they bore witness. They saw what he became.

"You are needed in this world," Laia goes on. "You should not be driven into hiding or to war by the greed of a human king from a thousand years ago. The jinn were wronged. The Nightbringer avenged that wrong. Let it end now."

"What do you wish us to do?" The jinn called Faaz steps forward, brown-haired and dark-eyed in his human form. "Serve your kind again? You will only return to thieve our powers."

"We will not." The Blood Shrike steps forward. "I am Blood Shrike of the Martial Empire and Regent to Emperor Zacharias. In his name, I vow that no Martial shall cross the border of the Waiting Place unless you will it, and no Martial shall raise arms against you, unless in defense. We will make no treaty with any nation that does not agree to do the same."

I look at the Shrike in surprise, but then consider what she said to me only days ago. *Another war. Will it ever end, Soul Catcher? Or will this be the legacy I leave my nephew?*

"We cannot go back." The crowd parts to let a jinn through. He is thin and stoop-shouldered, heavily cloaked, but I recognize him instantly. Maro—the jinn who siphoned the ghosts for the Meherya, who did nothing as thousands upon thousands of humans died. "Not after all we have done," he says. "Not after all that has been done to us."

"You can." I think of my father. "I have saved lives and taken them. I have been whipped and beaten and broken down. I have failed the world, failed in my duty. My mistakes will haunt me until I die. But I can still do good. I can pass the ghosts. I can vow to never make the same mistakes again."

In that moment, something shifts in the air, as if a door has opened on a long-shut room. Spirits flow from Mauth's realm into the Waiting Place. Hundreds—no, thousands. All those who died here, those who fed the Sea of Suffering this day.

The force of their presence nearly brings me to my knees. They will stay away from the jinn grove, for they dislike it as much as the jinn themselves. But soon enough, their cries will require the humans to find some sort of refuge.

As one, the jinn look to the trees. Maro steps toward them, perhaps feeling the same compulsion that is upon me. Then he shakes himself and turns, walking back into the Sher Jinnaat. Most of the jinn follow him.

But not all.

The jinn Talis stands alone, his human body slowly slipping into a deep carmine flame with a cerulean heart. He raises his hand to the trees, beckoning.

A group of spirits emerge and flow to him. The red of his flame deepens, and he walks with them into the Sher Jinnaat, head tilted as they speak their pain. When he reaches the first buildings, he stops and turns.

"Leave the bodies, Banu al-Mauth," he says. "They will not be tampered with. I will see them buried." Then he is gone, the knot of ghosts trailing after.

As he leaves, jinn voices rise on the air, a chorus with layer upon layer of melody, hair-raising and beautiful. The air quivers with the force of their song, and Mauth speaks.

A lament for the Meherya, he says. *An elegy for their fallen king.*

"Only one returned out of hundreds, Mauth." I glance toward the city, where Talis has disappeared. "I failed you."

Without you, all would have been lost, Banu al-Mauth. One is a beginning. And for now, that is enough.

«« «

Hundreds are injured and thousands are dead. The ghosts call to me, begging to be seen, heard, sent to the other side. But I must speak with Mamie and Shan, with Afya and Spiro, with Gibran and Aubarit. I must spend time with the *Fakirs* and *Fakiras* and give them guidance on how to move forward with so many of their elders lost. Quin, bleeding from a dozen wounds in the infirmary, demands my presence, and it takes hours to persuade the Paters to leave the bodies of the dead.

But by dawn the morning after the battle, the army is ready to march, and I have spoken with everyone I need to.

Well. Almost everyone.

Laia finds me near the road that will lead the army out of the Waiting Place. The Blood Shrike, Musa, and I are discussing how the troops should handle any rogue ghosts. When Laia appears, Musa kicks the Shrike in the ankle.

"What the *hells*, Musa—oh—"

The Shrike gives me a dark look—*Don't you hurt her, Elias*—and disappears with the Scholar man.

480

"You will not ride with us?" Laia pulls me toward the trees, for though Rehmat is gone, Laia's magic remains. Some part of the jinn queen still lives within her—within Musa and the Blood Shrike. Enough that most of the ghosts leave them be.

"The spirits call." I want to take her hands but restrain myself. Nothing will make this easier. There's no reason to make it more difficult. "Even with Talis, there are too many ghosts to pass."

I reach into my pocket. The armlet that she returned months ago is still with me, though far more intricately carved than before, as I've been working on it in every quiet moment I've had. Do I give it to her? Will she reject it? It's not done yet. Perhaps I should wait.

"Laia—"

"I do not—"

We speak at the same time, and I gesture for her to go first.

"I do not want you to grieve what we have, Elias." She lifts her hand as a Tala blossom drifts into it. "You are alive. Wherever I am, I will know that somewhere in the world, you exist, and that you are at peace. That is enough for me."

"Well, it might be enough for you," a voice rasps from the shadows of the forest, "but it's not enough for me."

Laia and I both stare for long moments at the figure that emerges from the shadows, small and white-haired, with ocean-blue eyes that are hard as agate, but that soften at the sight of her daughter.

"How—" Laia finally manages to choke out. "The Karkauns—"

"Didn't bother checking my body," Mirra of Serra says. "And I touched the Star, remember? We're tough to kill."

"But why did you not come to me?" Laia says. "Why would you not try to find me?"

"Because revenge mattered to me more than you," Mirra says. Laia, stunned, steps back. "I was never a good m-m-mother, girl. You know that. I knew no one would have a shot against the Bitch of Blackcliff unless she wasn't expecting them. Her spies told her I was dead. So I stayed dead. The only ones who knew I lived were Harper, who gave me a place to sleep in Antium, and the Blood Shrike."

At the outrage on Laia's face, Mirra holds up her hand. "Don't go getting angry at her now," she says. "Helped her in the tunnels of Antium, but she didn't know it was me. She didn't know I was alive until the night before the battle. After I'd had a little chat with Karinna."

"I didn't sense you—" I begin, and Mirra laughs.

"There were thousands of humans in this forest, boy," she says. "What was one more? I could trust Harper to keep his thoughts to himself. Had a mind like a steel trap, that boy did. As for the Shrike, I ordered her to keep her mouth shut—to not even think my name, lest the Nightbringer pick it out of her head."

"I believe your exact phrasing was 'If you breathe a word of this to anyone, girl, I'll gut you first, then wear your skin as a cape.'"

The Blood Shrike appears behind us. "I'm sorry." She looks worriedly at Laia, as if expecting her anger. "It was the only way to kill Keris."

Laia throws herself at her mother, who rocks back, surprised, before lifting her hands and holding her daughter close.

"I'm not alone." Laia buries her face in her mother's hair. "I thought I was all that was left of us."

My eyes get hot, and the Blood Shrike looks away, rubbing her hand against her cheeks and muttering about mud in her lashes.

"You're not alone," Mirra says, and her voice is gentler now. "And if I have anything to do with it, you never will be again." She detaches herself from Laia and turns to me.

"Soul Catcher. Can you call your master?"

"Call?" I say. "Mauth?" I should stop using single syllables. The mother of the woman I love probably thinks I'm dim.

"Yes." Mirra speaks slowly. "The jinn queen mentioned a certain vow you made to Mauth."

"You knew Rehmat?" Laia says.

"A moment, cricket." Mirra holds up a hand, gaze fixed on me. "Rehmat told me of the vow. Something about serving Mauth for all eternity. I'd like to speak with him about it. Call him."

Mauth? I reach out with my mind, and when there is no answer, I shake my head. Mirra snarls with such force that Laia, the Shrike, and I all flinch.

"Don't you ignore me, you pretentious brute," Mirra says to the forest. "I've walked the edge of your realm more times that I can count. I've stared into the Sea. You told the boy he will not be free of his vow until a human takes his place. Well, here I am. Ready to take over. And you don't even have to bring me back to life."

A long silence, and then Mauth's ancient rumble. *Do you know what it is you ask for, Lioness?*

Laia looks between Mirra and me, for she cannot hear Mauth. But before I can explain, Mirra answers.

"A few months of training from my future son-in-law—" She shoves me in the chest, and I nearly choke. Laia's cheeks turn red, and the Blood Shrike smiles for the first time in an age.

"The occasional argument with our fiery friends down in the Sher Jinnaat. A lot of excellent Tribal food, since I'll be their Bani al-Mauth.

And an eternity in this forest, passing on ghosts to the other side."

"Wait," Laia says frantically. "Just a moment. You cannot—"

"You want me in the world of the living instead?" Mirra asks. "Weighing it down with my hate? I killed Keris Veturia. Slid a dagger through her throat and watched her die. But all I dream about is raising her from the dead so I can do it again." Her voice drops to a whisper. "I am haunted, girl. By your f-f-father's eyes. Your sis-sister's voice. Dar—dar—" The Lioness shudders. "Your b-brother's laugh," she finally says. "I do not belong among the living. To be a Soul Catcher is to feel remorse, the jinn queen said. I am made of it. Let me go. Let me do some good."

Lioness. Mauth speaks before Laia can. *Will you, like the Banu al-Mauth, seek to hold to who you were? Or will you release your past, so that you might pass the ghosts more easily?*

"Just free the boy, Mauth. I'll do whatever you bleeding want." Mirra considers. "Except forget her." She nods to Laia.

You are her mother, Lioness. No power in the universe could wrest her from your heart. She is of you. Very well. Mirra of Serra, kinslayer and Lioness, hear me. To serve the Waiting Place is to light the way for the weak, the weary, the fallen, and the forgotten in the darkness that follows death. You will be bound to me until another is worthy enough to release you. Do you submit?

I notice that he does not threaten to punish Mirra for leaving the forest. Nor does he call her the ruler of the Waiting Place, as he did me.

Perhaps she won't be bound for an eternity after all.

"I submit," Mirra says.

Her vow is unlike mine, for Mauth does not need to bring her back to life. Still, her body goes rigid, and I know what she feels—the power of Mauth passing into her as he gives her a touch of magic that he can never take away.

A moment later, the Lioness shakes herself and turns to me.

"Right, then," she says. "You best start telling me what I need to know. And since you won't be Soul Catcher for much longer, don't mind me if call you Elias."

"The Mother watches over them all," I say. Cain and his bleeding prophecy. "I thought the Augur was talking about the Commandant. But it was you. You're the Mother."

"That I am, Elias." The Lioness takes her daughter's fingers in one hand and mine in the other. "That I am."

CHAPTER SIXTY-NINE

The Blood Shrike

Duty first, unto death. I learned those words at the age of six from my father, on the night the Augurs took me to Blackcliff.

Duty can be a burden, my daughter. My father knelt before me, his hands on my shoulders. He brushed his thumbs against my eyes, so the Augurs would not see my tears. *Or it can be an ally. It is your choice.*

After the battle in the Waiting Place, duty carries me through the negotiations with Keris's generals and the surrender of what is left of her forces. It keeps me flinty-eyed when Elias thanks and dismisses his army of Tribespeople and efrits, and asks me to take mine from the forest.

Duty gives me a straight back when Musa, his own eyes red at the loss of Darin, finds me and takes me to a line of bodies to be buried in the jinn grove.

But when I look down at the still form of Avitas Harper, duty does not hold me up. It offers me no comfort.

My knees sink into the mud on which he lies, though I do not remember kneeling. His face is as serene in repose as it was in life. But there is no mistaking that he is dead. Even with a cloak pulled over the vicious gash delivered him by Keris, he is blood-spattered, cut and bruised in a dozen places.

I reach out my hand to touch Harper's face, but pull it back at the last moment. Not long ago, he drove the chill from my bones, from my heart. But now he will feel cold, for Death has my love and all his warmth is gone from this world.

Damn you, I shout at him in my head. *Damn you for not being faster. For not loving me less. For not being locked in some other battle so you didn't have to risk yourself in mine.*

I do not say those things. I look into his face and seek—I do not know. An answer. A reason for all that has happened. Some meaning.

But sometimes, there is no reason. Sometimes you kill and you hate killing but you are a soldier through and through so you keep killing. Your friends die. Your lovers die. And what you have at the end of your life is not the surety that you did it for some grand reason, but the hard knowledge that something was taken from you and you also gave it away. And you know you will carry that weight with you always. For it is a regret that only death can relieve.

I put my hand on Harper's heart, and lift his to mine.

"You got there first, my love," I whisper. "I envy you so. For how will I endure without you?"

I hear no answer to my question, only his eyes that will remain forever closed, the stillness of his body beneath my hand, and the rain falling cold upon us.

« « «

It takes three days to get the army out of the forest—and another two and a half weeks to make our way across the rolling green hills of the Empire to the Estium garrison, tucked into a curve of the River Taius.

"Camp is set, Shrike." Quin Veturius, impeccable as always, finds me in my tent in the middle of the encampment. "Do you wish to have quarters readied in the garrison?"

I wish to be left alone, but my tent is full. Laia arrived first, bringing with her a tin of mango jam she dug up from skies-know-where. She's been spreading it on flatbread, with a soft white cheese on top, quietly handing it to whoever comes into the tent.

Musa is here too, gesturing with the flatbread while flirting with Afya Ara-Nur. The Tribeswoman is still pale from her injury, wincing even as she laughs. Mamie looks amused while Spiro Teluman watches with a dark glare. The smith shouldn't worry. Musa's heart is as shattered as mine.

"Blood Shrike?"

I bring my attention back to Quin, pulling him away from the others so they aren't disturbed. "No need for quarters in the garrison," I tell him. "Has everyone arrived?"

"We wait only on the Emperor," Quin says. The old man is a bit paler than before, having barely survived a brutal fight with his daughter.

"I have something for you," he tells me, fishing a silver object out of his cloak. He opens his hand to reveal a mask.

"Elias's," he says. "You gave it to me last year. It will join with you, I think. The way it never joined with my grandson."

I reach out to touch the living metal, warm and pliant. What a comfort it would be to wear a mask again, to remind all who encounter me of what I am.

"I thank you, Quin." I run a finger along the pale slashes that mark my cheeks. "But I've gotten used to the scars."

He nods and pockets it, before taking in my mud-spattered armor, my scuffed boots. About the only part of me that's neat is my hair, and only because Laia insisted on re-braiding it while I was eating.

"A bit of mud on my armor won't hurt, Quin," I say. "It will remind the Paters that we just won a battle."

"Your call," he says. "The Emperor is en route and will be here within the hour. We have a pavilion ready for you and him in the garrison's training grounds. Keris's generals are chained and waiting to swear fealty there. I've had the troops form up, as you requested."

Laia and the others join me, and we make our way through the empty camp, toward the vast training grounds, wide enough to accommodate the army: three thousand Martials and Scholars, and another two thousand Tribespeople—some of whom will settle in Estium while the Empire helps rebuild the cities of the Tribal desert.

A viewing area overlooks the grounds, and I make for a black canopy slung over a dozen chairs. Only a few yards away, Keris's allies kneel in a row, chained to rings in the earth.

The clatter of hooves breaks up the buzz of conversation. A column of Masks led by Dex enters the grounds, with a carriage following. When it rolls to a stop, Coralia and Mariana Farrar emerge, Zacharias held to Coralia's shoulder. He is fast asleep. Tas pops out afterward, and when he sees Laia, he runs straight for her.

"You're alive!" He nearly bowls her over with the force of his hug. "Rallius owes me and Dex ten marks. Rallius—" The boy runs back to the big Mask, who shifts uneasily under Laia's flinty gaze.

I'm inclined to run to my nephew, but I merely quicken my step, meeting him at the pavilion. Mariana murmurs a greeting, while Coralia drops into a half curtsy.

"Hail, Blood Shrike," she says. "He was in a bit of a mood when he fell asleep."

"Likely he's as excited as I am about sitting through this." I kiss my nephew gently on the head, hoping he'll sleep through what will no doubt be a great deal of gibbering and groveling from Keris's former allies.

Coralia winces when Zacharias shifts, fearful he will wake. But to my surprise, Mamie steps forward and takes the child with firm hands. He opens his eyes, looks around, and scowls, his tiny nose red.

"He should not be in such thin clothing." Mamie glowers at Coralia and Mariana, and holds a hand out to Laia. The Scholar offers her cloak without a moment's hesitation. Mamie wraps Zacharias in it, offering him her brilliant smile. He stares at her as if she is the most fascinating person he's ever seen. Then he smiles back.

"Do not worry for the child." Mamie dismisses Coralia and Mariana with a wave. "I will make sure he does not disturb you."

"Blood Shrike." Musa settles into a seat behind me and looks to the other end of the grounds. "Your audience has arrived."

I follow his gaze to the half a hundred Scholars in attendance—many familiar from Antium. Close by, hundreds of finely dressed men and women file into the viewing area. Paters and Maters from all over the Empire. Some are my allies, and some were Keris's. There are as many Mercators and Plebeians as there are Illustrians. All told, they represent nearly five hundred of the Empire's most powerful families.

Quin glances over and I nod approvingly. When those Paters and Maters witness Keris's most stalwart allies on their knees, they will know to never challenge our emperor again.

The Tribal *Zaldars* appear soon after, and once they are seated, Quin steps out from the pavilion.

"Paters and Maters, Scholars and Tribespeople—I beg your attention." Quin's voice booms across the training field and up the terraced seats.

"Five centuries ago," Quin says, "Taius was named Imperator Invictus for his prowess in battle. In time, he was named Emperor. Not because of his family. Not because he ruled by fear. And not because a group of white-haired mystics decided they knew what was best for the Empire. Taius was hailed Imperator Invictus because when our people suffered, he saved them. When they were divided, he united them."

I frown at Quin and glance at the Scholars. "United them" is a rather inaccurate way of saying "decimated and enslaved our enemy." This was not the speech he and I agreed upon.

"Like Taius, Helene Aquilla fought for our people—"

I start. Quin did not call me Blood Shrike. Instantly, I understand his intention.

"Quin," I hiss.

But the old man thunders on. "Helene Aquilla could have left Antium to suffer the yoke of Karkaun rulership," he says. "Instead, she rallied her troops and liberated the city. Helene Aquilla could have fallen to despair when her sister, the Empress Regent, was killed. Instead, she called up her army to seek revenge on the greatest traitor the Empire has ever known— Keris Veturia. Helene Aquilla could have stolen back the Empire for her nephew. Instead, she fought for all of the living—Scholars, Tribespeople, and Martials alike."

"Gird your loins, Shrike." Musa gives me a sidelong glance. "You're about to get quite the promotion."

"We have been torn asunder by civil war," Quin goes on. "A fourth of our standing army lies dead. We betrayed and destroyed cities in our own protectorate. Our Empire stands on the brink of dissolution. We do not need a regent. We need an Imperator Invictus. We need an empress."

He turns and points at me. "And there she stands."

At that moment, the sun, drifting in and out of the clouds all morning, breaks through, washing the training ground and the river beyond in pale light.

"Witness!" Quin isn't one to waste a moment of drama. "Witness how the skies crown her!"

The sun hits my braid and the crowd titters in awe. A part of me wishes Laia hadn't re-braided it, for if my hair was a mess, perhaps this nonsense would end.

"*Empress! Empress!*" The chant begins with the Martial army. It spreads to the leaders of the Plebeian Gens. Then the Illustrians. The Mercators.

The Scholars remain silent. So do the Tribespeople.

As they should. For I cannot accept the crown. My nephew still lives. *He* is Emperor, no matter what Quin says.

"I don't want this." I glare at Quin. "I don't even want to be the bleeding regent. We *have* an emperor."

"Shrike." Quin lowers his voice. "Your first duty is not to yourself or your Gens or even your nephew. It is to the Empire. We need your strength. Your wisdom."

The Martials still shout. "*Empress! Empress! Empress!*"

Harper, I think. *What the bleeding hells do I do? What do I say?* But he is not here. Instead, Laia speaks up from beside me.

"The Augur prophecy, Helene." And before I can tell her to call me Shrike, she grasps my shoulder, turning me toward her. "Do you remember? *It was never one. It was always three. The Blood Shrike is the first. Laia of Serra, the second. And the Soul Catcher is the last.* What is your beginning, Shrike? It is Blackcliff. And what are the words carved on Blackcliff's belltower?"

"*From among the battle-hardened youth there shall rise the Foretold, the*

Greatest Emperor, scourge of our enemies, commander of a host most devastating." I feel faint as I say it, because now, I see what Laia is getting at. For in her way, she, too, survived Blackcliff. She, too, is a battle-hardened youth.

The chanting goes on, the crowd hardly noticing the conversation going on beneath the pavilion."*And the Empire shall be made whole.*"

"I'm the second: the scourge," Laia says. "Elias was the last: the commander. And you—"

"The first," I say faintly. The Greatest Emperor. So Cain had known. Skies, he as good as told me, months ago, the first time I sought him out in his blasted cave.

You are my masterpiece, Helene Aquilla, he'd said, *but I have just begun. If you survive, you shall be a force to be reckoned with in this world.*

"*Empress! Empress!*"

"The Augurs knew, Helene," Laia says. "This is your destiny. *And the Empire shall be made whole.* It means you can change things. Make them better."

"But will you?" Afya says. "Will you renegotiate the Tribes' place in the Empire, Helene Aquilla? The Scholars'? If you don't, we cannot support you."

"I will," I say, for if I make this promise, I'll have to keep it. *And the Empire shall be made whole.* "I swear it."

"*Empress! Empress! Empress!*"

The sound echoes in my head, too heavy a burden, and I raise my hands, desperate for it to stop.

"If you wish me to be your empress," I call out, "then you must first know my heart." *Father,* I think. *Wherever you are, please give me the words.* "In the Empire's darkest hour, it was not a Martial who stood with

493

me, but a Scholar rebel." I nod to Laia. The crowd is silent.

"When Keris and her allies were determined to destroy our world, it was not the Martials who challenged them first, but the Tribespeople. We are nothing if we are not united. And we are not united if we are not equal. I will not rule an Empire intent on crushing Scholars and Tribespeople under its boot. If the old way is what you wish for, then choose another to lead you."

This is not what they want. I know it. For it is not simple or neat or clean. It does not sweep the sins of the Empire under the rug, or allow those who have always had everything to return to that life. But it is what they will get, if I am their empress. And they deserve to know.

"Moreover"—I glance at Quin—"I will not forsake my family. Citizens of the Empire." I rake the crowd with my gaze. "I will not marry. I will bear no children. For if I am Empress, then the Empire is my husband and my wife. My mother and my father. My brother and my sister. And I name Zacharias Marcus Livius Aquillus Farrar my sole heir." I draw my knife and cut my hand, letting the blood soak the ground. "This I swear, by blood and by bone."

There is a dead silence, and I look to Quin, waiting for him to give the order to have me removed. Instead, he offers a surmising glance before putting his fist to his heart.

"Empress!" he bellows, and the army joins almost immediately, for they, above all others, understand that fighting and dying together creates bonds where there were none. The Paters and Maters follow.

Behind me, Laia calls out. "Empress!" Then Afya. Musa. The Tribespeople. The Scholars.

Only Mamie is silent.

I glance at her, at Zacharias in her arms. By naming him my heir, I may be damning him to a life he will not want. He might hate me for it.

"He will not be safe in Antium," I muse aloud as the chant continues. "Not for long years, while I work to stabilize the Empire. His mother did not want him there anyway, amid the plotting and scheming."

"I have raised small boys before, Helene Aquilla." Mamie cuddles Zacharias close. "They haven't turned out half-bad. And if he is meant to rule the Empire, he should know its people. All of its people. The Martials, Tribes, *and* Scholars." She gives Laia a significant look, and at the question in my eyes, the Scholar speaks.

"Mamie is to train me as a *Kehanni*." Laia cannot hide her joy at the prospect. "Tribe Saif has agreed."

"Who better to watch over him than the woman who brought him into the world?" I say. "And the *Kehanni* who raised one of the best men I know. But won't it be a burden?"

Mamie meets my eyes with an arched brow, and I see the first tender shoots of forgiveness there.

"No, Empress," she says. "For he is family. As are you. As is Laia. And while family can cause pain and make mistakes, it is never a burden. Never."

The chant dissolves into a roar. Within it, I hear my father's voice and my mother's. I hear Hannah's and Livia's and Harper's.

Loyal, they whisper, *to the end.*

PART SIX

THE TALE

CHAPTER SEVENTY

Elias

The first few days after the battle are difficult, and my heart cracks more than once. First when I come upon Avitas Harper's ghost, tethered to the Waiting Place not because of his turmoil, but because of my own sadness at his loss.

"I hear our father's voice," he says quietly as we pass through a carpet of pink Tala blooms on our way to the river. Avitas is the consummate soldier, at peace with the fact that he died in battle, defending the woman he loved. "He awaits me. For years, I have longed to see him. Let me go, brother."

We had too little time together. Part of me wants to refuse to pass him, to make him stay. But whereas in life Avitas was guarded, he now has a sense of quietude about him. It would be wrong to keep him here.

At the river he pauses and tilts his head, a gesture I recognize with a pang, because I do it too. "Tell Helene I got my wish, please. Tell her she must live."

He fades into the river, and only hours later, I find Darin of Serra drifting near the promontory where he died. Seeing his spectral form drives home the finality of his passing, and I find I cannot bring myself to speak.

"Elias." He turns to me and offers a wry smile. "I'm aware that I'm dead. You don't have to give me the speech. All I want to know is if Laia is all right."

"She's alive," I tell him. "And she defeated the Nightbringer."

Most spirits who come to the Waiting Place are angry. Confused. Not Darin. His blue eyes shine with pride, and he walks willingly with me to the shores of the Dusk. We stare out at its glittering waters.

499

"You'll go to her?" he asks.

At my nod, he tilts his head. "I'm happy," he says. "If anyone can love her enough for everyone she's lost, it's you. I wish you joy, Elias."

Then he too steps into the river. After, I sit by its banks for a long time, mourning all that the war stole away.

The weeks pass, and as I train Mirra, as I soothe the spirits' pain, I try to put my own to rest as well. To find peace with the ghosts until I am free of them.

Spring oozes into summer, and the Waiting Place bursts with verdure. Beneath the drenching sunshine, the River Dusk carves its lazy path south, and the sweet scent of night jasmine perfumes every glen and clearing.

One day, when the breezes off the river are still cool and the stars are just giving way to a purple-bellied dawn, my grandmother, Karinna Veturia, finds me.

"I am ready, little one," she says. "To pass to the other side."

She is not alone.

"Hello, Keris." I kneel down and speak to the child beside Karinna. Mirra, trailing them, waits patiently for me.

When we discovered Keris Veturia's ghost among the thousands that Mauth had saved from oblivion, it was Mirra who offered to pass her on. Mirra who listened to my mother as she raged at her own death. Mirra who bore witness as Keris's spirit wailed, forced to feel every bit of excruciating torment she'd unleashed upon the world. And Mirra who ultimately eased away a lifetime of violence and suffering over the course of months, so Keris could return to her last peaceful moment, and remain there.

The Lioness is better for it. The weight she carried in her soul has lightened, and there is a distance to her now, a tranquility in her mien that has slowly replaced the vitriol.

Together with Talis, we walk Keris and Karinna down to the river, stopping to let the young ghost crouch in the woods and watch a spider build a web.

When we finally reach the Dusk, its banks are lush with greenery, and its waters run crystalline. Young Keris peers at it suspiciously, holding tighter to her mother. Then she glances back at Mirra.

"Are you coming?" she asks.

Mirra drops to her knees. "No, Keris," she rasps. "I have work yet to do."

"Do not fear, lovey." Karinna has a joyful glow to her now, for that which she waited for has finally come to pass. "I am here."

My grandmother looks back at me, and for the first time, I see her smile. "Until we meet again, little one," she whispers.

Then they step into the river, holding tightly to one another, and disappear. For a moment, the three of us listen to the water whisper in silent reverence. A step sounds behind us.

It is Azul, braiding her long black hair with flowers. Two months ago, she arrived at Mirra's cabin with Talis to break bread with us. That first time, she only observed. But within a few weeks, she began to walk again among the ghosts.

She nods to the southern woods. "A ship went down near Lacertium," she says. "The ghosts await us."

We make to follow her, but as we do, a voice speaks.

Banu al-Mauth.

We all stop in our tracks, for Mauth hasn't communicated with us since

Mirra took her vow. Talis and Azul exchange a glance, but the Scholar watches me. I know then that he's already spoken to her.

I thank you, my son, for your service to me. The Lioness is ready. I release you from your vow. You are Banu al-Mauth no longer.

I expect to feel different. To not be able to see the ghosts, or to not sense that low tingle of magic in the earth that lets me know Mauth is near. But nothing changes.

You will always have a home among the spirits, Elias. I do not forget my children. I leave you your windwalking as a remembrance of your time here. Perhaps one day, long years from now, you will serve again.

With that, the voice falls silent, and I turn to look at Mirra, feeling stunned, a touch sad, and uncertain of what to do.

"Well, boy, what are you waiting for?" She smiles her crooked smile and gives me a shove. "Go to her."

«‹«

Nur's streets spill over with traders and merchants, acrobats and jugglers, hawkers selling moon cakes, and children roaming in joyful packs. The thoroughfares are strung with multicolored lanterns, and dance stages gleam in the sunlight. A storm lurks along the horizon, but the people of Nur ignore it. They have survived worse.

Though there are still remnants of Keris's assault, the Empress sent two thousand troops to assist with rebuilding. Nur's structures have been re-painted and restored, debris has long since been carted away, and roads have been repaved. The oasis thrums with life. For tonight is the Scholar Moon Festival. And the people mean to celebrate.

At the Martial garrison where Laia and I faced the Meherya, Helene's banner snaps in the warm summer wind. She has arrived, then.

Tribe Saif's wagons sit in one of Nur's many caravanserais, and for a long time, I simply watch the bustle.

True freedom—of body and of soul. That is what Cain promised me, so long ago. But now that it is here, I do not know how to trust it. I am not a soldier or a student or a Mask. I am not a Soul Catcher. Life stretches ahead of me, unknown and uncertain and full of possibility. I do not know how to believe that it will last.

A whisper of cloth, and the scent of fruit and sugar. Then she is beside me, pulling me close, her gold eyes closing as she rises up on her tiptoes. I lift her, and her legs are around my waist, her lips soft against mine, hands in my hair.

"Oi!"

Mid-kiss, something smacks me on the back of the head and I wince and put Laia down, flushing as Shan steps between us.

"That is our *Kehanni*-in-training." He glares at me, before his face breaks into a grin. "And she will be telling her very first story tonight. Show some decorum, Martial. Or at the very least"—he nods to a brilliantly painted wagon at the edge of the caravanserai—"find a wagon."

He does not have to tell me twice, and as the girl I love and I tumble into her wagon, as I bash my head on the low roof and curse, as she kicks my feet out from under me and pins me to her bed, laughing, the tension in my heart unknots.

But later, when we stare up at the dark, lace-cut wood of the wagon's ceiling, I voice the question in my head.

"How do we trust our happiness, Laia?" I turn toward her, and she traces my lips with her finger. "How do we go on if we don't know if it will be taken away?"

I'm gratified that she doesn't answer right away, thankful that she understands why I ask. Laia isn't who she was. Her joy is tempered, like mine. Her heart tender, like mine. Her mind wary, like mine.

"I do not think the answer is in words, love," she says. "I think it is in living. In finding joy, however small, in every day. We'll struggle to trust happiness at first, perhaps. But we can trust ourselves to reach for it always. Remember what Nan said."

"Where there is life, there is hope."

Her answer is another kiss, and when we break apart, I am surprised to see that she casts me a dark glance.

"Elias Veturius," she says imperiously, "two years ago, on the night of this very festival, you whispered something quite intriguing in my ear. You have yet to translate it."

"Ah. Yes." I rise to my elbows and kiss a trail down her neck, to her collarbone, lazily making my way to her stomach, my desire spiking as she trembles.

"I remember," I say. "But it doesn't quite translate." I glance up at her, smiling as her breath hitches. "I'd really have to show you."

CHAPTER SEVENTY-ONE

Helene

The dancing begins before the sun has set, and by the time the moon is overhead, Nur's stages are full and the music is raucous.

Martial and Tribal guards patrol, but I survey the festival anyway, marking exits and entrances through which an attacker could escape. Alcoves and windows where an assassin could hide.

Old habits.

With two Masks at my back, I make my way through the crowds, meeting with a half dozen key Tribal *Zaldars* before Mamie Rila marches up to me.

"No more politics, Empress." She jerks a chin at my guards, and when I nod, they make themselves scarce. "Even empresses must dance. Though you should have worn a dress." She frowns at my armor, and then shoves me toward a slightly disheveled Elias, who has just appeared at the stage himself.

"Where's Laia?" I look behind him. "I'd rather dance with her."

"She's preparing to tell a tale." He takes my hands and pulls me to the center of the stage. "It's her first one, and she's nervous. You're stuck with me."

"She'll be incredible," I say. "I heard her tell Zacharias a story last night. He was rapt."

"Where is he?"

"With Tas, eating moon cakes." I nod to a cart near Mamie's wagon, where the young Scholar boy, who appears to have grown a foot since I last saw him, grins as my nephew stuffs a cake into his mouth. Musa, keeping them company, hands over another.

"How are you?" Elias steps away from me and turns, holding my hand overhead as I do the same a moment later. I remember when this was all I wanted. To hold his fingers in mine. To feel unfettered. That time feels so far away that it is like looking at someone else's life.

"There is much to do," I say. "I have to finish touring the Tribal cities, and then I'll go to Serra. Blackcliff is nearly rebuilt."

"Dex is Commandant now, I hear."

"Commander," I correct him. "There will not be another Commandant."

"No." Elias is thoughtful. "I suppose not. No whipping post either, I hope?"

"Dex said Silvius used it for kindling," I say. "They'll welcome our first class of female recruits in a month. Interested in a teaching position?"

Elias laughs. The drums pound a bit faster, and as one, we quicken the pace of our dance. "Maybe one day. I've already had a letter from your Blood Shrike." He raises an eyebrow, referring to his grandfather. "He wants the heir to Gens Veturia back in Serra. With a Scholar wife, if you'd believe it."

"She'd have to say yes first." I smile at the way his brow furrows in concern. "But indeed, Quin would say that." I glance around and find Musa moving through the crowd toward us. "The Scholars have quite the advocate at court these days."

Elias tilts his head, gray eyes sober. "How is your heart, Hel?"

For a long moment, I do not answer. The drummers cease and a group of oud players strums a slower tune.

After Harper's death, I wanted to rip out my heart to stop it aching. Learning what his spirit said to Elias—a message my friend brought to me himself—offered me no comfort. I paced the streets of Antium late at night, cursing my actions, reliving the battle. Tormenting myself with what I could have done.

But as the days turned into weeks and months, I grew accustomed to the pain—the same way I learned to live with the scars on my face. And instead of hating my heart, I began to marvel at its strength, at the fact that it thuds on insistently. *I am here*, it seems to say. *For we are not done, Helene. We must live.*

"Before she died," I say, "Livvy told me I'd have to reckon with all that I tried to hide from myself. She said it would hurt. And"—I meet my old friend's gaze—"it does."

"We're trailing ghosts now, Hel," he says, and there is strange comfort in knowing that at the very least, there is someone in the world who understands this pain. "All we can do is try not to make any more."

"Pardon me, Elias." Musa appears, moon cake in hand. I promptly steal it from him. I'm starving. "May I cut in?"

Elias bows his head, and Musa waits patiently as I devour the moon cake. The second I'm done, he takes my hand and pulls me close.

Very close.

"This is a bit inappropriate." I glance up at him and find myself slightly breathless.

"Do you like it?" Musa arches a fine, dark eyebrow. Surprised, I consider his question.

"Yes," I say.

He shrugs. "Then who cares."

"I hear Adisa's new king reinstated your lands and title," I say. "When does your caravan leave?"

"Why, Empress? Are you trying to get rid of me?"

Am I? Musa has been invaluable in court, charming Illustrian Paters as easily as he has Scholars. When we broke up the estates of Keris's top allies, it was Musa who suggested we award them to Scholars and Plebeians who fought in the Battle of Antium.

And when grief threatens to consume me, it is Musa who appears with a meal and insists we eat it out in the sunshine. Musa who drags me to the palace kitchens to bake bread with him, and Musa who suggests a visit to Zacharias, even if it means canceling two weeks of court.

I thought at first that the Scholar had wights watching me to make sure I did not fall too deeply into despair. But the wights, he told me, are no longer his spies.

Knowing too many secrets isn't particularly pleasant, he said when we were out riding one day. *How am I supposed to take the Pater of Gens Visselia seriously when I know he spends most of his time composing odes to his hounds?*

"Empress?" He waits for an answer to his question, and I shake myself.

"I don't want to keep you in the Empire"—I can't quite look at him—"if you don't want to stay."

"Do *you* want me to stay?" Despite the arrogance that he wears like armor, I hear a thread of vulnerability in his voice that makes me look up into his dark eyes.

"Yes," I say to his uncertainty. "I want you to stay, Musa."

He lets out a breath. "Thank the skies," he says. "I don't actually like bees very much. Little bastards always sting me. And anyway, you need me around."

I scoff and step on his foot. "I do not *need* you."

"You do. Power is a strange thing." He glances out at Afya and Spiro, clapping and spinning a few feet away, and at Mamie, feeding a gleeful Zacharias yet another moon cake. "It can twist loneliness into despair if there is not someone nearby to keep an eye out."

"I'm not lonely!" A lie, though Musa is too much a gentleman to call me on it.

"But you are alone, Empress." A shadow passes across his face, and I know he thinks of his wife, Nikla, dead six months now. "As all those in power are alone. You don't have to be."

His words sting. Because they are true. His usually mirthful face softens as he watches me.

"It should have been him dancing with you," Musa says, and at the raw emotion in his voice, my eyes heat.

In that moment, I ache for Harper's hands. His grace and his rare smile. The way I could look at him level, because I was nearly his height. His steady, quiet love. I never danced with him. I should have.

Part of me wants desperately to shove my memories of him into the same dark room where my parents and sister live. The room that houses all my pain.

But that room should not exist anymore. My family deserves to be re-membered. Mourned. Often, and with love. And so does Harper.

A tear spills down my cheek. "It should be her beside you," I tell Musa.

"Alas." The Scholar spins me in a circle, then pulls me back. "We're the ones who survived, Empress. Unlucky, perhaps, but that's our lot. And since we're here, we might as well live."

The fiddlers and oud players take up another tune, and the drums thump along, demanding a faster, wilder dance.

Though I was reluctant moments ago, now I find that I want to give in to that exuberant beat. So does Musa. So we laugh and dance again. We eat a dozen moon cakes and chase away the loneliness, two broken people who, for this night, anyway, make a whole.

Later, when Mamie Rila calls us for Laia's story, and as we settle with Zacharias and the rest of Tribe Saif onto the rugs and cushions strewn across the caravanserai, I lean in to Musa.

"I am glad you are staying," I say. "And I will be thankful for your company."

"Good." Musa flashes me his brilliant smile, and for once, it is not mocking. "Because you still owe me a favor, Empress. And I plan to collect."

My answering laugh is one of delight. Delight that I can feel a thrill when a man I care for makes me smile. That I can look forward to a story told by my friend. That I can find hope in the eyes of the little boy I hold in my arms.

That despite all I have survived, or perhaps because of it, there is still joy in my heart.

CHAPTER SEVENTY-TWO

Laia

Mamie finds me in my wagon, pacing in the small space, muttering the Tale to myself. The moon is high outside, and the smell of cardamom and honey and tea fills the caravanserai.

"Laia, my love," she says. "It is time."

When I step out of the wagon, she straightens my dress, a traditional Scholar kurta and shalwar, the clothes we wore long ago, before the Martials came. The cloth of the kurta is the same warm ebony as the close-fitting pants beneath, and falls to my knees. It gleams with geometric embroidery in silver and green thread, to honor the *Kehanni* teaching me. The neckline is low and square, the *K* that Keris carved into me clearly visible.

"It stands," I told Elias earlier, "for *Kehanni*."

"Do you know the story you will tell?" Mamie asks me as we make our way to the *Kehanni's* stage, where a massive crowd has gathered. Aubarit and Gibran spread blankets and rugs, while Spiro—who has made his home in Nur—helps Afya pass mugs of steaming tea from hand to hand.

"I know the story I wish to tell," I say. "But—it's not very fitting for the Moon Festival."

"The tale chooses you, Laia of Serra," Mamie says. "Why do you wish to tell this one?"

The crowd fades for a moment, and I hear the Meherya in my mind. *Do not forget the story, Laia of Serra.*

"This tale is the gibbet in the square," I say. "The blood on the cobblestones. It is the *K* carved into a Scholar girl's skin. The mother who waited thirty years for her child. The agony of a family destroyed. This tale is a warning. And it is a promise kept."

"Then it must be told." Mamie makes her way to her own spot in the packed crowd.

As I ascend the stage, the audience shushes itself. Elias leans against a wagon, his hair falling into his eyes, gaze far away. Helene sits near him with Musa, her guards close by, her attention given over to Zacharias, who bounces up and down in her lap.

I raise my hands and everyone falls suddenly, reverently quiet.

Do not be surprised at the silence, Mamie taught me. *Demand it. For you offer them a gift they will carry with them forever. The gift of story.*

"I awoke in the glow of a young world." My voice carries to the farthest corners of the caravanserai. "When man knew of hunting but not tilling. Of stone but not steel. It smelled of rain and earth and life. It smelled of hope."

I draw the story from deep within my soul, pouring my love into it, and my forgiveness, my anger and my empathy, my joy and my sadness.

The audience is rapt, their faces ever changing—going from shock to gladness to horror—as I take them through the unrelenting storms of the Meherya's life.

They knew him only as a murderer and tormentor. Not as a king or father or husband. Not as a broken creature, forsaken by his creator.

I realize as I tell the tale that I have forgiven the Meherya for what he did to me. To my family. But I have no right to forgive what he did to this world. His crimes were too great—and only time will tell if we heal from them.

When I arrive at Rehmat's mercy, at the Meherya's end, even Zacharias is silent, his hand stuffed in his mouth as he stares, wide-eyed.

"In that moment, the wind ceased." My voice drops, and everyone leans forward as one to hear. "All fell silent. All went still. For the Beloved who woke with the dawning of the world was no more. And for a single, anguished moment, the earth itself mourned him."

My shoulders droop. The tale is over, and it has taken its toll. No one says a word after I finish, and I wonder, briefly, if I have made some sort of error in the telling.

Then the Tribes erupt, clapping, shouting, stamping their feet, crying, "*Aara! Aara!*"

More. More.

In the long buildings that edge the caravanserai, figures shift in the shadows, sun eyes flashing. They disappear the moment I look at them—all but one. Beneath her hood, I catch a glimpse of dark blue eyes and white hair, a scarred face and a hand lifted to her heart.

Mother.

After the fires have dimmed and festivalgoers have gone to their homes and wagons, I leave the caravanserai and make my way into the desert. It is the darkest hour of the night, when even ghosts take their rest. Nur gleams with thousands of lamps, a constellation in the heart of the sands.

"Laia."

I know her voice, but more than that, I know the feel of her, the comfort of her presence, the cinnamon scent of her hair.

"You did not have to come," I say to her. "I know it's hard to get away."

"It was your first story." She does not stutter anymore, and exudes a gravitas that reminds me of my father. She has begun to forgive herself. "I did not wish to miss it."

"How are the jinn?"

"Grumpy," Mother says. "A bit lost. But starting to find their way, even without the Meherya." She squeezes my hand. "They liked your story."

We walk in silence for a time, and then stop atop a large dune. The galaxy burns bright, and we watch the stars wheel above in their unknowable dance, letting ourselves appreciate their beauty. She puts her arm around me, and I sink into her, closing my eyes.

"I miss them," I whisper.

"As do I," she says. "But they'll be there, little cricket, on the other side. Waiting for us when our time comes." She says it with a longing I understand. "But not yet." Mother nudges me pointedly. "We have much left to do in this world. I must go. The spirits call." She nods over my shoulder. "And there's someone waiting for you."

Elias approaches after Mother has already windwalked away. "She's about a thousand times better at soul catching than I ever was," he says.

"You were excellent at it." I turn for Nur and hook my arm into his, reveling in his solidity, his strength. "You just hated it."

"And now that I'm free," he says, "I was thinking I need to find something to do. I can't very well loiter about the caravan while you're hard at work becoming a *Kehanni*. I'd never hear the end of it."

"You will be maddeningly wonderful at whatever you choose, Elias. But what do you want?"

He answers swiftly enough that I know he's been thinking on this for a long while.

"Tas wants to learn scimcraft along with a few other children in the Saif caravan," he says. "And our future emperor will eventually need lessons in a dozen subjects."

The thought of Elias teaching Tas, the Saif children, and Zacharias makes my heart melt a bit. "You'll be an incredible teacher," I chuckle.

"Though I feel for those children. They will not get away with anything."

Elias pulls away from me, and I realize after a moment that he is holding an object, spinning it so fast that I cannot get a look at it.

"Before any of that, I—ah—have something for you." He stops and lifts his hands to reveal an armlet—intricately carved with apricot blossoms and cherry blossoms and Tala blossoms, a veritable garden of fruit. Along the edges, in vivid script, he has inscribed the names of my family. Words fail me, and I reach out to take it, but he does not give it to me. Not yet.

"I wish I could live a thousand lives so I could fall in love with you a thousand times," he says. "But if all we get is this one, and I share it with you, then I will never want for anything, if—if you—would—if you—" He stops, hands gripped so tight around the armlet that I fear he'll break it.

"Yes. *Yes.*" I take it from him and put it on. "Yes!" I cannot say it enough.

He pulls me up into a kiss that reminds me of why I want to spend my life with him, of all of the things I want with him. *Adventures,* I told him. *Meals. Late nights. Rainy walks.*

Later—much later—I lift my cloak from the earth and shake the dust off.

"You can't complain." He runs his hand through his hair, and a torrent of sand pours out. His smile is a white flash in the night. "You did say you wanted me to talk you out of your clothes in inappropriate places."

He dodges my shove with a laugh, and I pull him to his feet.

Elias laces his fingers through mine as we walk. He tells me what he hopes to do on his first full day home, his baritone thrumming in my veins like the sweetest, deepest oud playing a song that I wish to hear forever. What a small thing it seems, to walk with the one you love. To look forward to a day with them. I marvel at the simplicity of this moment. And I thank the skies for the miracle of it.

A thick layer of cloud rests atop the eastern horizon, and the sky pales, the deep orange glow of an ember breathed into life. High above, the stars whisper their goodbyes and fade into the depthless blue dome of the firmament.

Acknowledgements

How do I thank you, reader, for staying with me to the end? You create fan art and cosplay and wait for hours to have books signed. You name kids and kittens and puppies after Ember characters. You cheer with me and cry with me and lift me up. With all my heart and soul, thank you.

For thirteen years, my family has ridden the highs and lows of this journey with me. My loving appreciation to Mama, Emberling #1. Your duas have carried me farther than I ever dreamed. Daddy, thank you for the gift of willpower and for always asking how I'm doing, first.

Kashi—for letting me steal your softest shirts and our greatest memories, for gales of midnight laughter, for listening to me read and dwelling on the shape of a word, and most of all for believing, long before I ever did—thank you.

My boys, my always-little ones, your patience and positivity inspire me every day. All of it, every good thing, is for you.

Amer, late-night writing partner, calmest of voice, fiercest of allies. Thank you for helping me find my way through this book and life in general. I would be lost without you. Haroon, champion to end all champions. You are a badass, and every year that passes cements this further. Thank you for fighting on.

Alexandra, fellow warrior and worrier, she who always believes. I know this end is really just a beginning, but I cannot imagine any of it without you. May we reach ever higher.

To my sister Tala—with each book, I failed to find the words for us. So I'll just say that I will never hear a DM song and not smile and think of all we have survived together.

Great love to Heelah, for the laughter and memes; Uncle and Auntie, for your duas and belief in me; Imaan, Armaan, and Zakat, for reminding me why I write; and Brittany, Lilly, Zoey, Anum, and Bobby, for your prayers and love.

Cathy Yardley, mentor and friend, I am so thankful for your steady encouragement and for helping me make sense of my own weird brain.

Penguins, thank you, thank you, thank you: Jen Loja, for believing in and supporting me, but most of all for time, a gift I shall never forget; Casey McIntyre, Ruta Rimas, and Gretchen Durning, for your patience and for tirelessly going over this manuscript a million times; Shanta Newlin and the always-hustling publicity team; Felicia Frazier and the phenomenal sales team; Emily Romero and the wildly inventive marketing team; and Carmela Iaria and the awesome school and library team.

My deep appreciation also to Felicity Vallence, Jen Klonsky, Shane Rebenschied, Kristin Boyle, Krista Ahlberg, Jonathan Roberts, Jayne Ziemba, Rebecca Aidlin, Roxane Edouard, Savanna Wicks, and Stephanie Koven; and to the international publishers, editors, cover artists, and translators, for making the Ember books the best they can be in so many beautiful languages.

Ben Schrank, life takes us on unexpected paths, and I'm glad that for this bit, we walked together. Thank you for all that you have done for me and for this series.

Nicola Yoon, I could not have done this without you. Thank you for reminding me of all the beauty the darkness holds. You are an extraordinary friend and a beautiful person. Renée Ahdieh, beloved sis and always ally, thank you for your wisdom and love, for being you, through thick and thin. Lauren DeStefano—who was there with kind words on the hard days and a stern word on the lazy ones, my forever DRiC, I'm very grateful for you.

My heartfelt thanks to friends who have offered love, puppy/baby/ kitten pictures, chai, music, and advice: Abigail Wen, Adam Silvera, Haina Karim, Nyla Ibrahim, Zuha Warraich, Subha Kumar, Mari Nicholson, Sarah Balkin, Tomi Adeyemi, Samira Ahmed, Becky Albertalli, Victoria Aveyard, Leigh Bardugo, Sona Charaipotra, Dhonielle Clayton, Stephanie Garber, Kelly Loy Gilbert, Amie Kaufman, Stacey Lee, Marie Lu, Tahereh Mafi, Angela Mann, Tochi Onyebuchi, Aisha Saeed, Laini Taylor, Angie Thomas, and David Yoon.

A long overdue thank-you to journalists and writers who have left their mark: Philip Bennett, Terry Brooks, Milton Coleman, Alison Croggon, Tony Reid, Marilynne Robinson, Arundhati Roy, Mary Doria Russell, Antoine de Saint-Exupéry, Keith Sinzinger, Anthony Shadid, Jason Ukman, Elizabeth Ward, Emily Wax, Kathy Wenner, and Marcus Zusak.

My books would be pale shadows of themselves without the music that inspired me. Thank you to the National for "Terrible Love," Rihanna for "Love on the Brain," Zola Jesus for "Dangerous Days," the Lumineers for "Salt and the Sea," Aqualung for "Complicated," Kendrick Lamar for "DNA," Hozier for "Would That I," Arcade Fire for "My Body Is a Cage" performed by Peter Gabriel, Autumn Walker for "Barking at the Buddha," and the Nooran Sisters for their performance of "Dama Dam Mast Kalandar."

My last thanks, always, are to Him, An-Nur, the Illuminator, the voice that speaks in the lonely night, the hand that has spared me so much grief. All things, in the end, come back to You.